ALSO BY DALIA SOFER

The Septembers of Shiraz

MAN OF MY TIME

DALIA SOFER

—◆—

MAN
OF MY
TIME

FARRAR

STRAUS

AND

GIROUX

New

York

Farrar, Straus and Giroux
120 Broadway, New York 10271

Copyright © 2020 by Dalia Sofer
All rights reserved
Printed in the United States of America
First edition, 2020

Grateful acknowledgment is made for permission to reprint lines from
"Tablet X" from *Gilgamesh: A New Rendering in English Verse*, by David
Ferry. Copyright © 1992 by David Ferry. Reprinted by permission of
Farrar, Straus and Giroux.

Library of Congress Cataloging-in-Publication Data
Names: Sofer, Dalia, 1972– author.
Title: Man of my time / Dalia Sofer.
Description: First edition. | New York : Farrar, Straus and Giroux,
2020.
Identifiers: LCCN 2019054566 | ISBN 9780374110062 (hardcover)
Classification: LCC PS3619.O3797 M36 2020 | DDC 813/.6—dc23
LC record available at https://lccn.loc.gov/2019054566

Designed by Richard Oriolo

Our books may be purchased in bulk for promotional, educational,
or business use. Please contact your local bookseller or the
Macmillan Corporate and Premium Sales Department at
1-800-221-7945, extension 5442, or by e-mail at
MacmillanSpecialMarkets@macmillan.com.

www.fsgbooks.com
www.twitter.com/fsgbooks • www.facebook.com/fsgbooks

1   3   5   7   9   10   8   6   4   2

FOR MY FAMILY

The simple man and the ruler resemble each other.
The face of the one will darken like that of the other.

—*Gilgamesh: A New Rendering in English Verse*, by David Ferry

PART

ONE

1

AROUND ME WAS AN ANT COLONY of black motorcars. In my jacket pocket, hidden inside a mint candy box, were the ashes of my father—Sadegh Mozaffarian—dead for two weeks and estranged from me for thirty-eight years. And next to me, in the back seat of our sedan, was my boss, the minister of foreign affairs. The Iranian delegation—among them the Minister, myself, a couple of translators, and a half dozen security men—was confined to a few designated New York blocks, beyond which we were not permitted to go. "It's like a goddamn prison," I said to the Minister on the first day of the United Nations

General Assembly, when I realized the constraints of the phantom barbed wire fencing us in, and he said, "Hardly. You of all people should know."

His optimism had been tested throughout the trip. Once again American promises had been made to us and broken, the most recent excuse being a tiff between our respective navy ships in the Persian Gulf. The Americans pointed their fingers eastward, at our sphinxlike ayatollahs, who in turn stood at their Friday prayer pulpits and disclaimed involvement. Accusations and denials pinged back and forth, and made any notions of guilt or innocence mere afterthoughts.

"The sons of bitches are screwing us again," I said to the Minister that morning during a well-earned piss break from the procession of speeches. As the Saudi crown prince and the Pakistani prime minister had been hogging the bathroom stalls for over fifteen minutes, the Minister and I, despite the edicts of our religion, had no choice but to resort to the urinals. We stood with the others, a row of dark-suited men with passports from opposing nations tucked in our pockets, but all of us facing the wall like a firing squad, and sighing with relief in unison. "Resolute but open," the Minister said. "That's the only way to achieve anything."

"You know what else is resolute but open?" I said, zipping my pants.

He gave me an amused look in the mirror as he washed his hands. How I envied the Minister his forbearance. His presentation to the assembly had been so well received that for two days his face had been on the front pages of the newspapers. He had a good face, the kind that elicited trust because it suggested familiarity with the Western canon—Homer to Hemingway, Socrates to Žižek. His speech and diction, as contemplative as his face, were measured, thoughtful, and just evasive enough to suggest ambiguity bordering on mysticism. The press had parsed his every word, as if he were the holy pope himself.

The Russian ambassador was stooped over a washbasin next to us, leaning into the mirror to inspect a dark spot on his Cossack nose. Must have gotten too much sun while on holiday in Crimea. I nearly said as much but reconsidered. Leave the poor bastard alone, I thought. He probably doesn't want to be here any more than we do. This annual gathering of the world's kingpins was like a cross between high school and the Day of Judgment. We all showed up to bullshit our way out of the reckoning awaiting us, as clear as a lighthouse illuminating a black sea.

"Talking with the Americans," I said to the Minister, "is like getting butter from water. *Az āb kareh gereftan.*"

"Patience, Hamid," the Minister said as he combed his Van Dyke beard. "We've talked about this. When will you stop being a hothead?"

"My father used to call me *khorous jangi*—fighting cock," I said.

"Your father is a wise man," said the Minister.

"Was," I said.

I SPLASHED COLD WATER ON MY FACE, my father's ashes heavy in my breast pocket. I shut my eyes and saw him drinking tea by our kitchen window and reading the paper, cover to cover, as he used to do each morning. My father was always impeccably dressed—a necktie and a suit, even on the hottest days. He had an old-world air about him—he knew how deep to bow, how often to smile, when to engage and when to retreat. Doctor of art history, professor for a time at Tehran University, he was affable to all and an intimate of none. A constant melancholy, so thick it could have been rehearsed, made him seem at once fragile and impervious. The man, as I remembered him, was always alone.

Later, even as he accepted a top position at the Ministry of Culture and the scaffolding of his existence shifted, his aloneness remained unbroken. His days and nights, filled now with meetings and dinners, remained a hall of mirrors he never wished to fully enter. When he came home in the evenings he glided from the chandeliered world of ministers and artists to his hushed room, removing only his shoes and socks. At his desk, in his suit, tie, and slippers, he worked on his magnum opus, a compendium of Iranian art—preconquest, postconquest, premodern, modern, postmodern—and whatever else there had ever been or would ever be. At dinnertime, from the head of the table, he would interrogate the family on Sasanian glass, Samarkand pottery, Tahmasp miniatures, coffeehouse paintings. My mother disregarded him. My brother, Omid, and I tried to both appease and even conquer him. But as the right answer earned us no praise, the wrong answer earned us no reprimand.

SIDEWALK DEMONSTRATORS were slowing down traffic. Syrians. Some obscure Chinese sect. Liberal Americans singing their swan song for democracy. And most perplexing of all, Orthodox Jews calling for the destruction of the Holy Land. "What's *their* grievance?" I asked the Minister. "They're waiting for the Messiah to rebuild the Temple in Jerusalem," he said with his knowing smile, indicating acceptance of the world as the carnival that it was. I would have prolonged the discussion but sensed his stiffness as he resumed texting with his old friend, the former American secretary of state. How we all missed the man, the Minister more than anyone. "A minyan of decent Americans appeared in our lifetime," I joked, "and they came and went like Halley's Comet." The Minister nodded but didn't laugh. "How does a man like you know about minyans?" he asked. "A man like me has been through many lifetimes," I said, taking no offense. He resumed typing, with the fretful gaze of a teenager trying to resurrect a first love.

MY DAUGHTER, GOLNAZ, had that same look the last time I had seen her. Three years had passed since that accursed night, when she went to live with her mother, Noushin. And I didn't even try to stop her. Letting my daughter go was an act of pure benevolence. I didn't know I was capable of behaving this way.

With Noushin, who left me five years before my daughter did, I had been far more strident. In the farewell letter she left on the breakfast table, Noushin wrote that life with me *was like going deaf in increments, until you realize one day that the morning's birdcalls sound like children crying from a distance.* "Your simile is tortured," I said, holding the letter and following her to the bedroom, where I saw her tossing shirts and skirts and shoes into a valise. "I mean, *the morning's birdcalls sound like crying children?* That's ridiculous . . ." When she pulled the pale blue dress with the moonstone buttons from the hanger—the one she had worn to Golnaz's second birthday party, when together we had baked a Pink Panther cake and believed ourselves happy— I felt our future snap inside my chest. "You can't just renounce your husband like that," I told her as she put on her black velvet combat boots and shut the green suitcase, the same one she had brought on our first and only family trip—a visit to Isfahan.

A memory of the three of us eating ice cream under the

columns of Chehel Sotoun stung my heart with the loss that lay ahead of me, the way my reflection in the old Safavid palace pool had done, that summer afternoon. I ran to the front door and blocked it with my large frame. "You're no husband," she said, her black eyes hard as ice picks. "You're just a warden with a wedding ring." She pushed me aside and I let her. As I heard her scrambling down the stairs—she hadn't even waited for the elevator—I regained my senses and yelled, "Go back to whichever hell you came from, but understand that you just saw your daughter for the last time." From the stairs came a strange, aborted scream. She knew the law was on my side.

WHEN NOUSHIN LEFT, Golnaz was nine years old, on the edge of eviction from childhood. I vowed to give her a good life. I cooked dinner for her, took her shopping or to the movies, and dropped her off at school in the morning. I even sang to her from time to time. I had often been told that I had a soulful voice, and more than once I gave her my best impersonation of Dariush, which she found hilarious. There was a time when I would sing my Dariush renditions to seduce women, but that was a lifetime before. Going from seduction to hilarity didn't bother me—it was just the nature of time, passing. Often, after we would wash and put away the dishes, we would sit together at the kitchen table as she would finish her homework, and I, staring at her heart-shaped face, would be seized by the thought of losing her. When she wished me good night I would kiss the top of her head, reminding myself, each time as though it were the first, of the possibility for goodness on this earth. She smelled of powder and honey, vanilla and salt. It was her scent and it had been Noushin's scent. On nights when I couldn't sleep I would tiptoe into her room and stand over her bed, sniffing her head like a bandit before returning to the cold crispness of my own laundered sheets. I was addicted to laundry in those days and asked the housekeeper to leave the dirty wash to me. But instead of using the washing machine, I would fill the tub and soak the clothes and sheets in lye, scrubbing and beating the soiled cloth like some ancient washerwoman by the riverside, rubbing out memories with suds and ash.

SIRENS BLARED AS Forty-Second Street finally opened up, and we crossed, sedan after sedan, back to our hotels. From the tinted, bulletproof windows of the jet-black Mercedes I watched pedestrians struggling to make their way through their occupied city. *Serves them right*, I thought. *Let them squirm for a couple of days like the rest of the world.* In truth my favorite part of the entire trip was being in this mighty car. I called it our *māchin-e-zanbour assal*—the honeybee car, because it reminded me of a toy I played with as a boy. Back in the day, my brother and I had a collection of toy cars. Among them was a sleek, black Chrysler Imperial, modeled after the car in the Green Hornet TV series, with a majestic bee on its roof, green-tinted windows, a radiator grille that would open to reveal a red missile, and a boot that, once unlocked, would allow a radar scanner to fly upward. In the back seat was a figurine of the Green Hornet aiming a gun, and behind the wheel sat Kato, his assistant. It was a prodigious car, loved equally by my brother and me, but for different reasons. I was obsessed with the flapping grille and the missile underneath, while Omid adored the hornet set against the black sheen of the chassis. "The bee leads to the honeycomb," Omid would say as he'd maneuver the car within the arabesques of the century-old silk Kashani carpet of our bedroom, a hand-me-down from one of our rich maternal relatives. Poor Omid. He believed in improvement. Maybe he couldn't help it, with a name like that. *Omid*. It means hope.

THE MINISTER AND I arrived at our hotel. The concierge—a young man in a smart navy suit, doubtless a graduate of a Swiss hospitality school—alerted us that about a dozen people had left us a handful of miniature flags engraved with messages. As the Minister questioned him about these visitors I noticed the young concierge's cuff links emblazoned with a Warhol-style image of Mao—a wink of irony in his otherwise stern outfit.

He handed us the flags. They were of the old variety with a golden lion and sun in the middle, and carried such messages as "Down with the devil" and "One day the prince shall return," and other such nonsense. Of all the splintered groups of our nation, the royalists were the most pathetic.

On the way to the elevator the Minister tucked one of the flags behind my ear like a rose. I placed one in his plentiful head of hair and we cracked up. "Meet later for dinner?" he asked. Though I liked the idea, I declined. I told him I was tired, which was the truth. The other truth was that all I wanted was to have a drink at the bar, by myself, which obviously wasn't possible. Even though we were staying in a discreet hotel—the brochures called it "boutique"—a delegate to the Islamic Republic being spotted at the hotel bar with a glass of gin would have caused nothing short of an international scandal.

Alone in my room, I sat on the king-size bed. I sat for a good ten minutes, doing nothing, just staring at a wall and thinking that this New York visit really did feel like a prison sentence, only in a better decorated cell: fleur-de-lys wallpaper, pearl-white bed crown draped over an antique mahogany bed, gold-rimmed mirror, candelabra chandelier, all striving for a rococo effect. As though life prior to electricity were something worthy of being replicated. It was the type of room my mother would have swooned over, back in the days when we were an unbroken family and traveled together to such places as Paris and Barcelona and Rome. My mother, a sucker for anything remotely continental, was Swiss-educated and claimed royal ancestry. On that summer morning of 1979 as the three of them—she, my father, and Omid—headed to the airport to catch what ended up being their final flight out of Tehran, she kept wringing her bejeweled hands and saying, "To think that a Qajar descendant should be fleeing her own land with nothing but a suitcase, how outrageous . . ." And I, sitting in the back seat next to Omid to accompany them to the airport even though a few months earlier I had been among the unshaven bell-bottomed revolutionaries burning down the streets of our city, said to my mother what I had been dying to say to her for years, "Mother, you and half of Iran are royal Qajar descendants. After all, every Qajar king had a harem full of whores!"

We never spoke after that. Until a week before my New York trip, when she called me early one morning at the Ministry. When I picked up she said, like a stranger, "May I speak with *aghaye* Hamid Mozaffarian?" Between us stood suitcases, borders, and the stone wall of nearly four decades. The morning news on Radio Tehran was on; they were doing a segment on the health benefits of cardamom. I turned it off and held the receiver, wordless, for what felt like a very long time. She must have recognized me, too, even in the absence of speech, because she said, "It's your mother, Monir." As though I would have forgotten even her name.

When she told me my father had died—collapsed from a heart attack during a morning walk by the river—I felt nothing at first. "Which river?" I asked her, not knowing why such a detail should matter. "The East River," she said. "A block from our apartment in New York." That in almost four decades I had not once imagined my family's life with any kind of precision began to fill me with an ache that had to be interrupted. "So what do you want?" I asked.

She cleared her throat with the nervousness of someone about to deliver a rehearsed speech; I had heard many of these in my day. "I'd like you to meet your brother during your visit to New York," she said. "He will give you your father's ashes and I'd like you to take them back to Iran. It was your father's last, and to tell you the truth, only wish."

I had slept barely two hours the previous night. Insomnia had taken hold of me again and I had spent sleepless hours reading Ali Shariati's *Reflections on Humanity*, one of the texts held over from my revolutionary days. I clutched the receiver, watching a worker outside my window teetering on scaffolding and drilling the chipped horn of the Achaemenid-style bull capital on one of the columns of the portico. My head throbbed.

That my mother had tracked me down at the Ministry and knew of my position as the Delegate in Charge of European and American Matters pleased me. Then again, most likely she had done it not because she missed me, but because she needed me. I took a sip from the unmarked bottle I kept under my desk. The drink pierced my gut and steadied me. "Cremation is against the religion," I said. "You know that."

"Oh, stop that nonsense!" she said, her rehearsed cool showing its first cracks. "His wish was to be buried there, in his homeland, and this is the simplest way to do it. It's written in his will."

"Do you know what will happen if I get caught?" I whispered into the receiver. "I'll lose my post at the Ministry, and God knows what else. In fact, your calling me here was extremely careless."

"Where else was I supposed to call you? Do I know where you live?" She took a sip of something then continued, in a maternal command, "Do this one thing for us."

This *one* thing. She had forgotten the endless things I had done for them until I had discovered my cause and broken free—how I had gone to the schools they had chosen, made friends they approved of, spoke as they wished me to, read what they told me to, ate as they advised, took a piss when allowed, played the piano when summoned, accompanied them to social dinners at the Officers' Club and the Chattanooga, those nightclubs where I embroidered my speech with French and Italian words seemingly at random. Though there was nothing random about any of it. It was all part of the master plan, some belief in the ascendance to a social stratosphere higher even than the Tower of Babel. My irritation aside, I was secretly heartened that time had not eroded my mother's overbearing ways. And maybe out of some filial deference still living in my heart like a blind and forgotten old dog, I said, "All right. I will carry out *bābā*'s wish."

"One more thing," she said. "There will be a memorial dinner and I'd like you to attend."

"I'll be busy with meetings," I said.

"You can't make time for one dinner in your father's memory?"

"Fine," I said. We remained silent, neither of us volunteering a farewell. I looked out my office window at Mashgh Square, shimmering from the morning rain. A boy passed by on a bicycle, his wheels unsteady, wearing a T-shirt with a green comic book character I was too old to recognize. I remembered how my mother used to pick me up from school each Thursday with a new *Tintin* volume, which would be my companion for the entire weekend.

"Well, that's all," she said.

"Wait," I said.

"Don't overextend yourself," she said. "I am grateful that you agreed to take the ashes and that you will attend the dinner." After a long pause she added, "For years I accompanied your father on his walks. But this past year I couldn't, because of the arthritis."

She said *the* arthritis, as though I had been in her life all along and was privy to its misfortunes. "So he was alone when he collapsed?" I said.

"Yes, he was alone. A jogger found him and called for an ambulance. The hospital didn't notify me until two hours later." She lit up a cigarette. "Imagine, found like that by a river, as though he had no family."

I said nothing.

"Do you have a family?" my mother asked.

"A daughter," I said, leaving out the fact that I had not seen her in three years. "Her name is Golnaz."

"Good," said my mother. "Good for you." She hung up the phone.

AS THE ELDEST SON of the deceased I would need to appear appropriately mournful. Nothing less than gray would do. Or navy blue, at the least. I had three good suits, all light-colored.

I considered asking the Minister to lend me a suit but he was a head shorter than I, and besides, the last thing I wanted was to embroil him in my family drama. I had never spoken to him about my parents, except to give him the kind of information that could be readily found in a government dossier: names, dates of birth, dates of disappearance, and the like. This pursuit of the proper attire would encroach on my preparations for the visit to New York. I still had to revise the Minister's speech to the General Assembly, and come up with a book selection, in keeping with our habit of reading a volume inspired by each city we visited. This had been the Minister's idea, to prevent us, he said, from becoming "birdbrained handshakers," polluted with manifestos and resolutions. So in Paris we had read Balzac's *Père Goriot* and in Rome, a book of poems by Pasolini. For New York I had yet to make a selection. As the city that had engulfed my family, New York seemed to me the most foreboding place on earth, and also the most illusory.

In the end I bought a steel-gray suit I couldn't afford and I chose DeLillo's *Underworld*, as daunting, brilliant, and sinister as the city we were visiting.

AS I WAITED FOR OMID on the corner of Forty-Third Street and First Avenue, I half expected to greet the little brother I had seen for the last time under the fluorescent lights of Mehrabad airport, looking queasy and far younger than his sixteen years. When he approached, I shuddered, not because he still resembled that boy, but because he seemed the replica of my father as I had last seen him—a man in middle age, handsome still but with a paunch, tall and inwardly cracked like a Greek column, a memorial to some realm of expired grandeur. I could tell from his searching eyes that he didn't immediately recognize me, which did not surprise me.

After I let my daughter slip out of my life, my physical transformation began. My hair fell out, first by numbers then in clumps, with such speed that I stopped lamenting the loss of each strand and began reciting collective eulogies as one does when faced with a mass grave. When I had lost enough of it I decided to shave my head altogether. I don't know when exactly I began to lose weight—so preoccupied was I with my hair—but I remember coming out of the shower one morning and being stunned to find the man staring back at me from the steamy bathroom mirror: tall, broad-shouldered, deep black eyes cradled inside ashen crescents, a naked skull, and not a gram of excess fat—an exquisite, indignant creature.

"OMID!" I called out over the chaos of Midtown Manhattan at noon. "Omid, Omid . . ." Saying his name over and over soothed me like a refrain suddenly recalled. When he saw me, he froze for an instant, then his face opened up. He walked toward me with restraint. We stood facing each other, awkward, while journalists and cameramen bypassed us from all directions, visibly annoyed by our moment of inaction amid so much frenzy. We reached for each other, and if I were a religious man, I would have said that this was the closest I had ever come to experiencing God. There was a feeling of utter timelessness, a sense that nothing that had come before and nothing that would come after mattered. Only this.

"Shall we sit somewhere?" he said. "Did you have lunch?"

At a nearby bodega we got turkey sandwiches. He told me that normally the Halal Guys would be two blocks up but because of the General Assembly all the food vendors had been barred.

"The Halal Guys?" I said.

"Don't laugh," he said. "They've built an empire from kebab."

AFTER SOME BACK AND FORTH with the security office I finagled a visitor's pass for Omid. We found a subdued corner in the Rose Garden, in the shadow of the General Assembly building. Aluminum crinkled as we unwrapped our sandwiches, thirty-eight years of unspoken words between us. It was Omid who began. He told me about his studies in literature, the years he spent writing poetry before taking up translation, first of the literary variety, and later, when he decided to get married and have a steadier income, of the bureaucratic kind. Mostly, he said, he translated affidavits for those seeking green cards, and land restitution forms for those who had left home so long ago that they had forgotten even their language.

"And Mother?" I said.

"She carries on," he said. "But she lives in a time warp. She stays up into all hours of the night listening to old Sattar and Googoosh records and bidding on memorabilia on eBay. You should see her apartment. She has a set of plates from the 1971 gala in Persepolis, every possible banknote and coin, magazine clips about those final days in Panama and Cairo, a tea set that the seller swore belonged to Mozaffar al-Din Shah Qajar, and a silver gelatin print of one of Naser al-Din Shah's chubby wives. I call the apartment the Golestan Palace."

"*Bābā* didn't mind?"

"*Bābā* had lost his ability to mind anything," he said. "Especially during his last year."

When I asked him about his wife and child, his face darkened. "Divorced," he said. "She cleaned me out. All I do now is work and pay alimony. And I hardly see my son."

"Your ex-wife is American?" I said.

"No," he said. "The daughter of an Iranian real estate developer in Los Angeles. I don't know why the family fortune wasn't enough. She needed my meager translator's scrapyard, too. And you?" he asked. "What have you done since we left you at the airport? We heard rumors . . ." he said. "Are they true?"

"I don't know what you heard," I said.

"Rumors about your job at the prison," he said. "People said you were working for the Ministry of Intelligence, that you became an interrogator."

"It was complicated," I said.

"Hamid, are the rumors true?"

"Yes," I said. "They are probably true."

For a long time we sat in silence, our half-eaten sandwiches on our laps, like two awkward boys in a schoolyard at lunch hour. I worried that a photographer might take our picture for an amusing sidebar to the day's hard news—*look, even the Islamic Republic breeds humans!* It would be the kind of article Americans love, affirming their self-proclaimed ability to see humanity even in their enemy, and in so doing, reassuring themselves of their own magnanimous heart.

"What happened to you?" he finally said.

"I don't know," I said. "I meant well, I believe."

"Did you?"

"In the beginning, yes," I said.

"And later?"

"Later it became something else." I looked up at the September sky. The clean fall day reminded me of Tehran before the pollution.

"We all do what we need to do at any given moment," Omid said. "*Tout comprendre c'est tout pardoner*," he went on, quoting the old proverb—to understand all is to forgive all. His clemency had surfaced so quickly that I doubted its sincerity; I imagined it was an aphorism he had adopted to defend against the sorrows the world had inflicted on him.

He looked at his watch and withdrew a mint candy box from his pocket. "Here are *bābā*'s ashes," he said.

"This? That's all of *bābā*? I was expecting some kind of pewter urn."

"*Khar nasho*—don't be an ass!" he said. "You want to carry a ten-kilo urn of bone and ash back to Tehran? Of course it's not all of him."

"So where is the rest?" I said, the familiar outrage surging again. "A dead body must remain intact," I continued with the authority of a holy man. "You committed a sin, taking the poor man apart like that."

"The poor man?" he said. "Where were you all these years, you asshole, when the poor man was alive?" His voice was losing its practiced restraint.

It never failed. Push anyone hard enough and you arrive at the essence. I stared into my brother's black eyes, mirror images of my own, and said, "What happened to *understanding all and forgiving all*?"

Sirens sounded around us as a motorcade left the building. "The American president," I said. "His entire speech this morning was against us." I remembered how only a few years earlier this president's predecessor and the Minister had shaken hands in the hallways of the General Assembly, an unrehearsed, momentous event, as spectacular as Vito Corleone sitting down after all the bloodshed with the Five Families.

"Listen," Omid said. "I want to put the past behind us."

"Give me the candy box," I said. "I will take the ashes."

He placed the box in my palm.

"Where shall I scatter them?" I said.

"As you see fit. We only just found out that he wanted to be buried there."

"No one had seen his will?"

"He had a *mystic* will—the kind that's sealed until death."

"Leave it to *bābā* to have a *mystic* will," I said.

He laughed, that boyish chuckle of his that I had forgotten but which now assaulted me with a memory of the two of us one summer at the beach in Babolsar, building in the sand the city of Uruk, of the king Gilgamesh. We did this to impress our father, who had a fascination with *The Epic of Gilgamesh*, a Mesopotamian tale of friendship and kingship, immortality and mortality. It was, he said, the oldest known preserved written literature in the history of the world, and even though it was a narrative told from the point of view of our ancient enemies—the Mesopotamians who would one day become the Arabs—he read to us from it nightly, telling us, again and again, the tale of the mighty but tyrannical king who found goodness, and ultimately wisdom, through the death of his dear friend Enkidu. That summer day, Omid and I, giddy with the sun-drenched hours of freedom before us, carried pails of water from the sea from sunrise until day's end, and we fashioned the dwellings, date grove, clay pit, and even the temple of Ishtar, believing that we would forever live together within our own city of sand.

"Omid," I said. "Come back to Tehran. It's a different place now. So much is happening, pushing in all directions. It may be ugly, and wild, but it's alive, and in its wildness it reminds you that you're alive, too. You—all of you who left and never returned—are frozen in time. You have one final memory and you keep playing and replaying it. And you have already bred a new generation with no memory of their beginnings except for the occasional kebab they eat with their relatives in some restaurant in New York or Los Angeles, an old pop icon's record playing in memoriam. What's holding you here?"

"Nothing," he said, "but time. Too much time has passed. It's like a caesura in a poem. Once you have that break in the line, you can't go back."

"When did you become a poet?" I said.

WE PARTED WITH A PROMISE to make up for lost time, starting with lunch the following day. As he exited the UN gate he held up his hand in a Vulcan salute as he used to do when we were boys, then dissolved into the crowd on First Avenue. I held the cold tin box in my palm. My father.

2

L YING ON THE HOTEL BED IN THE DARK I stared at the
tin box, glinting in the red neon glare of the delicatessen sign
across the street. *Look here, old man,* I said out loud. *Even in your
last will and testament you demanded the impossible—to die in
one corner of the earth and be buried in the other.* I opened the
box and stared at the ashes, which were alabaster and grainy—
nothing like the gray cinders I had envisioned.

As a boy, I would lie next to my father as he would nap and
I would slide down on the bed until my feet were lined up with
his, pretending that his right foot was the best friend of my left.
Now I held the box and realized that I didn't even know the size

of his feet. All these years, a whole lifetime, and I could not tell you the size of my father's feet. An avalanche of things I didn't know descended on me. What time of day was he born? What was his favorite subject at school? Who was his first kiss? How did he feel the first time he walked into the university to teach art? And the day I was born, was he joyous or perturbed? I had spent so much time defending my own existence to my father that I had overlooked *his* existence.

I got up and stumbled to the fridge. Miniature Bacardis, Veuve Cliquots, and Johnnie Walkers, sized for a gnome, faced me with scorn. There was also a vial of Kahlúa liqueur: to mix with what, exactly?

Looking out the window, I saw pedestrians hurrying toward their encounter with their storied city, whose harshness, I imagined, stood in stark contrast to its promise. This, I understood, was the gamble of New York, the gamble that my own family had made. But like any gamble, it required luck to work out. And as the saying goes, the house always wins.

In the morning the Minister and I were to meet with the Americans over the return of stolen artwork, found in the possession of a Geneva-based dealer who had smuggled a drawing to New York some years earlier, and was about to sell it to a private collector for a considerable sum. Federal agents had seized the work and had stored it in a warehouse in Queens. The drawing— *The Pilgrim*, by Reza Abbasi, court painter for a time for the Safavid king Shah Abbas—portrayed an old man on pilgrimage to the Imam Reza shrine in Mashhad. It had been stolen from the shrine's museum, and the custodians, one of whom—Mostafa Akbari, a man who for decades had been my Rasputin but who no longer spoke to me—had in recent months turned its theft into a matter of national indignation. No friend of the Minister and his foreign policy, Akbari knew the artwork's repatriation could be used as gasoline to ignite the collective psyche.

Symbolism aside, Abbasi was important to me because he had once been among my father's preferred artists, and in later years—long after my father's flight—my own. With his signature calligraphic lines, he was the first to forgo princes and heroes in favor of the everyman—dervishes, merchants, pilgrims, and scribes—and to turn the ordinary into something worthy of depiction. Why the Americans refused to hand back the drawing can be attributed only to malice. While in recent years they had returned several stolen items, they had now resumed their vengeful ways. And the Minister and I, were we to return home empty-handed, would be offering the Mashhad grumblers fodder for their false grievances.

SOMEONE KNOCKED. "Room service," said the voice.

A young man in a three-piece suit entered and placed a silver pot of boiling milk and a lone glass on the table. "From the Minister," he said. "He wishes you a good night's sleep." I thanked him and gave him the compulsory New York tip, which was someone's daily salary in Tehran.

That a man of my age and history should need warm milk in order to sleep was absurd, but the habit had taken root in me decades earlier, when, sleepless, I would tiptoe into the kitchen in the middle of the night to find my father, also awake, in his pajamas and felt slippers, sipping boiled milk and reading. Something about the midnight darkness stripped my father of his veneer, and on those occasions he seemed to me as no more or less than a man, like a flower reduced to its anther. After pouring me a glass he would fetch my coloring book and pencils, and we would sit together in silence, I coloring, he reading, until sleep would overtake us both and we would retreat to our respective bedrooms to wait out the darkness, each taking comfort in the other's unspoken vigilance.

AS THE MILK BEGAN TO SOOTHE ME, my phone buzzed. A text from Noushin. She had been pestering me about a divorce and had dragged me to court three times. The judge would see us next Wednesday at ten in the morning, she informed me. "And Hamid, this time please don't play games. I want nothing from you. Only a signature."

When I thought of us as we had been in the beginning, I yearned for her, still. The night we met, some twenty years earlier, she had been rounded up with her hip friends at a loud party held in her apartment uptown. Because a bootlegged copy of the film *Z* by Costa-Gavras was found in her VCR, the police had sent the group directly to the detention center. I interrogated her as I did the rest of them, going through the routine questions—how much alcohol had she consumed, who supplied it, why were the women so scantily dressed, why did the men look like hoboes, and other inquiries that made me feel like a customs officer checking off compulsory boxes on a form. But there was something about her that made me pause. She had the sullen, angular beauty of Anouk Aimée, my mother's longtime screen heroine, and I imagined her driving at nightfall too close to the edge of a mountainous road, envisioning an escape from the tedium of the visible world. She answered my questions courteously but with a hint of annoyance, which charmed me. Annoyance rarely emerged during a first interrogation. But the times were changing. It was the summer of

1997 and reformists were high on their *labbādeh*-wearing candidate's victory to the presidency. I attributed her insolence to her relative youth, her graduate art degree, and her generation's newfound sense of entitlement. *Tolerance, civil society, dialogue among civilizations*—in those crepuscular years of the last millennium these words had infiltrated conversations, carrying echoes of the Austrian Hans Köchler and our own Ayatollah Haj Agha Nourollah, the old constitutionalist from Isfahan. I, too, was feeling more optimistic than I had in years, believing that we would, at last, align ourselves with what we had set out to achieve so long ago.

Still, I had a job to do. "The police report indicates that *Z* was in your VCR," I said. "Are you planning an insurrection?"

She laughed. "An insurrection?" she said. "Aren't you people revolutionaries? You above all should appreciate the film. Besides, it's set in a fictional country."

"Where did you get the bootleg?" I said.

"I found it on the street," she said, averting her gaze.

"What about the bootlegs of the Foo Fighters and Pearl Jam in your stereo? You found those on the sidewalk, too? You must be a very lucky gleaner."

She said nothing. It was past midnight and a sudden fatigue overwhelmed me. As though trapped in an infinity mirror, I saw before me multiplying reflections of my father in his suit and necktie, alternately facing me and looking away. *Z*, I remembered, had caused a stir in my own household when I was a boy. In 1969, the year the film was released in America and Europe, my father, recently employed by the Ministry of Culture as director of national archives, had also been recruited as a member of the Commission of Dramatic Arts, whose task, among others, was to censor films deemed offensive to religion, the monarchy, the government, the military, morality, and national unity. Not yet hardened by the ludicrousness of the Commission, my father had found the deliberations over the banning of *Z* particularly distressing. "It's a very good film," he would say, mostly to himself, at the dinner table or during a drive. "How can I, in good conscience, ban it?" My mother would remain silent during these solo negotiations, like someone waiting for hiccups to pass. In the end the film was banned, and decades later, with a new regime and another censorship apparatus in place, I bought a bootlegged copy and encountered, at last, what my father had banished, and what I—like my father—was forced to efface all over again.

But I felt too tired to revisit any of that. So I focused instead on her confiscated camera, a Leica M6 that sat like the black box of an airplane on the desk between us.

"You know that I have to ask you to give me your film, don't you?" I said.

"You don't have to," she said. "You may want to, but that isn't the same thing."

"What's on that film?"

"Will you believe me if I tell you?"

"Let's say I will."

"A series of self-portraits."

"For what purpose?"

"To understand myself better," she said.

"And do you?"

"What?"

"Understand yourself better?"

She looked around the room, which, except for the desk and the requisite posters on the wall of the two Ayatollahs—the original and his successor—was bare. "Allow me to photograph you," she said. "It would be for my series."

"You can't charm your way out of this," I said. "Besides, I don't see how I would fit into your self-portrait series."

"You are my interrogator," she said. "And as such you have already become a part of my biography."

"What goes on here must not be recorded," I said.

"There was a time when what went on here was prime-time television."

She was referring to the early days of the revolution and the videotaping of interrogation sessions, called *mossāhebeh*— interviews, recantations that were regularly broadcast on television.

"Weren't you a child back then?" I said. "How do you remember?"

"There was nothing else on television in those days," she said.

I KNEW THAT BY ASKING to take my photograph she was stoking my vanity, and slyly turning the table on me. But I didn't care. Something about her boldness reminded me of the revolutionary I had once been. Besides, for so long I had been the chronicler of other people's records. To be recorded felt like a kind of surrender.

She adjusted her camera and watched me through her viewfinder. I leaned back in my leather seat, my Captain Kirk's command chair, as I always joked. Most of my colleagues, villagers with religious leanings and a second-grade education, didn't get the reference, but a handful—those who like me had grown up watching American shows on their color televisions— appreciated it. This is how I had earned the nickname *Capitān Kir*—"Captain Prick"—a moniker I protested but which in truth pleased me. During lulls in the interrogation I killed time by telling stories of how my brother and I, addicts of the show, used to host *Star Trek* parties for the neighborhood kids, complete with Spock ears and blue-green drinks we made with grapes and a splash of blue curaçao.

I clasped my hands on my stomach but the pose felt forced. I leaned forward, my arms firm on the table, but that didn't feel right either. "How shall I sit?" I said.

"Any way you like," she said. "Be yourself."

"But how can I be myself in a place like this?" I said, looking up at her, and it was at that moment that she pressed the shutter.

I watched her from across the desk. Her metallic eyeliner exaggerated the blackness of her eyes and a trace of hastily removed lipstick stained her lips, making her look like a fading Roman mosaic. She stared back at me, then bent her head, smiling and biting her lower lip. *Here is a woman who knows how to look at a man*, I thought. *Audacity and reticence in just the right dosage.* I retrieved a gold-foiled chocolate from my desk drawer and offered it to her. She took it but didn't eat it. I got up and paced the room, unsure of what to do next. The fan on my desk spun against the summer night; a broken blade clicked at every rotation and threatened to come undone.

I stood back, enchanted with the ruby toes peeking out from her stiletto sandals; she hadn't had time to change her shoes when the party was raided. Taking a few steps forward I stood close behind her chair. She didn't flinch. Gently I placed my palms on her shoulders. She bent her head to the side and rested her right cheek on the back of my hand. Her skin was warm and throbbing with life. Her chiffon headscarf slipped off her hair and she let it fall to the floor. With my index finger I wiped the sweat near her temple, then I bent just a centimeter or two toward her head, which smelled of strawberries and cigarettes.

We remained like that a minute or two before I released her. "You're free to go," I said.

"And my friends?" she said.

"I'll have them released, too."

She took her camera and fixed her headscarf. But before she got up, she glanced at the dossier on my desk bearing her name (Noushin Taheri), her age (twenty-five), her address (Ziba Street), her job (associate at Anahita art gallery), the people she was arrested with (Mariam P., Shabnam S., Parissa A., Reza A., and Babak M.), where she spent her weekends (at a museum or in Park-e Mellat), her favorite café and drink (the cappuccino at Café de France on Gandhi Street), and other facts known only to her—and now to me and to the government archives. She walked to the door, but before leaving she turned around and said, with an inward smile, "Well, *aghaye* Mozaffarian, if you'd like to see a print of that photograph, you know where to find me."

Twisted, like me, I thought to myself. I was thirty-seven years old and I had finally met my match.

STUCK NOW BETWEEN REGRET AND REVENGE, I held the phone and read her text over and over. "I'll come to court," I wrote back. "Just so I can see you."

"I didn't want it to come to this," she wrote. "But Golnaz has agreed to testify on my behalf."

"Testify on your behalf or against me?"

"Isn't it the same?"

"Get lost," I wrote.

And she did. All that was left was the lifeless screen, and our final exchange—the epitaph to our history together. Soon even the screen went blank.

Here I was once more, in unbounded solitude, a place I knew better than my own address. When I thought of how hard I had worked to get there, I was sorry that I wasn't enjoying it more. I stared up at the ceiling, at the crystal chandelier glinting in the moonlight, and I heard the sound of my tired breath inside absences I had spent decades collecting, with the same diligence and fervor with which my father once amassed his beloved encyclopedia.

3

BY THE TIME OF MY ARRIVAL, in the summer of 1960, my father had been at work on his encyclopedia for nearly a decade. If I had to associate a smell with childhood, it would be the scent of buckram and paper—not the innocuous kind found in stationers, but from moldy manuscripts piled up in every corner of his office, the largest room in our small apartment on Pahlavi Street. My mother, who still only half-jokingly called herself Monir Farahani *Ed Dowleh*—this last obsolete suffix a reference to her supposed aristocratic heritage—endured his mania with the pragmatism of a jockey putting up with her thoroughbred's quirks. Though she claimed she was from old money, she had reconciled herself to the fact that having married an academic, the best she could now hope for was not wealth, but recognition from the band of university highbrows she couldn't tolerate. Her father, Ardeshir Khan Farahani, a man with a Shah Abbas–style mustache who was our family's supplier of French porcelain, had cut off all financial support, as he had never cared much for his impractical son-in-law, likening him to Don Quixote and calling him "Don Mozaffarian, man of Shatt al-Arab." This moniker, a reference to the circumstances of my father's birth, was an unconcealed attempt to estrange him: my father had been born two weeks early on a ferry crossing the contested river named "Shatt al-Arab" by our Arab neighbors and "Arvand Roud" by us. The exact spot of the birth, as the ferryman later described it, was past the juncture with the Karun but before the fork of the Tigris and the Euphrates, leaving my grandparents, who in those days lived in my grandmother's province of Khuzestan, with a harrowing story and a stateless baby. And even though the matter was eventually resolved and a birth certificate was issued, my father, throughout his life, was branded with a fishy provenance teetering on the border of an Arab land.

To all appearances my father ignored my mother's peacockish family and labored on his encyclopedia with the precision of a scribe, becoming, over the years, the mythical simorgh toward whom art history disciples, like Attar's fabled birds, made their pilgrimage. In 1972, four years into his stint at the Ministry of Culture, he received an endowment from the government. He expanded his study to the apartment above ours and hired three scholars who showed up with their Samsonite briefcases every morning at seven o'clock with the fidelity of the three magi bearing gifts. I had nicknames for all three: the bumbling Frenchman with a penchant for Pierre Cardin trench coats became "Monsieur

Hulot," the stout Englishman with the bulbous nose was the "Earl of Sandwich," and the Persian reputed to be a genius who consumed copious amounts of marzipan became "Yasser Maghz-Pahn—big-brained Yasser."

Seven years later, when everything came to an end, M. Hulot and the Earl packed up and returned to their respective homes, but Yasser Maghz-Pahn, who maybe wasn't such a genius after all, decided to remain because, he said, he had been only a scholar and had committed no crime. He must have forgotten that before becoming my father's minion he had for years been a critic denigrating the artists of the Saqqākhāneh school, who integrated in their works local motifs from mythical lore, religious symbols, or objects found in the bazaars—amulets, zodiac signs, astrolabes, and even the lowly *āftābeh*—the toilet ewer. "Marcel Duchamp," the eminent Yasser had written in 1964 following the Fourth Tehran Biennial, "born in the land of Molière, Montesquieu, and Voltaire, could permit himself to proclaim a urinal as art, but we, already regarded as Hajji Babas on flying carpets, can hardly afford to do so. I suggest we let the toilet ewer do what it was designed to do: wash our behinds." The poor fool is buried in Behesht-e Zahra cemetery, in an unmarked grave not far from the old prime minister Amir Abbas Hoveyda's.

4

LOOKING AT ME NOW, one wouldn't guess that I started out in this world as the kind of boy who would crouch in a corner of the kitchen, softly biting into a cookie and catching crumbs in my cupped hand. That I arranged my colored pencils according to shade—light to dark—and my books according to size, the spines aligned and facing the same direction like a field of sunflowers. That going to sleep I counted to ten to keep death at bay, and upon waking each morning I placed one hand on my heart to make sure it was still beating and the other on my penis to make sure it was still there, a habit that earned me a few slaps from my mother.

From my earliest years, I was in love with glass. I had a

collection of nineteenth-century sulfide marbles—transparent globes with porcelain figures inside. My father would help me send for them from Germany through one of his art magazines. My favorite marble, the one that contained a milky snow owl, was, according to my perfectionist father, faulty, because the owl was cracked. This defect didn't bother me; it only made me love that marble more. When one afternoon after school the marble went missing, I searched frantically, first in the vicinity of the crystal ashtray on the coffee table—where I had left it—then inside drawers and under furniture and even behind the toilet, where I discovered a ladybug, dying.

At the dinner table that evening my father confessed that having found the marble in the crease of the sofa the previous night, he had thrown it out. "The thing was broken," he said, serving me a second helping of the eggplant stew that I had eaten under duress the first time around. I shook my head no, but my voice wouldn't come. The memory of my chipped snow owl, now gone, made me cry with an intensity that embarrassed me. My father reached over his plate and handed me his monogrammed handkerchief. He promised to order more marbles from the magazine.

"Remember, dear boy, harmony!" he said afterward. "Without it things collapse." He explained that to make those sulfide marbles a glassblower would heat the tiny figure at the same temperature as the molten glass globe that would encase it; even the slightest difference in temperature would cause either the marble to shatter or the figurine to crack.

I longed for harmony but didn't believe in it. The world had presented me with too much incongruity: my father, the hermetic scholar, versus my mother, the unfulfilled socialite; my devotion to a prayer stone my uncle Majid had given me shortly before he died in a car accident, versus the stone's complete indifference to me; the uninterrupted presence in my mind of the vanished uncle Majid, of whom I remembered only his knowing smile and his black bowler hat; and the fact that pleasant things, like the smell of burnt sugar, sometimes made me cry.

In glass I found my own deliverance. I saved used bottles and arranged them like soldiers on the bathroom windowsill, where they would catch the afternoon light and refract it back on the floor as dancing shadows. That they had once contained such remedies as pennyroyal and rosewater and marjoram pacified me. The bottles, I believed, protected me from the world.

I loved glass because it didn't want to be defined. Was it solid molten earth or a liquid that moved so slowly that it seemed not to move at all, like the earth itself? I loved it, too, because through it I learned to see—the world appearing to me not as a smooth continuum but as a series of erratic shapes, reflected and refracted, changing color according to the time of day or the light in the sky. And I knew, besides, the heartbreak everyone experienced at the sound of shattering glass. A chipped pitcher, a splintered breakfast bowl, a shattered mirror—no other broken thing triggered such sorrow.

My father, believing that I was exhibiting the characteristics of glass, offered me a book, John Amos Comenius's *Orbis Pictus*—a children's pictorial encyclopedia from the seventeenth century—which he hoped would inject me with a dose of reality and make me more solid, less translucent. The full title was *Visible World, or a Nomenclature, and Pictures, of All the Chief Things That Are in the World, and of Men's Employments Therein.* It was, said my father, the forebear to all subsequent children's picture books, and pulling it out of his suitcase after a business trip to London, he placed it in my hand with the reverence one may devote to a prayer book. "Take good care of it," he said, and kissed my forehead. Thinking that we might be performing some kind of religious ritual and hoping to live up to the moment's gravity, I brought the book to my lips and kissed it. My father watched me for what felt like a very long time. "What is this nonsense?" he said, as he poured himself a glass of Cointreau. "Sentimentality, as Oscar Wilde observed, belongs to one who wishes to have the luxury of emotion without paying for it."

That a book could contain the "visible world" seemed to me like an undeliverable promise. And soon I found that like all things in the visible world, this book could not fulfill its pledge: already in the second chapter there was a discussion of God, the most absent of all absentees, described as "a Light inaccessible . . . Everywhere and nowhere." The accompanying drawing was nothing like the paintings of the white-bearded old men of Michelangelo and Benvenuto Tisi printed in my father's reference books, but a sun with a triangle inside, along with letters in some undecipherable, extinct language. After an initial sense of betrayal, during which I convinced myself that I had been the victim of an inexcusable lie, I gradually came to admire the book's lapse. Allowing the absent to enter the tyrannical assembly of the present was a silent concession by the author that the dead are not very far away, and it assured me that my own marble, with its snow owl cracked since birth, remained, despite my father's casual murder of it, somewhere in this world.

After much deliberation I accepted John Comenius as one undertakes a new friendship. For many afternoons I sat fully clothed in the bathtub under the bottles and read his book, cover to cover, discovering its catalog of a seventeenth-century world, which had remained largely unchanged from my own—*fire, air, clouds, water, earth, metals, stones, trees, flowers, corn, shrubs, singing birds, ravenous birds, water fowl, laboring beasts, wild beasts, serpents and creeping things, sea fish and shell fish, the outward parts of man, the head and the hand, the flesh and the bowels, the channels and bones, the outward and inward senses, the soul of man, husbandry, the making of honey, bread baking, fishing, fowling, butchery, cookery, the shoemaker, the carpenter, the mason, a house, a mine, the blacksmith, the traveler, the horseman, carriages, passing over waters, swimming, shipwreck, writing, paper, the book binder, a book, a school, geometry, the aspects of the planets, moral philosophy, prudence, diligence, temperance, fortitude, patience, humanity, justice, liberality, the tree of consanguinity, a city, judgment, the tormenting of malefactors, a burial, a stage play, the kingdom and the region, the army and the fight, the besieging of the city, religion, the last judgment, the close.*

I didn't initially grasp that the book was in Old English, and for weeks afterward I recited my favorite passage, which I dutifully memorized in my very poor English, to anyone who would listen, never understanding why it garnered so many laughs from the adults—namely my parents and my father's associates from the Ministry—whom I had hoped to impress rather than amuse. The passage, which I still remember, was in the section describing man, and went as follows:

The inward Senses are Three:

The Common Sense, (under the forepart of the head), apprehendeth things taken from the outward Senses.

The Phantasie, under the crown of the head judgeth of those things, thinketh and dreameth,

The Memory, under the hinder part of the head, layeth up every thing and fetcheth them out: it loseth some, and this is forgetfulness.

Sleep is the rest of the Senses.

TO PROVE TO MYSELF the existence of the world I followed the book's example and began to draw. I drew my father's eyeglasses, my mother's faux fur coat, my grandfather's imperial mustache. I drew the chipped porcelain Harlequin on the piano and the tarnished silver samovar in the kitchen. I drew winter coats hanging limp on the rack by the front door and hollow gloves stacked palms up on the console in the foyer, like hands outstretched and waiting. I drew my mother's wedding dress, wrapped in an ink-blue cotton shroud, like some precious relic that could disintegrate if exposed to daylight. I drew, one summer afternoon, a bruised apricot fallen from the tree in our yard.

I tried to draw Uncle Majid, but I could not remember him as he had been. *The memory loses some*, I thought, *and this is forgetfulness*. With charcoal I traced the jagged outline of a black bowler hat and propped up the drawing by my bed.

"What's this?" asked my father when waking me for school one morning.

"It's Uncle Majid," I said.

"That's not Uncle Majid," my father said. "That's a hat."

"It's Uncle Majid," I said again.

FROM THAT DAY ON my father ridiculed my drawing of Uncle Majid. I cried, publicly and shamefully, and my father introduced the storyline that would accompany me for the rest of my childhood: that I had a penchant for cracks, scraps, and splinters. That I was very thin-skinned, that I would break before long.

But I held on to my drawing of Uncle Majid. I needed it in order to be in the world.

5

UNTIL FIVE DAYS BEFORE HE DIED Uncle Majid was a house gardener who held no aspiration to be anything else. To my father—his older brother—this was a disappointment, and to my mother, it was one more familial humiliation. Why a man may wish to spend his days with rakes and hoses was, for them both, beyond comprehension, but my uncle insisted that the toil was good for the soul and until one has spent hours with hands dipped in earth one cannot know the meaning of existence. He had three clients in north Tehran: a Jewish steel industrialist, a wistful widower with a passion for tulips, and a professor of mathematics with a blond Irish wife whom everyone called "the Englishwoman." More than once my father offered to use his connections at the Ministry to get his brother a job at one of the city's municipal parks, say, the Niavaran garden or Shahanshahi Park, but Uncle Majid declined. "I would never work for anything named Shahanshah—king of kings," he said. "Be it man or park."

In addition to his modest ambitions my uncle exhibited few vices. He didn't drink, didn't smoke, couldn't go anywhere near opium because he was prone to migraines. His food intake was measured and his clothes even more so; his collection of wool cardigans—hand-me-downs from the professor with the Irish wife—along with his bowler hat, made him look like he was perpetually stepping out of a Marks & Spencer catalog. His speech embodied the restraint of his outfits: he didn't care for gossip and never trespassed anyone's privacy. Of current events he was adequately informed but he read few books; even in his intake of information he was cautious, as though too much knowledge consumed at once could induce in him a fit of indigestion. No storyteller at the dinner table and certainly not a wit, his main virtue was kindness, which meant that all in all, Uncle Majid was deemed by society—our family included—to be rather dull.

But what he lacked in eccentricity was made up for by his wife, Azar, a professional grumbler who carried a small bottle of ethyl alcohol in her bag to disinfect surfaces the world forced her to come into contact with—a stranger's telephone, an armrest, the door handle of a haberdashery, where she could be found on any given afternoon buying ribbons, buttons, or trimmings for her homemade outfits. According to Uncle Majid, she washed all the paper money in her wallet each night before going to bed and hung the bills to dry in the bathroom, pinned to a clothesline. "What about *him*?" my father would joke, pointing at Uncle

Majid. "Do you dip him in ethanol each night before bed, too?" Azar would shrug, indicating that there was no danger of her ever coming into direct contact with her husband, and my uncle, who had fairer skin than any of us Mozaffarians, would turn red, and surrendering, would bow his head.

Until an incident in the fall of 1970, when my father returned from Germany with a Märklin train set, I had no definitive opinion of my uncle. His presence in our house was comforting in the way that a pair of woolly slippers tucked under the bed can be. When my father, galvanized from his visit to Cologne, where he had attended an art fair with the unpronounceable name Kölner Kunstmarkt, stacked the train boxes on the coffee table, Omid and I looked on with disbelief. The set had a steam locomotive, several passenger cars, dining and baggage cars, and stretches of track, some straight and others curved, all designed to link to one another and create a world so magical that no child—not I, certainly—was worthy enough to enter.

And I was, in fact, denied entry. My father enlisted Uncle Majid to help him assemble the set, allowing us—the children and the wives—to watch from a safe distance. My mother, who had no interest in toys and gadgets, turned on the television and busied herself with some old French film; it was *Children of Paradise*, a three-hour epic she had seen multiple times, twice with me. Dolefully she chewed a slice of pineapple, glancing every now and again with dismay at the bowl of towering yellow fruit masquerading as her dinner. She had been following, since the summer, "the Sexy Pineapple Diet," which instructed its adherents to eat nothing but bowlfuls of pineapple for two days every week. Like a teenager replaying a tragedy song, my shrinking mother, who repeated the diet weekly despite everyone's objections to it, was beginning to resemble a yellow trumpet fish and was turning our house, with its growing heaps of Brazilian pineapples, into the Tropicana. My father called her Carmen Miranda.

Azar sighed and slumped into a chair, fidgeting with the uneven sash of her orchid dress. "Do you know," she said to no one in particular, "that I could have become a fashion designer? Who knows where I could be now—London or Paris or even Amsterdam . . ." No one answered. I examined her gaunt face and her downturned mouth. *By all means*, I thought, *go! Walk across London Bridge, play the accordion on the Eiffel Tower, buy yourself some clogs and twirl with a Dutchman along the canals of Amsterdam, or better yet, hop on a Märklin train and huff your way out of our lives.* The unkind trail of my thoughts liberated me, and I could have carried on, were it not for my uncle who, watching me and Omid seated on two dining chairs side by side with our hands idle on our laps, said to my father, "Let the boys help us, Sadegh. After all, isn't all this for them?" My father, sleeves rolled up and tie undone, shook his head and said, "Do you know to what lengths I went to get this? It's expensive, and vintage besides. I won't have it ruined by these two clowns."

Omid and I watched as the men tinkered for hours with the cars and rails, constructing and deconstructing the set on the dining room table. Throughout it all, my father treated Uncle Majid like an orderly, but more than once, when Uncle Majid was the one who solved an engineering conundrum, he reluctantly shut up, though he never went so far as to grant his brother due credit. I ignored their bickering, listening instead to the sound of the television in the background, to the smart-alecky voice of Arletty playing Garance, the woman who receives the love of four men—including the mime, Baptiste—but who, in the end, must relinquish all.

As the film's final scene played and the carnival music drowned the cries of the lovelorn Baptiste calling out Garance's name in the crowd, Azar bid everyone farewell. My aunt's one laudable trait, a consequence of her fear of germs, was that she never kissed anyone goodbye and disappeared from any gathering with little ceremony. To keep the men awake my mother brought glasses of tea, and to us she offered cookies, then apricot *lavāshak*—a fruit roll-up—and finally nothing, because it was midnight and she was going to bed.

Omid and I were allowed to stay up, as the following day was a holiday marking the birthday of Imam Mahdi, the twelfth Imam who is believed to have disappeared and who, it is said, will reemerge prior to the Day of Judgment to rid the world of its ills. Often I wondered why occultations, like resurrections and parting seas before them, no longer happened in our own lackluster time. It was as though God, now a cynical adolescent in leather jacket and shades, had outgrown his tricks, opting instead for cigarettes and Jean-Paul Sartre—whose books occupied half a row on my father's bookshelf. Still, we had this: in memory of those bygone marvels, school was closed.

I had intended to stay up as long as I could, but as I watched my father meticulously placing the dining car on the rail, the room began spinning around me and I felt unsteady on my chair. I got up and followed my mother to her bedroom. "You don't want to stay until they finish?" she said. I shook my head no, feeling inside my body a widening crack. I told her I wanted to sleep in her bed, but she laughed. "You're ten years old," she said. "Too big for that." She led me to my room and stayed while I changed into my Batman pajamas and wiped my toes with my socks. Sitting on my bed, she buried my head in her chest, which smelled of her perfume—a bittersweet scent of orange blossoms. "When you see the train set all finished in the morning," she said, "you will forget that tonight you were sad."

Even this, I thought, *my sadness, they want to take away from me.* I burst into a sob, and my mother, stiffening against me the longer it lasted, continued, "You are a big boy now and must learn to contend with the world. To survive in this life one needs an armor, like a soldier." She left a cold kiss on my forehead and walked away, shutting off the light after her. I lay alone in the dark, wondering where I was supposed to buy this armor and whether anyone was going to help me find it. And if I were to be a soldier, didn't I need a regiment? What kind of war can you wage with an army of one?

I heard Omid collapsing on his bed. "Are they done?" I asked him. "No," he said. "They are trying to make the traffic light flicker." I contemplated enlisting Omid into my army, but he was too young, and besides, I could never be sure of his loyalties. I turned to my side and stared at the blank wall. "I hate that train set," I said. Omid was quiet for some time and I thought he had already fallen asleep. "I like the bridge," he suddenly said. "The bridge is all right."

"You Kölner Kunstmarkt," I said to him as though it were an insult.

"Kölner Kunstmarkt yourself," Omid said, and we laughed out loud in the darkness of another indifferent night.

I WOKE UP, startled, to a figure standing over my head. From the silhouette of the bowler hat I understood that it was Uncle Majid. "It's finished," he whispered in my ear. "Do you want to see it?" Placing a finger on his mouth he added, "Be very quiet. Your father already went to bed."

Groggy and parched from too much *lavāshak*, I followed him to the dining room. There, on the table, were the train cars running along their faultless tracks, stopping at the traffic sign, like a memory retrieved from a dream.

"It's perfect," I said.

He brought two chairs and we sat side by side. The longer I stared, the more real the train set became and the farther my own life receded from reality. In the electric sound of the wheels rolling along the tracks, I heard, with remorse, an echo of my father's love. I was sorry for having begrudged him earlier.

"It's two in the morning," said my uncle. "You must go back to bed and I should go home. Azar is going to throw a fit."

"Yes," I said, without taking my eyes off the blinking traffic light.

"Hamid . . ."

"Just a few minutes?"

"All right," he said. He showed me the Off switch for the train and kissed me on the top of my head. "Goodbye. Tomorrow night I'll be on a real train. Azar and I are going to Tabriz to visit her family for two weeks."

"Goodbye," I said, wondering why he was so dutiful toward such a sour woman.

THE FRONT DOOR BANGED SHUT. I had never been up and alone in the middle of the night. Objects innocuous in the daytime—the porcelain figurines in the vitrine, the wall clock shaped like a hot air balloon, and even my own sweater draped over a chair—became uncanny at this hour. To distract myself I walked to the kitchen and there, as I opened the fridge and examined the contents, my earlier terror left me, replaced instead by a rush of freedom. I poured myself a glass of milk and to it I added two heaping tablespoons of cocoa powder and as much sugar as it could absorb, then I walked back to the dining room and sat patrolling the train, drunk on my sickly sweet drink and my own sovereignty.

WHEN I WOKE UP, I was facedown on the dining table. Lifting my achy head I saw my father sitting before me, in his suit and tie, staring me down. From the kitchen came the usual sounds of the morning—the clink of breakfast dishes, the news on the radio, Omid reciting some school tale to my mother.

My father said nothing. A fly was on the sun-drenched window, busy configuring for himself an exit. I sat up and rubbed my eyes. The night's events arranged themselves in my memory, and there, before me, I saw it: the catastrophe—chocolate milk drowning the rails, several cars, and the power switch. Next to it was the toppled glass bearing my fingerprints. I looked again at my father, who sat as still as the marble bust of Omar Khayyam in his study. "Explain," he said.

"I guess I fell asleep."

"Who told you to sleep here? And the chocolate milk, where did it come from?"

"The kitchen," I said.

I saw rage in my father's eyes. But after my initial fear, a strange exhilaration followed. It occurred to me to blame Uncle Majid—it was, after all, partly his doing—but I decided to do better. "Accidents happen," I said.

"You know what else happens? Nights spent without a roof. You will sleep in the garden tonight."

"The whole night?"

"It will teach you that a house is a covenant and a covenant has rules."

"Sadegh, you're going too far," said my mother as she rushed from the kitchen, cooking oil staining her white dress. "And what will the neighbors say? That we leave our son in the yard like a dog?"

My father put on his shearling jacket and left without a word. Minutes later the engine of his Paykan filled the morning air.

Sitting before the ruined train, I flipped the power switch on and off, but nothing happened. "Go wash your face," said my mother. "Your breakfast is ready."

How does one go through an entire day knowing that doom awaits him at night? Omid nagged me all morning for destroying the train set but finally agreed to help me. He blew my mother's hair dryer over the power switch in an attempt to undo the damage; it didn't work. I spent the rest of the day contemplating my defense, then my escape, and finally my surrender. "We may as well play ball," said my brother, who, bored with my misfortune, urged me to give up sulking. But given the diminishing hours of the day, playing seemed juvenile. That I was a condemned boy filled me with self-pity, followed by a sense of grandeur; there was something consoling about being maligned, having a grievance, and maybe even dying misjudged. Many great men had thus met their end. Cicero, Galileo, and our own toppled prime minister, Mohammad Mossadegh, who, as my father never tired of explaining, had been brought down by a British and American–led coup d'état after nationalizing the country's oil. Sentenced to house arrest, he had died after a long illness, secluded and alone.

IT WAS THE MIDDLE OF OCTOBER, that time of the year when nightfall arrives with stealth in the late afternoon. In that brief, liminal space between light and darkness I headed to the garden in anticipation of my banishment. The evening was clear and there would be no rain. For this I was grateful.

I sat on the grass, under the apricot tree, which since late summer had lost its fruit. Omid joined me. "Are you scared?" he said.

"Don't be ridiculous," I said.

"Do you think *bābā* will really make you spend the whole night here by yourself?"

I shrugged.

"Maybe there are wild animals roaming at night," he said. "And thieves."

"Shut up," I said. "There are no wild animals in a city."

"But there are thieves," he said. "It's too bad I never saw the train running," he added. "I wish Uncle Majid had woken me up, too."

My brother's blameless face made me envy his untarnished status in the family. "Go away," I said. "You're a selfish idiot. All you care about is yourself."

MY FATHER WAS, among other things, a man of his word. After dinner that night he told me to get a sweater and a blanket and head outside. My mother protested again, but he ignored her. I lingered at the kitchen table, chewing in slow motion in order to postpone the hour of my exile. "Hamid," he said, "I am not doing this to amuse myself. I am doing it to make you understand that the world is a chaotic place, and one must learn to live by rules in order to contain it. Otherwise the descent is inevitable." I stared at him, not understanding a word. "Will you write it down?" I said. "So I can remember." His face softening, he pulled his fountain pen from his pocket and reached for the Pan Am matchbook near the stove. He flipped it open, and in the blank space he wrote down in a miniature script what he had said.

IN THE GARDEN I wrapped my shoulders with the blanket and stared at the moon, asking it for illumination. Something bristled against the geraniums and a stray cat appeared, his green eyes glinting in the night. I called to him, extending my hand, and he wobbled toward me on his three good legs. He was white with black patches on his face that made him look like a diminutive Batman. I placed my palm on the crown of his head and he curled up against my knee, his chest heaving. I felt sorry for all the times I had chased an animal with a water hose or disrupted an ant colony with a stone. I decided to give him a name. Pofak, I called him, after my favorite potato chip, and as I said his name I was overcome with the foreknowledge that I would lose him.

As I spread the blanket on the ground, the cat, perturbed by the commotion, hobbled away. I lay on my side, the smell of grass heavy in my nose. For some time I could see Pofak's eyes shimmering in the night like memorial candles. In the distance an ambulance siren sounded; somewhere, I imagined, someone was dying. I thought about everything that had happened to me— the train disaster and the long day spent in anticipation of this night. And what, after this? I had arrived at a precipice, an ending that I could not name.

"Hamid!" I heard my uncle in the dark.

"Uncle Majid . . . I thought you would be on the train to Tabriz."

"We're leaving in the morning. By car. After your mother

called and told me what happened, I couldn't go. I'm sorry about all this."

"It's not your fault," I said.

"I explained to your father that I was the one who woke you up."

"I guess you couldn't change his mind."

"No. Never. Not even when we were boys."

Thinking of my father and Uncle Majid as boys was like looking through a telescope from the wrong end. My uncle sat on the blanket, poured a cup of tea from a thermos, and handed it to me. I took the tea though I didn't want it. On a night like this I felt I should accept any offering—a moon, a cat, a cup of tea, a kind uncle.

"What was my father like as a boy?" I asked.

"He was smart, and serious. He won all the prizes. I think he always believed that he was destined for something great."

"Doesn't everyone?"

"I didn't," he said, removing his hat and twirling it with his finger. "I never felt I could compete with him, and I didn't want to. I would finish my homework as fast as I could and go play. But your father . . . Did he ever tell you he tried to memorize the entire dictionary?"

"No. What did he do that for?"

"That was my question. I would tell him, *The dictionary has one job, and that's to remember words, so that we don't have to.*"

"Did he finish it?"

"No, he got to the letter *dāl*—D. He stopped when he fell in love with your mother."

The night was getting cooler and I began wondering if my blanket would be enough. I refilled my teacup.

"Look, don't let this incident separate you from your father."

From his pocket he pulled a prayer stone and handed it to me. "I'd like you to have this. I've carried it ever since I was a boy."

"Why have you carried it?" I said.

"It's made of earth and it has helped me stay anchored in this world."

I held the clay stone in my palm. It was cool and light, and was engraved with some Arabic letters. "Do you pray, Uncle Majid?"

"I pray when I am so inclined."

"Will you pray for me?" I said. "That I may survive this night?"

He placed his hand on the crown of my head, as I had earlier done with the cat. Then he removed his shoes and socks, performed his ablutions with the water hose, placed the stone on the blanket, and began praying, his body folding and unfolding in the moonlight. I knelt next to him and shadowed his gestures, but I had never prayed before and did not know the words.

My mind wandered off to an episode I had witnessed two weeks earlier, through the keyhole to my father's study: Uncle Majid sitting stooped in a chair, and my father, standing over him, slipping into his hand a stack of banknotes. "Thank you, Sadegh . . ." said my uncle, as my father walked to the window, hands in his pockets. "You're a fool," said my father, "not to accept the position at the municipal park. It would change your situation." Uncle Majid shook his head. "I can't work for this government," he said. "It's a question of integrity, don't you see? I am not like you." My father turned around, his face flushed. "What does that mean?" he said. My uncle, looking down, answered, "Did you forget what you did to your friend Houshang? To work for this government one must relinquish integrity." My father stared him down for some time. Finally he said, "What good is integrity if the price is your dignity?"

His head in his hands, my uncle, silent, began sobbing; he left the banknotes on the table and stood up.

"Take the money, you fool," said my father. "What are you going to live on, your tulips?"

WHEN MAJID FINISHED PRAYING, he slipped the prayer stone in my pocket and lay down on the blanket.

"You're not going home?" I said.

"I'm staying here with you," he said, holding out his arm to form a pillow for my head.

"On the way to Tabriz," he said as we both looked up at the sapphire sky, "there is a mountain range called Aladaglar. It's red and yellow and copper and green, like a giant birthday cake from some fairy tale. Imagine, centuries of eroded limestone and volcanic rock have formed it. It's one of the most beautiful spots on earth and it's my consolation prize for enduring two weeks with your aunt's family."

"Uncle Majid," I said. "Why did you marry Aunt Azar?"

"I made a mistake," he said.

I had never heard an adult speak so frankly. No justifications, no explanations. Only an admission of a truth. I placed my hand in my pocket and held on to the prayer stone. Something warm settled against my leg—the cat had returned. I shut my eyes, feeling the moonlight above me, and as I sensed my own breath dissolving in my uncle's snores and Pofak's purrs, I was, for the span of a night, happy.

WHEN THE TELEPHONE RANG at 4:59 in the afternoon five days later, my mother was out shopping with Omid and my father was in his study, listening as he often did to some musical transmission on Radio Golha. I was alone in the living room in front of the television, waiting for the end of the daily broadcast of the national anthem and the beginning of the children's program. I picked up the receiver; it was Azar. "Get me your parents," she said, out of breath.

I turned off the television and called out to my father, but the music was too loud and he couldn't hear me. "They're not here," I told her.

"There was an accident," she said. "It's Majid."

My heart pounded in my ears.

"Are you listening?"

"Yes."

"Tell your parents there was an accident. Majid went for a drive and he crashed."

I reached for the prayer stone in my pocket.

"You heard me, Hamid? You tell your parents, okay? They can call me at my family's house in Tabriz."

"Okay."

I stood for a long time by the phone. My father finally emerged from his study to refill his glass of tea in the kitchen.

"What is it?" he said when he saw me.

"Aunt Azar called. It's Uncle Majid . . . There was an accident."

He brushed me aside, looked up Azar's family's number in my mother's phone book, and picked up the receiver. When he hung up he sat on the sofa, his forehead in his palm. "Majid's car crashed by a mountain range near Tabriz," he said.

"Why wasn't Aunt Azar with him?" I asked.

"They had a fight. He went for a drive by himself."

I wondered whether, at the moment when his car began capsizing and Uncle Majid saw the Aladaglar Mountains upside down—the rainbow-colored limestone of centuries passing before his eyes—he had reached in his pocket for the earth that was his prayer stone, and, not finding it there, had bid the world goodbye.

"*Bābā*," I said. "I think this is my fault. Uncle Majid gave me his prayer stone before he left."

My father didn't hear me. "That fool," he said, staring out the window. "How many times did I tell him he was a lousy driver?"

TWO MONTHS AFTER Uncle Majid died we received, by postal mail, his black bowler hat and a wingtip shoe, also black; his body, it was said, could not be retrieved, except for a right foot, for which my father decided to hold a funeral at Behesht-e Zahra. The sprawling cemetery had just been built on the city's edge, and my father, in a leap of faith, had already bought three plots—for himself, my mother, and Uncle Majid.

6

THE ONLY ONE IN THE FAMILY to attend Uncle Majid's funeral was my father. My grandparents refused to go. *How do you bury a foot,* they said, *when you've lost a son?* Azar appropriated this lament to the point of exhaustion, telling anyone who asked—and those who didn't—*It's one thing to bury a husband, another to bury . . .* And here her voice would fade and her eyes would water, a performance that, in my father's words, would have impressed Stanislavski himself. My mother, who had bought a dress for the occasion and shoes to match, woke up on the morning of the burial with a headache that was "blinding" and stayed in bed. And Omid and I, deemed too young to come so close to death—especially one so abrupt and untimely—were not allowed to attend.

If anyone had bothered to ask me, I would have said that I, of all people, should have been present, as I had been the one accountable for my uncle's death, having accepted the gift of his prayer stone. No one asked. A week later, with a collective desire for redemption, everyone—my grandparents from both sides, and several aunts, uncles, and cousins—gathered in our home for a memorial. It was, they agreed, the least they could do for poor Majid, who died unheard and unseen, just as he had lived.

The two sides of the family rarely came together, which was just as well. I had always thought of them as soccer teams of unequal prowess. On one side, my mother's family, something like the Spanish team Real Madrid, armed with the legacy of Alfredo Di Stéfano and the deftness of Francisco Gento, winners of the Copa del Rey and six European cups. On the other side, my father's family, embodiment of some obscure team, say, Guam.

My maternal grandparents arrived first, theatrically morose. My cashmere-coated grandfather, Ardeshir, handed my mother a porcelain bowl filled with dates, and French pralines thrown in for good measure. She lifted the dish as discreetly as she knew how, looking for the telltale sign, the twin blue interlaced *L*s— the mark of the magnificent, authentic porcelain of Sèvres. This was a specialty of the antique shop owned by my grandfather, who reminded us, again and again, that Sèvres porcelain came into being in the eighteenth century with the patronage of King Louis XV and his mistress Madame de Pompadour. My grandmother, Ziba, the link to our own supposed royal but defunct heritage—a progeny of one of Fath-Ali Shah Qajar's one hundred and fifteen surviving children—was the shop's accountant and all-around manager. Their home, in north Tehran, was filled with everything porcelain—vases and clocks, tea sets and ice pails—and I was always stunned, when walking through it, to be among fat seraphs and pink-cheeked amoretti, wistful shepherdesses and naked nymphs, gemstone flowers and fantasy fish, all set against creamy backdrops haloed with twenty-four-carat threads of gold and splashes of brilliant color—fuchsia, turquoise, celestial blue, jade green, and jonquil yellow. Being in that house was like watching the real world from the inside of a Fragonard painting.

On the sofa, squeezed side by side, my grandparents seemed out of place, like a crystal chandelier hanging in a child's playroom.

"Such misfortune," my grandmother said.

Everyone nodded.

"Was the Simca very old?" my grandfather said. "People riding old cars play Russian roulette."

"The car was fine," my father said. "Majid was a lousy driver."

My mother's four siblings arrived, with husbands, wives, and children, people I had seen once a year throughout my life, if that. They filled the room, a flock of flamingos, the women in shift dresses and the men in Italian-cut suits, the kind my father also wore. There were enough diamonds in the room to fill the treasury of jewels in the National Bank. Foldout chairs were brought to accommodate the arrivals. Tea and sweets were passed around, and people spoke of the weather, which had suddenly turned cold, and of forthcoming trips. Two aunts and their brood were planning a ski vacation in Chamonix. I pictured them in their circular pattern Emilio Pucci skiwear and matching knee socks, rolling down the slopes of Mont Blanc like kaleidoscopic macaroons.

When my paternal grandparents arrived with Azar, the room shifted. People offered seats and expressions of pity, the kind you see in volunteers doing charity work for the first time.

"We are sorry for your loss," Grandfather Ardeshir said.

My father's mother, Grandmother Nasrin, cried in a handkerchief, while her husband, Grandfather Ahmad, sat impassive. For years a shift supervisor at the oil refinery in Abadan, my grandfather had, a few years after my father's birth, worked his way into a government job in Tehran. He became a clerk in Edareh-ye Sabt-e Ahval—the Office of Statistics and Civil Registration—where he was the issuer of birth certificates and collector of population statistics. This job had left him in a perennial state of tabulation, and my grandmother, born in Ahvaz and part Arab, in a perennial state of justification regarding her origins and her right to be counted among her husband's census tallies. That their eldest, my father, had entered academia and later the Ministry of Culture made them proud, you could tell by the way they dressed up whenever they came to see us—my grandfather in a suit one size too large, my grandmother in some shapeless geometric patterned dress and black patent pumps. Now they sat silent in a corner, in black versions of these outfits. Next to them Aunt Azar, in her self-made polyester knit skirt, appeared to have lost, in the presence of my mother's formidable family, all the dramatic flair she had acquired in the previous week. Shriveled and spent, she was no longer the exalted widow. She was now the dead gardener's wife.

From time to time my father, visibly irritated, glanced at his sobbing mother. He got up, finally, and interrupted her grief with a box of tissues. She blew her nose, and looking up at the room she said, "Forgive me."

Pity gained pitch, and with it came annoyance at being trapped in gloom. Someone commented on the beauty of the porcelain bowl. Grandfather Ardeshir explained that it dated from 1768 and offered an unsolicited and obscure story about Madame de Pompadour's affair with Louis XV, whom he simply called "Louis." My grandfather played up his faux-Frenchness every chance he got, quoting freely—and often erroneously, according to my father—from Molière and Racine. He spoke at length about the delicacy of the porcelain of Sèvres, of the divine quattrocento blue of a Lanvin gown, of the sanctity of bread made daily in the French home. As he spoke, guests reached for dates and pralines and other edible distractions.

MY FATHER, silent during this monologue, suddenly began reciting,

"Dar kārgaheh kouzegari raftam doush
Didam do hezar kouzeh gouyā va khamoush
Nāgāh yeki kouzeh barāvard khoroush
Koo kouzeh garo, kouzeh kharo, kouzeh foroush?"

"Who doesn't love a quatrain from Khayyam?" Grandmother Ziba said.

The cousins grumbled about my father's poetry recitation. "I don't understand," said Teymour, the wildest and the fattest, the one who used to taunt me with plastic snakes when I was small.

"The poet goes to the potter's workshop," my father explained. "He sees two thousand pots, and one of the pots speaks. It says, *Where is the potter, and where are the buyer and seller?*"

"I still don't understand," Teymour said, denting a date with his chipmunk teeth.

"My interpretation is that the potter symbolizes God," said my father. "The poet is wondering where God is, and where humanity has disappeared."

My father's spirituality only revealed itself in the presence of his in-laws, who could elicit in him humiliation and exasperation, a combustible combination that turned even him—reader of Sartre and Nietzsche—into a mystic. The room went quiet and my mother, who all afternoon had perched on the sofa armrest next to her family, gave him one of her disapproving looks, the kind she reserved for the butcher who cheated her out of a few grams of lamb each week.

"I'm sorry if the porcelain bowl makes you so despondent about humanity," Grandfather Ardeshir said to my father, smirking under his venerable mustache.

"It's not the bowl," said my father. "An object is never at fault."

My grandfather replenished his tea.

Silence. As the referee would say, it was a fifty-fifty ball.

"But how did our Don Mozaffarian," said my grandfather, "born on the Shatt al-Arab, become such a fine reciter of Khayyam? This I'll never figure out!"

Any reminder of his origins never failed to expose the fault line in my father's backbone. Invariably he would withdraw into an eggshell of shame.

AS NIGHT FELL and bottles of wine were poured, my mother's family, trapped in some hilarity, listened to Grandfather Ardeshir as he recited a passage attributed to his wife's so-called eighteenth-century ancestor, Fath-Ali Shah.

"'Some fool or other has been telling you about my wealth,'" my grandfather the baritone was saying with imperial panache. "'It is true that on the Nowruz they send me presents, but what are they?—not money—but horses and camels, mules, sheep, shawals, pearls, and such sort of trumpery. The first, as you see Mr. Ambassador, enables me to move about and then,'" here he added a stately flourish, "'the women coax me out of the two last.'"

Everyone laughed. The assembly never tired of the patriarch's performance.

MY GRANDFATHER AHMAD watched them with both deference and distaste. Maybe he was thinking that the price for his clerical job in Tehran, and his son's ascent to the peak of the social order, was the endurance of afternoons such as this. I had once asked him, during a summer trip to Babolsar, what his job entailed, and he explained that the Office of Statistics and Civil Registration had been created by the Shah's father, Reza Shah, to ensure that all births were duly recorded. This, he said, was part of the plan to centralize, systematize, and organize, and followed an earlier edict, the "Law of Identity and Personal Status," which had made the bearing of a surname a civic obligation. Bewildered families, until then content with honorific suffixes and pseudo-military titles, had to select a name that would define them for generations. Some chose their city as surname—Tehrani, Shirazi, Hamadani (of Tehran, of Shiraz, of Hamadan)—others their profession—Saatchi (watchmaker). Intellectuals flaunted their erudition—Daneshvar (learned)— and the clergy boasted religious knowledge—Shariatmadari (expert in Sharia law). It was my great-grandfather Lotfollah who selected our family name, Mozaffarian—of the family of the victorious.

"Us? Victorious?" I said.

"Why not?" said my father. "Do you know how Reza Shah selected his own name?"

I had never considered the possibility that a king could have become king without his name. "How?" I said.

"An ordinary man originally named Reza Khan," said my father, "commander of a Cossack-trained brigade who toppled the Qajars—your mother's alleged ancestors—he chose for himself the surname 'Pahlavi'—the name of the Middle Persian script practiced until the Arab conquests. This is how he offered himself an ancient lineage and gave his subjects the myth of imperial potency, a crafted historiography, a continuation of the narrative of the Book of Kings."

As usual, I didn't understand my father's words, but I memorized them nonetheless, because I believed my father the encyclopedia man was an actual encyclopedia. "What is historiography?" I said. "Do you mean history?"

"It isn't history itself," said my father. "It's how history gets written."

NO ONE TALKED to my grandfather the tabulator, who sat counting the lipstick-stained cigarette butts in the ashtray. Maybe if they had known that he, the mourner, would soon become the mourned, they would have made some effort to address him. In exactly sixty-two days, having left a friend's house at three in the morning after a game of poker, he would be blinded by the headlight of an oncoming car and would slip into a puddle of icy water, cracking his skull on the pavement at Sarcheshmeh Crossroad, right by Bahar Confectionery, which still makes the best *koloucheh* in Tehran.

TO BREAK HIS SOLITUDE I brought him tea; it was all I had to offer. He thanked me. My grandmother, next to him, cried intermittently. Her legs, two swollen buttresses in black tights, and her puffy feet crammed in her patent pumps, filled me with an ineffable ache.

"Uncle Majid and I spent a night together in the garden," I said to them without knowing why. "And there, we made friends with a three-legged cat who kept us company until sunrise."

They smiled, no doubt thinking that I, too, was fabricating some tale to outwit the specter of death.

ACROSS THE ROOM my mother was regaling her sisters with the story of how, on her Roman honeymoon with my father, she had hyperventilated and nearly collapsed in the Sistine Chapel—God's hand reaching out to Adam above her head. "One minute I was admiring the Last Judgment frescoes, the next I was sitting cross-legged, right there on that marble floor, my skirt hiked up above my knees. On the site of the papal conclave, imagine! Guards came, offered water, ice, a handkerchief. But it was all a scheme. To get these handsome Italians fussing over me! I was very operatic, once upon a time, wasn't I?"

The sisters laughed as they cracked open sunflower seeds with white teeth. But my father watched as if she were a tedious movie he had seen many times and was being forced to sit through again. I never dared ask him if my mother had really collapsed in the Sistine Chapel, as she claimed. From their honeymoon the only witness was a miniature replica of Michelangelo's Pietà, buried in the recesses of an overstuffed vitrine.

7

THE YEAR AFTER I LOST MY SNOW OWL, the Märklin train, and Uncle Majid, I developed an obsession with bugs. More precisely, it was an obsession with their demise. Capturing them in glass containers and shutting them in with airtight lids, I monitored their undoing, which lasted hours, sometimes days. The humble housefly was a stalwart fighter, but the mindless mosquito circled itself for so long that I usually ended its turmoil by flushing it down the toilet. Moths were the most theatrical and therefore the most hysterical of insects. Butterflies were too delicate to harm, and ladybugs, for which I held a particular affection, were exempt from my list.

Forced to witness these slow deaths, Omid opened the jars one summer afternoon, rejoicing as six houseflies, four mosquitoes, and a moth took flight in our bedroom, in the direction of an open window. I watched them as they exited, fancying themselves free, and I let my brother savor his budding righteousness. No matter. In another house, just a few doors down and a few hours later, a shoe would smack a fly's head flat, or a puff of bug spray would halt the mosquito's final breath.

THAT SAME YEAR my father's work on his encyclopedia took on a frenzied pace. It was at this time that he became a true insomniac, one who no longer found solace in warm milk. And I, sleepless like him, would lie in bed and listen to the midnight tap-tap of his typewriter filling the hours as I tried, again and again, to reconstruct Uncle Majid's final moments in the car— was the window rolled down, was the radio playing, did anyone witness his fall as the aquamarine Simca transformed into a coffin? Of these things no one spoke.

What we did talk about was my father's gallbladder. The sharp, unannounced pains, which he called "knife attacks." Bile, stones, indigestion, biliary obstruction. It seemed fitting that my father should have a disease of the "humors"—melancholy and rage, appropriately medieval. He banished butter from breakfast, forswore red meat, ate half the portions he once did. He grew gaunt and gray, but the attacks persisted and he gave in, at last, to his doctor's urging to have the gallbladder surgically removed.

During his hospital stay my mother, Omid, and I carried on with our days, but we circled around his absence with a jagged calm. Unable to sleep one night I tiptoed into his study, hoping to better understand the man who introduced himself to the world as Sadegh Mozaffarian. A smell of tobacco, paper dust, and anise candy lingered by his desk. On shelves along the wall were black binders in alphabetical order, where he stored encyclopedia entries as he compiled them. Next to these were a dozen editions and translations of *The Epic of Gilgamesh*, and newspaper clippings on the discovery of one more clay fragment of the reconstructed epic.

A few months earlier during our summer vacation he had explained to me that early strands of the narrative could be traced back to Sumerian poems, but the best-known version was the Babylonian, written in Akkadian, a cuneiform script. The eventual vanishing of cuneiform wiped out the story of Gilgamesh, and for two millennia the sunbaked clay tablets lay buried, along with tens of thousands of other cuneiform texts, under the remnants of the Library of Ashurbanipal in Nineveh. In these rediscovered tablets, said my father, was, among other tales, the story of the flood, precursor to the biblical account of Noah.

"How can that be," I said, "since the story of Noah is the genesis of the world?" We were sitting on the patio of the Caspian house my father had bought a year earlier, after receiving his post at the Ministry of Culture. A nest of bees—an octagonal sac that threatened to unleash an army of stingers—had formed that summer on the exterior wall; the insects buzzed and whirred as my father spoke. "The story of Noah is the one we all know," he said, "but there were other versions long before that one. In Gilgamesh the immortal man, survivor of the deluge, is Utnapishtim."

As my father carried on about the deluge, a sharp pain stabbed my stomach, pain that for weeks had been coming and going with no explanation. Doctors had found nothing wrong with me. Aching, they concluded, was part of my theatricality. And maybe, they said, I was emulating my father and his gallstone attacks. I dismissed the sensation now as best I could, and argued instead with my father, for always undoing what I thought I knew. "Are you saying everyone is wrong?" I said. "My teacher and the textbooks and even the movies?"

"The story they tell," he said, "originated elsewhere. And our job is to reconstruct from the lost fragments new versions of our origin."

"But what if more tablets are found, even older than these? How can we ever know where we started?"

"We'll never know," said my father, oblivious of the three bees dancing near his ear. "So we compile, we compile, as I do with my encyclopedia . . . We go back as far as we can see. That's all we can do."

Sitting now at his desk I wondered how he was managing at the hospital without his encyclopedia or his papers. From his bookshelf I picked up a translation of Sartre's *Nausea* but could not get past the first paragraph. I placed the book back where I had found it, next to translations of works by people whose German-sounding names I could neither read nor pronounce. Above these were several volumes by Sadegh Hedayat and a collection of stories by Gholam-Hossein Sa'edi, whose name I recognized because his story "The Cow," which had recently been adapted into a film, had earned him considerable fame. And then there was the translation of *Gilgamesh*, which he used to read to us at bedtime when we were younger. Opening it to a random page I read, of Gilgamesh pleading with Utnapishtim,

Enkidu, my brother whom I loved, the end of mortality
has overtaken him. I wept for him seven days and nights
till the worm fastened on him. Because of my brother I
am afraid of death.

To say that I was moved by this passage would be a half truth. I was, to be sure, as moved by it as any mortal would be, and briefly I wondered if the loss of my brother would similarly devastate me. This train of thought agitated me, and I grew increasingly annoyed, not by the passage itself, which I had to admit was beautiful, but by the incessant reminders of dissolution wherever I looked. Maybe grief, that exalted realm of humanity, was as tedious as any dictator.

In his top drawer I found postcards from people unknown to me—his friends and acquaintances from Yerevan or Istanbul or Rome; a moonstone *tasbih*—string of prayer beads; Air France towelettes; a dark Polaroid of a painting with the inscription, on the back, "*Caravaggio, The Calling of Saint Matthew, San Luigi dei Francesi, Rome, August, 1952.*" I remembered that my father had traveled in Italy as an art history student. What else did I know of his youth? In the back of the drawer, inside a Kodak manila envelope, was a black-and-white photograph of two boys, arms akimbo, standing under a cypress tree. The caption: "Abbas and Majid by the *Abarkuh* tree, Yazd, 1943."

AFTER THE SURGERY, still in the postanesthesia fog of half-consciousness, my father stared at nothing, his eyes empty of resolve.

"How are you, *bābā*?" I said.

He didn't answer, and I wondered if he had already forgotten me.

"How did I not see it?" he said.

I looked around. Bleached walls and white curtains enclosed the two of us. "See what?" I said.

"Majid. I didn't save him."

"*Bābā*, he died in a car accident."

He stared at the ceiling. "Did I ever tell you that when we were boys I made him carry my schoolbag? And he was so little . . . I had all the good grades, so I got away with so many things. I think," said my father, "that I made my brother suffer."

I said nothing.

"But we had good times, too," he continued. "We would ride on our bicycles to Lalezar and sneak into movie theaters. Majid loved *The Mark of Zorro* with Tyrone Power. How many times we saw that film! . . . But how could I not see it?"

"Uncle Majid died in an accident, *bābā*," I said.

"Oh yes," my father said. "The accident."

WHEN HE RETURNED HOME from the hospital, my father appeared to have no memory of our conversation. Regret seemed as elusive to him as the completion of his encyclopedia. And so he carried on, the faultless man in search of the genealogy of objects, his vision extending back to the beginning of time but unable to stretch wide enough to accommodate us, his mundane family.

8

TIME SOON BECAME MY MAIN PREOCCUPATION: I wasted it, lost it, measured it, beat it, marked it, passed it, filled it, killed it, waited for it to tell, to counsel, to heal. But I could neither forget it nor abide by it. Lessons designed to intrigue left me indifferent—another king, another massacre, territories forsaken, lands won, new nations traced and old ones erased from the world map—it all evened itself out in the end.

Omid and I diverged further; puberty was unmasking our dissimilarities. While my brother obeyed every house rule, I began disregarding them. I went alone to the shops—ignoring my mother's warnings that child predators lurked at every corner—and I bought bags of tamarind paste, sucking on them until my teeth were as rusty as a copper *kashkul*. For each piece of gum we were allowed I chewed five—all at once—and to each relative we were obligated to kiss I turned my head, so expertly that at the moment of contact all they got under their puckered mouths was a sweaty knot of unwashed hair. The rare occasions when Omid and I attempted a joint adventure ended badly, like the time we snuck into a movie theater to see Chaplin's *The Great Dictator* but got caught because Omid cried in the back—from guilt, he said—or the time we fed a feral dog the shank bone of a lamb but got bitten, Omid on his ankle, I on my hand, all because Omid could not run fast enough and I, in brotherly concord, had to slow down and suffer with him.

From the school biology laboratory one afternoon I stole a cow's eyeball and hid it in Omid's schoolbag. That night, when my brother reached into his bag to retrieve an uneaten apple and pulled out an eyeball instead, he dropped the eye on our bedroom floor and ran through the house like a madman. The eye, a milky, gelatinous ball with a giant brown iris, wiggled before settling into the geometric motifs of the carpet. As I doubled over, laughing at the absurdity of the prank and pleased with my triumph, Omid returned to the bedroom and threw his physics textbook in my direction. I dodged and counterattacked with a pencil, which pierced the top of his head, releasing a trickle of blood that stained his forehead. Bodily injury was the point at which my parents, like good NATO allies, intervened. I received the predictable admonishment from them both and it was then that I earned my most enduring nickname, *khorous jangi*—fighting cock—which, I soon learned, carried far more prestige than my previous incarnation as the boy who exhibited the properties of glass.

AND ALWAYS, I DREW. With charcoal I drew animals and plants—monkeys and elephants, cypress trees and tulips. The apricot tree in our garden, under which I had spent a night with my uncle, made a cameo appearance every now and again. When I was done with the animals I drew humans—bakers and cobblers, dancers and drifters. By eleventh grade I adopted caricatures—the most recurrent was a contemplative man with a turned-up raincoat collar, prominent sideburns, and a 1970s-style pompadour, smoking a Gauloise—my Iranian incarnation of Albert Camus. I named him "Everyman Jamshid" and autographed each drawing not with my own name, but his.

9

AFTER MY PROMOTION TO *FIGHTING COCK*, I became my father's designated companion on visits to Doctor Albert. For decades my family's dentist in Tehran, Doctor Albert, a man resurrected from the Victorian age, had drilled and crowned my grandfather's molars, extracted my father's canines, assessed my mouth more than once as one appraises a horse. To this day I owe my impeccable oral hygiene to my terror of this man. His clinic was on Lalezar Street, on the second floor of a ramshackle building flanked by a row of fish stands through which I walked with my chin tucked into my shirt collar and my nose appended to a tin of Nivea cream that proved powerless against the stench.

My father, egging me on, likened me to a fussy marquis with a snuff box and shamed me into keeping up with him. "Such affectations," he would say, "belong to your mother's side of the family." And so we would walk past the fishmongers and the still-pulsating gills of the condemned fish, and up the shabby wooden stairs where we would be greeted by the gatekeeper and makeshift secretary, Ali-*agha*, who would hand us an appointment number from his deck of cards. Naturally, a banknote slipped into Ali-*agha*'s scaly hand would nudge one to the front of the line.

In the fall of 1973, I accompanied my father to Doctor Albert's office for the extraction of a wisdom tooth. Holding on to his swollen chin my father walked with me almost obediently, not as my better but as my equal—a friend in pain. His reliance on me that afternoon both flattered and burdened me, and by the time we made it to the top of the stairs and received a three of spades from Ali-*agha*, I almost missed the father in whose eyes I had until then been immaterial and therefore free of obligations. Attempting to rise to the occasion I pulled his wallet from his coat pocket and slipped a twenty into Ali-*agha*'s clammy palm, receiving in exchange an ace of hearts, which moved us up accordingly. My father's eyes brightened; I don't think he had expected such slyness from me. Thirteen years old and puffed up with recognition, I understood, on those rickety stairs of Doctor Albert's clinic, the meaning of filial loyalty and moral malleability.

After the doctor greeted us in his starched laboratory coat and head mirror, my father submitted to the examination chair and I made my way to the waiting room—a replica of Louis Pasteur's nineteenth-century office complete with mahogany furniture, velvet drapes, and marble busts. In the wood-framed vitrines were dental tools from bygone centuries, some of which,

I was quite sure, the good doctor still used from time to time. Two patients were waiting, an ancient man holding on to his last tooth, and a woman with frumpy clothes and skin scarred from some unforgiving childhood disease. The cruelty of having to go through life with a face like that made me restless, and to distract myself I picked up a French magazine. I could read well enough in French to understand a chronicle of a five-month-long volcanic eruption in Iceland.

From the treatment room came the sound of drilling and the rising pitch of my father's scream. Doctor Albert didn't believe in anesthesia, or even in ether. He believed in suffering, and in his own ability to inflict it.

I looked up from the magazine. The old man played with his worry beads and the scarred woman looked mindlessly at a shoe shop sign out the window. I returned to the magazine and moved on to another article, this one a twentieth-anniversary commemoration of "the fall of Mossadegh." I read of the deposed prime minister's battle to nationalize the oil, of the British and Americans who collaborated to unseat him, of his supporters and detractors at home and the clashes between them, of the Shah's "retreat" to Rome—no one called it an escape back then—and of the monarch's return to Tehran, when, choked up and weary, he said of his people, "I knew they loved me." One had to feel sorry for such a man. The article quoted a *New York Times* account of the prime minister's defeat, on August 21, 1953:

An eyewitness to the surrender said the former Premier was wearing pajamas. The surrender took place in an emotionally-charged scene in General Zahedi's office on the third floor of the Teheran Officers' Club. The three who surrendered with him were Safollah Moazami, former Minister of Posts and Telegraph; Dr. Ali Shayegan, Dr. Mossadegh's former spokesman in the Majlis (the lower house of Parliament) and a chief adviser, and Dr. Gholam Hossein Sadighi, former Minister of the Interior.

The deposed Premier was driven into the courtyard of the Officers' Club and then helped from his automobile. He appeared tired and depressed. He emerged from the car, leaning heavily upon a yellow malacca cane.

On the way home I asked my father about the life of Mohammad Mossadegh; all he ever talked about was his death.

"He got his start in the Constitutional Revolution in 1906," said my father. "Later he became a member of parliament, then minister of justice, then finance minister, and again a parliamentarian. As prime minister he introduced social security and land reforms, and his downfall, as everyone knows, was his nationalization of the oil industry, which until then had been controlled by the British."

"Did you like him?" I said.

"I was among his supporters and demonstrated on his behalf and against the system. We were all accused of being Communists."

I had never envisioned my father a protester. "You, a Communist?"

"I was no Communist," he said. "I only believed in justice. But the Shah and his supporters had pegged Mossadegh as a devotee of Communism."

"Were you there on the day he surrendered?" I said. "The magazine said he was wearing pajamas."

My father held his swollen cheek and didn't answer. "I had a friend," he said after a while. "We met at the university. His name was Houshang Habibi. Still is, of course, but now he is simply known as 'H.' We were inseparable. We believed our time had come. Democracy. Self-governance. A constitution. In our future we saw these things, and more."

"What happened to your friend?" I said.

"He became an artist," said my father. "A political satirist. His drawings are in galleries all over Europe. Even here, his work sneaks its way in. But since we last saw each other, twenty years ago, he has been imprisoned three times."

"What did he do?"

"He drew."

"Why haven't you seen him in so long?" I said.

"In life you have to make certain choices," said my father curtly.

Swallows were flying overhead and a smell of burning wood hung in the dusk. "But how is it that all these years later you work for the Shah's Ministry of Culture?" I said. "Didn't you say you were against the system?"

"My dear boy," said my father. "Slowly, slowly, I became the system."

10

TO DISCUSS THE FATE OF *THE PILGRIM*, the drawing impounded in a federal warehouse, the Americans sent a low-level functionary, an assistant to the ambassador to the United Nations. He apologized for the absence of the secretary of state, citing some absurd last-minute scheduling conflict, something about the secretary's child having food poisoning and his wife being out of the country. The functionary, red-faced and tight-lipped, was the kind able to mouth meaningless words until his adversary surrenders to the farce he has been trapped in. *So be it*, I thought. *We, too, know something about farce.*

"We understand this drawing is of some importance to you,"

he began. "It's unfortunate that current circumstances prevent us from engaging with you."

"I'm glad you appreciate the value of the drawing, which is symbolic, rather than simply monetary," said the Minister. "Returning stolen property—which your own federal agents have deemed this object to be—would hardly qualify as an engagement. It's simply a restoration."

"A restoration," said the functionary, "must recognize the opposing party as worthy."

"Isn't a theft a theft, regardless of your assessment of the aggrieved party?" the Minister said. "Consider this," he continued. "That drawing depicts a pilgrim to Mashhad, resting place of our eighth Imam, Reza, and the shrine built in his name. It is one of the holiest sites of our religion, visited by millions of pilgrims every year. The artist who drew it, Reza Abbasi, was for a time court painter of Shah Abbas, who in the late sixteenth century decreed Shi'ism the country's official religion. To mark his devotion Shah Abbas made several pilgrimages to the shrine and bestowed on it sizable *waqfs*—charitable donations. So you see, the artifact we are talking about is of national symbolic significance, and your returning it would not only signal your country's acknowledgment of our heritage, but also your willingness to discuss matters of far greater consequence. We all know that this meeting is not really about a drawing."

"Look," the functionary said. "You may have gotten used to sweet-talking our predecessors. But we are in a different time now."

"If I may," I said. "What animal has the most powerful hearing capacity?"

"How should I know?" he said. "A bat?"

"Actually the moth beats the bat, by one hundred and fifty times. Do you know how it got that way?"

He shrugged.

"The moth is the primary food source for the bat. But over time it evolved to outsmart its predator. Call it nature's arms race, if you like."

"You're wasting your time," he said. "And mine."

"Why did they send you to meet with us?" I said.

He smiled with bloodless lips. "So we could tell the press that we invited you to talk," he said. "And here we are, talking. Are we not?"

OMID WAS ALREADY at the diner when I arrived. I slid into the booth and a burly waiter with a bald spot and a ponytail handed us menus as thick as his forearms. "What is this," I said, "lunch or the *Shahnameh*?" My brother smiled as he once used to. "Sometimes I get so overwhelmed," he said, "that I randomly open the menu and point at a dish."

"*Fal-e Hafez*," I said.

When we were boys we followed the tradition of seeking guidance from the *Divan* of Hafez, which involved opening the volume at a random page to find the answer to a dilemma in the verses of the fourteenth-century poet. But instead of turning to Hafez, Omid and I used as oracle *Dayee Jān Napoleon—My Uncle Napoleon*—a bestselling novel whose popularity had naturally turned our father into its critic, and us into devotees.

I remembered the time Omid came home in a panic because he had seen our father huddled over a monograph with a young woman in a trench coat and lace-up boots in the art history aisle of the bookstore. When he told me that he wanted to inform our mother, I tried to dissuade him, not so much for my parents' sake but for my own; I was in no mood for domestic quarrels. "It's a bookstore, for God's sake," I said, "not exactly Shahr-e No." Omid wouldn't have it. "For *bābā* the bookstore *is* the red-light district," he said. "There is no greater aphrodisiac in that man's life." He paced the narrow width of our bedroom. "I'm telling you, Hamid," he continued. "There was something in the way they held that volume together, their hands making love on the page. She was very pretty," he continued. "In a bookish way. She looked the very part of the sexy postdoctoral student."

I knew the kind of girl he was referring to—I had plenty of them in my own class. Beautiful, high-minded, snobbish, they unleashed volatile sexual energy in spurts as intellectual discourse, like hair spray from an aerosol can. Making love to one of them, I imagined in my still-virgin brain, would be as exhausting as being trapped in a conference on Michel Foucault. That only a year later I would fall in love with the poster child for these girls, and with Foucault himself, was unthinkable to me then. But that's how it goes in life. One often surprises oneself, at least in the early years. "What's the point in ratting on him?" I said.

"The point?" said Omid. "To let the truth be known."

I was sitting on my bed, playing a game of solitaire. "There is never one single truth," I said, "but a pandemonium of truths within the same man."

Back and forth we went, neither one of us letting go, until I pulled out *My Uncle Napoleon* from the shelf and presented it to Omid, who opened it at random and read, "Suddenly Dear Uncle remembered the treachery of those who were near him . . ." He closed the book. "Well?" he said, to me, the interpreter.

"Let the man breathe," I said. "And in any case, the bigger question is, what was a louse like *you* doing at the bookstore?"

"My research on Charles Dickens for my final paper," he said.

"I've been at it for months. But when have you not been oblivious of me?"

THE WAITER LOOMED, NOTEPAD IN HAND. In our indecision we both ordered burgers, which neither of us wanted.

"How was the morning meeting?" Omid said.

"Useless. They sent some lightweight to meet with us. His job was to refuse. They're just being vindictive, since the drawing is in a warehouse collecting dust. The custodians of the foundation that runs the Mashhad shrine will make a big ruckus, and of course they'll blame the Minister."

"For a charity foundation they make a lot of noise," Omid said.

"Religious charity foundations control the economy," I said. "It's like in medieval Europe, when the pope and his cardinals, claiming to speak for God, owned every piece of land and property."

"It's the same here," he said. "Except here, instead of holy shrines, there are corporations."

"Yes, every nation has its sermonizers. They are just in different costumes."

"So who spoke at the Assembly today?"

"The Saudi prince. I kept dozing off like we used to during *bābā*'s John Wayne movies."

"Did you know that John Wayne was a lot funnier dubbed in Farsi?" Omid said. "In English he is just a ruffian. I was very disappointed the first time I heard his real voice."

Our burgers arrived—behemoths of ground meat— accompanied by mounds of French fries, two bowls of pickles, and a full bottle of ketchup. There was enough food on the table to feed a congregation of worshippers at a Friday prayer in Qom. As we ate in silence, I felt once more the familiar weight of time, its incapacity to contain the past. Every minute spent chewing was a minute added to the cenotaph of lost hours.

"Did *bābā* ever mention that young woman, the one at the bookstore?" I said.

"The woman at the bookstore?" He paused, then said, "My God! And you tell me *I'm* frozen in time. She was a footnote in our family history."

"Sometimes the footnote is the main story," I said.

"No, Hamid," he said. "The main story was always you."

"For *bābā* I was not even an idea, much less a story," I said, wondering if my father's ashes, still in my pocket, could hear me.

"After we left all he ever talked about was what had happened to you and how you would fare all alone in that revolutionary chaos," Omid said. "We sent you many letters. You didn't answer a single one. And we tried calling you. But there was never an answer."

"I changed the phone number after you left," I said as I pulled the sports bottle from my bag and took a few sips.

"Why don't you order a proper drink?"

"You know very well that I can't be seen drinking alcohol."

"And you think you're fooling anyone with that plastic bottle?"

"Every other person in Tehran walks around with one of these. We all know what it is and we all pretend not to know."

"What the hell are you still doing there, Hamid?"

I took several sips. "Yes," I said, "I could have left that polluted world long ago, as so many have. But in leaving I would be forfeiting my self."

"What self?" he said. "You forfeited your self long ago, if the rumors about you contain any truth."

"All right," I said. "I've made many mistakes, and I've committed many misdeeds. I can't undo any of that. But I also know this: were I to leave my birthplace, I would be done for. Freedom with no lifeblood has no meaning for me."

Omid nodded and a tender smile appeared on his face. "'*Somehow the change wore out like a prescription,*'" he recited. "'And there's more to it than just window-views and living by a lake. I'm past such help—'"

"What?"

"Robert Frost," he said. "You know, I tried hard to find my place on this earth, and I think I am old enough now to accept that I failed. I spent my entire youth in the dusty stacks of libraries researching my doctoral dissertation—'The Reconciliation Between Word and World in *The Waste Land.*' But I got restless and left school with thousands of pages of notes. I tried some odd jobs—for a few years I was a copy editor at an agricultural magazine, *The Farm Gentleman*; then I became a ticket seller at the Metropolitan Opera, then a bartender in the East Village, back when it was home to junkies and dealers. Finally I packed up my bags and went to a Buddhist retreat in California, with the knowledge that I was becoming a cliché but unable to stop myself. There I met a man who called himself Denpa, a Colombian whose real name, I later learned, was Alvaro. We quickly became friends, I think because we were the only foreign, dark-skinned people at the retreat, and we were relentlessly called on by our well-meaning but sadly dim fellow bodhisattvas for an education on Otherness. Alvaro and I had patchouli-infused midnight conversations about the difference between pain and suffering. He encouraged me to purify my diet and to do body cleanses, and I spent many sleepless nights meditating cross-legged on a pillow, dizzy from a juice fast, my back stiff and my mind aching.

I believed that if only I tried hard enough I would transcend my sense of alienation, this feeling of exile from which I could never fully extract myself. But the truth is that I felt like a charlatan."

"That was *bābā*'s word—*charlatan*," I said.

"Yes," he said. "He liked that word. Everyone to him was some kind of con artist. And maybe he was right, after all. In any case," he continued, "when I returned to New York, Alvaro, who had been trying to pursue acting in Los Angeles, decided to settle on the East Coast, having had an epiphany during the retreat that he was ill-suited to the film world and would do better in the theater. We rented a ramshackle apartment in an old walk-up on East Eighty-Fifth Street, where the smell of Chinese food from the restaurant below stifled the air. Alvaro hung up beaded curtains and burned incense all day long. I remember coming home from some temp job one winter night, broke and frozen, to find him meditating in the dark on a buckwheat pillow. Not wishing to disturb him, I lay on the couch contemplating the usual plate of General Tso's chicken, and I was half-asleep when the buzzer rang. 'I'll get it,' I mumbled, but couldn't get myself to stand. He interrupted his meditation, turned on the light as he teasingly cursed me in Spanish, and answered the intercom. 'FedEx,' a voice announced from downstairs.

"'A package from my cousin in Bogota,' he said to me as he signed the slip and handed it to the courier. He had never mentioned this cousin, and I made a mental note to ask him about it over dinner. But as soon as the FedEx man had left, two police officers appeared, flashed their badges, and handcuffed Alvaro. 'What's going on?' he protested. One of the officers calmly said, 'You are under arrest for possession of cocaine,' and dragged him away with the package. Running after them into the hallway I yelled, 'I know this man. There must be a mistake.' The other officer—a red-faced man with a crew cut and bloodshot eyes—looked up from the stairway. 'Lucky for you,' he said, 'that you weren't the one who signed the slip. I'd keep my nose out of this, if I were you. Because you're not in the clear, Mr. Mozaffarian.'"

"You, in trouble with the law?" I said to Omid. "I can't imagine you entangled in such a mess."

"I couldn't either. But I was his roommate and therefore a suspect. Anyway, I got myself a lawyer, and after many months of court proceedings and lost dollars, I was cleared."

"And your friend?"

"Turned out that the cousin in Colombia had been using family members in New York to send the stuff, and was asking them to deliver the packages to a local contact. During the trial it became clear that Alvaro had no idea what the packages contained. But as he had received five ounces of cocaine, he got convicted of criminal possession in the second degree and was sentenced to eight years in prison."

"Eight years?"

He nodded, with the kind of resignation that appears only after outrage has long congealed; I knew that look well.

"Anyway, with Alvaro gone," he continued, "I sat at the kitchen table one morning and I thought, *I am a middle-aged poet with no job and no family and no home.* That's when I decided to take up legal translation, move out, and get married."

"You capitulated," I said.

"No," he said. "I surrendered. To capitulate you must believe that what you have given up was of great value. I had no such belief in my own talent. I can't say that I became happier after my marriage, because I soon realized that in my hurry to turn my life around I married the wrong woman."

"Like Uncle Majid," I said.

"Yes . . . But at least I no longer felt at war with society," he continued. "To get society off your back is no small triumph. Especially expat society."

The waiter cleared the table and slapped the bill down like a summons. "There is one thing," he said, getting out his wallet, "that feels true to me, and that's my love for my son."

"You never told me his name," I said.

"Arash," he said.

"*Arash the archer*," I said. "You haven't forgotten your mythology."

"Mythology is all I have left," he said.

"Omid," I said. "I missed you all these years."

"I did, too," he said. "You were my best friend, you jackass, and you disappeared on me."

"But don't you see?" I said. "*You* disappeared. I didn't go anywhere. For all of us who stayed home, it was the others who vanished."

He nodded, unconvinced, then put on his newsboy cap. "You sound as virtuous as a sailor's wife."

"Those early days were mad," I said. "Don't judge me by them."

"I am no judge," he said. "But look," he continued, "I have to go. My dog is old, and he hasn't been well lately." As he got up he pulled out a slim volume from his coat pocket and handed it to me. "A chapbook of my poems. I'd like you to have it."

I held the book, titled *Two Sons*. "Meet me again tomorrow morning?" I said.

"Come to my place," he said. "I live near the UN, in a neighborhood called Tudor City. You can't miss the fake Elizabethan gargoyles and cartouches on the buildings." Laughing, he added, "This country has scant history but plenty of shtick."

As I watched my little brother put on his reading glasses to write down his address, I was flooded with the regret that for so many years I had forsworn.

"By the way," he said, "Mother wants you to speak at the memorial dinner."

"Me? That's absurd."

"She wants both of us to say something."

"But what could I possibly say after all this time?"

"You'll come up with something," he said.

ON MY WAY BACK TO THE HOTEL I passed demonstrators with placards and slogans and megaphones, voices annihilating one another amid the steel towers of midtown. I made my way through them, disbelieving that in a different time and place, I had been one of them—a man with a grievance, trusting the possibility for rectification: strongmen would be banished, the fraudulent punished, forgers vanquished, and the friendless— like me—at last cherished.

In my room that afternoon I locked the door, undressed, placed my father's ashes and Omid's book on the nightstand, and slipped my body under the covers. The sheets were icy against my bare skin, but I was burning from inside. I turned on the television. There was a documentary on the eightieth anniversary of the Anschluss, Germany's annexation of Austria and the beginning of the last world war. Eighty years. What had changed since then? The world was yet again splintering, and nations, once more bewitched by ideas about racial purity, were decrying the wretchedness of the other. Newspapers said children had dropped dead like cicadas amid the scorched ruins of Aleppo and in the waters of the Mediterranean, but these deaths were no more to me than a bothersome idea I had to contend with. I shut my eyes and imagined someone somewhere preparing to attend a funeral for a body part, as I had done many times, for a few I had loved and for many I had wronged, and occasionally both at once. I knew that what was happening in the world, despite its absurdity, would one day be written up as history, as everything up until that moment had been. Maybe someday, history, like a fly-by-night lover, would send us all an apology. The message would read, "I am sorry for my ways." It would be signed by everyone who had ever lived, myself included. Suddenly, I felt in my heart a piercing pain that foretells a loss. It was a stab not for the vanishing of people, but of places, those that were mine— like the bakery near my apartment that was shuttered one morning and a month later turned into a hair salon—and those that weren't. And for memories, those that were mine—like the first time I kissed Noushin under the willow tree in the park—and those that weren't. For life—my own and others'—I felt pity but not sorrow, since its destination was already known; my father's ashes next to my pillow were proof of this.

The world may be splintering, but hadn't it been doing so since its conception? The breach had begun long before, with a million wrongs that like hairline fractures on an ancient urn finally crack it from within. I reached for Omid's book of poetry and opened it to a random page, and in the half-light of the September dusk I read.

I have two sons, my father says
addressing me, one of the sons.
I don't remind him who I am.
Lost on his way home, he calls me, says,
frantic, I don't know where I am.

I, the younger of the two sons,
say, shush, shush, like a father.
Why did you go all alone?
Walk to a corner, read me a sign.
There are no signs, says my father,
only a river and a lone
crow, and, oh, yes, one big sign,
Pepsi-Cola, red neon rising against an orange sun.
I have two sons, says my father.
And your brother will save me from you.

11

IN THE SPRING OF 1976 Minoo Levy shuffled my life like a veteran croupier. I first noticed her on a May afternoon, before the summer break, when she joined our all-boy soccer game, uninvited. Though the boys protested, she positioned herself at defense on our team; Omid, normally on defense, was sick that day.

The ball happened to be with me, and I found myself kicking it, hard. This is how the game resumed, with Minoo in it. Afterward I went up to her and introduced myself.

"I know who you are," she said. "Hamid Mozaffarian, right?"

I wiped the sweat off my forehead, maintaining a good distance. "I didn't know I was famous," I said, and she laughed. "It's your drawing that has become famous, an icon throughout the school," she said. "Didn't you know?"

I had seen photocopies of my caricature of Everyman Jamshid—my Iranian Camus—pasted inside the boys' bathroom stalls and in the courtyard, lined up in a row like mug shots above the garbage bins, but I had no idea he was anything other than a joke. "An icon of what?" I said.

"An everyman on the brink of consciousness," she said.

Not wanting to appear dumber than my own creation, I smiled knowingly and made my way home. What did it mean to be on "the brink of consciousness" and how had my drawing portrayed it? Had I intended this without fully understanding it, or were people projecting meaning onto a senseless caricature? The questions circled my mind, but as the afternoon hardened into dusk, that odd hour still unresigned to the day's conclusion, my thoughts shifted to Minoo, who was far more captivating to me than my cartoon. I thought of her white shorts and red-striped Adidas, of the improbable curl of her eyelashes and of her eyelids light as a dragonfly's wings.

THE NEXT DAY, THE LAST OF THE SCHOOL YEAR, I went down to the tenth graders' floor every chance I got until the pursuit became as thrilling as the prize. In the final hour I saw her with her friends by the school gate. Normally I would have been too timid to pierce a circle of girls, but remembering my newfound celebrity I took a deep breath, said *Besmellah*, and went in. "I wish you ladies a beautiful summer," I said. They stood silent, cheeks flushed, with their cigarettes and Levi's, looking at me wide-eyed as though I truly were some kind of luminary.

"We're all going to a secret meeting tonight," Minoo said. "Six o'clock. Come with us."

"A meeting about what?" I said.

She glanced around for prying ears. "*Gharbzadeghi*— westoxification," she said.

This was one of those words that had of late entered the lexicon of the intellectual class, among whom I did not count myself. The term, suggesting a contamination, denounced our national infatuation with the West. I had not until then given it much thought, and in truth, it mattered little to me. The meeting could have been about grasshoppers and I still would have gone just to be with Minoo. "I'll pick you up in my car," I said.

"You understand that you can't tell anyone," she said. "The meeting is at a safe house, the vacant apartment of a professor who is abroad."

"I understand," I said.

As she scribbled her address I schemed to borrow my mother's Fiat coupé, the only gift of note that she had received from her father. The alternative was my father's beat-up Paykan.

She handed me the paper and when I read her surname, Levy, I stood wordless.

"Something wrong?" she said.

"You're Jewish?"

"Is that a bother?"

"Not if it isn't to you," I said.

"I make do," she said, with irony that disarmed me.

"I meant no disrespect," I said.

"I expected better from Jamshid's creator."

"All creators are imperfect," I said as I reached for her hand and kissed it.

"Pick me up at five-thirty," she said.

TO COAX MY MOTHER out of the house I bought her a ticket to a French film showing at a theater nearby, along with a box of Swiss chocolates. The manual to my mother's heart, I had long ago discovered, was Gallic. When I arrived home I found her on the terrace cleaning the birdcage as she did every afternoon and chatting with the canary as though the bird were an old and dear friend. I handed her the chocolate and the ticket. "What's the occasion?" she said. Her face was flushed from the afternoon heat and her hair, normally styled in Charlie's Angels cascades, was up in a ponytail, making her look girlish. I felt a pang of sorrow for my scheme to take her car. "A modest present for a beautiful mother," I said.

"You want me to drop everything and go to the movies?" she said. "And with Omid still not feeling well? He is in bed."

"Live a little," I said. "I'll look after Omid."

She kissed me on the forehead, shut the birdcage, and headed to her bedroom to change. I stood on the terrace, the world open before me, the canary in full song. I didn't know what was more thrilling, the prospect of an underground meeting or of seeing Minoo. I had found a girl and a cause, all at once. What more could a man ask for? One of my father's oft-recited verses came to me, "I'm in love with the whole world, for the whole world belongs to my beloved." I could not remember who the author was but assumed it was one of the usual suspects—those medieval mystics people refused to renounce. A million verses had since been written but we all clung to the bards like the nostalgic progeny of a fallen dynasty.

With her heels clicking and echoing in the courtyard, my mother looked up and blew me a kiss, then rushed down the street to catch the five o'clock showing. During the previous months she had been softening, spending more time with me and Omid and the bird, cooking elaborate meals and ironing every last bit of linen and clothing, even our underwear. It was all overdue—I was nearly sixteen—but I appreciated the maternal effort despite the late hour. I attributed her newfound kindliness to loneliness. The deeper my father burrowed into his encyclopedia, the more attentive my mother became to us. I waved goodbye to her and held on to the moment.

To the ailing Omid I brought a cup of tea, and I made him promise not to rat on me. Green as an unripe mango and running a fever, he was in no condition to refuse.

WHEN I SHOWED UP AT MINOO'S in the convertible Fiat she leaned over the car door and said, "You do realize what the talk is about?"

"I realize," I said, making no comment about her Levi's and Ray-Bans. "Get in."

We drove off, leaving skid marks of hubris on the streets. The evening sun warmed our skin and the smell of hollyhocks and jasmine from the June gardens filled the approaching dusk. We were running away from something and reaching for something beyond, both sides as infinite and unknowable to us as the beginning of time and the end. Circling the five-year-old Shahyad Tower that embodied our pre- and post-Islamic past— its parabolic arch, echoing the ruins at Ctesiphon, interspersed with pointed arches reminiscent of mosques—we marveled at our own still unrealized possibility. Three years later the tower would be renamed Azadi—freedom—and its architect, a young Baha'i, would flee the country in that mass exodus of the persecuted and the fearful. But his creation would remain, a witness to decades of demonstrations and counter-demonstrations, to collective hopes and their stillborn offspring, to crowds converging to cry out an ancient despair and dispersing, just as fast, under batons of one creed or another.

The meeting at the safe house was as I had expected: a roomful of smoke, and opinions on rights, liberty, equality, and other lofty words that raised our emotional temperature. There were communists, socialists, constitutionalists, and historians of all stripes, reminding everyone that we had arrived at this juncture many times before, most notably in 1906 and again in 1953, and had each time been thwarted by foreign powers in our efforts to democratize ourselves. Someone recited entire paragraphs of Samad Behrangi's *Little Black Fish* by heart. Others paraphrased Marx and Hegel and Voltaire. Still others spoke of Ahmad Fardid, who had coined the term *gharbzadeghi*—westoxification— and Jalal Al-e Ahmad, who had popularized it, and of how the machine-made goods of the West were destroying our agriculture and handicrafts. The soil and the soul were invoked, again and again, and we all nodded, again and again, intoxicated with the prospect of our rebirth.

AFTERWARD I SAT in the Fiat with Minoo and held her hand. The meeting had gone on far longer than I had expected and I knew that my mother was no doubt home by now and had noticed the empty space where her car should have been. But for the first time, I didn't care. The moon was full and low in the summer sky. Anoushiravan Rohani's "Soltane Ghalbha (Emperor of Hearts)" was on the radio. I leaned over and kissed Minoo, and it was in that kiss that I forgot the hours of solitude I had already amassed and the desolate hours that I would go on to collect. Love was a sweet interruption in the lonely march toward nonbeing.

I drove for a long time afterward, aimless, postponing as long as possible my return home—humdrum territory of television, dirty dishes, a tiresome encyclopedia, and familial fences. I drove by the shops on Shahreza Street, past the convergence of *chadors* and miniskirts, and steered us downtown, where the dilapidation made us feel magnanimous for having ventured there. Near the bazaar a group of men were reciting prayers and beating their chests—another day of mourning in the endless procession of days punctured by national bereavement. "It's the martyrdom of Fatima," Minoo said, and remembering her Jewishness I said, "Well, it doesn't concern you very much, does it?" She looked away and said, "I don't see you beating your chest either."

"I don't have to," I said, one arm cockily resting on the wheel. "Chest beating is my patrimony. I have nothing to prove."

"And I do?"

We remained silent, the first incision of separation already between us.

"To be a bystander to a procession of mourners is worse than being a participant in the procession," she continued. "The mourner carries his grief like a birthright; the bystander can claim nothing but his exclusion."

The conversation was getting too sober. I would have preferred to talk about her Ray-Bans. "Let it go," I said. "Your people have their esteemed place. You are, after all, Esther's children!"

"Yes, that's our claim to fame," she said. "Esther. The beautiful slave who became queen and saved her people. That story legitimizes us as a museum validates relics."

"As far as I know," I said, "relics don't build factories or become scientists and professors. You can insist on being a victim if you want. But the fact is that I said nothing wrong."

In the pounding silence, I took a turn, headed back north, and held out my hand to her. After a long pause, she took it.

FROM AFAR WE SAW the lights of the Ferris wheel in the night sky. I drove toward them and Minoo didn't object. We parked and made our way into the amusement park, where the air carried the din of children, laughter, and electronic chimes. Minoo wanted cotton candy so we bought some, and as she held the stick and took small bites from the spun sugar, I felt an old ache rise in my heart. I dragged her to a corner and kissed her, the taste of sugar still on her tongue. We were standing behind the house of mirrors and could hear people inside marveling and giggling at their distorted reflections. Holding hands, we rushed in, laughing at the tall and lanky and fat and swirling images of ourselves, complicit in the deceit of mirrors.

From the Ferris wheel, suspended in midair, I watched the feverish city below us, four and a half million people colliding and colluding, resisting and yearning. And here we were, just two of those millions, spinning in a yellow plastic booth. "Minoo," I said. "You're the best thing that ever happened to me." I held her close and we remained like that for the rest of the ride. Dawn, I knew, would break like eggshells. But that was a long way off.

HOME WAS WHERE I found my parents, as expected. In the living room my father was reading a book on the looting of Lorestan bronzes in the 1920s and my mother was watching *Rang-arang* on television—a mind-numbing procession of pop stars in ball gowns and tuxedos delivering the latest hits, fingers snapping, bodies stiff, faces suitable for Puccini. I served myself some leftover *tahchin* and sat with them, but for some reason I could not swallow; the chicken kept sticking below my throat, refusing ingestion. I tried to make it go down with Coke, but the sweetness burned my throat while leaving the bird intact. "Are you unwell, Hamid?" my mother said. "I'm fine," I said and continued chewing. I felt myself floating about the room, swinging from the chandelier, dusting my father's gold griffin-headed goblet—some Achaemenid antique bestowed on him by the government.

"Who gave you permission to take my car?" said my mother without looking away from the television.

"*Hichkas*—nobody," I said, relishing the nihilism of the word.

Her face glowed blue in the glare of the screen. I found her beautiful, just then, more so than usual. Maybe it was the knowledge that I had at last stirred her. From the bedroom came the sound of Omid's latest coughing fit. Though I regretted having abandoned him, I reasoned that everything I had gained that evening and everything I had lost, merited my transgression. Collateral damage, as they say in the military.

"Do you know that the French movie you sent me to was almost pornographic?" my mother said over a funereal Googoosh singing "Gomshodeh."

"What, *Emmanuelle*?" I said. "Everyone says it's an amazing film. And you're always singing that Pierre Bachelet song around the house."

"I wouldn't sing it if I knew what the film was about," she said.

"I figured you would appreciate anything French," I said.

My father gave me a disapproving look, then resumed reading. He was slumped in his chair, his face lit by the ludicrous table lamp: a marble bust of Marie Antoinette with a wide-hipped linen shade. My mother had bought it at a Parisian flea market some years before, and she had been so pleased with her find that my father had finally allowed her to display it.

"What do we have to do with that old queen?" I said. "Why is she in our living room?"

"Now you have a grievance against the lamp?" said my mother. "It's just a piece of art."

"Art?" I turned to my father. "You, of all people, are not going to challenge this absurd statement?"

"I don't live alone in this house, Hamid," he said with his exasperating poise.

"You could have fooled me," I said.

He pretended not to hear.

My mother retreated to the kitchen and arrived some time later with orange cake and three cups of tea, offering a truce. Her music show ended with an abrupt beep, giving way to the color bars that appeared each midnight at the end of programming. *So long, viewers. We have nothing left to distract you with. We've shown you all our tricks, lulled you with our electronic embrace for as long as we could. Go now and face the night.*

With the television off, we drank our tea and ate our cake, the crumbs falling onto our plates. My mother, nibbling on a sliver, sat on the sofa, her legs crossed, her elegance bordering on boniness. The bitterness of the baked orange peels calmed me, and I felt sorry for having sent her to that movie, but not sorry enough to apologize. My father put his empty plate on the coffee table and extended his legs, hands clasped on his paunch.

Listen! I wanted to tell them as the excitement of the evening surged once more inside me. *The city is cracking.* For the first time I imagined myself alone in the world, without them, without Omid, even. Me. Just me. I felt a longing for that world, then panic about its possibility, then a deep sadness at its inevitability. But soon, the thought of Minoo returned to me. The white shorts, the eyelashes, the kiss in the Fiat. And these, her first words to me: *I know who you are.*

12

IF I WERE TO ASCRIBE MY FEUD with my parents in that summer of 1976 to a single trigger, it would be the event that became known in our household as the "Campbell's Soup Incident."

At the invitation of the Iranian ambassador to the UN, Andy Warhol had arrived in Tehran with his white wig and Polaroid camera to photograph the Empress, an art enthusiast who was building the first museum of modern art with a collection that Western critics deemed "worthy of MoMA." Woe to the face that becomes a Warhol print, I had thought, for its days as a human face are numbered. I ignored the fuss about Warhol, but when an evening at the Ministry of Culture was arranged in the artist's honor, my mother, dusting off her Saint Laurent shoes, insisted that I go, too. My father, who made no secret of his contempt for Campbell's soup cans, was only attending because of his position at the Ministry. "You do as you see fit," he said, a directive that back then I interpreted as indifference.

HIDING AMONG A GROUP of young admirers, the artist glanced at his hosts seemingly petrified, though the one trait he displayed with impunity was his weakness for the caviar that circled the room on silver trays carried by unsmiling waiters. The other guests, most of whom—in the artist's own words—appeared to have stepped off a Visconti set, didn't seem to care so much about the man himself as they did about his name; they were pleased to be in the same room as the words "Andy Warhol"—those ten letters that symbolized for them the holy number of creation and completion.

I walked around the room drink in hand, nibbling on canapés and wrath. My mother's Francophile performance was grating me more than usual, and my father's coolness, as predictable as the arrival of his morning paper, sent me into a silent tantrum.

I had spent the summer with Minoo as a tourist of revolutionary thought. I had read transcripts of Ali Shariati's lectures and had begun tackling Leninism thanks to the translated text of *What Is to Be Done?*, printed in a miniature font on a pamphlet, which I had found in the bathroom of a gas station during a family drive to Karaj. Sometimes I even perused Minoo's library, filled with volumes of Voltaire and Diderot and Montesquieu, those mainstays of the Enlightenment. But like travelers who perennially declare that they wish to move to the city they last visited, I would read a few paragraphs of each and spontaneously decide to adopt its philosophy, a vow that would last only until my next excursion. This vacillation troubled me. What kind of man doesn't know what he thinks? When a frustrated Minoo asked me if I admired anyone at all, I said, "As a matter of fact, I do. Masoud Ahmadzadeh." I said this not so much out of conviction but because that morning at the bus stop I had found and read Ahmadzadeh's pamphlet, *Mobārezeh-ye mosallahāneh, ham esterāteji ham tāktik*—"Armed struggle, both strategy and tactics"—which echoed ideas of Mao, Che Guevara, and Régis Debray. I said it also because Ahmadzadeh's group was part of the Fadaiyan-e-Khalq, the Organization of Iranian People's Fedai Guerrillas, which had arrived on the scene with the assassination of the chief military prosecutor, and had conducted armed robbery of several banks. In other words, they were, by far, the most iconoclastic of the subversives. Minoo, a devotee of liberal democracy and nonviolent resistance, didn't approve of my choice, and I, who in those days still wished to please her, conceded that, as Gandhi had said, "non-violence and truth are inseparable and presuppose one another."

IN THE MIRRORED HALL of the Ministry, opposite Warhol and his youthful entourage, men in military uniforms studded with medals stood erect, drinks in hand. Others in more casual clothes and metal-rimmed glasses assumed a more scholarly air. In the center of the room was a gathering of businessmen and their emerald-studded wives standing on a diagonal like Balanchine ballerinas and listening to a confectionary tycoon boasting of his latest factory in Qazvin. Next to them were my father and his research assistant, Yasser Maghz-Pahn, discussing pop art.

"His brilliance," said Yasser, referring to Warhol, "is that he has embraced consumerism wholeheartedly." My father stirred his whiskey, the ice clinking against the Baccarat crystal. "Where's the brilliance in that?" he said. "That's capitulation . . ." Yasser cut him off. "But don't you see? Instead of colluding with the system through hypocrisy, he's putting it all on the table. There's the brilliance!"

"Maybe it's time *we* put it all on the table and called out the system for what it is," I said.

My father looked at me, switchblades in his eyes. He glanced at the government men surrounding us and whispered, "This is hardly the place!"

"This *is* the place," I said. "It's the lion's den!"

"Gentlemen," said Yasser, trying to defuse the situation, "I woke up this morning with this rash on my finger." He held up his chafed index finger. "Now what do you suppose . . . ?"

"Maybe if you stopped sticking it up your nose, *aghaye* Yasser," I said.

"What's the matter with you?" my father said. "You're back to your *khorous jangi* ways. My son, the fighting cock."

"*Bāz gardad be asleh khod har cheez*—everything goes back to its origin," I said. "Forgive me, Yasser-*agha*," I continued. "That was inappropriate. But why do you change the subject? Weren't you just saying that the brilliance of this man is that he has done away with hypocrisy and embraced the system? Why don't we do the same? Why don't we come out and shout from a rooftop, 'We live and thrive in corruption; we are, all of us, puppets and puppeteers.'"

People had gathered around us now, among them my mother, whose enthusiastic display of cleavage had played no small part in fueling my drive all evening. "Quiet down, Hamid!" she said, her voice cracking with humiliation.

"You're the one who insisted I come," I said.

"I'd like you to leave immediately," said my father.

"Finally, we agree on something," I said.

I WALKED FOR A LONG TIME, toward Minoo's house. Though it was a flawless summer night I felt myself at the edge of a precipice, aching for an encounter with my own spilled blood. What I had said about government corruption qualified me for an arrest and interrogation by the secret police, but my father had no doubt already finagled a way out. This enraged me further; I wanted them to question me, maybe even beat the hell out of me. Only then, I thought, would my circumstances match my anguish.

Pedestrians out on strolls filled the streets—a family with ice cream cones, a couple kissing next to the red-and-white glare of a Kentucky Fried Chicken window, a lone man in a suit running to catch the last bus. We were, all of us, funambulists skywalking between the myth of our ancestral greatness and the reality of our compromised past, between our attempts to govern ourselves and our repeated failures. We were a generation doused in oil and oblivion, the city expanding in steel and glass around us, erasing at dizzying speed the alleys of our grandfathers, hemming us in along the way.

MINOO OPENED THE DOOR wearing cutoff shorts and a camisole. "Weren't you supposed to be at the Campbell's soup party?" she said.

I entered, and when I realized that she was home alone I kissed her more forcefully than I ever had, pushing her slowly toward her bedroom. While we had fooled around countless times, we had never ventured beyond. She half resisted, half acquiesced, which was all the permission I needed.

I was sweating, from the nighttime heat and the scent of her summer skin. I removed my shirt and shoved her on the bed, continuing to kiss her on her neck and ignoring her aborted protests. I wanted to love and harm her at once, the weight of my body on top of hers intoxicating me with my own sentience. We carried on like that for a while, but as I unbuttoned her pants and slipped my hand inside, a smack landed so violently near my right ear that I felt my brain rattling against my skull. I sat up, my skin throbbing. It occurred to me that this pulsating pain was what I had been after all evening, and letting out a long sigh, I lowered my body to the floor and collapsed on my bare back, eyes shut so as to hold back my childish tears. She sat next to me, her legs tucked beside her. "I didn't want it to happen like this," she said.

As I lay there, on Minoo's carpet wrapped in the scent of old wool, I whispered to her, though I don't think she could hear me, "Forgive me."

"Look," she said. "Outrage alone is useless."

"What else is there?" I said.

"You haven't understood anything," she said. "Please go. I want to be alone. And Hamid," she added, "don't ever come back. You and I are through."

13

WERE IT NOT for the tilting of our house a few months later, my life may have taken a different turn.

That fall, after weeks spent in the void of Minoo, I began classes at the university. I was not, I told myself, made of political cloth. Better stick to my germinal love: drawing, and the history of drawing. Walking home from class one afternoon and considering that day's lecture on the difference between seeing an artwork in and out of context—for example, witnessing a Giotto fresco in the Basilica of Saint Francis of Assisi, versus encountering a reproduction of that same fresco in a magazine—I noticed the house leaning to the left, a bizarre slant that made it look like something Magritte might have painted. I wrote this off as an optical illusion; discussions about perspective, composition, and visual acuity were no doubt making me more perceptive of the world's irregularities. But the longer I looked the more I became convinced that this was an architectural scoliosis that would, sooner or later, lead to graver conditions.

My father laughed this off. "*Meymoun balad nist beraghse migeh zamin kajeh*—the monkey doesn't know how to dance, he says the floor is crooked." At his desk in his top floor office, in his suit and necktie and slippers, he looked up from his papers, and in a gentler tone he added, "The house is fine, Hamid. Maybe you just want to believe it's crooked?"

Maybe, maybe. What did I know, in any case? I had been proven an idiot in my pursuit of sentiment and political philosophy, so why not architecture, also? I dismissed my apprehension of a structural collapse, but as fall became winter and cracks in our apartment began expanding like spiderwebs around doorframes and windows, I knocked on the forbidding door of our landlord, a bachelor from the Imperial Air Force. He was a tall man of about fifty, soft-spoken, with a collection of Lacoste polo shirts. We never saw much of him, since on weekdays he left before dawn and he returned home in the evenings just in time to sleep. According to Yasser Maghz-Pahn, the gossiper who knew anyone worth knowing, the General spent weekends reading Leonardo Sciascia novels at a teahouse near the bazaar—a peculiar location given his military rank—or went horseback riding at the Shaki riding club in the Evin district.

That afternoon, on account of the announced snowstorm, he was home early and opened the door in his pajamas.

I peeked inside the living room. On a console in the foyer a Germanic ivory statue of a jester on a wooden plinth stood impish and sinister. I remembered that he had received his military training at some air base in Bavaria, near Munich.

"Forgive the intrusion, General," I said. "But I think the house is slanting."

"Excuse me?" he said. "I don't understand."

"The house is leaning to the side."

"Which side?" he said.

I wasn't sure why the direction should matter. "I think the left side," I said.

He asked me to wait while he went in to put on his pants and boots, and we walked back out, with me following the General like one of his cadets. From across the street he examined the house, moving his head this way and that as one does after hanging a picture on a wall. I noticed the outline of my father's torso in the top window, his face, a blur of discontent, staring me down.

"I don't see the tilt," said the General.

"It's possible," I said, "that I see things that aren't there. Forgive me."

He continued examining the midcentury façade. "Wait," he said. "Look, the house number over the front door. It's indeed tilted." Noticing my father behind the window just then, the General offered him a military salute, which my father returned with a noncommittal civilian wave.

Back in the house the General opened a creaky door and we walked down a spiral staircase to the basement. There was a dank smell, of old things and overspent decades. He lit up a match (from the Officers' Club) and held it up to the wall, up and down and up again. I had no idea what he was after. Soon, I saw them: deep, horizontal cracks, running across several walls. "This is bad," the General said with no explanation. None was needed. His affirmation of my suspicions was good enough.

In the morning the world was unchanged, except for twenty centimeters of snow on the ground and the brooding silence of my father, the sore loser. He refused breakfast—even tea—and attached snow chains to his tires, setting off for the Ministry even before the General had wiped his windshield.

Feeling grateful to the General for taking me seriously, I helped him clean his car and offered to skip class in order to receive the contractor he had scheduled to inspect the house. He thanked me formally, as was his way, and asked that I report back to him at a number that he scribbled on the back of a receipt.

Hours later the contractor arrived with an engineer and two laborers. After a lengthy assessment they began to work: the foundation, they said, was sinking because of poor drainage and soil pressure, and the house was at risk of collapsing. Naturally I was afraid, but what was fear against vindication? I called the General at the number he had specified—it turned out to be his direct line at the Imperial Air Force—and I was filled with a sense of my own importance as I relayed the contractor's diagnosis. He thanked me coolly as he had that morning, and added, "Your father should be proud."

My father was neither proud nor pleased. At the dinner table that night his fork lingered in his rice and stew before he said, mostly to himself, "Maybe I should move my encyclopedia papers . . ."

"Your only concern is your papers?" my mother said.

He looked up, and pointing the fork in my direction, he said, "Why do you always create trouble?"

THE FIXERS WERE a brotherly duo named Mirza and Morteza. Mirza—the older of the two by at least a decade and clearly the boss—dictated the rhythm of the day, outlining goals and keeping track of breaks. He could have been thirty or forty years old, I couldn't tell, and were it not for the pockmarks on his face and the premature curvature of his spine he might have been considered good-looking. His brother was both less scarred and less handsome, a balancing act of familial fate that kept the two of them tethered to modesty.

I ignored them as one ignores workers, meaning that I said hello whenever our paths crossed, and feigned minimum interest in their presence out of sheer politeness; I may have been a mediocre student at school but I had, at the very least, learned good manners. As the months went by their presence in our building was reduced to a pattern, no different than a carpet motif you see daily without actually seeing it. The holes they drilled and the dust they produced were the only reminders that they in fact existed.

AS SUMMER ARRIVED and I sat in the garden one morning reading the newspaper, I came across a cartoon by Houshang Habibi, my father's old friend, also known as "H." His caricatures of corrupt men and dirt-poor workers and fat kings with their henchmen were increasingly seen in the papers, a sign of the government's efforts to distribute crumbs of freedom in the face of escalating discontent. I felt a pang of loss for my revolutionary days, and for Minoo, who had led me to them. I wanted to share the image with someone, but no one was around—they were all inside getting dressed for the annual trip to the Caspian. Given my father's ongoing ill humor toward me, I had refused to go, and my father hadn't objected, a snub that only strengthened my resolve to stay alone in Tehran.

When the brothers arrived in their pickup truck I showed

them the drawing—a man hanging from the gallows looking down at his balloon stand, surrounded by a king and his viziers. The caption read, "The balloon seller missed the king's jubilee." Morteza shrugged and walked away. Mirza laughed with a half-shut mouth; he was trying to conceal a missing tooth. Afterward we remained, awkward, neither of us knowing where to go from there.

"My family is driving up north today," I said.

He looked at me, puzzled by the disclosure. It was the first time I had spoken to him directly. After a while he said, "You're not going?"

"I decided not to, this year," I said. "Usually we go as a family, but sometimes it's easier to be alone."

"I wouldn't know," he said.

"Do you have a family?"

"A wife and four children. All healthy, thank God."

"Thank God," I said. "May they be blessed. What else can we ask for but good health?" But who was speaking? I sounded nothing like myself.

"Well, I'll get to work now," he said, "if you'll excuse me."

AS MY FAMILY LOADED THE PAYKAN I stayed in the garden. I considered helping with the luggage but didn't; I knew my father would interpret that gesture as a concession. When they were done I walked over to them, and as they said their goodbyes—my mother advised me on what to eat and how to water the plants and where to put the laundry—I turned to my father, and showing him the cartoon I said, "Your old friend H. is in all the papers these days, have you seen?"

"I've seen," he said flatly.

"I guess no one is locking him up anymore."

He didn't answer.

"Changes must be under way," I said.

"Why don't you ask your new friend, the General?" said my father as he opened the front door and sat behind the wheel. He ignited the engine before my mother and Omid had even gotten into the car.

"Why should I ask the General," I said, "when we have a government man in the family? Surely you know what's happening just as well as he does."

Omid gave me a sad look; for weeks he had pleaded with me not to disrupt our annual family vacation.

"All right, we're going," my mother said. "Take care of yourself, Hamid."

"Maybe the house will collapse while you are on holiday," I said, "and you'll find me in the rubble when you return, buried with your encyclopedia."

"I have no doubt you will remain alive and well," said my father. "And don't even try to get near the encyclopedia. In any case, the office door is locked."

OVER THE ENSUING DAYS a ritual emerged: I sat with the paper in the garden with a glass of tea, and when the brothers arrived I showed Mirza the daily cartoon, usually drawn by H. Sometimes he laughed and other times he stared at the image for a few moments before smiling vaguely, which I knew was an indication that he hadn't understood the cartoon but was too embarrassed to admit it. This mattered little; the point was that we had something to share.

When Mirza would begin his work, I, who in those days was

not the expert in solitude that I would later become, would fall into restlessness. Deliverance from family could only go so far.

I'd like to believe that it was a longing for justice that made me reach, in those empty hours, for the old Lenin and Marx pamphlets I had hidden in a hatbox under my bed. But this would be untrue. What made me uncover these texts, at least initially, was boredom, or more accurately, loneliness. How I missed Minoo.

I read, getting lost not in language, but in ideology. If the former is water, fluid and transmutable, the latter is a boulder— hard, heavy, and unyielding. Both are made of words, but if in language words are the masters, in ideology they are the servants. This seminal difference evaded me in those days, and it was with the words of ideology that I gradually formed a self, a process that was of great comfort to a boy such as I, erratic, untethered, and, above all, ordinary. The challenge now was to find a stage on which to enact this new self, and it was at this juncture that Mirza, my morning co-browser of newspaper cartoons, became for me something more and less than a man: he became a project.

I began visiting the brothers with pomegranate juice, tea, and cakes while they drilled the foundation's footing to install piers that would push up the sunken section of the house. Morteza accepted my offerings without interacting with me; he drank and ate and returned to work. But Mirza lingered during the breaks, and judging by how his face brightened whenever I appeared with a tray, I understood that he enjoyed my visits and in time even looked forward to them. In the beginning we spoke of the work, of how the faulty drainage of rain gutters had caused the soil beneath the house to expand and rupture the foundation. "People forget," he said, "that the soil they build on is a living thing. It breathes and expands and contracts, like any human being." His respect for the soil reminded me of Uncle Majid and slowly transformed my curiosity toward him into affection. Over the ensuing weeks, as we grew closer and the formality between us lessened, he disclosed many details of his biography. He was from Anzali, from a lineage of fishermen. From the days of his great-grandfather, he said, until his twelfth birthday, the Caspian fisheries were controlled by Russian families of one creed or another. By the time the fishing industry was nationalized in 1953 and the fishermen's condition began to improve, his father had developed lung trouble and could no longer spend hours at sea. He took a job at a caviar plant, filling gold tins with sturgeon eggs. "I remember visiting him at the plant when I was a boy," Mirza told me, "and watching as the big, sad fish would be brought in a gurney by two men. They would lay her down on a table, slice open her abdomen, and scoop out a giant, congealed mass of black eggs. It frightened me so much that I would freeze in my corner, not even moving to avoid the blood dripping on the tile floor."

It was the first time I had thought of caviar, that centerpiece of my maternal grandparents' table, as actual eggs, unborn, and sourced from an animal's ovaries. The fleshiness of it disturbed me.

"Watching my father canning those tins for hours on end with his bad lungs made me want to do something, anything . . ." Mirza continued as he sat on the bottom step of his ladder, sipping his tea. He slurped as he drank, a sound that irritated me, but which I pretended to ignore. The absence of social graces, I decided, was not going to upset our budding friendship. "I was the first in my family," he added, "to leave the region and relocate to Tehran, a move that my brother followed. But I had only a second-grade education . . ."

I asked him if he was happy with his decision and for some time he didn't answer. "It hasn't been easy," he finally said.

This was my opening. I spoke to him—as I had once been

spoken to at so many safe house meetings—of the proletariat and the bourgeoisie, of the polarization of the classes, of the corruption of the educational system by capitalist societies such as our own. For the first few days he seemed intrigued. But as my lectures became longer and more fiery, he began drifting away, finding excuses to cut me short and return to work, because, he said, the General was on their backs to finish up.

"Why be afraid of the General?" I said one evening as he was gathering his belongings and preparing to leave for the night.

"The General pays my wages," he said.

"He pays you," I said, "but not enough. He is exploiting you. Didn't you tell me that you and your wife and four children live in two rooms, like so many canned tomatoes?"

"I did tell you that we live in two rooms," he said. "But the thought of canned tomatoes is yours, not mine. The General's money feeds my family," he continued as he walked past me. "Who else will pay, you?"

"You're missing the big picture," I said. "It's not about the General, or you, or any other individual. It's about a system."

"I don't know systems," he said. "I know that I have a wife and four children who need food and clothes and medicine." He got in his car and rolled down the window. "Oh, and I lied about their health," he added. "My youngest has bad lungs, like her grandfather, and needs a special drug from France. I don't have time for your lectures, Hamid-*agha*. *Shab-bekheyr*—have a good night."

14

THIS MUCH WAS TRUE: I had meant well, in the beginning. After the stinging words with Mirza I decided to set off on a trip. I could not become a real revolutionary by lecturing to one man in my own backyard; to change the world I first needed to witness it. But where to go, and how? After a day or two of brooding, I concluded that the destination didn't matter; the point was to act. Access to cash wasn't an obstacle either—my parents kept an emergency stash in a lacquer box in the second drawer of their bedroom dresser. The bills added up to a respectable amount, though not enough for a car and expenses. I considered taking the bus or the train, but there was something pathetic about public transport in a situation like this.

That's when I had an idea.

At the bakery I had seen a flyer announcing the sale of an old motorbike—a refurbished Harley-Davidson XA, a World War II souvenir left behind by American troops. When I called the listed number, the seller, a French diplomat whose appointment had come to an end, explained that though he had painstakingly revamped the motorcycle and had grown fond of it, he wished to be rid of his belongings as quickly as possible and would offer a good price. I bought the motorcycle that same afternoon, and after practicing nonstop for two weeks, I set off on an exploratory mission, imagining myself a modern-day Che. I rode northward, to Mazandaran and Gilan, then south, through Sanandaj, Kermanshah, and down the coast to Bushehr, then back north through Yazd, Isfahan, and Qom. I met, along the way, workers and merchants, itinerants and hashish smokers, snot-nosed rural children with barefoot mothers who tricked me into believing that I was a benevolent man. In Anzali, the birthplace of Mirza, an old fisherman told me that Qajar rulers once leased bulk fishing in the Caspian provinces to local governors who then would sublease them to private entrepreneurs. For decades, he said, the fishing lease belonged to the Russian-Armenian Lianozov family, and later to another Russian named Vanitsof. "They say the Lianozovs made half a million rubles before the October Revolution. They went on to build a massive petroleum company in Baku. You see," he said, "the Qajars used the land like their private bank account."

I asked him what he thought of the current situation. He looked around, cautious. "There has been some improvement," he finally said, "but the profit, in the end, is always elsewhere.

You understand?" I said that I understood very well. "Still," he added, "we are lucky up here. We have the beautiful sturgeons and their black pearls, and so much bounty besides. Rice, chicken, milk . . ." As we parted I offered him a photocopy of the Lenin pamphlet. He accepted my gift but confessed he couldn't read. His son, he said, might be able to make out a word or two.

IT WAS IN QOM that my imagination made a turn. By the seminary gates, where I had parked, a young man in a robe and turban stood admiring my motorcycle. "It's an old clunker," I said, "but has served me well. I've been riding all over the country."

He asked me what had prompted my road trip and I told him that I was searching for answers, which, being a seminary man, he interpreted as a quest for God. "It's a different kind of quest," I said. "I want to understand what's happening in this land. The dam is about to break. But there are many questions. Why is it breaking, why now, and how best to direct the floodwaters that will come pouring?" He asked me how I was educating myself on the pesky questions of injustice, and I told him about my readings, of Marx and Hegel and Lenin.

"You are imposing Western ideas onto Eastern problems," he said. "We have to arrive at social justice our own way. The foundation of our religion is social justice—think of Imam Hossein, martyred as he was. Or Imam Reza. We are the religion of the downtrodden. Everything we seek is in our own house, yet we insist on being elsewhere." He then spoke of an Ayatollah—"the light of the nation's eye," he called him—in exile in Najaf since 1965. "Have you heard of him?" he said. I told him I hadn't. "No matter," he continued, "you will soon."

He explained, with much excitement, that two summers earlier, on the fifteenth day of Khordad in the year 1354, right there in the holy city of Qom, hundreds of seminary students—himself included—had gathered to commemorate the anniversary of the Ayatollah's exile, calling for his return. Rightly assuming that I was not fluent in the Hijri calendar and would be more comfortable with the Gregorian one, he added with a smile, "That's June 5, 1975, for you."

The police, he continued, secret and otherwise, responded with water cannons and tear gas, and they closed off all the roads leading to the seminary, so that the townspeople could not join the protests. But the fight continued into the night, and by morning everyone knew that the regime had violated the seminary. Newspapers—meaning the state—blamed Communist forces for the protests. "This was absurd," my young interlocutor said. "And yet, if you think about it, what we and the Ayatollah want isn't so different from what the Marxists and all those liberal democrats are calling for: social justice. On this we can all agree, can't we?"

I neither agreed nor objected. The mere fact of my standing in Qom discussing social justice with a seminary man felt to me like a small miracle. I offered to take him for a ride and he accepted, as he, too, seemed pleased by our incongruous connection. He sat behind me, taking care to prevent his *qabā* from getting caught in the spokes, and as he looped his arms around my waist, we set off together, an unlikely duo, riding through the streets of Qom with the freedom of two young men out on the town. In that brief period, as he held on to me for fear of falling, I felt an openness until then—and since—unknown to me.

I dropped him off at the seminary, and as he got off the bike—again mindful not to trip over his robe—he slipped a cassette tape in my pocket. "The Ayatollah's speech," he said in a low voice. I thanked him, and as we stood facing each other on the street corner, we must have both borne the flushed look of two people who have had a one-night stand and must now reenter the austerity of the known world.

In my hotel, not far from the Fatimeh Massoumeh shrine, I asked the concierge—a middle-aged man in an outdated suit and oversize eyeglasses—for a cassette player. He obliged after considerable grumbling; I think he mistook me for a brat from Tehran with a sudden craving for the Bee Gees. "Not too loud," he said as he placed the cassette deck on the counter. "If you bother the other hotel guests I will send you back to your parents."

"Don't worry, stealth is my specialty," I said.

I had intended to amuse him. For some reason—maybe because of his frumpy style—I had assumed him to be on the side of the seminary men. But he stared at me now, his eyes humorless; one never knew, in those days as in the present, where another's loyalties lay. I held on to the tape in my pocket, trying my best to calm my heart's pounding.

For some time he continued staring, then shrugged, as though concluding that I wasn't worth the trouble of further consideration.

In my room I closed the curtain, sat on the bed, and played the tape. The voice I heard was that of an old man, determined but fatherly, with a provincial accent that could sound appealing or objectionable, depending on who you were. Among the many arguments in favor of a religious judiciary there were also lucid tidbits. This one, for example, regarding the penal system under the monarchy: *"They kill people for possessing ten grams of heroin and say, 'That is the law,'* [. . .] *The sale of heroin must indeed be prohibited, but the punishment must be in proportion to the crime . . ."*

Such eloquent statements were interspersed with incoherent arguments calling for the rule of God over human affairs, and I found myself tuning in and out, alternately convinced and distressed, unable, as had become my habit, to form an opinion. But the crucial fact, I told myself, was that the Ayatollah spoke of an end to oppression, something that, as the seminary student had argued, we could all agree on. Wasn't this, I wondered, the voice—and more crucially the words—that would speak to a man like Mirza, far better than my academic lectures had managed to do?

I lingered in Qom for a week, spellbound by the number of mosques and seminaries and clerics walking around in their robes as naturally as ducks in a pond, a reality that was in plain sight but remained forgotten by most of us outsiders. Had they always been there? My ignorance was like that of a medieval Roman oblivious of the existence of the Vatican.

MY FAMILY HAD long been back from their summer holiday by the time I returned. I ignored my parents' outrage about my disappearance, the missing money, and the Harley in the garage. "Heartless!" my father said on the first day. "We were worried sick about you, and you didn't even have the decency to let us know your whereabouts. What kind of halfwit does something like that?" On the second day he called me "a con man." By the third I had graduated to "bandit," and by the fourth, when he named me an "outlaw," it seemed that it was only a matter of time before I would reach the ranks of Butch Cassidy and the Sundance Kid. He seemed unaware that by escalating the insults and aggrandizing my transgression, he was glorifying me. I had already become a minor hero for Omid, and maybe even for the basement brothers: Morteza had become obsessed with my motorcycle, and Mirza with where the motorcycle had taken me. "For some time," he said one morning as I sat with the newspaper in the garden, "I've wanted to make a pilgrimage to Qom. It has been my wish to take my daughter to the Fatimeh Massoumeh shrine, so that, God willing, she may be healed. But I can't afford not to work, not even for a week."

I told him that at the shrine I had seen pilgrims on crutches and in wheelchairs, praying, asking for patience, for blessing, and maybe even a cure. This supplication, I added, initially struck me as preposterous, but the longer I stayed in Qom, the more my certainty began to shift, so that by the end, I thought, *Why not? Isn't the world populated with ex-votos and the hair and teeth and fingernails of this or that saint? What would a human being become without belief in something other than himself?* I am not sure if this thought had truly occurred to me in Qom, or if I was simply saying it now because I knew that it would please Mirza and would entice him, once more, to pay attention to my revolutionary discourse. When he asked if I had become a believer, I said that my incapacity for unadulterated belief was beside the point, and that one had to admire the raw power of faith in keeping the world whirling, in allowing, say, a woman in a war-torn country to desire a child, or a man to embrace his wife even as his mother lies dying in another corner of the same room. "God willing *agha*-Mirza," I told him, "you will go to Qom." He nodded, pensive, with more conviction than he generally displayed. As he was about to resume his work I showed him the day's cartoon and he laughed as he once used to. I believe it was this—the resumption of our old routine—that restored my confidence and made me slip the tape into his pocket. "A seminary man in Qom offered this to me," I said. "Listen to it."

In the garden the following morning he embraced me like a father. His eyes were bright, trusting. "Thank you," he said. "For the first time in my life, I see a way out for us. We need to rid ourselves of this puppet regime. As the Ayatollah said, 'Imperialist countries think they are better than us because they have conquered even the moon. Let them go all the way to Mars or beyond the Milky Way; they will still be deprived of true happiness, moral virtue, and spiritual advancement.'" He stood for some time, wistful, then smiled at me kindly, forgetting to hide the missing tooth.

15

WHEN I SAW YOU AT THE POETRY READINGS, so serious . . ." she said. "I was happy. You seemed changed."

Dear Minoo. I had run into her at the poetry readings of the Goethe-Institut a week earlier. That we should have found each other in a crowd of thousands seemed to me like an intervention of providence.

We were having coffee at Café Naderi, by a window overlooking the garden. The cappuccino machine fizzed in the background, filling the room with the heady aroma of fresh coffee beans and frothy milk, while the framed portraits of the writers and poets who in times past had been café regulars—Hedayat,

Yushij, Daneshvar—kept vigil over our words. We met there because the coffee was good. Maybe we also met there so we could insert ourselves into the café's past, and in this way, or so we thought, write ourselves into the national history.

"Since we parted," I said, "I've met many people and seen many things. Something is about to happen, don't you feel it?"

"Yes," she said. "The ten nights of poetry convinced me. The thousands showing up, night after night! And how easily the literary evenings turned political. To hear allusions to freedom of thought and equality on loudspeakers was surreal. And the way the police just stood back and watched . . ."

"We will fly or falter," I said. "But nothing will remain the same." I reached for her hand and a current ran wild through my body. Was it carnal or political? Maybe the two were identical? "In the words of Ali Shariati," I continued, "*What if Iranian society consisted of twenty-five million Hallajs?*"

"Who is Hallaj?" she said.

"Ah . . . It's finally my turn to teach *you* something."

"Don't gloat," she said. "Just explain."

"Mansur Al-Hallaj," I said, "was a medieval mystic who was executed by orders of the Abbasid Caliph al-Muqtadir, because he is believed to have said, '*ana al-Haqq*—I am the Truth,' which was considered a heresy. The French philosopher Louis Massignon wrote about him in his four-volume work *The Passion of Al-Hallaj: Mystic and Martyr of Islam* . . ."

"Look at you," she said, "making references to Massignon . . . You really have changed."

"Do you or do you not want to hear about Hallaj," I said as I inched my chair closer to hers and placed my hand on her knee.

"Yes," she said, her face flushed. "Tell me."

"Shariati's brilliance is that he infuses, through Hallaj, an element of spirituality into the Western language of oppression and justice. He is merging discourses of East and West to present a new way of thinking, a new vocabulary. But he isn't speaking of religion as a stagnant, corrupt institution, the kind that has colluded with kings and rulers from the time of the Safavids until now. He means religion as an expression of social action."

"I think," she said, "that religion, all religion, should be left out of the democratic discourse. How can you impose religion on a secular society? The two can't coexist."

"You're too committed to Western philosophy," I said, "and to *laïcité*, that sacred ideal of the French. Secularism is an off-spring of their experience, not ours, and it belongs to their lexicon, not ours. By ours," I continued, "I don't mean you and me. I mean everyone. A new way of thinking is what we need, and from that will come a new way of being."

"But where would that leave those who prefer their religion in small doses and on the side?"

I wanted to say, *That's nothing more than an afterthought, a footnote at best.* Instead I said, "This is like worrying about the buttons on an overcoat before it has even been sewn. Details can be figured out later. Can we agree, for now, that it has been a long, cold winter, and we desperately need a coat?"

"Fine," she said, "if we must speak in allegories . . . But what will that coat look like? What kind of fabric? How many pockets? Double-breasted or single?"

"Dear God!" I said. "For such a brilliant person you're so myopic."

"'*Caress the detail, the divine detail*,'" she said. "This was Nabokov's advice regarding memory, but I think it also applies to what is yet to come . . . For my part, I've joined the National Front, the party of Mossadegh."

"Mossadegh is an inspiration to all of us," I said. "But it's time to improvise."

"Liberal democracy," she said, "is the best system we have come up with so far, and I think . . ."

I kissed her, midsentence, and she closed her eyes, her lips soft, her hand warm on my knee. With so much rhetoric in the air, the future was murky. But who could consider the future, when the present was so bewildering?

16

SEPTEMBER 8, 1978—"Black Friday"—was the day that would begin the intricate frostwork of my soul. That morning, Mostafa Akbari—also known as "The Lizard"—ordered me to strike a soldier. He is sacrosanct now because he converted so many leftists back in the day, and now sits among those at the helm of the foundation governing the holy shrine in Mashhad. But he was a sort of false god, a *div*.

WHEN I FIRST NOTICED HIM, he was standing by the shuttered kiosk in ill-fitting corduroy pants and a mustard-yellow jacket with all but one button missing, smoking and surveying the crowd of protesters in Jaleh Square with the detachment of a hierophant. A purple antler-shaped birthmark jutted from his neck to his ear. I was standing in the bowels of the crowd, all of us behind a barricade. People think of protests as all freedom of movement and adrenaline, but anyone who has demonstrated will tell you that they are mostly boring affairs, figures trapped within the inertia of a mob, hypnotically repeating slogans. Until, that is, the decisive moment, the moment when bodies from all directions spill beyond the barricades, the moment of contact of flesh with baton, flesh with tear gas, flesh with bullet, flesh with flesh.

ON THE RADIO THAT MORNING they declared martial law beginning at six. When the news was announced I was sitting at the kitchen table with my father, whose breakfast was untouched; his head was buried in the newspaper. Mother, by the window, smoked her Gauloise. Omid was asleep.

"You heard the announcement?" my father said. "Martial law means a military government. You can't go to the demonstration."

"On the contrary," I said. "Now I must go."

I was still rattled from a chance encounter I had had the previous day, when, dizzy from the headlines I had gleaned at the newsstand, I stopped outside a café to light up a cigarette—a recent habit that I believed suited my image of a man in revolt. Through the window of the café a vintage map of the Persian Achaemenid Empire could be seen, a map whose long-held truths, Caspia, Parthia, Susa, had no particular meaning to any of us. Beneath the map a man wearing a navy suit was having soup. He looked up. It was Yasser, my father's associate. Out of politeness—a trait I had difficulty discarding—I waved hello and bowed slightly, and he, perhaps out of loyalty to my father, motioned for me to join him. I demurred, he insisted, in that familiar dance that we all knew too well, until I had no choice but to do as he asked; his seniority made my refusal a flagrant offense.

"Shall I order you something?" he said as I sat.

I thanked him and declined, but he ordered me a tea nonetheless.

"Your father tells me you've become quite the revolutionary," he said.

"I didn't realize he had such interest in my activities," I said.

"Hamid," he said, putting down his spoon. "He's worried about you."

"He's only worried I'll ruffle some feathers in his beloved Peacock throne."

"You don't know what you're talking about," he said. "This government can finish you off in a minute if it wants to. Your father knows something about this."

"Oh yes," I said. "I've heard about my father's so-called activism."

He removed his hexagonal black-rimmed glasses that made his eyes look like tiny bees in a hive, and pinched the bridge of his nose. "I'm going to tell you something I was never meant to mention," he said. "I'm doing it because I'm hoping it will knock some sense into your thick brain. In 1953, a few months after the coup, your father's apartment was raided by the secret police because he had written some articles on Mossadegh's behalf. In his room they found an art book he had borrowed from the university library, and the name preceding your father's on the attached borrowers' card was the name of a prominent member of Tudeh—the Communist party that had earlier tried to topple the Shah. So they arrested your father, because of a stupid library book! He was held in jail for several weeks while they investigated to make sure that he had no ties to the previous borrower. They put him through hell, and forced him to disclose information about friends and acquaintances. For a long time he refused, until he no longer could."

As he spoke a sharp pain stabbed my stomach and shot down to my foot, where it dulled into a throb. To numb it I reached for another cigarette. Remembering the conversation I had had with my father years earlier after the visit to the dentist, I said, "Was Houshang Habibi, the artist, among these *friends*?"

Avoiding my gaze, Yasser sipped his Coke. "I don't know," he said.

"Tell me the truth, Yasser-*agha*. My father ratted on his best friend?"

"You idiot!" he said, banging his glass on the table. "Why do you insist on simplifying everything? History is painted in shades of gray."

"As far as I'm concerned, treachery has only one shade," I said as I left the table and walked out.

"Fighting cock!" he called out after me. "Just as your father always says. I should have known you'd be too dim-witted to understand this story."

I DIDN'T TELL MY FATHER of my encounter with Yasser. Quietly I finished my omelet and retrieved the six-foot banner I had prepared for the rally, unfurling it on the kitchen floor, in front of my parents, wanting them to witness my creation. On the left side I had drawn, with a charcoal stick, a portrait of Mossadegh—deep, dark, with shades of gray filling his oblong face—and I watched my father with satisfaction as he examined my rendering of the abandoned hero of his youth, whose image, I imagined, inflamed the ache of his private history. He folded the newspaper and looked on as I wrote on the banner, in the most refined calligraphy I could manage, a slogan I had picked up from the previous demonstration, "*Mikosham, Mikosham, ānke barādaram kosht*—I will kill, I will kill, he who killed my brother!"

My mother stubbed her cigarette in the sink. "I'm going back to bed," she said.

AT THE SQUARE, soldiers with rifles encircled the protesters. I had come alone, as Minoo was sick with the flu. I squeezed one end of the wooden pole attached to my banner with a clammy palm and a woman next to me—a pretty collegiate with platform shoes—held on to the other. A man in front of us had a small boy riding on his shoulder, and this comforted me; if a child was present, I told myself, then providence would not allow anything bad to happen. The same thought had always quieted me before boarding airplanes.

As our numbers grew the crowd's velocity could no longer be contained, and we began spilling out, slowly at first then frantically, men and women dispersing across the square in all directions. Suddenly, the woman dropped the pole and the left side of my banner, slack on the ground, was trampled by the stomping feet of the protesters.

When I heard the first shot I didn't think it was real; it sounded like a metallic hiccup. But as the sound of rifles reverberated in the September sky and I saw the pavement splattered with bodies and blood, I dropped the banner and ran—toward the man with the antler-shaped birthmark still standing, unshaken, by the kiosk. He gestured at me to crouch low beside him, and reaching into a bowling bag he pulled out a bottle, lit it with a match, and hurled it in the direction of the soldiers. "Run!" he said to me, as he, too, began running, and I followed him through the broken doors of the cinema and into the lobby, turning my head every now and again to witness the fire of his Molotov cocktail, and the soldiers, running, running—terrified as we were.

The cinema lobby was deserted. The last time I had been there was some months earlier to see *The Spy Who Loved Me* with my father. Though the two of us were barely speaking by then, we had maintained our ritual of seeing James Bond films, which, despite his scholarly airs, my father adored. Remembering how we had sat side by side, a bag of sunflower seeds between us, transported by spies and submarines and a henchman with metal teeth named Jaws, I felt a violent regret for what I knew I had to do.

"DID YOU SEE HOW I BLASTED THEM?" he said, catching his breath. "Like a bug bomb in an infested house." He wiped his flushed face with a washcloth stained with oil. His Stalinist mustache made him seem older than he was, but up close I could see that he was no more than six or seven years my senior. "I am Mostafa Akbari," he said, as he opened his bowling bag and pulled out another bottle filled with gasoline, into which he inserted an alcohol-infused wick. He handed me a matchbox and the bottle. "Your turn," he said.

I took the bottle, placed it on the floor, and lit a match. But my hands were unsteady and I couldn't ignite the wick.

He blew out my matchstick. "After you light it you have one second to throw," he said. "Or else it will blow up right here and turn the two of us into *abgoosht*."

I thought of Minoo, just then, running a fever. What would she say if she saw me with a Molotov cocktail? "I can't do it," I said.

"You don't look like a cripple. But are you?"

"It's a philosophy," I said. "How shall I explain? A commitment to nonviolence."

His surly laughter dissolved in the gunshots and screams outside the cinema. "The nonviolent ones are history's losers," he said. "Gandhi, and that black American stooge. Where did they end up? Wake up! Look what's happening in that square." He lit the bottle's wick and threw, this time decimating a military car.

As we walked toward the crowd, I wanted to see who had fallen near the military car, but people had already congregated there and not much was visible. I thought I saw the girl in the platform shoes, hobbling, but Akbari shoved me along. We passed a soldier firing his rifle at a group of students, and Akbari, producing a baton from the bowling bag, hit him on the head from behind. The bloodied soldier fell to the ground; the students ran. Another soldier was crouching near a hair salon, his head in his hands. Akbari handed me a stick. "Hit him," he said.

"But he isn't doing anything," I said.

"You fool," he said. "You think so small. Hit him, before he rises and hits you."

I held on to the baton with both hands and raised it, but I couldn't act.

"If you can't do it then go home," he said. "You're not made for this."

THE BATON CAME DOWN and something crackled, like cellophane. His neck. He grabbed it and fell sideways on the pavement. He looked up at me, the shadow of a mustache framing his upper lip. He was young—eighteen or so, my own age. I knelt beside him, sorry for what I had done, but relieved, too, that I had finally done it, that from that moment on, I could go on doing it.

17

IN THAT TURBULENT AUTUMN OF 1978, I saw Akbari at
all the demonstrations. He was from a village in Khorasan and
had for three years worked as a petroleum inspector at the oil
refinery in Abadan. Until the uprisings his goal had been to rise
to a managerial role—anything that required a suit, a necktie,
and a desk—but he had since understood, or so he claimed, the
absurdity of his desires. He was, by all appearances, a peculiar
man. He never smiled, had the thin-skinned pride of a peasant,
and wore an assortment of ill-fitting corduroy pants and black
turtlenecks that failed to hide his antler birthmark. He owned a
pet lizard named Spaghetti, drank a glass of raw eggs and heavy

cream every morning, and did thirty rotation planks each night before bed, followed by ten Superman planks and one hundred crunches.

When we met he was a member of the Mujahedin-e Khalq, and were it not for Minoo, who remained committed to nonviolent resistance and mistrusted Akbari from the start, I would have joined his group. After the government's collapse and the arrival of the Ayatollah we drifted apart, but I ran into him in the summer of 1979, when he played a brief but ruinous role in my family's breakup.

IT ALL HAPPENED HAPHAZARDLY and without warning, like a slip on black ice. I had gone shopping at the bazaar—since the closure of the Ministry of Culture and my father's unemployment, the family finances were faltering and my mother had asked me to stock up on cheaper goods downtown. On my way home the Paykan huffed and suddenly died. A car honked behind me, impatient. After several minutes the driver cursed then backed out of the street and disappeared. I sat livid, turning the ignition to no avail, my mind circling back to a bitter exchange with my father.

Late in the afternoon on the previous day, as I was cleaning my closet, I had stumbled on a box filled with the old Märklin train set. The dusty compartments and rails—several of them bent and badly chipped—made me yearn for Uncle Majid, and for the night I had shared with him and the three-legged cat beneath the clear, moonlit October sky. As I placed the train components back in the box, another feeling gripped me, an unexpected warmth toward my father, whose spirits since the protests and the regime's collapse had been diminishing. No longer the know-it-all professor, he had relinquished his encyclopedia, and he sat for hours in the living room, unshaven and often in pajamas, staring at a glass of tea that my mother periodically replenished.

Despite the hostility between us, I went to him, and finding him forlorn on the settee, I offered to take him for a drive.

"Where do you want to go?" he said, stunned by my invitation. "Everything has been destroyed." The whites of his eyes were a pale yellow, making me wonder if his digestion was acting up again.

"Don't exaggerate, *bābā*," I said. "Everything is in transition, that's all."

My mother, reading a magazine by the window, looked up, shocked by my unusual act of benevolence toward my father. "Sadegh," she said, "get up and get dressed. Your son has kindly offered to take you out."

After grumbling for a while my father acquiesced. Half an hour later he emerged shaven, in his suit and necktie.

"No need for a tie," I said. "We're just going for a ride. And besides, we don't want to attract any undue attention."

"Oh yes," he said. "I forgot that a tie is now a symbol of royalist affiliations." He uncoiled the tie from around his neck and threw it on the floor. "Now we have to dance to the tune of a bunch of illiterates."

I was already regretting my invitation. But we walked together down the street to my father's Paykan.

As I was about to get into the driver's seat my father said, "You're driving?"

"I thought I would," I said.

"Do you even know how?"

"You forget I rode around the country two summers ago on my motorcycle," I said as calmly as I could.

"Yes," he said. "How could I forget your motorcycle, which you bought with the money you stole from *us*." He got into the passenger seat. "All right," he said, "let's see what you can do."

I had driven that car scores of times, but as we set off my hands felt unsteady on the wheel. I headed north along Pahlavi Street—now named Valiasr. "I thought we could go to Shahan-shahi Park," I said.

My father didn't object.

"The new name is Park-e Mellat," I added.

"The *people's park*," my father mumbled, grimacing. "Well, *the people* are in for a surprise."

"I know things haven't turned out well so far, *bābā*. But give the revolution a chance."

"*Āb az sarcheshmeh ghel āloud ast*," he said. "The water is turbid from its source."

The lush summer plane trees flanking the boulevard lulled us into silence. My father watched me drive as though he were grading me for a road test. The more he watched the more nervous I became, and when I accelerated and forgot to change the gear, he said, "Gear, gear! My God, you're as lousy a driver as Majid was."

I fought back tears. I'm not sure what had caused them, my longing for my uncle, triggered by the train set, or the feeling swelling in me as I sat beside my father—a sense of becoming small, of wanting to disappear.

We continued north in silence. I turned on the radio to distract myself, but all I found was a sermon by the Ayatollah. I shut it off.

"What are you planning to do with yourself when things settle down?" my father asked. "You can't continue being a so-called revolutionary."

"I guess I'll go back to the university and resume my studies."

"You intend to stick with drawing?"

"I enjoy drawing," I said. "I'd like to become a cartoonist."

"But you're not very good at it," he said matter-of-factly.

I made no reply. I thought of my drawing of Everyman Jamshid, how it had been photocopied and pasted throughout the school. But my throat felt shut and I couldn't speak.

"Look," he said. "What we want and what we're good at don't always match up in life. You've got to make smart choices from the outset. Otherwise you'll end up useless and poor, like Majid."

"What do you have against Uncle Majid today?" I asked.

"*Against* him? Nothing. But he lived badly and he ended up even worse. I don't need to remind you."

For the rest of the ride we didn't speak. We hit traffic near a checkpoint, and by the time we made it to the park, dusk was already settling and two militiamen advised us to head home.

NOW, AS I SAT near the bazaar in the idle Paykan, the memory of the afternoon with my father played in my mind repeatedly. The car was sweltering despite the open windows, and a pungent smell of urine was trapped in the noontime August heat. I banged on the wheel and kept on igniting the engine, but it refused to start.

To my relief, I was soon joined by volunteers pushing the car from behind. I ignited, they pushed, I ignited, they pushed, their numbers growing with each traveled centimeter. The fact is that nothing unites my countrymen better than unforeseen bad luck. As I pressed on the gas with my tired foot, sweat running down my forehead and chest, I was stunned to find, among the multiplying faces reflected in my rearview mirror, the big, irritable, unmistakable peasant mug of Mostafa Akbari. I sank low into my seat so he wouldn't recognize me, but soon another impulse, in complete opposition to the first, made me stick my head out the window and call out his name. He walked over. "Still in Tehran?" he said, a rifle hanging from his shoulder as casually as a tennis racket.

"Where else would I be?"

"I had counted you as one of those talkers who would pack up and leave as soon as things got messy."

"You underestimate me," I said.

"So I did," he said. He had trimmed his Stalinist mustache and now sported a full beard.

"Who are you with now?" I asked him, and he said, "I am with whomever Allah sees fit. And you?" he added. "You're still with Gandhi?"

I smiled, acknowledging the naiveté of my ways. "No, my brother," I said. "I am with whomever you are with." Pointing at the rifle I added, "Is God handing out Kalashnikovs now?"

Narrowing his eyes he smiled tepidly, like a schoolteacher who has decided to indulge a student's juvenile joke. "I've joined the Sepah, the Revolutionary Guards," he said. He glanced at the shopping bags stacked on the back seat of my car. The head of a chicken, just butchered, stuck out from one of the bags, and from another sprang the wet tails of two fish. "What's all this?" he asked. "Looks like enough food for an army. You're not still running around with the Communists, are you?"

How could I tell him that I, self-professed revolutionary, was still the errand boy for my parents? "Listen, now that you're with Sepah, I have a favor to ask," I said.

"Ask, brother," he said.

"I'd like you to come by with a friend or two to seize . . . my father's papers."

"You're asking me to raid your house?"

"My father's house."

"Your father still hasn't left town? Wasn't he with the Ministry of Culture?"

"He hasn't left. He seems to believe that the arts hover above politics and that he is therefore immune."

"You're turning in your own father?" he said incredulously. "What kind of papers are we talking about?"

I hesitated. "Notes for an encyclopedia," I said. "Three decades' worth of research in his study and in an office space one floor above our apartment."

I believe it was not the gravity of the task, but the extent of the intended injury, that made his black eyes soften with delight. "Consider it done," he said. "How about Tuesday at three in the afternoon?"

We shook hands. I wrote down my family's address on the back of the receipt from the bakery, where I had just bought my father's favorite sweets: a box of *koloucheh*, which he liked to eat with his afternoon tea.

The car finally started, and as I pressed on the gas I watched the volunteers wishing me well and dispersing in various directions. All with the exception of one man: Mostafa Akbari, in his tattered corduroy suit, the bakery receipt dangling from his hand.

AT THREE O'CLOCK SHARP the following Tuesday the knocks came. His promptness stunned me; it was as though he had come for a job interview or a bank loan. My mother was napping on the sofa under the hum of the air conditioner, and my father sat silent on the settee, staring at his tea and cookies and playing with his *tasbih*, dazed by the vertiginous bounce of one bead on the next. "Who could that be?" said my alarmed mother, sitting up and straightening her hair. "Will you get it, Hamid?"

I had hoped that this task wouldn't fall to me. But I did as I was told, allaying my hesitation with reminders of Yasser's story about my father's betrayal of his friend H.

Akbari stood before me, as promised, with two fellow Guards. On his face I found only a trace of derision. They walked past my speechless parents with their rifles and made their way to my father's study. "What is this?" *bābā* said, walking after them. "What do you think you're doing?" They ignored him as they ransacked his books, collecting whatever they thought may be viable evidence for a future case against him. "Hamid!" said my father. "Talk to them. They'll listen to you."

I stood beside him like a besieged moth before a praying mantis. "Hamid, Hamid, do something . . ." my father carried on. Akbari dangled a key in my father's face and said, "We understand you have an office dedicated to your encyclopedia upstairs?"

"Yes, but what can you possibly want with an art encyclopedia?"

"You let us be the judges of that," Akbari said as he headed upstairs with his men.

We sat in the living room in silence, listening to their footsteps and the rattle of furniture above us. It was another oppressive summer afternoon. My mother stroked my father's forearm. "It was bound to happen to us, too," she whispered. "After all, why not?" My father muttered something, his voice hoarse. Woozy, as though wasted, I walked to the window and looked out on the street, at cars headed to half-empty office buildings or desolate restaurants, at a city built by one regime and awaiting ordinances by another, suspended in disorder. My knees trembled as I stood, and a sinking feeling made the room spin slowly around me. Breathless, I took small steps to a chair, and as I sat down, my mother said, "Hamid-*jan*, you look so pale . . . It will be all right, don't be scared." From the kitchen she brought two glasses of water, one for my father and one for me.

Akbari and his men emerged hours later, and hauled away three decades of *bābā*'s writings in thirteen garbage bags. "You're lucky your son is a friend of the revolution, *aghaye* Mozaffarian," Akbari said on his way out. "Or you would be sharing the fate of your papers." My father remained on the settee in his pajamas and slippers, his hands on his lap visibly shaking. He cleared his throat several times in an attempt to speak, but his voice wouldn't come. Finally, in a barely audible voice he said, "History will not be kind to you, *aghaye* Akbari."

"Professor," Akbari said. "Don't concern yourself with history, because history has the memory of a baboon. Agonize instead over your own destiny."

He walked out, leaving dusty prints on the carpet, and I followed him to the foyer, unsure of how to bid him farewell. His face was even more sallow than usual, his antler birthmark more inflamed. "How would you like to join Sepah?" he said. "I'll put in a good word for you." I hesitated. "I am honored," I said, my voice breaking. "But I've decided to resume my commitment to nonviolence."

"*Māshāllah*—bravo!" he said. "But I'm afraid you crossed that line today, a hundred times over. Think about it, brother."

As he walked out he noticed a crumpled piece of paper on the console. He glanced at it and put it in his pocket. It was, I remembered, the General's phone number at the Imperial Air Force; the General had given it to me when the house had tilted and was at risk of collapsing. The number was useless now; like so many others, the General, too, had disappeared.

The front door slammed shut, the sound of heavy bags thrown inside a trunk filled the afternoon, a car engine boomed. Then came the sound of nothing, which follows all else.

Running into the garden, I crouched under the apricot tree and sobbed. When I was done I got up and frantically looked for Pofak the crippled cat, whose magical appearance, I felt, would signal that things would turn out all right in the end. But there was no cat.

In the living room my father sat stooped on the settee, his hands clasped on his bony knees, staring blankly at the untouched plate of *koloucheh* before him.

It was the first and last time I saw him cry.

18

WHEN I LEFT MY FAMILY at the departure gate at Mehrabad airport in that summer of 1979, it was they who called out my name, and not the other way around. "Hamid, Hamid! . . ." cried my father amid the footsteps of travelers and the public address system blaring departures, arrivals, delays, cancellations. I didn't turn back. I allowed my father's broken voice to inoculate me against loyalty, and I kept on walking, one foot in front of the other, facing a splintering city promising solitude. A hot wind filled my father's old Paykan as I drove home with the windows rolled down, dust and pollution making everything—the abandoned construction sites and the rusted cranes—feel like the yellowing sketches of a dead architect.

I parked the car on Shahreza Street, renamed Enghelab—Revolution—and walked toward the apartment. The old frame shop still displayed in its window prints of docile kittens, London Bridge, and alpine forests. The cassette seller next door played one of the Ayatollah's old speeches.

When I opened the door to the empty house my reflection in the foyer mirror startled me. I looked at my hard, haggard face and asked myself a question that would haunt me for the rest of my days: how does the stone stand being a stone? The hollow gloves stacked palms up on the console were as solemn as an undertaker's handshake. In the living room my mother's red cardigan draped over the sofa, my father's slippers abandoned at the foot of the settee, and my brother's favorite vinyl—Boney M.'s "Ma Baker" single—left behind on the coffee table, all bore the fingerprints of familial heartbreak. On the floor, next to my father's slippers, was the last book he had read in that settee—a monograph on Caravaggio. I picked it up. It was bookmarked at a page on *The Calling of St. Matthew.* I stared, mesmerized, at the photograph of the painting, remembering the old Polaroid I had once found in his desk drawer. It was the grit that now drew me in—the seedy tavern, the weathered faces, the bare, dirty feet of Saint Peter. I loved the image, in all its soil and unsaintliness. I loved, too, the outstretched arm beckoning in the ray of light, and the stunned face of Matthew pointing at himself. I closed the book, wondering why I had shirked, countless times, my father's attempts to share with me his love of Caravaggio. I wanted to call Minoo, but felt unqualified for both sympathy and love. Instead I went to the kitchen, where an unwashed teacup sang a requiem from the sink, and I made myself two sunny-side-up eggs, the heady smell of frying butter convincing me that I had done the right thing. At my father's seat near the window, I ate ravenously. His morning paper was still on the breakfast table. I did not read it.

IN THOSE EARLY DAYS what preoccupied me above all was dirt. I dusted the apartment daily, washed my hands at least a dozen times a day. I played Omid's Boney M. record over and over as I painted the walls hospital white and wiped the floors with bleach, all the while singing along, *Ma Baker, she never could cry . . . Ma Ma Ma Ma . . . Ma Baker, but she knew how to die . . .* I sorted the closets and tossed out my family's belongings like a widower at once grieving and jubilant. I did the same with friends and acquaintances, liquidating those I deemed unfit for the portrait I was drawing of myself. Though I tried my best to carry out this selection in a manner that caused as little offense as possible, a few discarded friends took their dismissal to heart; one old Baha'i classmate wept.

There were items I could not cast off. The honeybee car. My collection of sulfide marbles; my mother's hideous Marie Antoinette lamp; my father's Caravaggio book; his monogrammed cigarette lighter, and his spare reading glasses, which I began using some two decades later; the prayer stone Uncle Majid gave me before the car accident; the shortwave portable radio, around which my family had huddled in those final months to pick up staticky transmissions of the BBC; the Pan Am matchbook with my father's inscription, given to me the night he exiled me to the garden; bins of family photographs; and this: a shoebox I found under my parents' bed, containing dozens of photocopies of caricatures, all initialed "H." Among these were facsimiles of two typed letters from the Ministry of Culture, addressed to Houshang Habibi, informing him that should he not desist the political nature of his work, he would suffer severe consequences. The signatory on both letters was my father.

Throughout this liquidation my mother's canary sang, having neither memory nor foreknowledge of misfortune. As was my habit I berated my mother for neglecting those who depended on her, in this case her beloved bird. Why had she not entrusted it to a friend? But soon I remembered that I was the one who had precipitated my family's exit, leaving them no time to settle accounts, make peace, say goodbye.

19

WITH MY FAMILY GONE, I talked Minoo into moving in with me. This caused a disturbance in her household, especially as I had no intention of marrying her, and as far as I knew, marriage—so petty and bourgeois an institution compared to our riotous exploits—wasn't on her mind either. With the revolution now accomplished, we set out each evening with cans of aerosol paint to imprint the city with graffiti. I drew, Minoo wrote slogans. But as the nimbus of the victorious regime seeped its religion into the marrow of our lives, dictating ideals, laws, and eventually habits, our guerrilla-style living arrangement gradually became illegal, and Minoo, whose affronted father refused to take her back, effectively became a fugitive in my home. She kept her head down and limited her comings and goings to off-hours, and we made sure never to be seen together outside the apartment, a dichotomy mirrored in countless households, a harbinger of a nation's collective psychosis. Our slapdash street art was soon deemed unacceptable, too, replaced instead by government-sponsored propaganda murals.

Ask any child who has played musical chairs: finding your place in the shifting order of vanishing chairs is no small task. So it was for us. Would we keep whirling to the tuneless clapping of a new regime and grab a seat at someone else's expense, or would we relinquish the game and disappear? Minoo's family, as mine had a year earlier, decided to surrender and leave for America, and she, wavering for weeks, chose in the end to stay. I was pleased with her choice but only hoped that it had not been made on my account.

One week before their departure date, her father, Ebrahim Levy, son of the late rabbi Baruch Levy and owner of a mirror shop on Lalezar Street, amateur interpreter of the Babylonian Talmud and lover of pistachios from Rafsanjan, died of a heart attack on his way to the synagogue, where he had hoped to pray one last time for his family's safe passage. I accompanied the devastated Minoo to the funeral, and sat in mourning with her for seven days in her family's home, where their last remaining friends and relatives gathered nightly to recite the Kaddish. On several occasions, when the required ten Jewish men were not present to form a minyan, the rabbi, seeing the exceptional nature of our time, allowed me to stand in as one of the ten. In the circle of praying mourners I felt both privileged and alien, honored to have been included but not wishing to make a habit of it.

THE ENVELOPE OF CASH my father had left on my pillow on the day he fled soon lay like a deflated balloon on the dining room table, along with our abandoned spray paints and revolutionary banners. And Minoo's savings, courtesy of her bereft mother, would in a matter of weeks become nothing more than a chilly memory of familial refuge. With the threat of destitution pushing us toward pragmatism, Minoo decided to take over her father's boarded-up mirror shop, determined to support us in our solitude.

For two days we cleaned the shop, wiping dusty glass with vinegar and rags, sieged once more by our own reflections as we had been in the house of mirrors at the amusement park, on that summer night that now seemed centuries ago. Convex, cheval, swing, and oval mirrors, Venetian mirrors rimmed with rosettes, gold-plated Beaux Arts mirrors—all stood taciturn along the walls, unstained and chaste.

ON THE MORNING of Minoo's first workday I got up before dawn and, as had become my habit, didn't bother to put pants on. While I was grateful for her sensible decision to overtake the shop, this descent into normalcy unnerved me. Not only were we going to play house, we were going to do it under a government that wished to erase us—its progenitors—as it expunged its own footprints. To fill the hours until sunrise I placed the kettle on the stove and picked up a newspaper from the stack piling up on the kitchen counter. It was a one-week-old *New York Times* that the kiosk down the street had somehow managed to get. I read,

Tehran, Sep 29, 1980—
Tehran at night appears like a ghost town.

Like most other cities in the country, the capital is dark because the authorities switch off the city's electrical generators to assure that a blackout is enforced and perhaps also as a conservation measure. Iranians live by candlelight behind thick curtains.

Thousands of militiamen, on foot or in cars with dimmed headlights, circulate in silence. Shadows loom to intercept a lone pedestrian to check his papers or advise him to return home.

MISSILES LIGHT SKY

Every evening since the beginning of last week an air raid siren has broadcast the presence of enemy planes over the city. Ground-to-air missiles and machine gun fire light the sky, making an enormous racket. Last Sunday's raid warning and the firing lasted more than two hours, but not one enemy bomb was dropped on the city. In fact, the only verifiable bombing of Tehran came last Monday, the first day of the war.

Iraqi planes have aimed rockets at the Tehran airport, but they have not succeeded in damaging the runways. According to witnesses, from two to eight people have been killed in these attacks . . .

The shortage of oil, which until now was the only commodity that had been rationed, has become a very serious problem for Iran. Travel between Tehran and the provinces has diminished to a trickle, and on the highways one encounters mainly supply vehicles and military trucks.

In Tabriz on Saturday the long lines at gasoline stations came to a halt when the electrical power on which the pumps run was cut off. At one station hundreds of orange taxis were lined up for several kilometers.

SHORTAGE OF PUBLIC TRANSIT

The scene is similar in Tehran, where private cars are forbidden to operate. Drivers of buses and taxis have trouble getting gasoline, and people often wait up to two hours before they can find transportation to work. Many are not able to return home at night. Nevertheless there is not the slightest complaint or sign of ill humor . . .

Rendered with a Western pen our troubles sounded almost poetic. I pictured us as described, good-humored and philosophical, lining up at bus stops and gas stations as sunset dipped us in wistful postcard colors, our militiamen bidding us good night like benevolent uncles.

MINOO APPEARED IN the kitchen groggy and ill-tempered. She poured herself a glass of tea. "Don't you think it's unsanitary to walk around the apartment naked?" she said, lighting up a cigarette.

"Not more unsanitary than that smoke in the kitchen."

"You're one to lecture me on smoking," she said. She nudged me aside to grab a pan, tucked her head inside the fridge and moved its contents—the butter and the milk and the eggs—like mahjong tiles. The cigarette, still in her hand, spewed smoke inside the fridge.

"Omelet?" she said. Despite the shortages we had finally gotten a dozen eggs the day before.

"Sure, thank you." I stepped aside to give her full reign of the stove. She glanced at my nakedness before cracking the eggs open in the sizzling pan.

"It didn't use to bother you, my walking around like this," I said.

"Well, it does now," she said.

I folded the newspaper and left to cool off in the shower. Was she feeling the same agitation I was—she, who after all had surrendered her family in order to sustain the idea of us? I washed quickly—the water refused to heat up—then dressed and returned to the kitchen table, where she had laid out two plates. She knew I would return to eat with her because that's what I always did.

Daylight arrived reproachfully, exposing our aimlessness. From the floor above came a squeaking sound, which had begun weeks earlier and magnified with each passing day. I wondered if mice had set up house in my father's old office, but I was too cowardly to check. Minoo glanced up at the ceiling then at me, but said nothing. A dozen times she had asked me to go upstairs; she wasn't going to ask again. We ate in silence, the omelet leaving an ashen taste on my tongue, no doubt from her cigarette.

"Thank you," I said, releasing my fork, my plate half-empty.

She examined the uneaten half but didn't speak. I detected the hint of a shrug. Her own plate was nearly full and she was already reaching for another cigarette. I poured a teaspoon of sugar on the table and traced a smiley face inside it with my finger.

"I feel very sad today," she said. "There is so much darkness. I miss my father."

I reached for her free hand and kissed it. She resumed smoking and looked beyond me, at the ashes-of-roses face of the porcelain clock on the wall. It was almost seven o'clock. "I have to go," she said. "Before the neighbors see me."

I strapped her purse to her shoulder and walked her to the door, as though I were sending her off to school. "Thank you for taking care of us," I said as I watched her descend the staircase, disappearing and reappearing along its spirals.

AT THE KITCHEN TABLE the smiley face stared back at me until I could no longer stand it. I dipped my fingertip in the sugar and sucked it, then scattered the remaining granules all over the table. Unsure of what to do with myself I paced the apartment and stood by the living room window. Another day was unfolding on the street below. A woman walking her daughter to school, a bookseller unlocking the metal gate of his half-censored shop, an unemployed man returning home in a crumpled suit with *sangak* bread. The meagerness of it all made me yearn for the bloody days of protests, when possibilities still lay ahead of us. I considered going up to my father's study to check on the mice. But not having entered it since Akbari had paid it a visit, it remained as unapproachable to me as a looted mausoleum.

I lay back on the settee, that same settee where my father had sat trembling as he watched the abduction of his life's work. I shut my eyes. Homemade alcohol, black-market gasoline, glassy-eyed addicts, smugglers, pushers, sweaty men passing the hours in downtown teahouses amid the clatter of saucers and cups, people blindfolded and spirited away only to be distilled days later into names on execution lists in newspapers—these things, which I, like others, had been witnessing, flashed in my mind. These were the makings of an underground parallel city shadowing the so-called pious city above, the scaffolding of a professed republic that like the monarchy preceding it did not dare to look at its own reflection save in a draped mirror.

So our revolution had been accomplished, but what of it? And what of us?

I sank into a fretful sleep and dreamed of a cockfight in which I, one of the combatants—half man, half rooster—pierced my opponent's eyes with gaffs attached to my legs, and my adversary, in turn, punctured my lungs with the precision of a curved ice pick, drawing out the air as in a deflated zeppelin. Faceless spectators cheered as my opponent and I outdid each other, surrounded by smoke and the smell of whiskey and sweat. I looked at my blinded rival and said, in the voiceless voice of someone struggling to speak in a dream, "But how is it, brother, that we have been trapped like this? We—you and I—have been for millennia emblems of spirituality, harbingers of new beginnings. Left to our own devices, we may at worst do a cockerel waltz. How have they defaced us, as they themselves have been defaced?" As I spoke, I felt my lungs collapsing and I woke up with a start, breathless, as a dreamer about to fall into a black crater. *Bābā*, I cried. *Bābā! What have I done?*

How I wished to tell Minoo of how I had betrayed my father. Sweet Minoo, who had cried for months over her own father's death and the grief she believed she had caused him. But I could not tell. Would not. A week earlier, as the sound of fighter planes reverberated through a blacked-out city and we huddled together under the kitchen table, a candle flickering between us, I nearly said, "Minoo, you have bound yourself to a traitor. Walk away, while you can." But that, I knew, would be the end of us, an end that in any case would come sooner or later.

I idled in the apartment for the rest of the day, then set out on my motorcycle as the sun began to forsake a liquidated city, glittering like mica on tar-bound rooftops. I rode all night, defying the curfew and going nowhere, my last drops of gasoline taking me through streets bereft of the memory of streetlamps, past houses where people slept but didn't dream. Daylight broke as sharply as a wishbone, and as the first rays of sunlight shimmered on treetops, I parked the bike near the apartment and walked along Valiasr Street, intent on making up to Minoo for my nocturnal absence by returning home with pastries for breakfast. I had forgotten that because of the war and the shortages, no bakeries were open.

THE APARTMENT WAS EMPTY WHEN I ARRIVED. I called the mirror shop but there was no answer; I figured she must be somewhere along her tortuous commute.

Filling a backpack with spray paints I set out again, hands in my pockets, and along a quiet alley shooting off Enghelab Street, I pulled out a can of red paint and sprayed an image I had sidelined but not forgotten, that of Everyman Jamshid—the same turned-up raincoat collar, prominent sideburns, and pensive mien. But in accordance with the times I tamed his pompadour, changed his Gauloise to a Bahman cigarette, and gave him a beard. Stepping back, soothed once more by the act of drawing, I signed the bottom "Everyman Jamshid, Man of Revolt" and kept on walking, replicating the image a few steps down, and again in the next alley, on the shuttered metal gate of an abandoned shop. With a sense of aliveness that I had relegated to times past, I walked all morning, spraying my everyman along the streets of Tehran like a scorned cat pissing in forbidden places to reclaim lost territory.

This ritual I repeated every morning for about a month, without telling a soul, not even Minoo, who since my disappearing act on my motorcycle had been giving me the cold shoulder. Those who witnessed my transgression were too preoccupied with their own lives and misfortunes to care. And so I carried on, repeating the image like a mantra, hoping to reach shore on the lifeboat of subversion.

During this time, a strange thing happened: I mistook every tall, middle-aged man for my father. More than once I followed a stranger down several avenues, my footsteps echoing his quickening pace, convinced that the chase would culminate in some reconciliation. After following a man in a checkered scarf inside a tobacco shop one foggy afternoon, I stood idle as he bought himself a bag of rock candy, and I shadowed him back out, monitoring his movements as he opened the bag and popped a candy into his mouth every couple of blocks. He slowed down, finally, allowing me to catch up, and turned around. "May I help you?" he said.

"Oh," I said. "I mistook you for someone."

"What is your name?"

"Never mind," I said. "I made a mistake. Forgive me." I began walking away.

"Hold on a minute," he called after me. "Who said you could go?"

"Who said I couldn't?" I said as he reached for something in his coat pocket. I stood still. Though his face—the thick eyebrows arched over the horn-rimmed glasses, the outturned ears, and the dark scrape on his forehead, which had of late become the seal of piety because it signified repeated friction against the prayer stone—seemed vaguely familiar, I could not place him. "Who are you?" I said.

He approached me and stood very close, his godly forehead

almost touching mine, his breath reeking of onions and candy. From his pocket he did not pull out a gun—as I had feared— but a worn-out wallet, from which he deftly produced a driver's license. I recognized the name; he was the chief prosecutor of Tehran, in those days something of a celebrity.

"So I ask you again," he said. "Your name, brother."

"Hamid Mozaffarian."

"Providence has its way," he said. "I was about to send someone to pay you a visit. Come with me."

We walked together along the pavement, my knees buckling, and got into his car and set off. "Where are we going?" I said.

"I ask the questions here," he said, putting the bag of candy in my face.

"No, thank you," I said.

"I know . . . You're supposed to have them with tea, but I just eat them like this, one after the other. I'm ruining my teeth."

I said nothing.

"So it appears you are quite the artist," he said.

"Me?"

"Aren't you Everyman Jamshid?"

"Me?"

"Are you half-witted or something? Yes, you. Many of your old schoolmates are now, shall we say . . . my guests. And they've all identified you as Everyman Jamshid. So what are you thinking, you jackass, doodling that stupid face all over town? Is he supposed to symbolize something? And why is he red? Is that a nod to your old Marxist friends?"

"No, it's just a face," I said. "And red is just a color."

He scoffed. "And what about 'Man of Revolt'? What does that refer to? Are you plotting against the new regime?"

"That . . . That's just my homage to Albert Camus."

"Who?"

"Never mind," I said. "Some French philosopher. He believed that revolt is one of the essential dimensions of human nature. At the same time, he cautioned that this urge has to be reined in, so as not to lead to excess, as happened, for example, during the French Revolution, or . . ."

"Save your *cherto-pert*—your gibberish—for a poor fool who will be impressed," he said. "I know your kind. You've read half a book on some French writer and you're suddenly the expert."

He was smarter than I had supposed. I had to change tactics. "Brother," I said. "You are right. I am no expert on Camus, or on anything else for that matter. I'm just a university dropout killing time. But I do know one thing. The images of raised fists and droplets of blood and Kalashnikovs that you guys are sponsoring are already becoming tired. No one even notices them anymore. You have to offer people something to think about."

He stared at me, and the realization that I was trapped in a car with a man whose tribunals lasted about as long as it took to unload a washing machine seized me. I sank low, the seat belt chafing my neck.

"Consider yourself lucky," he said. "You have a friend in high places who has been speaking well of you, and of the sacrifices you have made for the cause of the revolution. He is the reason you have so far been allowed to roam free, despite your doodles all over town."

I kept my head down, picking at my cuticles.

"I know of your denouncement of your father," he continued. "One of my judicial officers, Mostafa Akbari, has told me all about it. The capacity for such a betrayal, in my opinion, is a rare thing, and precious." Turning into an alley he stopped the car. "I was going to take you in for interrogation, but I've changed my mind. I'd like to offer you a job, instead."

"What job?"

"A job in the prison. As an interrogator."

"Me? Why me?"

"Because I like you. I see in you a beautiful mix of brutishness and naiveté."

I made no answer.

"Well?" he said. "This offer has a quick expiration date. Otherwise I'm taking you in for interrogation."

"I am at your service, *sarkār.*"

FOR MANY WEEKS, maybe as many as seven or eight, long after I became an interrogator for Akbari, I told Minoo nothing about my new job. I slipped in and out of the house always with the excuse of roaming the city. The deeper I sank into my alternate life, the more I longed to resume my studies at the university. But when I shared this with Akbari, he had a good laugh. "Be a man," he said, "and leave the art degree for the homosexuals."

We were standing outside branch six, cell block two. "But don't you also want to go back to your old job?" I said. "We could both pick up where we left off."

"Listen to me," he said. "Every man must sooner or later reckon with what he is. I, for instance, know that I am no oil company man. And you . . . you have to get that fancy idea of yourself as some iconoclast artist out of your head. You put an end to that the day you asked me to raid your father's house. On that day, whether or not you realized it, you chose a new course, from which there is no return. So just keep on going, brother. That's all you can do." He pinched my cheek in that patronizing way of his and added, "One more thing: you may want to get rid of that Bolshevik Jewish girlfriend of yours. The path you've chosen cannot accommodate her."

I carried on as instructed, convincing myself that better days were ahead, that the revolution, after all, was still only an infant crawling its way to maturity. Akbari, pleased with my compliance, asked me to witness my first execution—that of Yasser Maghz-Pahn, who had been detained some months earlier—on *shabeh yaldā*, the winter solstice, the longest night of the year, a night normally celebrated with friends and family until dawn, a night holding the promise of darkness defeated.

That afternoon I bought Minoo a box of sweets and visited her at the shop, where the lone customer was a lanky militiaman with a unibrow. His gruff reflection in the Murano glass of a gold-rimmed Venetian mirror was a strange sight. "Why is the glass scratched in the corner?" he asked Minoo reproachfully. Minoo, unruffled, replied, "It's an antique from Italy, from the early nineteenth century. That's the beauty of it, you see, the history . . ." He cut her off. "What kind of discount will you offer then? It's clearly faulty." She resisted. "It's an antique," she repeated. "It's not faulty. The scratch is the mark of time, nothing more." He sneered at her and left the shop.

"You should be more careful when you talk to these guys," I said.

"They don't scare me," she said, as she prepared tea and set out the pastries I had brought next to the register. We sat together in the empty shop, sipping tea, our reflections in the scores of mirrors along the walls persuading us that we were guests at a midnight revel.

"Why did you bring all this here?" she said. "I was hoping we could have a little winter solstice celebration at home."

"Minoo," I said. "I won't be coming home tonight. There is something I must do."

"What thing?"

"You can't ask me that," I said.

"I can't?" she said. "You've never talked to me like that."

"I am now. Get used to it."

"What's going on, Hamid?"

I retrieved my backpack. "Bye," I said.

"This is how you talk to me, after everything?"

I turned around. "After everything what?" I said. "Are you going to deliver your monologue about how you renounced your family and stayed here for me? Go ahead, because I've been waiting for it for months."

"Don't flatter yourself," she said. "I didn't stay for you."

"You stayed for your love of turbans, then?"

"You may find this absurd. But I stayed because two thirds of the Jewish population has left. And if everyone leaves, then what? We've been here for two thousand years. Someone must persevere until things settle down."

"I thought all that synagogue talk of Cyrus and Babylon and Esther made you feel like a relic. What happened? Suddenly you've become more Jewish than the Chief Rabbi."

"In the words of Italo Svevo," she said, "'it's not race that makes a Jew, it's life.' And by the way, even the Chief Rabbi has left. I hear he is now driving a Mercedes on Sunset Boulevard."

"Well then, congratulations," I said. "You're single-handedly going to be the savior of Middle Eastern Jews! You must be the first anthropological martyr history has yet produced."

"Who are you?" she said. "Who have you become? You and I used to be on the same side. We fought the system together. This one as much as the old one."

"Well, my love," I said. "Slowly, slowly, I've become the system." I strapped my bag to my shoulder and jumped on my motorcycle, and as I rode in the icy air toward the prison, I remembered how my father had said those very words to me a decade earlier.

MINOO WAS GONE when I returned home the next day. I didn't go looking for her. Instead, over the ensuing weeks, I retreated into the memory of sound. The sound that emanated from the firing squad on that winter morning—deafening, dull, single-minded, smoke-filled. The sound of my own boots on the snow as I walked the dozen steps to Yasser's corpse; the sound of swallows flying overhead afterward; the sound of a man's dead weight as it is placed on a stretcher; the sound of a lifeless arm scraping a trail in the snow with a fingernail; the sound of my breath vibrating in my thorax; the sound of shrapnel dropped into a metal bucket by a janitor using his bare hands.

The tribunal, perhaps displaying gratitude for my good behavior, honored my request to keep Yasser's body safe at the morgue until his family claimed it. After a couple of weeks a pimply nephew named Ali, who couldn't have been older than sixteen, showed up at the prison. I assumed he had some sob story about his parents, but I didn't ask. Still, his bewildered face made me feel sorry for him and I offered to drive him to the morgue. When he saw the body—which, except for a bullet hole lodged near the spine, looked quite ordinary—he said, "I imagined he would be bigger." I almost made a joke about how his uncle's supply of marzipan had been cut off in prison, but I thought better of it. "Well . . . Good luck," I said and walked away, but the boy's scrawny arms were now trembling before his uncle's corpse and I felt sorry for him again.

To put him out of his misery I drove him to the cemetery for a secret burial that same night. I carried the shrouded body out of the morgue and dumped it in the trunk as they do in movies, marveling at the absurdity of my life and of Yasser's death. Everyone has heard how heavy a lifeless body is but no one knows what the weight feels like until he has carried a dead man himself. Like lifting a hundred-kilo burlap sack of rice, tightly packed and stiff as a cello.

The boy insisted on sitting in the back, as though this would shield him from the man I had become. I let him. The last thing I cared about was some heartbroken adolescent's misgivings about the way of things. As we drove I thought of Yasser's trial, which had lasted no more than fifteen minutes, of his surprise and relief upon seeing me in the room and of his anguish when he understood that I would be of no help to him. I thought of the tremor in his right hand as he nervously tapped his knee and the twitch beneath his emaciated jaw. I thought of Akbari reciting the charges against him—*declaring war on God, colluding with the West, insulting government officials, lying to the authorities*—and repeating, again and again, "Is this true?" I thought of Yasser refuting the charges until only minutes later when, shutting his eyes as a man who has had a quick word with his own death, he said, "Yes, it is true. Everything you say is true."

At the cemetery I bribed a gravedigger to dig a hole and waited in the car for an hour with the boy and the body. From time to time I glanced at the boy's face in the rearview mirror and noticed the strain of aborted tears in his eyes. Crickets sang in the starless night, but the boy said nothing. To distract myself I turned on the radio, but the only audible transmission was a religious sermon and I was in no mood for that. I imagined the boy wasn't either; I switched it off. "Did you know your uncle well?" I finally said.

"He used to teach me to draw when I was a kid," he said, his voice as hollow as a beggar's bowl. "And he always brought me gifts. The best one was a giant box of colored pencils."

"Yes," I said. "My father also brought me those beautiful pencils."

WHEN THE GRAVEDIGGER tapped on the window Ali helped me carry the body to the grave. After we lowered it into the ground he threw on it a fistful of soil, as was required of him. For some reason, perhaps out of nostalgia for the days when Yasser Maghz-Pahn and the others gathered in my father's office, I, too, threw a fistful of soil on the corpse and recited the prayer for the dead, "*one always returns to Allah and ends with Allah.*" The gravedigger covered up the body with more soil and I sprinkled rosewater on the grave. In the car, on the way back, I offered the devastated nephew a piece of halvah I had brought for the occasion, as one does after a burial. He refused it.

FOR WEEKS AFTER THE BURIAL I searched for an antidote to my restlessness. I undertook another house cleaning, rode my motorcycle longer and farther. I began attending the Friday prayer weekly, but unable to sustain this attempt at religiosity, I let go of this, too.

20

IN THE HALF-LIGHT OF THE HOTEL ROOM I checked my phone. Nothing from Noushin, not even a rebuke. Would my daughter testify against me in court? My Golnaz, who had for a time been my dearest friend, maybe my only friend. I thought of our third summer alone together—after Noushin had left—of our visit to Ramsar, and of the brilliance of the water that July.

We had rented a small house near the old hotel, the mountain on one side and the sea on the other. The days were hot and humid, but in the nighttime winds scratched the windows. Golnaz was afraid. She said there were spirits all around us. I told her she only knew the exhaust of Tehran, the sirens, the soot, that's why she thought this. She conceded, but more than once she snuck into my bed during the night, and I let her. She had just turned twelve and we got along like old friends, taking turns making breakfast and driving to nearby villages every morning to pick up raw milk and pails of yogurt. In the afternoons we took walks along the palm-lined promenade that led from the hotel to the sea, where the air carried the sound of waves and crowds and children. Sometimes, when we tired of the water, we drove to nearby forests and foraged for wild mushrooms and starflowers.

During the summer break she rarely wore the mandated manteau and scarf, and since she was still young enough, I didn't protest. But it was on one of those afternoons that I noticed, as I walked behind her, a bloodstain on the back of her pants. I stepped ahead of her and walked on as though I had not seen the blood, and she, silent, dragged her feet to keep up with me. Finally, she asked that I stop and she bent over holding her stomach. When she noticed the stain she looked up at me with the guilt-ridden face of a criminal. "Is it your first time?" I said, embarrassed for not knowing and even more embarrassed for having to know. She nodded, avoiding my eyes as she removed her sweater and tied it around her waist. Back at the house, she locked herself in the bathroom for what seemed like an eternity. When I knocked gently on the door, asking if I could help, she said, "I wish Mom were here."

If the father in me wanted to quiet her pain, the man in me felt a pang of betrayal. My daughter's blood became for me a declaration of an unspoken mistrust between us. I knocked again. "Come out, *azizam*—my dear," I said, regretful now that providence had not given me a son instead. "Let's get groceries for dinner. It will take your mind off."

She unbolted the door and came out, looking mournful. She had changed into pajama pants and thick socks. The years of hormonal volatility ahead of us made me suddenly breathless. How was it that I had not considered this earlier, when I had insisted that she stay with me? She wobbled to the living room and sank in a corner of the sofa, curling her legs under her and making herself small. Though I found her needlessly thespian, I made her tea and brought it to her with a tray of cookies. I sat down at the other end of the sofa, and for some time we remained, not speaking, in this rented house that suddenly seemed to me as cold as an interrogation room. An old clock with Roman numerals that I had barely noticed ticked loudly on the wall. It was six-fifteen in the evening.

In the uninterrupted silence between us, the knowledge that here, in Ramsar, we were in one of the most naturally radio-active spots in the world thrust itself to the forefront of my mind like the centuries of radon carried by hot springs to the earth's surface, seeping into the limestone with which this house, as so many like it, had been built. I had read of tests showing that the area's inhabitants had through the generations developed an ability to adapt to this radiation, like sea turtles continuing their deep, slow swim across time.

Moving closer to me she rested her head on my chest as she used to do when she was a toddler. I held her close and we fell asleep like that until nightfall, when I woke up with a start, and scanning with my eyes the edges and curves of the unfamiliar furniture in the dark, I decided that our time here together was over. We would drive back to Tehran in the morning, our windows rolled down, the taste of saltwater on our silent tongues, between us the shared memory of blood that neither one of us could ever forget.

OMID'S APARTMENT, as he had described, was in a cul-de-sac of Tudor-style buildings with fanciful gargoyles and heraldic cartouches. In the dimly lit lobby a doorman with a cowlick surrounded by stained-glass windows broadcast my visit over the intercom.

When Omid opened the door I said, "Did I see Henry the Eighth in the lobby?"

"I warned you," he said, laughing, then added, "The rent was cheap."

I entered the overfed apartment. A cabinet facing the sofa bore everything from dictionaries with cracked spines to a pen collection to piles of letters. In one corner of the room paper-filled shopping bags formed a tower of Pisa, while in another boxes marked "Affidavits" were haphazardly stacked. A miniature lemon tree stood under a light fixture, and a vase of wilting white roses dripped onto the dining table every time the dog, a spotted Labrador, brushed against it.

"This is Luca," Omid said affectionately of the dog, who eyed me with suspicion.

Omid looked haggard. Deep, gray crescents shadowed his bloodshot eyes and a two-day-old beard darkened his chin. He prepared tea in a kitchen the size of Golnaz's old make-believe stove. As I stood back, imagining my brother's life in this medieval-styled shipping container, the dog sniffed my pants then settled in his bed, observing me like a jaded volunteer militiaman of the Revolutionary Guard. "Your dog is watching me like a worn-out Basiji," I said.

Handing me the teacup Omid sat on the sofa, dread in his eyes. "Luca is dying," he said. "This morning when I woke up he didn't stir from the foot of my bed, as he usually does. I walked over and sat beside him, but he just looked at me with tired, crusty eyes. His breathing was uneven and labored. Finally, with great effort he lifted one paw and placed it on my knee. For the past few months his heart disease has been worsening, and I understood that the end must now be near. From the bathroom I brought a wet towel and wiped his eyes and coat. He let me tend to him, surrendering his weakness to our friendship. Then I sat with him, watching the sunrise and stroking his head—those beautiful ridges and valleys of his skull that I know so well."

"How long have you had him?"

"Thirteen years. We got him when Arash was just three. He was a two-year-old rescue that we picked up from a shelter in Brooklyn. Anita, my ex, was dead set against getting a pet, but Arash and I prevailed. When we brought him home, I felt an old sadness lifting from my heart; it was like encountering, after decades, a childhood home you thought had been destroyed.

"Arash, too, was changed. He had been a fussy child but in the dog's presence he became more spirited. At the time we lived in an apartment on the Upper East Side, not far from Central Park, and on Saturdays I would take Arash and Luca to the park. At the pond, where Arash would race a model sailboat along with other children, Luca would bounce excitedly, his eyes following the boats. He was a fantastic swimmer, and once, on a scorching afternoon in July, he did jump in, swimming back and forth with his wiggling paws from one sailboat to another, much to the delight of all the children gathered around the lake, who laughed and clapped for him. Afterward we walked together, the three of us, to the statue of Alice in Wonderland, and as Arash climbed on top of the Mad Hatter, Luca cheered him on, circling the statue as the kind and beautiful dog that he was."

Omid began crying, releasing unrestrained tears that alarmed and embarrassed me. "For so long I've wanted to take him to the beach but I never got around to it," he continued. "There was always something—a deadline, a house project, a school meeting, an argument with Anita, or just inertia. Luca would have so loved to run along the seashore . . . And now it's too late."

I knew better than to say, "It's just a dog," so I said nothing. Seeing my brother bereft over an ailing animal made me realize, in a way I hadn't until then, that I no longer knew him. Time had washed away the traces of our familiarity. I decided to give him a few moments of self-pity. Silence, I had learned, quickened the sufferer's transition from disbelief to surrender.

I walked to the bookshelf in the corner and examined the volumes, most of them American classics—Fitzgerald, Hemingway, Faulkner, and Cather. He had clearly gone through some phases, too. There had been the black phase, when he had spent time with Baldwin and Wright, and the Jewish phase, when he had consumed Roth and Bellow. These books, I thought, contained all the kilometers and decades that stood between us. That my brother had read them here, in the place and language where they had been written, had transformed him into a man different from the one he would have become had he read them in another land and in translation. As I scanned the volumes I noticed a name that sounded familiar but I could not place it: Ali Rahimi. The book was called *A Man Named Yasser.*

"Who is Ali Rahimi?" I said.

"That's the nephew of *bābā*'s old associate, the guy you had nicknamed Yasser Maghz-Pahn. Remember him? He died a bad death, as Ali tells it."

I felt my heart lodged inside my rib cage as a stone. Reaching for the shelf to steady myself I said, "So that pimply louse has written a book, too?"

"You know him?" Omid said.

"Does he give any details about how Yasser died?" I said.

"He knows it was by firing squad, but he says no more than that. He does describe the burial in detail. Some revolutionary drove him and Yasser's corpse from the morgue to the cemetery for a secret burial. It's a gruesome scene."

I couldn't tell if Omid was trying to break me down for a confession, or if he truly didn't know the role I had played in this so-called scene. An aftertaste of the greasy diner eggs I had eaten for breakfast surged in my throat and gradually subsided. I picked up the book. On the cover was a stock black-and-white photograph of a man in a suit, pictured from the back, holding a briefcase and standing on some kind of ledge.

"Does Ali name the revolutionary?" I said, still facing the bookshelf.

I could feel Omid's gaze flagellating my back. "You know who it was?" he asked. The dog shifted in his bed and growled a few times.

I made no reply.

A deep, muffled sound escaped my brother's throat—the kind Noushin emitted from the staircase the last time I saw her—and he said, "Get out."

"It was so long ago, Omid," I said. "Another lifetime."

"No, Hamid," he said. "You're mistaken. It was this lifetime. It was *our* lifetime."

21

I LEFT OMID'S APARTMENT with the taste of rotten eggs in my throat. The dog barked in my wake, and I wondered if animals, known to foretell disasters, could also sense the oxidized scent of bygone betrayals. In the lobby the doorman was now in deep conversation with a tenant about the promiscuities of a new resident on the seventh floor. Life everywhere was the same. People informing, judging, being judged.

Midtown crowds were trickling into the little park across the street—pale women in colorless suits and sexless flats, anonymous men in white shirts and dull pants, all carrying bags of plastic food containers and settling on benches to take in their noontime ration of fresh air. Briefly I imagined myself among them, in an alternate life where I had become, like many of my countrymen, an office worker in New York.

I walked along First Avenue, where two Africans in bright peach kaftans were rushing somewhere, dossiers in hand. The Syrian ambassador, a tall striking figure with his Omar Sharif mustache, was arguing something with his retinue. Not far behind was a Saudi government man in a starched dishdasha and Gucci aviator glasses, flattering someone. The Israeli ambassador, being interviewed by a television crew at the street corner, defended his government's forgetfulness of the circumstances of its own birth. Policemen dotted the sidewalks, hands on gun belts. I made my way back to the hotel, feeling dizzy.

An image of Omid and me on our way to school in the clean morning light looped in my mind. We used to stop at a tobacco shop for *Khorous Neshan* chewing gum with the rooster on the packet. Sometimes I would confiscate his packet just to annoy him. *It's tax day*, I would tell him. And at other times, far less frequent, I would offer him mine, an act that he interpreted as generosity but which was actually designed to unsettle him.

THE MINISTER WAS ALONE in the hotel lobby, staring at a teapot gone cold.

"What are we doing here?" I said. "We're like funeral guests who must remain until the body is carried out."

"And we have another problem," he said. "Akbari. He is at it again."

"What now?"

"He is delivering speeches about how I capitulated to the West. And he is making up things I supposedly said during a closed meeting—all fabrications. The trouble is, the more the Americans backstab us, the better the case for Akbari and his clan. Of course the hardline press is already all over it. Haven't you received my messages, Hamid? Where have you been?"

I had forgotten to check my phone all morning. "I was with my brother," I said.

"Your brother?" the Minister said, uncharacteristically caustic. "This is a state visit."

"I'm sorry," I said. "I think I'm losing my bearings." I sat beside him. From our first encounter, a decade earlier, the Minister had been for me a kind of hope, like the promise of a green, open field at the end of a road paved with deceit. The night we met we had adjacent seats at a puppet show on the grounds of Teatre Shahr—the City Theater—both of us accompanied by our daughters, who were about the same age. The show was a representation of *The Epic of Gilgamesh*, and I, who despite everything could not forsake this last filial loyalty, had decided to bring Golnaz, to instill in her, as my father had in me, the permanence of loss.

We stayed in our seats, our backs perspiring against the foldout chairs, our somnolent eyes following the shadows of the paper puppets before us. The warm light behind Gilgamesh and Utnapishtim glowed against the black sky; something about the August night reminded me of my father's final days in Tehran. When a firefly emerged leaving phosphorescent trails in the black night, I whispered, softly, *bābā*. The Minister, who at the time was not yet the Minister, must have heard me, for his face reflected an anomalous kindness. "It's true," he said, "the firefly is beautiful."

How does one explain the shame of being mistaken for a man who can see, as he once did in boyhood, the beauty of things? I sat silent, feeling myself an impostor, but after the shame a strange elation came: if I was capable of seeing beauty in the world, then I was, despite everything, still a man.

When the show ended we trickled out of the theater grounds, walking against the summer heat. The Minister and I spoke together, as did the girls, who had quickly bonded in the way that children do. Mostly, I was the one asking questions, and the Minister answered amicably, like someone at ease with himself and with his life. He told me that he was a professor of political science at the university, and that he was born in Tehran but was from an old conservative family of merchants from Tabriz. His father had been among the first to import cutting-edge medical equipment into the country, and despite his religious leanings, had sent all his children to study abroad. The Minister, who had left in the fall of 1978, had completed his studies in America, first at Berkeley, where he majored in international relations, and later at Yale, where he received a law degree. After working for a few years at the Council on Foreign Relations, he decided to move back to Tehran, because, he said, "a job at a think tank was ossifying me into Rodin's Thinker. After a decade away, it was time to come home."

As he spoke, it occurred to me that perhaps his departure just prior to the country's implosion and his return ten years later had left him unsullied by that initial decade that had so tainted the rest of us. Inevitably he, too, began asking questions, and I deflected these as best I could, offering brief answers or making some comment about the children. As we reached the outer boundary of the theater grounds and the crowds began dispersing, we came across vendors selling vintage puppets. Golnaz pointed at a medieval European jester with brilliant blue, downcast eyes, and a shimmering crimson collar. There was something in the marionette's face, a certain palpable sorrow—made more astonishing by the fact that this sorrow was chiseled in wood—that made me want to offer it to her. The Minister, too, bought one for his daughter, and we walked on, the Minister and I chatting, the girls cheerfully holding on to their jesters—a foursome briefly unperturbed and improbably free.

As we parted we exchanged phone numbers with promises of day trips and picnics with our wives, and though in the ensuing months he attempted several times to reach me, I never took his calls, feeling myself incapable of replicating the man I had been for a few hours on that summer evening, the amiable and gentle man who was not me.

It was only a year later, in 2008, that I finally got in touch with him, after hearing that the Tehran Urban & Suburban Railway Operation Company had without notice fenced off the theater grounds one night, turning it into a construction site for a new metro station. Already in 2003 the municipality had damaged the complex to build a new mosque. I am not sure why I dialed his number on hearing the news of the metro, but I was feeling despondent in a way that had become increasingly familiar, and visions of the gutted theater complex felt to me like stakes through my own ribs.

We met for lunch in a small eatery. It was a gloomy day in December—cold and damp—and because of the weather, the place was mobbed. The windows were sweating from soup steam and ancient radiators and cigarette smoke and human breath. I apologized for not returning his calls, offering the usual excuses people offer when they have avoided someone, then asked him if he had heard about the gutting of the theater grounds.

"First they took the parking lot to build the mosque," he said. "Now it's the grounds. They want to gut the theater because it symbolizes everything they are against: poetry, beauty, ambiguity—in a word, humanity. They say the new metro station is needed. Maybe. But couldn't it be five hundred meters down the street?"

"Everything is going backwards again," I said, "ever since that buffoon became president. The old posters and murals are back, and the Basijis are out again with a vengeance."

He nodded in agreement, and it was then that I decided to tell him the truth—that for many years I had been an interrogator, formally known as a judicial officer, with *Vezarat-eettela'at*—the Ministry of Intelligence. As I spoke his face turned pale and he leaned back. Clearly he was speculating whether he had been trapped in some kind of setup, and his mind was fast surveying past activities that may have landed him in a jam such as this.

"I didn't mean to alarm you," I continued. "I've never spoken so candidly with anyone. But I am tired, and there is something about you that signals mercy, if not understanding. I've done many things I'd rather not talk about. I have been in it deep, as they say, and since I can't get out, I decided long ago that the best I could do was to try to influence things from inside."

For some time he was quiet, idly stirring his soup with a spoon. "A piece of shit can't clean a cesspool from inside," he finally said.

I swallowed my pomegranate soup, unsure of how to react to this rebuke by a man who was ordinarily so unruffled that he made you forget he was fallible, let alone mortal.

"Hear me out," I said. "I accepted the job because I had to. Later, when I could no longer exit, I reasoned that at least by having access to detainees' files I could occasionally circumvent the fate that had been assigned to them. In the final years of the last millennium, I hoped, like many, that a government of moderates would at the minimum steer us in the right direction. But now, eight years into this new millennium, that administration has been eviscerated and it seems we are turning back again."

The clink of noontime dishes in the uncarpeted room made the space feel even tighter. "Since you claim to wish to speak candidly," he said, "I'll honor your wish. Here is what I think: a man can make himself believe anything he wants. He may convince himself that he is wielding influence from inside, that in fact he is doing good, or whatever fairy tale he tells himself to fall asleep at night. But as long as he remains in that pothole, he is nothing more than a collaborator."

I DIDN'T SPEAK to him again after that lunch, until an afternoon in 2013, when, after the election that at last ousted the unhinged president and once more brought a moderate man to the presidency, I called to congratulate him on his appointment as the minister of foreign affairs. I had, by then, fallen out with Akbari, and quit the Ministry of Intelligence. When I asked if he would consider employing me, I was certain he would refuse. After all, this was a new era that would best be served by fresh faces. Why select this scarred face of mine? But I had little left to lose. As I spoke he cleared his throat several times but remained quiet. Then he said, "Yes, I would like to extend you this chance. After all, *kessi az dele kessi khabar nadārad*—no one knows of another's heart."

AT THE HOTEL reception a Dutch family was checking in— mother, father, two boys. They lingered by the brochures in their Dr. Martens, contemplating the options of monuments, plays, museums. I envied them their togetherness, the inevitability of their tour bus afternoon. The Minister ordered another pot of tea and stroked his forehead. I remembered my father making the same gesture at the airport terminal that summer morning as he waited for their final flight out of Tehran. "What does Akbari even want?" the Minister said.

A few months after I had resigned as judicial officer, Akbari—who by then had long been the prosecutor general of Tehran—moved to Mashhad to become assistant to the custodian of the city's largest charitable foundation, which controlled two thirds of the urban land, along with scores of businesses that included mines, a bus factory, a pharmaceutical plant, a sugar refinery, dairy farms, cattle ranches, and orchards. "Akbari believes in nothing, except power and money," I said. "He wants to thwart you because he knows that relations with the world will encourage foreign businesses to invest in our country, and this, in turn, will mean less political and economic influence for foundations such as his."

The tea arrived, and the waiter served us with pomp and fuss, as though we were Englishmen on holiday. As we sat back with our cups, I thought of my years at Akbari's side when he was a public prosecutor and I was obliging his requests, doing everything short of pulling the trigger myself. That, even I could not do, a failing for which he reproached me, and one that, he prophesized, would be my undoing. But I was made to watch, relentlessly and against my will, and thinking of him now filled me with revulsion, not for him but for myself.

I remembered the summer of 1988, when the then deputy Supreme Leader, who in those days was nicknamed *Gorbeh nareh*—the Cat—because of his round face and scruffy beard, pleaded with us not to carry out planned executions of thousands of political prisoners, many of whom, once members of the Mujahedin, had been imprisoned for years. He had sent multiple letters to his superior, the Ayatollah and Supreme Leader, to no avail, and in an unusual display of dissidence, he had met with members of the judiciary to voice his objection. Akbari was at this meeting and had brought me along, and I, for reasons that I could not then name, secretly recorded it. Maybe I had sensed, even then, that its significance would one day surpass my own.

In the forty-minute recording, which I had listened to only once, the Cat could be heard speaking to us—several judges; the Intelligence Ministry's representative to Evin; Mostafa Akbari, by then promoted to prosecutor general; and me, his shadow. "The worst crime in the history of this Republic," says the Cat on the scratchy recording, "which will be condemned by history, is happening at your hands."

It was a scorching summer afternoon. Fruit flies congregated around a bowl of overripe apricots, among them a blowfly in a colonel's uniform—a green, metallic body and a red-dotted thorax. Unlike his homelier brethren, the blowfly showed no interest in the fruit; I knew from my childhood fascination with insects that he must have earlier feasted on a carcass somewhere—a dead mouse or a stray dog crushed in a roadside accident.

Drenched in sweat and at our wits' end, we listened to the good cleric. After nearly a decade of delirious revenge, rations, war, and death, we saw the world in shades of blood. We had begun by killing our own, and in this we had been joined by killers across our western border. We had witnessed our oil fields engulfed in flames, our cities shot through with bullets, the enameled walls of our mosques perforated like diseased brains on their way to forgetfulness. We had known, along the banks of the Karun, the chilly, scentless scattering of bones.

The scheduled executions were claimed as retribution for another attack on the government by the Mujahedin, now armed by the very enemy we were fighting. The Cat spoke of justice and legacy and the judgment of each man for his own actions. He argued that though the attacks on the government were reprehensible, the condemned prisoners had played no part in the latest bombing, making their execution absurd and morally unacceptable. We grew impatient and deemed him irrelevant. Akbari, determined to follow through with the executions, delivered a soliloquy worthy of Macbeth, and he became, toward the end, so belligerent that he cursed all who should stand in his way. And I, seeing the error of his ways as clearly as a rooster senses the dawn, did not oppose him. I remained silent, knowing that the episode would one day—perhaps long after our deaths—lead to both our ends.

"DON'T WORRY ABOUT AKBARI," I said to the beleaguered Minister. "We will draft a statement and put him in his place."

"Yes," he said, unconvinced. "But tell me," he added. "You said you missed my calls because you were visiting your brother. What brother? How is it that you never mentioned him?"

"My brother has been an absence for so long," I said, "that I made myself believe he didn't exist."

The Minister was silent. What was to be said? Absence was our country's chief commodity, and we all had, at one time or another, traded in it.

22

THE MINISTER RETREATED TO HIS ROOM to make calls
before the Russian president's speech that afternoon; I stayed
in the lobby, with two hours to spare. I began drafting an official
statement in response to Akbari, but after multiple false starts I
abandoned it and dialed Omid's number. There was no answer,
so I left a rambling message. As I was about to hang up, the machine, as if sensing the ineptitude of my words, offered me the
option to review what I had said. I accepted. "Omid . . ." I heard
myself saying. "Just let it go. You can't possibly understand. It was
all a long time ago. Let it go, brother. You know, there are things
in this life . . . And situations. Okay . . . Call me." The machine

asked if I wanted to confirm my message or delete it and begin again. I chose the latter, and the voice victoriously confirmed the erasure of my words and prompted me to try again. As the beep sounded, I froze and hung up.

A woman in a white shirtdress and sky-blue espadrilles sat before me with a glass of water. She looked like she had stepped out of an advertisement for a holiday on the Amalfi Coast and I wondered if her life was as carefree as it appeared. I envied her this lightness. A few minutes later she left the water on the table, adjusted her crushed turquoise necklace around her swanlike neck, and walked out, a white figure dissolving into the sunlit afternoon. I stared at the empty chair facing me; had I made her up? I felt sleepy, and hollow. My eyes watered and burned like the exhaust pipe of an overworked transit bus. All I heard within the barbed wires of my mind was one name—Ali Rahimi. I walked to the concierge and asked where the nearest bookstore was. A couple of blocks south, he said.

THE BOOK WAS IN THE SHOP WINDOW, wearing a dictator's jacket of accolades and endorsements. "A remarkable meditation on suffering," said one reviewer. "Psychologically resonant," said another. A poster announced the author's appearance at seven o'clock that same evening. I entered the shop and found the book on a front table, propped up with a dozen identical copies that made me think of the reverberations of a man's howl in an empty room. How many copies were out there, settling as dust motes on the world's polluted sills? I reached for the top copy but could not bring myself to pick it up. "May I help you?" a store clerk said. I looked into his sophistic eyes, and made my way to the exit, where a security guard wished me a good afternoon. I thanked him and wished him the same, permitting myself a moment of blamelessness, when I could pretend to be nothing less than a book browser.

Back at the General Assembly, I buried myself in the drone of the Russian president's speech, self-absolving and familiar, a fifty-minute oration on the new world order and the might of his nation, a sermon that could have been delivered by Tsar Nicholas II himself.

AFTERWARD, I declined the Minister's offer to ride the honeybee car back to the hotel and returned to the bookstore. Rows of listeners were seated before the empty podium as congregants awaiting a holy man. Next to the podium were stacks of orphaned books expecting reunification with their creator. I settled into the back row and stared at the book's jacket, wondering who was the man in the stock photograph standing in for the deceased Yasser, toward whom I suddenly felt oddly proprietary, as though my role in his secret burial had somehow bestowed on me a privileged status.

A bookseller introduced the author. For twenty-five years he had been a film critic and had written several books on film history. He had won many awards and this was his first memoir.

Ali Rahimi stood up to reverent applause and nervously approached the podium. His studious appearance had a calculated air about it, not unlike that of his so-called intellectual brethren in New York—navy blue sweater over striped shirt, tortoiseshell glasses, a three-day-old beard. In his bag was no doubt the same weekly magazine read by all his cohorts, making the lot of them uniformly well-versed in ivory poaching or the Sinaloa Cartel for about a week, when the next issue would appear and they'd all move on to Norwegian cuisine. I had come to know his type. They had of late been visiting Tehran more frequently, speaking in their accented and faltering Farsi, reclaiming their homeland after so many decades as though they had never abandoned it in its hour of need. They viewed their absence as their birthright, not realizing that their collective forsaking was a betrayal of the worst kind.

Rahimi thanked the audience for sacrificing a beautiful autumn evening for his sake. Time may have aged and polished him, but if one looked closely one could detect the scrawny teenager terrified of his uncle's corpse at the morgue. And now, just as decades before, I wanted to walk out on him, but could not help feeling sorry for him. So I sat back, like the others, and listened to him read. Because the truth, when I finally cared to admit it, was that I, too, had come to hear him.

23

A MAN NAMED YASSER
By Ali Rahimi

Long before he had gone to study art history in Paris, Yasser, my mother's younger brother, dabbled in a string of odd jobs. Beginning as a taxi driver after high school, he later became a motorcycle mechanic in a downtown garage, then a window washer in Plasco—Tehran's first skyscraper. As a waiter at the Shokoofeh No' Club, he was known to have carried on romances with more than one dignitary's wife. With the money he made, saved, or once or twice usurped, he bought himself an Alfa

Romeo Giulia that he painted dark blue, adding red stripes and a white roof—a wink to the Italian carabinieri. His mischievous reputation was only elevated during his years in France. Instead of rumors of liaisons with the "colonel's wife" or the "mistress of the minister of education," he now was believed to have had associations with a certain "Madame de La Boulay," a widow with a withering château in the Loire Valley, and with a nameless ingénue whose most memorable performance had been as an extra in the French war film *Forbidden Games.*

All of this was history by the time I was born, and as with all histories it contained within it a dose of myth. He himself neither confirmed nor denied the allegations, because, as he explained to me when I was old enough to spend time alone with him, the charges were both true and untrue. "How can that be?" I asked him, and he said, "Do you know that a diamond and a pencil are made of the same material?" I told him I was getting too old for such jokes. "No joking," he said. "Both objects are made of carbon. The only difference is the way their atoms are bonded. Think of a man in the same way, Ali. One day the man can be a dazzling jewel, the next day he can be as serviceable as a pencil."

This was too much metaphysics for my preadolescent brain. I suspect my uncle did not fully buy his own assertion either. But curious declarations such as these added to his mystery, an element lacking in my own household, which lived within the grip of budgets, boredom, routine. My father, a sports aficionado who loved wrestling matches and considered soccer a second religion, was a house painter whose ambition did not transcend his evening meal of *ghormeh sabzi.* My mother, a hairdresser who collected decades-old European magazines for hairstyle inspiration, was anything but satisfied. In the evenings she pacified herself with a bowl of pumpkin seeds and Iranian B films, which in the 1970s had become as ingestible as automobile exhaust.

When Yasser began showing up to our weekly Friday lunches, by then a middle-aged art scholar in a tailored suit, cosmopolitan and discriminating—everything that my family was not—my parents treated him with the reverence reserved for an imported truffle that spoils an otherwise simple but delicious meal; they understood his worldly value but did not much care for him. Around him there was also the gossamer of a story about a certain Simin, a woman whose name could not be mentioned outside the house. When they spoke of her, my parents whispered as though she were a venereal disease for which there was not, as of yet, either a vaccine or a cure. I learned, from their example, to keep my mouth shut.

ANOTHER ELEMENT LACKING in my household: birthdays. When I asked my mother why mine, unlike other children's, was not celebrated, she said, "What did *you* do to bring about your own birth that's deserving of celebration? If anyone should get a present on your birthday, it's me. I was in labor for twenty long hours."

Yasser was the only one who brought me a gift and sweets every year, much to the displeasure of his sister. My favorite gift was the giant box of Swiss Caran d'Ache colored pencils that he offered me on my seventh birthday, with the snowy alpine mountains and virginal fields etched into the cover of the tin box. Second in line was the most impressive Lego set I had ever seen—Lego no. 8—with enough pieces to construct an entire make-believe city. The more my mother objected to the presents, the more extravagant they became. By my twelfth birthday, when Yasser arrived with a Bianchi Celeste racing bicycle and my mother almost refused him entry into the house, I understood that the gift-giving ritual was no longer about me. Maybe it had never been.

On my thirteenth birthday, my uncle arrived empty-handed. My mother, interpreting the gesture as a truce, tried her best to be something more than cordial. But when after lunch Yasser turned to me and said, "Get your jacket, we're going out," she stiffened once more. "Where?" she said. "To see a movie," he said. "What movie?" she said. "A movie, for God's sake!" he said. "Stop treating him like a baby, he is thirteen years old."

My mother sat back in her chair, twisting her fork. "I'll come, too," she said. "No," Yasser emphatically countered. "This wouldn't be your kind of film." My mother looked in my father's direction in the living room, but my father, engrossed in a soccer match on television, was as responsive as the maroon sofa he was lounging in. "Just because you've been too much of a Casanova to settle down and have your own child," said my mother to her brother, "doesn't mean you can play *bābā* with other people's children." Yasser lit up a cigarette and said to me, "Get your jacket, Ali-jan, we're going out."

I was certain that my uncle was taking me to a foreign pornographic film, a prospect that thrilled and unnerved me. What happened was the opposite. We saw an Iranian film unlike any I had yet encountered: stark, slow, shot in deep, throbbing hues of black and white, sexually charged and frustratingly abstinent—a film about the impossibility of consummating a passion. Made a few years earlier, it was called *Zir-e Poost-e Shab—Under the Skin of the Night*—and was playing at a small art-house cinema retrospective dubbed Mirror on Society. The plot was simple: A young man from the lower classes meets a girl—an American tourist scheduled to leave the next morning. The two communicate through sign language and decide to visit Tehran together for the following twenty-four hours. As the day unfolds, mutual attraction grows between them, but they are unable to find a suitable spot to consummate their romance. After a scuffle with some ruffians, they are arrested and taken to the police precinct. The girl is sent to the airport and the man is imprisoned. Alone in his cell, the man masturbates as the girl's plane takes off, an act that I suspect the entire audience would have liked to indulge in to alleviate the film's unabashed withholding of gratification.

Afterward my uncle and I sat in a teahouse, between us a bowl of pistachio ice cream. The film had made me antsy, needling me with the reality of my own loneliness. And yet I felt fully alive, because for the first time I had glimpsed the possibility of depicting impossibility, which, in the end, was so much truer to life than the nonsense on television.

"That film was a cocktease," I said.

"What do you know about cockteases?" my uncle said, laughing.

I blushed. "I know nothing," I said. "I've seen it in movies. But in the movies there is always a satisfactory resolution."

"You probably think this film was all about frustrated sexual desire," he said. "And of course it was about that. But it was about so much more."

My hormonal mind came up empty. "What else?" I said stupidly.

"The young man, you noticed, was of the lower class," Yasser said. "The film shows how Western ideals of emancipation are unattainable to the average Iranian, who is a product of his own society and its mores, and whose life is dictated by its confines."

This was a side of my uncle I had not yet witnessed. "Uncle Yasser," I said. "Don't you work for that fellow at the Ministry of Culture? I don't understand how you could be involved with the government and still admire films like this."

"The Ministry of Culture itself funds some of these films," he said. "But on the other hand it bans many more."

"I don't understand," I said.

"I told you, Ali," he said. "Most things are true and untrue at the same time. A man can be a diamond one day and a pencil another. So can a government. Did you know that when Beaumarchais wrote *The Marriage of Figaro* mocking aristocrats, the entire court of Louis XVI eventually found it brilliant, the king included?"

WE SAW MORE FILMS IN THE SERIES, films whose protagonists were downtrodden men and women from even more downtrodden parts of the city and the country, moody films that made me grasp the smallness of the life I had been living. "This also is one side of the story," Yasser said of the retrospective. "It's a side they don't tell you about."

Afterward I sought out my uncle as one may seek the riddle of the Sphinx. I believed he contained all the questions in the world, if not necessarily the answers. Each afternoon after school I would ride my bicycle to his house on Vanak Square and he, already back from work and wearing a white T-shirt, would greet me with fresh-brewed tea and a plate of marzipan and dried mulberries. We spent hours speaking of school, idiotic classmates, insipid teachers, polyester, plastic, pleats, monarchies, democracies, the Enlightenment, encyclopedias. He told me of the project he was involved with, doing research for a compendium of Persian art—the interminable, mad design of Sadegh Mozaffarian of the Ministry of Culture.

What we never talked about was love, and the more I got to know him, the less he resembled the image of the playboy the world had drawn of him. He seemed to me rather lonely, and what he found lacking in human affection he made up for in drink and opium, both of which he would break out after six o'clock in the evening, according to some self-imposed regulation he had instituted to keep himself in check.

One night that summer, as we sat on his terrace cooling ourselves with watermelon and stories of his encounters with some *kola makhmali* hooligans from the bazaar, a knock on the door interrupted us. It was ten in the evening; I had stayed far later than usual. More knocks followed, frenzied. Yasser hesitated, as though he already knew who the visitor was. "Stay here," he said, and went to the door. I heard a woman cursing, and my uncle's baritone failing to appease her. Minutes later he appeared on the terrace, pale and frightened. "I have to go," he said. "I need to take someone to the doctor." I followed him to the living room, where I found a young pregnant brunette, pretty but in cheap, provincial clothes, a white flowery chador sliding off her body. She could barely stand up. Uncle Yasser was frantically looking for his car key. "Maybe we should call an ambulance?" I said. "No! Mind your own business," he said. He grabbed towels from the linen closet and hooked her arm around his neck. "Find my keys," he commanded me. "I'm going to help her to the car."

I rummaged through his belongings, feeling guilty as I opened and closed drawers. I thought it a strange irony that the one time that the celebrated Alfa Romeo could have been of actual use, its key remained elusive. Finally I found the key in his underwear drawer, on top of a stack of T-shirts; he must have accidentally placed it there that afternoon while changing. At the bottom of the drawer was a letter. I hesitated, then unfolded it. It was from my mother, dated almost twenty years earlier. As I began reading I remembered that a sick woman was outside, waiting. I glanced quickly at the final line: "While you enjoy yourself with widows and actresses, your father lies here dying. Will you please come home, Yasser?" I placed the letter back where I had found it, and on the way to the car I did the math, which was not complicated. Yasser had returned from France four years after that letter had been written.

HE SLID THE WOMAN into the back of the Alfa Romeo as I arranged a towel under her. Was the towel there to protect the car or the woman? She was olive-skinned, with black eyes and a moon-shaped face, and with her chador off I could see that she was very pregnant. I sat in the front next to Uncle Yasser, and as we sped through streets overstuffed with summer crowds I thought about the strange concept of family, its intimacy and unknowable gaps. The woman moaned in the back, and Yasser, swerving through traffic like the taxi driver he had once been, kept on repeating, "Simin, *azizam*, for the love of Imam Reza, keep quiet."

Our speed was short-lived. Shahanshahi Expressway was a desert of unmoving, honking cars. Yasser whimpered, the woman cursed. I had no idea where we were headed and was too afraid to ask. When we finally snaked our way out of the expressway the car became eerily silent. I turned around.

The woman was crouching in a pool of blood, holding on to a tiny human knotted to a hideous ropy thing. Yasser must have seen it, too, because he was already turning into a dark residential street, thick beads of sweat on his forehead. When he parked the car he ran out and opened the back door, then stood, stunned, staring at the fetus, whose mouth opened and closed like a fish. The woman handed him the creature and as it turned purple, then blue, my uncle rocked it as though it weren't dying. A light turned on in a nearby house and someone peeked from behind a curtain. Somewhere beyond, a dog barked. "He's beautiful," Simin said. My uncle placed the dead child on her chest then returned to the front seat. As he began to shift the gear he paused, rested his head on the wheel, and wept.

We arrived at our destination—the house of an obstetrician who was my uncle's good friend—past midnight. "You're mad," said the doctor when he saw the wreckage inside the car. "Why didn't you go to the hospital?" Yasser looked sheepish. "Please help me," he said. "I couldn't take her to the hospital, and still can't. If this gets out it will be the end of me." I was not sure if "this" meant his relations with Simin or the dead baby or both. The doctor, obliging, brought more towels and some medical gear. He sliced the umbilical cord and the two men carried the tottering woman inside, leaving behind the lifeless baby.

I picked him up—he could not have weighed more than a grapefruit. I wiped him with a towel and wrapped him in a fresh one. Then I cleaned the car as best I could, though the job called for a forensic team. I kissed the baby on his forehead, no wider than a man's thumb. "I'm sorry," I said, recognizing that he was also my cousin.

YASSER EMERGED ALONE from the house. "She'll be fine," he said, "but she needs to rest. I'll come back for her in the morning."

We drove with the dead baby on my lap. The roads were

hushed. "Simin is a woman I've loved for years," my uncle suddenly said. "But I could not give her what she wanted."

"What did she want?"

"For me to marry her. And this would be impossible, you see? Marrying a woman of her social standing would be the end of my career. And not marrying her would be the end of me, because her family is very religious. That's why we kept the affair secret all this time." As he spoke I noticed the creases around his eyes and wondered if they had been there all along. "Ali," he said. "No one can know about tonight, you understand? Especially your mother. Promise me."

"I promise," I said. "And the baby? What shall we do with him?"

"We will bury him," he said.

"What, in a cemetery?"

"In the park," he said.

AT SHAHANSHAHI PARK, which was empty except for a couple making out on a bench, we buried the baby in a shallow grave that we dug with our bare hands at the foot of a cedar tree. Yasser covered the child with soil and knelt on all fours to kiss the ground where he lay.

Three years later, long after a new regime had renamed the park where the baby was buried Park-e-Mellat—the People's Park—a letter arrived in the mail. It read,

Yasser Ehsan, 52, was executed yesterday at 2:35 in the morning. His body is being held at the municipal morgue. We are extending his next of kin a rare chance to come and retrieve it.

MY MOTHER READ THE LETTER and said, "He caused enough trouble while he was alive; I won't let him do it now. Who knows what will happen if we show up? This could be a trap." The letter lingered on the pantry for weeks, next to jars of cumin and saffron and cardamom, until one morning, when, remembering the baby as I ate a sunny-side-up egg at the kitchen table, I decided to get my bicycle and ride to the morgue. Every being, I said to myself, must be claimed, sooner or later.

LIKE HIS SON BEFORE HIM, Yasser was buried in the blackness of a sibilant night, his grave unmarked and unnamed. Months later I saw a revolutionary riding around town in the Alfa Romeo with the windows rolled down. Ray-Bans on his suntanned face and a harlequin-green bandanna around his head, he tapped the wheel to a dreamed-up tune.

24

ALI RAHIMI ABSORBED THE APPLAUSE. People asked him about trauma and post-trauma and writing as catharsis and other fashionable words leaked from psychology manuals into the vernacular. Some wanted to know the fate of the suffering Simin, and many more requested details about the luckless baby: how many seconds had he lived, had he made any sound? One young man with a hipster beard wondered if Ali had considered telling the story from the baby's point of view. Ali answered diplomatically. Yes, the writing had been a kind of deliverance. He did not know what happened to Simin—during the three years that separated the baby's death from Yasser's, he,

Ali, had had limited contact with his uncle. As for questions of time, he could not say for sure how long the baby had lived—the entire night felt to him like a dream. But of one thing he was certain: the baby had made no sound. Finally, in response to the bearded man he said, with a smirk, that had the book been written from the baby's point of view, it would have been, in the words of Thomas Hobbes, *solitary, poor, nasty, brutish, and short.* Everyone laughed.

Afterward, as he offered the last autographs, I approached him and congratulated him on his book's publication. He acknowledged my words with the chronic politeness he had maintained all evening. He didn't remember me, and why would he? I had changed in the intervening decades, and in any case, on the night in question he must have regarded me as nothing more than another revolutionary in khaki clothes. But having at least recognized me as a fellow countryman he said, "We all lived some version of this, didn't we?"

"Our shared story," I said.

The bookseller who had earlier introduced him collected the few unsold copies, dismantled the microphone from the podium, and thanked him profusely.

Ali nodded. "I hate these events," he confided in me, mistaking our common heritage for intimacy.

"Do you have to do many?" I said, feigning sympathy.

"Tomorrow I fly to the West Coast. I have a few in San Francisco and Los Angeles."

"Glamorous," I said.

"As glamorous as an airplane bag of peanuts. I feel like Arthur Miller's salesman."

I assumed that by alluding to literature's archetypal salesman, he wished to prove that he was not a dull interlocutor. To reciprocate I said, "Things ended badly for *that* salesman, as I recall."

He laughed, appreciating my retort. I stood patient as he gathered his belongings and packed up his messenger bag.

"From what I gleaned from the reviews, much of your book is about your uncle's experience in prison, and his eventual execution. Is that right?"

"Yes," he said. "I did my best to put myself in his place, to imagine what he endured."

"But how could you imagine such a thing?" I said. "Since you weren't there."

"I'm a writer," he said, defensive. "It's what writers do."

"Something else occurred to me," I continued. "You write that your uncle asked you never to disclose the events of that unfortunate night with the baby."

"That's right," he said. "And I didn't. For decades."

"That's admirable. But now you have. You've disclosed it to the whole world."

"Not an easy decision," he said.

"You know, our beloved salesman kills himself at the end of the play in order to cash in on his life insurance for his family. What is it he says? . . . Oh yes, 'A man is worth more dead than alive.' Or something like that. One could argue that you also cashed in, not with your own death, but with those of others—your uncle and the baby."

He stared at me, a flash of recognition in his eyes. "Am I being interrogated?" he said. "Who are you?"

"I am the asshole who buried your uncle," I said. Without waiting for his reply, I walked out of the bookshop, sensing an ancient, muffled rage, more familiar to me than my own sorry face. I had revealed myself to him not for atonement, but to undo the congratulatory mood of the evening, to dismantle his delusion that loss could be conquered, that grief could be packaged and labeled, applauded and peddled. It seemed that every person who spent an hour in or even near our detention centers had gone on to pen a bestseller detailing the dignity of his affliction. What poseurs, the lot of them, hailed in America and Europe as modern-day Dostoyevskys and Solzhenitsyns and Koestlers, building an empire of grievance on the ruins of our disillusion. Were they, in the end, any better than we had been?

Footsteps echoed behind me. I slowed down to let him catch up.

"What do you want from me, *aghaye* Mozaffarian?" Ali said. "You undid me once, all those years ago. I won't let you do it again."

"You give me too much credit," I said. "It was history that undid you, as it did me, and millions of others. I had nothing to do with your undoing."

"No, that is too easy," he said. "A man has a choice in how he responds. You played a part in that history."

"And what choices have you made, *aghaye* Rahimi?" I said. "I've read all about you. It seems you are not shy about giving interviews. I know, for example, that you live with your wife and two daughters in a brownstone in Brooklyn Heights, which I understand is very fashionable these days. I know that your wife owns an organic bakery in Williamsburg that has won multiple awards for making the best bread, and that you spend Sunday mornings reading the paper and drinking a pot of Darjeeling tea and your wife a pot of Ceylon. I know that in the fall you enjoy apple picking in Dutchess County with the girls. Summers you like to spend on Shelter Island, where your family has become known for its paella dinner parties. But I'll tell you something. When you are on your deathbed, *inshallah* many years from now, and your wife brings you a sliver of organic apple pie that you are no longer able to eat, you will be thinking not of Hart Crane's bridge or of your seaside paella soirees or the century-old moldings of your Brooklyn brownstone, or even of your darling daughters who by then, God willing, will have offered you many grandchildren, but of your uncle's corpse being lowered into the ground, and of the baby, who died gasping for air in the Alfa Romeo like a fooled fish. And you will recognize, at last, that these things cannot be subdued. There is, in the end, no deliverance."

HE WALKED AWAY, tears in his eyes and hands in his pockets, so consumed that he was nearly hit by a speeding taxi as he crossed the street without noticing the red light; the stunned driver, who had braked just in time, rolled down his window and cursed in Bengali.

25

I RETURNED TO OMID'S. The nighttime doorman, less chatty than his daytime counterpart, called to announce me.

"This is not a good time," Omid said at the door.

"Will you let me in?"

"I'm not well," he said. "My dog collapsed this afternoon. I took him to the vet and had to put him down. I lost *bābā* just weeks ago. And now Luca. I'm devastated, and I have no stamina for you."

"Both of us lost *bābā*," I said.

"Both of us?" he said. "You didn't even know he was living."

"I'm leaving tomorrow," I said. "Right after the memorial dinner. Let me be with you."

He shifted his body and half-heartedly let me in.

THE DOG'S ABSENCE overwhelmed the living room. An unclaimed leash, an empty pet bed, a half-eaten bowl of congealing food, a scattering of squishy balls, a Mr. Spock chew toy. I picked up the Vulcan doll. It carried a soft scent of the vanished animal. "Remember our *Star Trek* parties?" I said.

"I remember," he said.

"And those awful blue drinks we made for all the kids?"

"Yes," he said. "I remember."

"Grapes and blue curaçao."

"That's right," he said.

"At my old job people called me Capitān Kir—Captain Prick."

"You've earned many nicknames," he said.

"Have you had dinner?" I asked.

"I can't eat," he said.

"Let me cook for you."

He neither accepted nor declined. His grief was too vast to allow room for decisions. I grabbed a pot and browsed the fridge and pantry; he had most of the ingredients for *ghormeh sabzi* and rice. As I chopped the parsley and fenugreek and chives it occurred to me that the last time I had cooked for anyone was for my daughter, three years earlier, on the night she left home. For myself I could not bother.

The stew simmered. Neither of us spoke. I noticed three framed photographs on the bookshelf—one of the dog running in snow with a young boy who I assumed was Omid's son, Arash, another of the same boy and the dog dressed in matching

Gryffindor Harry Potter costumes, and the third of an old man on a terrace with a cup of tea, book in hand. "Is that *bābā*?" I said, pointing at the third photograph.

"Yes. In the summertime he sat on the terrace of their apartment for hours, looking out at the river and reading. I think it was the only place where he was happy."

A line from a Leonard Cohen song looped in my mind, *Everybody's got this broken feeling, like their father or their dog just died.* I had gone through a Leonard Cohen phase right around the time my daughter left me. Dear Omid, my brother. I envied him his suffering, the palpability of it, as clean and impenetrable as a white shroud. I sat with him in silence. From the open window came a rustle of a deflated halogen birthday balloon caught on a naked branch of a September tree.

"And the other two photos are of Arash with Luca?"

"Yes. Luca was a good sport. He let us dress him up for Halloween, and came trick-or-treating with us. I remember how Arash would stand by each door, behind the other children, half-apologetic, half-entitled, caught between the aberration of his foreign parents and the certainty of his American birth. On these annual candy pilgrimages the dog was his sidekick, offering him the courage and levity that I so sorely lacked. Afterward Arash would cradle his harvest—the Hershey's Kisses, the Kit Kats, the Skittles—each candy, like collateral, escalating his worth, making him feel like he belonged to something greater—and maybe better—than our family. Anyway, that photo is from the last Halloween we were together, before Anita and I separated and she moved back to Los Angeles with our son."

"It must have been difficult for Arash to let go of the dog," I said.

"It was. But he had no choice. When Anita got custody, the

first thing she said was, 'At last I can be rid of both dogs.' Obviously she meant me and Luca."

"I'm sorry," I said.

He nodded but didn't answer.

I looked again at my father's photograph. In his old age he had come to resemble an ailing Mossadegh—the same oblong face, the bottomless black eyes of a man undone by his own kin.

"In case you were wondering about the will," Omid said, "he left you no money or property."

"I wasn't wondering," I said.

"But he did leave you something." He walked to his bedroom and returned with a book, which he handed me with reticence, as someone fulfilling an obligation. The book was an old edition of *The Epic of Gilgamesh*. Inside was an inscription: *To my son, Hamid, this was my first copy of this timeless tale, which I studied in school, in 1948. I hope you will one day receive from it all the beauty that I failed to teach you. With love, Sadegh Mozaffarian.*

A pang of sorrow rose in my heart, but I contained it just as quickly. This was my father's master plan, to present himself as the seraph that he was not. Puppetry from the grave—ingenious. I remembered a summer evening when at the dinner table, surrounded by his arty friends from the university, he commanded me to bring my drawing of Uncle Majid for all to see. He never tired of mocking the hat I had drawn in place of my departed uncle. "Leave him alone," my mother said, but he ignored her, encouraged by the cheers of the men, among them Yasser. Defeated, I presented my drawing like a *qhorbāni*—a sacrificial offering—and my father, basking in the hilarity in the room, held it up and said, "I present to you my son, the next Walter Gropius. Already at this tender age he has shunned *art for art's sake*." In fairness, they had had more than a few rounds of Chivas Regal, and I was nothing more than a cog in the evening's machinery of show-and-tell, which included a dramatic reading of some blank verses of Omid's budding poetry and a photo of someone's sister's amateur bronze bust of Ferdowsi.

"Remember how *bābā* used to read to us at bedtime?" Omid said.

"He never read normal children's stories. It was all epics and mythologies."

"You complain now, but you loved Gilgamesh. You used to cry for the dead Enkidu every time, as though you had never heard the story before."

A vague memory of my father sitting by my bed assaulted me. Scent of cigarettes and Paco Rabane cologne, indigo pajamas, warm hand on my forehead. "Gilgamesh was a Mesopotamian, like *bābā*," I said.

"Stories have nationalities?" Omid said.

"Never mind that," I said. "What I remember are the dinner table humiliations."

He shrugged.

"You were not immune, as I recall."

"There were humiliations," he said. "But Hamid, there was so much more."

Was my brother's clemency mere reverence for the dead? If you were to judge humankind from epitaphs, you would think that only saints had walked this earth. Nowhere in a cemetery can a neglectful father, a selfish mother, a drunken uncle, be found.

"Do you remember when *bābā* had his gallbladder surgery?" I said. "I think I was about eleven, so you were eight. Do you know what my biggest fear was as he began waking up from the anesthesia?"

"That he would quiz you on Seljuk pottery?" he said.

"I was afraid he wouldn't remember me."

"I want to tell you a story," Omid said. He picked up a squishy ball from the floor and squeezed it, causing it to whimper. "In the summer of 2003," he went on, "New York suddenly went dark. It was the biggest blackout in the history of America. *Bābā* and I were at the Metropolitan Museum, for an exhibit on the art of the third millennium BCE. It covered all the land from the Mediterranean to the Indus, and there was even a section devoted to Gilgamesh."

"He must have been ecstatic," I said.

"He was. For months he had wanted to see it, but his heart troubles had already begun and we had spent the summer in emergency rooms and doctors' offices. This was our last chance, as the show was to close just days later. So there we were, at last, among the lion-headed birds and lapis lazuli eyes and cuneiform clay tablets. When the hall went dark, we were standing before a statuette from eastern Iran. They had named him 'Standing male with a scarred face.' His black body was covered in scales and a deep gash sliced the right side of his face. One eye was hollow, the other was encrusted with a white substance, which the caption said was calcium carbonate that once upon a time might have been a shell. It was a small statue, no more than twelve centimeters, but it was one of the most frightening things I'd ever seen. When *bābā* saw it he stood before it transfixed, and he remained there long after the lights went out, long even after the guards with their flashlights began ushering everyone out of the museum halls. He said, 'Omid, I saw this man in a dream.'

"It was a hot afternoon, sweltering without air conditioners, and with the museum lights gone I was feeling tired and apprehensive. 'Let's go,' I said. 'The city has gone dark. There is nothing left to see.' *Bābā* said, 'I'm telling you that years ago I saw this man in a dream. He came to me, exactly like this, a man with a scarred face, one eye hollow, the other encrusted. And in this dream the man was in his essence your brother.' I dragged him away and we followed the throngs out of the museum, exiting through the medieval gallery, where the guards' flashlights flickered on the altarpieces and tapestries once housed in European cathedrals. I felt as though all of us, withdrawing from that dark museum with alarm and awe, were contemporaries of the objects surrounding us."

"Did you believe him?" I said. "That he had seen the man in a dream, and that I was that man?"

"I did. He was so perturbed by the dream that I had to believe him. Later I asked him when he had had that dream and he said, 'I don't know. Perhaps it was the summer of 1988. I remember that we had just bought the apartment and were still deep in renovations. Throughout that summer your mother and I slept among slabs of sheetrock, wooden tiles, and dust. I was feeling unsettled. It was as if by building a new house we were gutting the memory of the old one in Tehran, and, along with it, the memory of my sorrow over Hamid. Maybe that's why I had that bizarre dream.'"

Omid's tale unnerved me. Signs and symbols still held meaning for me. Broken mirrors, black cats, crossed telephone lines, the beloved's face at the first appearance of a full moon—all of these carried messages from a universe I did not seek to control. Had *bābā* known, without actually knowing, what I had become, by that summer of '88?

"When we came out of the museum," Omid continued, "the city was hushed and in disarray. The subways had shut down and with no traffic lights cars rolled down Fifth Avenue, confused, interrupted occasionally by hordes of pedestrians forcing their way through. *Bābā* and I made our way down the museum steps, tiptoeing around the hundreds of people who sat perplexed, trying to devise a way home. We walked downtown heading eastward, passing by grocery stores whose shelves were quickly depleting.

An ice cream shop was selling gelato cones for one dollar apiece; it was, said the manager, a 'blackout sale.'

"With *bābā*'s heart condition we had to keep pausing along the way, sitting on benches or in the lobbies of buildings whose doormen improbably welcomed us with grace. As night fell, an eerie mix of jubilation and disquiet filled the streets. *Bābā* said, 'Look what happens when the system is disrupted. Chaos, euphoria, madness. This has been the logic of crowds, throughout time and all over the world.'

"By the time we arrived home Mother was sitting in the dark listening to a shortwave radio, an anemic candle casting shadows on the opposite wall. My heart sank; I felt like we were back in the revolution, back to the curfews, back to you. *Bābā* must have had the same sensation because he said, 'Monir, you would not believe it. We saw Hamid at the Metropolitan Museum.' My mother looked up, perplexed. In the flicker of the candlelight I saw that she had been crying. 'Yes,' *bābā* went on. 'We saw him. Our elder son. Right there inside one of the vitrines.'

"As he removed his shoes and stretched out on the sofa, Mother searched my face, bewildered. I shook my head no, and she, retreating once again into her grief, where she now spent most of her days, turned up the radio. 'Treat the day like a snow day,' the mayor of New York was advising."

"Your story frightens me," I said.

"What I'm trying to tell you," Omid said, "is that he never stopped looking for you. He looked for you until the end, among the living and the dead."

I ran my hand over his beat-up sofa. Dog fur stuck to my palm. "Omid," I said, "how do you put down a dog?"

"The same way you put down a man," he said. "You hold him down and inject him with poison. The vet kept assuring me that it was the right thing to do, that the disease was killing my dog, not me. But I felt like a murderer nonetheless."

"The vet was right," I said. "The dog was already dying."

"No matter how you reason," he said, "witnessing a killing leaves you filthy."

"Yes," I said.

He looked at my face intently, his eyes searching for the brother he had once known.

"Let's call Mother. Maybe she'll join us for dinner," I said.

"I don't think she wants to see you."

"Yet she wants me to come to the memorial, and she wants to hear a speech from my lips."

"That's only for *aberoo*—to save face. Believe it or not, after all we've been through, what people say and think still matters to her."

I reached for Omid's phone. There was a long pause after I said hello. In the background I could hear the lament of one more exiled singer—probably Sattar.

"It's you," my mother said.

"I thought you might not pick up if I called you from my phone."

"What do you want?" she said.

"Would you like to come over to Omid's for dinner? We've cooked *ghormeh sabzi*."

There was no answer.

"Well?"

"I'm tired," she said. "And my arthritis is acting up."

"Wouldn't you like to have a family meal, together?"

"A family meal?" she said.

"I leave for Tehran tomorrow, after the memorial," I said.

"I'm looking forward to hearing your speech," she said, and hung up.

"She refused, didn't she?" Omid said as I put down the phone.

"Does she know about Luca?" I asked him.

"No. I've learned not to tell her such things. She has a way of lacerating other people's pain. She thinks it competes with hers."

"Omid," I said. "You've been so alone."

"I have," he said. "But we are a family of soloists, aren't we?"

26

I T'S ONE OF THE PARADOXES of this life that to fully grasp the extent of your aloneness, you must not be entirely lonely. In the winter of 1982, as my own loneliness became acute, I remained ignorant of this fact. But I did realize that I was developing bizarre habits: at work in my office, for example, while reviewing files or speaking on the phone, I would tap my foot loudly against my desk or move my chair brusquely for no other reason than to make it screech against the concrete floor—to prove to myself that I was still capable of producing an original sound, that I, in fact, still existed.

That winter, the war had made bananas disappear, an event

I considered a private calamity. Already I'd made myself accustomed to drinking condensed milk—the regular kind was now scarce—and thought nothing of washing with Soviet coal-tar soap. But come three o'clock, when I would normally pause my work and walk to the prison kitchen to retrieve my banana, I would find myself hankering in the empty hour, my blood sugar plummeting along with my morale. As a bad cold was going around that winter and the heating was intermittent, several clerks had taken to boiling turnips daily to heal their congested lungs. I didn't partake in their communal meal; in those days I felt myself leagues away from them in erudition and disposition. But I developed a taste for the raw turnip greens they left behind, snacking on them until I thought I tasted bile. Increasingly, thoughts of my departed family trespassed my mind, and their unbroken absence mingled on my tongue with the bitterness of turnips.

FROM THE TIME of my recruitment until that winter I had been an auxiliary interrogator, brought in to assist a superior. *Good interrogator, bad interrogator*. This was and still is a tactic commonly used, and I was often cast in the role of the "good" one. My assignment was to offer unexpected gestures of kindness to the prisoner, to catch him off guard, as it were, at the very moment when, having endured despite himself, he had lost hope. An aspirin, some freshly brewed tea, clean underwear, a fig or a date, these things could disarm a human being, so much so that in his longing for connection he would offer the prized confession that would lead to his demise.

What I had witnessed in those months, and what I had, myself, more than once dispensed, I wrote off to the chaos of transience, the birth of a black hole from which no particle—not even light—could escape. I had read somewhere that a black hole is born when stars collapse at the end of their life cycle, and that it continues growing as it absorbs other stars and merges with other black holes. But despite its invisible interior, a black hole transforms matter that falls into it into the brightest object in the universe. This, I still believed, was what our revolution could become: the brightest object in the universe.

Between interrogation sessions I would read up on our ever-changing legal code. The constitution of 1905, for decades ignored, had been replaced by a new one in December 1979. This document was endlessly revised and amended, and I, ever the earnest believer, studied its nuances as though they truly mattered.

ON JANUARY 23, 1982, at 3:25 in the afternoon, I received a dossier marked "Urgent." I remember the exact time because in the absence of my banana I was feeling lethargic, wondering how many hours separated me from the close of the workday. When I opened the file, I didn't immediately notice the name of the accused; my mind was preoccupied with my motorcycle's tire, which had gone flat that morning on the expressway on my way to work. I considered it a miracle that I had survived the accident with only a few bruises, since the bike had toppled over, throwing me in the air before landing me on the pavement on my right rib cage. Cars had stopped on my account, and a woman who reminded me of my mother offered to call an ambulance. It was beautiful, to be cared for by multitudes, to be, once again, on the side of the injured, of the mortal. I almost wished I had been more seriously harmed.

I STARED AT THE NAME on the front of the dossier: Houshang Habibi, known as "H." I remembered the newspaper cartoons I once shared with the laborer Mirza, and the story Yasser had told me about my father's betrayal of H. Based on the charges brought against him, H.'s case would be tried by the Revolutionary Court— a formalized version of the makeshift tribunals of the early months. As I read the dossier—address, date of arrest, names of family members—the words blurred on the page and my head began throbbing. I shut my eyes, but when I opened them the room was spinning, and the items on my desk—the plastic yellow clock and my father's monogrammed cigarette lighter, which I had started using that winter—appeared to be floating in the air. I wondered if my accident that morning had not injured me more than I realized.

Air, that's what I needed, and a good smoke. But as I reached for my jacket the phone rang. I had a premonition it was Akbari, so I let it ring, one arm already in a sleeve. The shrillness of the ring resonated in the recesses of my body. Finally I picked up, dread rising in my chest.

"A new arrest," he said. "A prominent artist. You must have received his file."

"Yes."

"I did you a big favor, to send you such a high-profile case. Consider it a vote of confidence. It will get you noticed."

I tried to regulate my breathing so he wouldn't detect my state.

"You heard me?"

"Yes. But am I to interrogate him by myself?"

"He's all yours," Akbari said. "Don't stall. I need the confession fast. This case is important and will be very good publicity for us."

I took a deep breath.

"What's the matter? Are you unwell?"

"No . . . I'm fine," I said. "I had an accident this morning on the motorcycle. I think I'm still in shock. It was a flat tire."

"Fix it then."

"Yes . . . It's complicated. It's an old Harley-Davidson. A World War Two relic. There are only a couple of tires that suit it. Pirelli makes them. And of course they aren't available anymore."

"Everything is available," he said, "if you go with a recommendation. Go see Asghar-*agha*. He has a shop on Meydan-e Shush. If you tell him I sent you, your tire will be fixed."

"*Sepās gozāram*—I'm grateful."

"That's two favors in one afternoon," he said. "But who's counting?"

I SAT BACK DOWN and studied the dossier. In his drawings H. had replaced monarchs and their henchmen with mullahs and their henchmen. Photocopies of several drawings had been placed in the file, and I examined these, remembering the days when I, too, would bring pencil to paper and produce some original image. Now the best I could do was to compose a requiem for originality, which I delivered daily, with the time-honored repetition of formulaic questions, accusations, and threats.

The mechanic shop, on Shoosh Square, was south of the bazaar. Tires and tools overpowered the room with the sour smell of rubber and rust, and a poster of a sparrow hung under a sickly yellow light. An old man, grease-stained, greeted me. When I told him what I wanted he walked away. "Where have you been?" he said. "The days of Pirellis and Michelins are over." I lit a cigarette with my father's monogrammed lighter, slowly and deliberately. "That's too bad," I said. "Because Mostafa Akbari told me you wouldn't let me down." His eyes filled with dread, a look I recognized, especially from my own face, whose changing reflection stunned me a little every morning as I trimmed my growing beard. "Why didn't you say so from the beginning?" he said. "Leave the bike here. Come back in two hours and you will have a brand-new set of Pirelli tires. And I will check the engine and all the parts besides."

"*Ghorbāne shomā*," I said. "You are too kind."

"No kindness is too much for dear friends," he said, in the language of masquerade that had infiltrated our mother tongue.

MY GIDDINESS as I left the shop slayed my earlier anguish over the case of H. Favors, promotions, considerations—in my future I saw these things, and more. I decided to return for the bike in the morning. I hailed a taxi and asked the driver to drop me off at a bakery near my home; I was in a celebratory mood.

Pistachio nougats and rosewater *faloudeh*—I bought a box of each as though I were hosting a wedding reception—and I walked home, the white packages tied with crimson string tucked under my arm. Twilight was dipping the city in hazard, announcing the hour of nothingness or air raids, one spent in anticipation of the other. Icicles hung from treetops along Revolution Street, and I could smell in the air the scent of snow, born from the communal frost-death of all other scents. It was the clean scent of absence.

In the apartment I arranged the nougats and *faloudeh* in glass bowls and set them on the kitchen table, powdered and ghost-white. I sat at the head of the table, in my father's old chair, which I had until then avoided. The cushion, having memorized the contours of his body, now rearranged itself around mine. Three empty chairs besieged me. One, at the table's other end, was the seat of my childhood. Briefly I saw myself there as a boy, an apparition that frightened me. In the dusk I ate a succession of nougats, the sweetness delighting me before numbing my taste buds, and as night fell I filled my mouth with spoonfuls of rosewater noodles, syrupy ice assaulting my tongue with oblivion.

I fell asleep at the table and woke up an hour later, my stomach a sinkhole. In the bathroom I knelt to the floor and leaned over the toilet, breathless, waiting for relief. Nothing came. I got up, brushed my teeth and rinsed my mouth, over and over, but an acrid taste resurged in my throat each time I stepped away from the sink. My body had begun its decades-long revolution against me, and I sensed, that night, that my slow, silent war with my own flesh would one day culminate in our inevitable destruction.

Restless in the apartment, I hailed another taxi to return to the repair shop. Two women already in the back seat eyed each other with alarm when I got in the car. I had of late been getting such looks from strangers, and I wondered if my façade was beginning to hint at my metamorphosis. I sat in the passenger seat next to the driver and rolled down the window, though the temperature had fallen and the snow had begun. The women sighed in the back but said nothing. The driver, too, was silent.

At the shop, a small black-and-white television on top of a painter's ladder was broadcasting a recantation. This jolted me, as I recognized the man: he was a tailor, a member of the tailors' union, and had been, until then, an unrepentant Marxist. I had not had much interaction with him, except for offering him an orange one morning after his overnight interrogation session. As he had been too weak to peel it, I had done it for him, removing the pith so as to spare him any unnecessary bitterness. I remembered how his face opened up as he placed an orange slice in his mouth, holding it on his tongue without chewing, just squeezing his jaws, gently, allowing himself no more than a few drops of juice at one time. Afterward, as though the act of eating had suddenly made him conscious of himself, he looked down at his soiled pants and ran his fingers along the tears in the legs. I promised to get him a needle and thread. I remembered now that I had forgotten my promise.

"ALMOST READY," the mechanic said.

"Take your time," I said, with none of my earlier swagger. I felt dejected now, and the deeper I sank into this dejection the angrier I became. Why did I need a new pair of Pirelli tires when no one else could get even one? What kind of privilege was this, exactly, and at what price? Every meter traveled on those tires would take me that much farther from decency. If I could have annulled my order I would have done so at once, but it was too late; the bike was almost finished. I sat in a corner on a low stool and listened to the television's drone in the background, the Marxist reciting passwords of atonement, bartering lies for life.

"You've had the shop for a long time?" I shouted to be heard over the television.

"Thirty years," said the old man. "We are castaways here. But it's never tedious. That eatery down the street? All the *lutis* used to gather there for *dizi* and water pipes. The gangsters, the street fighters, the *dash-mashtis*, the *javanmardan*. Tayeb Haj Rezaei used to go there—*khodā biyamorzatesh*—may he rest in peace. And his brother, Haj Ismael Rezaei. Shaban Jafari, too. Everybody called him Shaban *bi-mokh*—brainless Shaban. And of course the wrestler Gholamreza Takhti, the Olympic gold medalist."

"I remember when Takhti died," I said. "I was a kid. Everyone talked about it, even at school."

"Yes, the government said he committed suicide at the Atlantic Hotel, but that made no sense. It was obvious they'd finished him off because he had been a member of the National Front, was a supporter of Mossadegh, and was making too much noise."

I remembered my father's face as he had read the news of the wrestler's death that January morning, regret puncturing the indifference that he had cultivated over the years. My mother, who had just returned from the butcher, said, "They're all mourning as though he were some hero. All that for a ruffian from the *zoorkhaneh*. This country baffles me, sometimes."

"He was no ruffian," my father said. "He wrestled with ethics. That's an art, knowing not only how to fight, but how to fight honorably."

"Since when are you an advocate for the *jonoub shahri*—the backwater lowlifes from downtown?" my mother said. "Wasn't it enough, growing up with them?"

My father folded the newspaper in quarters until it was reduced to the size of his palm. I thought he was going to say something, but he didn't. He fixed his necktie and left for work.

"THE BIKE IS AS GOOD AS NEW," the mechanic said. "May you ride in good health."

"I'm grateful," I said. "How much do I owe you?"

"Friends don't owe friends anything," he said, a hand on his heart. "The only thing a friend asks is that you look out for him." He tilted his head toward the television broadcast.

"What else can we do," I said, "but look out for one another?"

PAPER-THIN SNOW already covered the streets. I rode for some time on the bike aimlessly, aware of the fullness of my tires, thinking again of the case of H. In the morning, in just a few hours, they would bring him to me, blindfolded. "Sit down and face the wall," I would tell him, hovering over him as I had been instructed to do. And so would begin the game, the mind-fuck of coercion and resistance, barter and cheap philosophy, defamation and defacement, all of which was designed to culminate in one thing: the confession, the final words that would carve out the mote in his own eye.

Not wanting to return to an empty house, I turned onto Ferdowsi Square to visit Judge Emami. He had a reputation for thoughtfulness, and unlike most of the quickly appointed judges with a few weeks' worth of seminary studies to their credit, he held degrees in law and theology from the Qom Seminary. We had once chatted in the prison kitchen, by the pot of steamed turnips that the ailing clerks had prepared. When he realized that we were almost neighbors he extended a brotherly invitation, a polite gesture that I knew, like most such invitations, was disingenuous. But my predicament—or more precisely the predicament of H.—was worthy of a transgression of manners.

The judge's apartment was on the top floor of a four-story building overlooking the square. The snow was now coming down harder, and my motorcycle skidded a few times as I slowed down to park. Achy and feverish, I wondered if I should not have gone straight home to bed.

He didn't immediately buzz me in. After I announced my name along with an apology for my impromptu visit, he hesitated. "Come up," he said. "But you must walk. The elevator is broken."

My footsteps echoed in the stairway. A clammy sweat was spreading over my chest and neck and I felt as though I were on a night train trapped in a tunnel. I stopped multiple times along the way, hanging on to the icy balustrade. Several lightbulbs on the stairway had come loose, and they flickered, on and off. The smell of fried fish from an apartment on the third floor reminded me of my nausea. Why had I come? What would I tell the judge when I finally reached his apartment? What did a kid like me have to say to a jurist from Qom? My heart pounded, and I considered turning around and going home, but it was too late; the judge was already expecting me.

His door was left open. I walked into an empty living room, sparsely furnished. White floor cushions lined two walls, and in the center an Isfahani rug, in brilliant shades of blue, sparkled under the prisms of a crystal chandelier. In the corner were papers, neatly stacked, a leather-bound notebook, and a fountain pen.

"I'll be with you in a moment," he called out. I followed the voice to the kitchen, where I found the judge kneeling on the floor in a pool of soapy water, a rag in his hand and a red pail of water beside him.

"The washing machine broke down," he said. "I walked in a minute ago and I see this flood."

I knelt down beside him with a kitchen towel, soaking up the water and wringing the towel over the pail, a repetitive motion that soothed me.

"Forgive me," he said after some time, as though he had just noticed my presence. "I'm sure you didn't come to wipe my floor. What can I do for you?" Without his cloak and turban he seemed an ordinary man. Average height, moon-shaped face, full beard, widow's peak, gray slacks, button-down shirt.

"It's my honor to wipe your floor, *Haj-agha*," I said.

"Let's take a break," he said, rising from the floor with exertion. He could not have been more than fifty, but his bones appeared to have aged before him. He poured tea from a samovar into two glasses and we carried these with a bowl of sugar cubes to the living room.

"*Haj-agha*," I said. "Where shall I begin?"

"What is troubling you?"

"I have been assigned the dossier of an artist named H."

"I am familiar with H.," he said. "Akbari told me about him."

"That's precisely it. Akbari is rash, for lack of a better word. I have been privy to his investigations, and maybe because I had until now been no more than an abettor to the interrogations, I had not felt the weight of my participation. But the case of H. has been assigned to me exclusively, and I am finding myself incapable."

"If the man is guilty then he shall pay for his crime," the judge said. "And your job is to obtain the confession."

"But *Haj-agha*, what is he guilty of? Drawing? For decades he was hounded by the old regime's men—men like my own father—for the exact same charge. How can we become the very beast we combatted?"

Slowly, he sipped his tea. Had I been out of line? Would I find myself, in a couple of hours, not facing H., but beside him? Again I broke into a sweat, this time a burning one. "Will you," I said, if only to say something and appease my anxiety, "oversee this case?"

"What difference would it make," he said, "if I oversaw the case?"

"Everyone knows of your judiciousness. You are fair-minded and believe in the law."

"These days the law itself is the beast," he said.

"The law?" I said. "But we finally got what we wanted, what many, in any case, wanted: a judiciary that's an amalgam of French civil law and Sharia jurisprudence."

"It was in theory a great invention," he said. "But the two sets of law aren't always in harmony. And in practical terms, none of it matters. Since we consecrated the *Velayat-e Faqih*—Guardianship of the Jurist—we have one supreme jurist who conducts the affairs of the State in accordance with God's laws during the absence of the twelfth Imam. And that person, as you know, is the Ayatollah."

"Are you saying it doesn't matter what the judge says? That's impossible, *Haj-agha*, it has to . . ."

The lights went off as I spoke. Another blackout. We sat together in the dark, wondering if this would be the night for air raids. The judge's windows overlooked the square, where the marble statue of Ferdowsi, snowcapped and solitary, stood against the moonless night. "I will look for candles," he said as I followed him to the kitchen, both of us sidestepping the soapy puddle on the floor.

He opened and shut cabinets. "Those candles . . ." he said. "Where did I put them?"

"But *Haj-agha*, how do we reconcile?" I said.

"Reconcile what?"

"What we could have been with what we are becoming."

"What we envisioned was not to be," he said. "Now we are in this labyrinth . . . Ah, yes!" He retrieved a candle, wax-dripped, and he placed it on a plate. "Now the matches . . ."

I pulled out my father's lighter and ignited the wick.

"Good, we have light," he said. "You can't leave during the blackout so we may as well be comfortable." He opened a box of chickpea cookies and began setting them on a plate.

The memory of the sweets I had eaten earlier made me queasy. "If you won't oversee the case of H.," I said, "then maybe you could remove me from it?"

He set aside the cookies and placed his hand on my shoulder. It occurred to me that since my family, and since Minoo, I had had no physical contact with another human being. I am not sure if it was the unexpected warmth of his hand, or the blackness of the night, or the chills and fever that coursed through my body, but I began crying, and, ashamed, I turned away from him and stepped back.

"It's difficult," he said. "I feel the pain, too . . ." He walked toward me, hands outstretched, and it was at that moment that it happened. The slip, the thud, the knock, the scream. The clamor of pots, shattering of glass. Then silence.

I stood in the half dark for some time, frozen, staring at the soundless body on the floor. "*Haj-agha?*" I said. "*Haj-agha?* Are you all right?"

Silence. The candle burned indifferently on the countertop. I picked it up and knelt to the floor, casting light on his face. His eyes were open; his mouth, too. Blood oozed from a deep gash in his head, and the puddle had turned bubblegum pink. He had slipped on the suds with his socks and had hit his head against something, probably the door handle of the washing machine. Around him were shards of dishes, bits of ceramic and glass. I shook him. But I had seen enough death to understand that the judge, too, was gone. I sat on the floor in the suds, shut his eyelids with the palm of my hand. His mouth, as though in midsentence, was locked open.

Call for an ambulance? What would be the point? The police? What if they suspected me of wrongdoing? And what of Akbari? Were he to discover that I had gone behind his back to visit the judge, he would have me arrested on one pretext or another. As I sat in indecision, the cold, bloodied water seeping into my pants, I remembered that before the judge's fall, I had been crying.

ELECTRICITY RETURNED with the sunrise. There had been no air raids, only blackness. I had spent the night by his side, the designated corpse watcher.

A bright, morning sun cast its rays along the countertops. To look at it one could have been fooled into thinking that it was time for tea and breakfast. His clothes lay inside the washing machine like witnesses. I wanted to remove and hang them, were it not for the judge's body still on the floor, reminding me that we had arrived at the endgame. Nothing more could be done.

Soaking wet, I got off the floor. In the judge's bedroom I opened his armoire, pulling from it a pair of clean slacks; they were too wide around the waist. I cinched them with a belt, also his. My own bloodstained pants I folded and placed in a plastic bag, wondering how to dispose of them.

I left Judge Emami lying stiff on the kitchen floor and ran down the stairs with the bag, past the man with a briefcase on the fourth floor, and the woman on the third, who had left the doors and windows of her apartment open, allowing fresh air to wash out the night's cinders and fear. Snowdrift blocked the front gate, so I pushed gently, trying my best to remain unnoticed, to be, once more, an ordinary man.

Back in my apartment I picked up the phone and called in sick, like a malingering schoolboy. "Serves you right," the clerk said. "For refusing to eat our turnips."

For a long time in the shower I let the hot water run over my body. Afterward, naked in front of the fogged-up mirror, I waited for patches of my face to connect under the vanishing steam, which seemed, just then, like human breath.

27

THE DOORBELL RANG. How long had I been asleep? Ten minutes or ten hours, I couldn't tell. I sat up in bed—my parents' bed. The room was half-dark, and my eyes had watered in my sleep, sealing my eyelids. I brought a finger to my mouth, wet it with saliva, and rubbed my eyes, removing the salty crust. Knocks interspersed with the doorbell. Dear God, the judge's body on the kitchen floor; had I dreamed it? But there, on the dresser, was the silhouette of the plastic bag. I got out of bed and threw it in the back of the closet, then wobbled to the front door as everything whirled around me.

Akbari was holding a pot swaddled in a red gingham kitchen

towel. "You look like death," he said. He entered casually, as though he had been expected, and carried the pot to the kitchen. "The place looks different since I last saw it," he went on. "You liquidated it."

Was I delirious from the fever? Akbari was not a man one would expect on a doorstep with soup. But no, he was there, standing by the stove, stirring. "Sit down," he said. "When was the last time you ate?"

I sat at the kitchen table as a stabbing pain shot through my head. He placed a sloppy bowl of ochre-yellow soup before me. I brought a spoonful to my mouth; it was watery and bland, leaving on my tongue a gelatinous film.

"When the clerk told me you had called in sick," he said, "it occurred to me that you are, despite everything, still a boy. You are, after all, only twenty-two. Someone needs to look after you." He poured me a glass of water and sat down, in my mother's old seat. "You need a friend. No, more than a friend. You need family."

His words comforted me, and briefly I allowed myself to crouch under them, as one crouches under a stairway during an air raid. Chewing on a tasteless drumstick it occurred to me that he was doing what I had been doing for months: he had cast himself as the good interrogator, offering me kindness in exchange for a confession.

"Why are you here?" I said.

"That's some way to thank me," he said.

I pushed back the bowl. "The soup, the compassion, what kind of performance is this?"

"You think me incapable of soup and compassion?"

"I think you capable of much more," I said.

"Very well," he said. "Since you insist. While you were

sleeping, strange news emerged. Judge Emami was found dead in his apartment this morning."

I tried to look him in the eyes but couldn't. This, I knew, already incriminated me. "That's terrible," I said.

"Yes. Such a fine judge. And so beloved. A real shame."

"How did he die?"

"At first glance," he said, "it looked like an accident. It appeared as though he had had a mishap with his washing machine and slipped on soapsuds. But when one looks more closely, there are clues . . ."

"What clues?"

"Where were you last night?" he said.

"I picked up the bike from Asghar-*agha*, then I came home."

"You came straight home?"

"Is this an interrogation?"

"Answer me," he said. "Straight home?"

"Yes. Can't you see I'm sick as a dog? Where else would I go?"

From his pocket he produced a photograph and placed it on the table. It looked like an image of snow; I didn't understand.

"Like I mentioned," he said. "When one looks more closely . . . Pick it up. Tell me what you see."

The fever interfered with my vision. "It's snow," I said.

"In the snow," he said, "there are tire tracks, of brand-new, perfect Pirelli tires. These were right by the judge's doorstep."

"So what?" I said.

"How many people have new Pirelli tires, nowadays?"

I didn't reply. Wasn't I still wearing the judge's pants?

"And if that doesn't convince you," he said, pulling another photograph, "maybe this will."

It was an image of my father's monogrammed cigarette lighter; I must have forgotten it on the judge's countertop.

"The rest is clear," he said.

"Yes, I was there," I said. "But it was an accident. He really did slip on the soapsuds."

"Why not report it then?"

"I was afraid that I would be considered a suspect."

"You are no mere suspect," he said.

"That's absurd," I said. "What motive could I have?"

"Motive is meaningless," he said, "when guilt is obvious. Why did you go to see the judge in the first place?"

I said nothing.

"Never mind," he said. "I already know. Your loyalties, my brother, are still with the left. You wanted to have H. released, by whatever means you could. And for this you went behind my back."

"It's not only H.," I said. "It's us. It's everything. Didn't the Ayatollah say he wanted justice, equality, democracy? All his tapes, all his discourses . . ."

"The Ayatollah laid it all out," he said. "But people like you listened selectively. You projected onto his words whatever you wished to hear."

"Akbari, what are we doing?"

"We're doing what we must," he said. "Yet you have designs to thwart our efforts." He helped himself to the leftover nougats in the bowl. "As I mentioned," he added, sugar dust on his beard, "intent makes no difference, when guilt is clear. Do you know that Judge Emami was being considered as the next chief justice?"

"I didn't know."

"I could have you arrested right now. And you already know what would happen next."

"Please," I said, "have mercy. What can I do?"

"You can follow the line. No one knows about the tires, or the cigarette lighter. To keep it that way you will do as you are asked."

"Yes," I said, "I promise." The tailor's recantation from the previous night's television broadcast looped in my ear.

"So get me that confession from H.," he said. "Because I already have yours."

28

THE CONFESSION. Its supremacy in the fate of the accused clarifies the meaning of the interrogation, which we called *mossāhebeh*—interview. The word imbued the proceedings with a sterile, altogether banal sound. But when you understand, as I did that winter, that the confession was the grand prize, the laurel crown of our Pythian games, then you can surmise that the "interview" was as unsterile as circumstances demanded. The confession was the sole evidence required for a conviction, the "proof of proofs," as one of our jurists called it. And who better than the accused to provide the words necessary to marshal his own case to its inevitable conclusion?

Confession. *Confiteri*—to acknowledge, from *fateri*, to speak. *E'terāf*, from *ta'rif*, to recount.

I WOULD, if I thought it useful, offer the account of my *interview* with H. I would write, for example, that when he entered my confessional and sat blindfolded facing the cement wall, listening to me as a Catholic hears the disembodied voice of the priest, he brought a finger to his forehead and placed it between his eyebrows, the spot known as the "third eye," gateway to spiritual purity and the point of contact between the forehead and the prayer stone. That he whispered something under his breath, and when asked to repeat it, he said, "It's just a line from a poem; it's useless here." That the tremor in his hand worsened as the day gave way to dusk, when, at last, he told me of his hypoglycemia and I offered him three pieces of rock candy. That when I removed his blindfold, and against all rules, I revealed to him the name of my father—and my own—his green eyes narrowed and he said, "Pigeon flies with pigeon, hawk with hawk." I would write, too, of how I pressed him, for names and monikers, dates and hours, opinions and dreams, beliefs and philosophies, crimes and sins, lovers and friends, and of how, by day's end, he looked at me across the table, between us my glass of tea, and said, "Do with me what you will. But you will see me every time you bring a glass of tea to your mouth, because I will be right there, sitting across from you, a face you will be unable to get rid of. For the rest of your days, *aghaye* Mozaffarian, you will be having a discourse with me."

I will not write of those things. Instead I will write of a bizarre memory that came to me as I sat across from H., failing to obtain his confession. As I showed him a forged newspaper with a fabricated story on a colossal fire in Bandar Anzali, the port city of his birth, and I blabbered something or other about the death of his mother in this fire, I was seized by the memory of a restaurant in Paris that I had visited as a child with my family—La Tour d'Argent—where we ordered, on my mother's insistence, the famed dish, *Canard à la Presse*. The waiter, with the pride of an army general, explained that the duck, once plucked, is strangled, then roasted, stripped of its liver, breast, and legs, and pressed in a contraption similar to a wine press. The resulting carcass juice is flavored with the duck's liver, cognac, and butter, then served with the aforementioned breast, and, for the second course, with the legs. At meal's end diners were presented with a memento bearing the butchered bird's serial number. Our family, we learned as my disgruntled father paid the exorbitant bill, had eaten duck number 486,557. Days later, in an old bookshop near the Comédie Française, I found a history book with a full page devoted to this storied restaurant and its ducks. I memorized the most illustrious of them: number 328, served to King Edward VII in 1890; number 14,312, served to King Alfonse XIII in 1914; number 112,151 served to Franklin D. Roosevelt in 1929. One day, I thought, anatine historiography would teach ducklings about the massacre of their forefathers. I don't know why this memory, out of so many others, presented itself to me at that moment, but I think that like H., I, too, was becoming delirious. In the end, long past midnight, long after I had concluded that I had no choice but to call in help, H., whose body bore the final traces of his commendable but vanquished stamina, collapsed from his chair to the floor, from hypoglycemia and forfeiture. Akbari, when informed, was livid. "I didn't want a corpse, you idiot," he said. "I wanted a confession so chilling that it would make the likes of him relinquish their pencils for the rest of their days."

"What could I do? He had hypoglycemia," I said. "And apparently a bad heart."

"You let it drag on too long," he said. "You had to intervene, before his blood sugar plummeted."

"Intervene how?" I said.

"Intervene in such a way that he would have had no choice but to speak. You were soft, and a fool."

"I'm sorry," I said.

"I'm losing my patience with you," he said. He stared at me, and in his black eyes I detected a trace of emotion. Not love—as I don't believe he was capable of it—but a certain affinity for the man he still thought me capable of becoming.

"You have one last chance at redemption," he continued. "Mess it up and I give you my word: you will go down in history as the judge's butcher."

A WEEK LATER I received an anonymous envelope from France, with multicolored postage stamps depicting Marianne, so-called "Goddess of Liberty." It contained a newspaper clipping of an obituary of H.:

DEATH OF AN ARTIST KNOWN AS "H."

Houshang Habibi, 54, illustrious cartoonist and satirist, died by suicide (according to his captors) while in detention in Tehran.

The youngest of five children, H. was born in 1928 to Pirouz Habibi, a carpenter in Bandar Anzali, and Afshin Kazemi. Growing up in the 1930s he witnessed many of Reza Shah's reforms, including infrastructure projects such as the construction of the Trans-Iranian

Railway, the banning of the chador for women, and the establishment of modern education, exemplified by the creation of Tehran University. He was seven years old when, in 1935, a backlash erupted in the Mashhad shrine, led by the clergy, who denounced the monarch's innovations and corruption; this protest was heeded by the *bazaaris* and villagers, who also took refuge in the shrine. After a four-day standoff dozens were killed and hundreds injured, prompting many among the clergy to resign their posts at the shrine. When asked by his father what he thought of the clash, H. drew a caricature of the Keeper of the Keys of the Mashhad shrine releasing a giant gilded key while being chased by a rabid dog wearing an imperial crown. This drawing is now in the collection of the Museum of Modern Art in New York.

After graduating from high school, H. enrolled at Tehran University's School of Fine Arts, and was later sent by the Ministry of Culture to France to pursue a graduate degree at the École Nationale Supérieure des Beaux-Arts.

In 1949, along with the artist Jalil Ziapour, the writer Qolam-Hossain Qarib, the playwright Hassan Shirvani, the art historian Sadegh Mozaffarian, and the musician Morteza Hannaneh, he cofounded Khorous Jangi (The fighting cock), a literary and art society, whose name was coined by Qarib, and its logo of a Cubist-style rooster was designed by Ziapour. The fighting cock symbolized the society's mission to "fight against the obscurantism and traditionalism that was detached from the realities of present-day." Espousing a new language in art and literature, the society hosted gatherings and presentations by modernist artists and writers, and published an eponymous journal, whose first issue included "Khorous mikhānad (The rooster sings)," a poem by Nima Yooshij, the founder of "new poetry" whose renouncement of classical poetry echoed the efforts of modernist artists.

In the 1950s H., a supporter of the deposed prime minister Mohammad Mossadegh, contributed regularly to *Towfiq*—the leading satirical journal of the period—with drawings that shed light on the plight of everyday people and mocked the regime's corruption. He was not, however, immune to the government's continued efforts to silence him: on multiple occasions in the ensuing decades H. was arrested and interrogated, and he served three terms in prison.

In 1971, H. traveled to Paris and collaborated with *Le Rire*, a satirical magazine. Having gained international acclaim, his drawings were increasingly featured in leading magazines such as *Graphis* (Switzerland) and *Communication Arts* (USA).

Drawing upon Persian folk art, miniatures, religious lore, and nineteenth-century lithographic illustrations, H.'s work is remarkable for its simplicity and minimalism. His drawings, often curvilinear, also reference the work of the artist Reza Abbasi (1565–1635).

H.'s numerous solo and group exhibitions began with his participation in the First Biennial Art Exhibition in Tehran in 1958, and culminated in a major solo exhibition at Galerie 66 in Paris in December 1981, just weeks prior to his latest arrest and alleged suicide.

I slipped the obituary into my pocket and went for a walk. So my father had betrayed his cause and his friend H., and I, the *khorous jangi*—namesake of their expired cause—had betrayed them both. But who had sent me this clip? An old classmate, an acquaintance from bygone underground meetings, someone who had heard what I had become?

At a café I sat at a corner table and looked out the window. Umbrellas were unfolding on the sidewalk as rain picked up momentum. A group of high school students arrived, laughing and drenched. They noisily pushed together several tables and gathered around it.

The older I get the more I dislike young people, I thought. *And I am only twenty-two. Why do I feel so old?* I lit a cigarette and brought it to my mouth. The students, who were discussing Attar's *Confederacy of the Birds*, talked over one another. One said, "As with most Sufis, Attar is saying that to become one with God, the self must be destroyed." "But God to him is not religion; it's truth itself," said another. A third, a good-looking kid with flaxen hair who made you want to invent your life all over again, said, "What about love? For Attar, passionate love is essential to the destruction of the self . . ."

I remembered my own readings of the medieval poem, after the fateful motorcycle trip in the summer of 1977 that had made me long for unity and utopias. Locking myself in my stifling room, I had read Attar—a spiritual descendant of Mansur al-Hallaj—and I had traveled with the poem's thirty bickering birds, led by their wise and humorous guide the hoopoe, who steered them to their spiritual king—the mythical bird simorgh, a kin of the phoenix. As it turned out, this spiritual king was none other than the traveling birds themselves: *si* means thirty, and *morgh* means bird—thirty birds. Where, I now wondered as I built a pyramid of sugar cubes on the wobbling table, was the hoopoe that could lead us back to the simorgh?

Feeling the damp and cold of the room, I put on my shearling coat—my father's. At that very moment, a small mirror on the opposite wall fell to the floor, unprovoked. Everyone jumped, startled by the crash. "Lucky," someone said. "No one was hurt."

Two waiters arrived with broom and bucket, sweeping up first the large pieces, then the glass dust. They apologized and offered everyone free tea and sweets, a distraction that lightened the mood. I remembered my mother's pronouncement about broken mirrors—*There will soon be a catastrophe.*

Superstition. Nonsense.

Fortunately, the mirror wasn't mine. It was a communal mirror fallen in a communal room. I was, at worst, a witness. Or so I told myself. I remained at the table and sipped my tea, the scent of bergamot and cardamom soothing my nerves. But when I looked up, before me I saw H. Mine was the last face he had seen in this life. What had he seen? What kind of face?

The rain stopped and a pale sunset broke through the smoky sky. The students left and the place quieted down. I looked around the café, at the people who, like me, were trapped in the trajectory of some unknowable misfortune. And each person, I knew, already harbored within himself his own private boneyard.

29

AFTER MY BOTCHED INTERVIEW WITH H., I was, for a decade, Akbari's diligent subordinate. I lived, in those years, in an inlet, caught between recklessness and terror. I became a man unknown, every hour transporting me further from the flower bed of my self. To make my existence more bearable I instituted rules: never allow an interrogation session to surpass five hours; keep water and sweets at hand should someone in the room—myself included—be on the verge of collapse; never aggress physically, but establish from the outset that aggression is possible.

At regular intervals I received letters from my family, thick envelopes bearing my father's calligraphic script. In the top left corner, a strange address in New York. In the center, his old address in Tehran—now mine. I opened none of them. I was terrified of what the letters might contain, words of rancor or kindness or both, words that would undo me, and the life I was so feverishly not living.

To counter these letters I came up with a ritual. Each week, from the boxes of family photographs I had saved, I would select a few images—of the four of us on picnics or driving north to the Caspian; of my parents drinking cocktails at the now outlawed smoky nightclubs; of Uncle Majid in his bowler hat and woolly cardigans; and of my paternal grandparents, both dead, and my maternal ones, now residents of Paris in an apartment on Avenue Montaigne. I would place these photographs in a manila envelope validated with the newly issued stamps bearing the likeness of the Ayatollah, and mail them to a fictional person residing at my family's address in New York. I didn't write my father's actual name so as not to arouse the suspicion of the authorities, who might have concluded that weekly packages addressed to someone in America bearing my own surname might signal some covert, nefarious activity. And so I would perform my weekly triage, deciding which memory should take precedence over others, which moment of the past should be granted the right of passage. My favorite part of this ceremony was inventing the name of each week's addressee. I selected these at random, from the phone book or from mythologies. One envelope went to a Mr. Reza Esfandiari (with myself as the sender), another to a Mr. Rostam Sistan (with the sender a Mr. Sohrab Samangan), and still another to a Professor Gilgamesh (with the sender a Mr. Enkidu Khodābiāmorz). Later, I addressed the envelopes to those who had once sat across from me, whose dossiers I had examined more thoroughly than my own fingernails. These names, I imagined, would be as anonymous to my father as names picked from the phone book, except for this one, the last: Mister H. Habibi (with the sender, Mister Khorous Jangi).

After that, my family's letters stopped, and I, too tired of being the trickster, resumed the role I knew best: humorless arbiter of fates.

IN THE ABSENCE of the letters and my own mailing ritual—the final filament of contact with my family—the house became an uninterrupted eulogy. I lived in it year after year as a ghost, aging and ageless. In August 1990, a year after the death of the Ayatollah, Akbari and a dozen prosecutors and interrogators showed up one evening at my place with a cake and a present wrapped in newspaper, to surprise me for my birthday. They sat around the dining table, rowdy, pouring freely from the bottles of vodka they had wangled from somewhere. I tore open the newspaper wrapping—it was from earlier that summer, with some headline about the arrest of the members of the Freedom Movement—and I was stunned to see a single-breasted houndstooth overcoat, with notched lapels and fully lined in chocolate brown silk. I had not thought these men capable of such largesse.

"Well?" Akbari said.

"It's beautiful," I said. "Thank you."

"It's time you stepped out of the 1970s and said goodbye to that sad shearling coat. It's 1990, my brother, and you're thirty years old!" He pinched my cheek.

One of the men—the Intelligence Ministry's representative to Evin—who two summers earlier had also been present at the meeting with the Cat—arranged thirty candles on the cake, taking care not to mess up the chocolate-hazelnut icing. Akbari shut off the lights and they all sang "Happy Birthday" in the dark. "Make a wish!" someone said.

I sat in front of the flickering candles, surrounded by the men's silhouettes. What could I ask for, and from whom? Unable to come up with anything, I made from providence this lone request: *May I find my way to the simorgh.*

I wore my new overcoat throughout that winter while my father's shearling hung in the closet, over the box that contained his reading glasses, the Pan Am matchbook, the Marie Antoinette table lamp, and all the other knickknacks that testified, when I myself could no longer believe it, that even I had once belonged to a family. The following winter, when Akbari caught me wearing the old shearling again, he said, *"Bāz gardad be asleh khod har cheez*—everything goes back to its origin."

30

To enter a father's home for the first time on the occasion of his memorial can unhinge a man. Standing in the living room in my steel-gray suit, stiff and alone, I found myself surrounded by scores of faces, a few vaguely familiar, containing something of the young selves they had been when I had last seen them. Oddly, my mother was not present.

They were huddled in clusters, older ones on the teal settee, younger ones standing in tight circles, the women in three-inch heels holding tall drinks next to their metrosexual husbands who reached now and again for hors d'oeuvres circulated by a silent Hispanic woman—the housekeeper, I assumed. I was neither greeted nor spurned. I walked, invisible, across the living room, and stood by the pier glass, in front of which was a framed portrait of my father in his middle years, stern and defiant, but with an inward smile, which disturbed me, because it was a negative of the image I had stored in my memory all these years, of my father, unsmiling. Next to the photograph was a memorial candle flickering in the breeze of an open window. No one seemed to notice that it was about to throw the sage silk curtains into flames. Normally I might have said something to the host—in this case, my mother— but I felt myself nothing more than a witness to this assembly.

In a vitrine nearby were the memorabilia Omid had told me about, china plates and framed defunct banknotes and gold Pahlavi coins displayed like war medals—the spoils of my mother's sleepless hours spent bidding on loss. I peeked at my watch; I had been present for only fifteen minutes. This night, I warned myself, would have no terminus. The looming hour of my speech made me anxious, so I rehearsed it in my head. Was the quote from Shamlou too much? I felt now that it would go over the heads of this crowd, and I imagined them staring at me, bored, baffled, contemptuous even. I should have chosen something more popular, maybe a quote from Rumi. Surely even they had come across a few poorly translated verses of the poet on a meditation pillow.

"Well, well . . ." A voice rose behind me. Female, hoarse, bitter. My mother.

I turned around. It's one thing to witness a parent's gradual decay across decades, another to see it all at once, with no forewarning and no prologue. She, my once-girlish mother with the lustrous black hair and wide-set chestnut eyes, seemed no different to me now than an old lady with a dyed bouffant to whom you might offer your seat on a crowded bus.

"What happened to your hair?" she said. "There are no bald

men in our family. Both your grandfathers had a full head of hair until the end. And your father, too, *khodā biyamorzatesh*. He may have lost much in his life, but not a strand of hair ever went missing from his beautiful head."

Before I could reply she said, "But you've kept your figure. That's something, at least. And you are taller than I remember. Have you grown? Well . . . what will you drink?"

"Water," I said.

She eyed me with suspicion then called the housekeeper. "Sandra," she said. "Bring a glass of water for this gentleman. Apparently he is more pristine than the rest of us." She walked off, toward the front door, which presented her with new guests: Ali Rahimi—celebrated author of *A Man Named Yasser*—accompanied by a no-nonsense blond woman in cargo pants, who I assumed was his wife, and two anemic girls in pigtails and metallic leggings. The woman offered my mother a white box. "An organic pecan pie from our bakery," she said. "We get the nuts from a small family farm in Louisiana." My mother thanked her lavishly though it was obvious to me that the offering was a disappointment.

Seeing me, Ali bit his lower lip and whispered something in his wife's ear, and together they walked to the opposite corner of the room, where admirers assailed them with congratulations on Ali's book publication. I looked out the window at the ashen river, the lone witness to my father's final breath, and I thought again of my mother's words when she told me of his death, *Imagine, found like that by a river, as though he had no family.* Along the promenade, just slipping into dusk, joggers ran back and forth with no aim except to postpone their mortality. A woman was practicing yoga, her body in a half-moon pose like the hands of a frozen clock. Another sat alone on a bench, an unread book on her lap, watching the sun's descent behind the dimming city.

A trembling hand took hold of my arm. It belonged to a centenarian, veiny and shrunken, leaning on a cane with a gargoyle ferrule. "I don't know if you remember me," he said. "I am Doctor Albert, the dentist. You used to accompany your father on his dental visits."

"How could I forget?" I said.

"Don't worry," he said, laughing. "I haven't practiced since I came here. But how did you get away from me? You never gave me a chance to work on your teeth."

"I'm surprised you recognize me, after all this time."

"I'd recognize those eyes anywhere," he said. "I used to look at you when you were a boy, and I would think to myself, *If one took the time to see beyond the sorrow in that child, one might even see kindness.*"

"I must ask you," I said. "Why did you refuse to give anesthesia?"

"It was my training. I studied dentistry in Austria in the late 1930s."

"But you were practicing until the 1970s."

"I suppose I believed that pain should not be masked."

The housekeeper brought him a chair and he sat. He surveyed the room, which, aside from the framed photograph of my father and the memorial candle, seemed no more muted than any New York party. "I kept in touch with your father over the years," he said. "I had always been very fond of him. There was a seriousness to him, the way he studied and worked on that encyclopedia all those years. You'd think he was doing God's work. But he was not the same man after he came here. Something cracked inside him."

"What's done is done," I said.

"Yes . . ." He sat quiet for some time, spinning the gargoyle-tipped cane. "Do you know," he said, suddenly upbeat, "that some years ago, maybe ten, a small plane crashed into that building across the street? Right there, on the thirtieth floor. I happened to be visiting your parents that afternoon. I remember that your mother was watering her gardenias by the window and your father and I were playing backgammon. And there it was, a terrible explosion. Boom! . . . The entire block shook and fire broke out. Black smoke rose to the sky. In the plane were a Yankees pitcher and his flight instructor. Both were killed, of course. A woman inside the building was scorched by a fireball. An Iranian woman, the wife of a cardiologist. But she survived."

I imagined the baseball player mumbling some prayer as his plane shattered the walls and windows of the ill-fated woman, whose life, until that moment, had probably been unremarkable.

"I was heartbroken for the pitcher," he continued. "You know, when I arrived in this country, I took to baseball right away. Even though it's all about money now, there is still something innocent about the game. To tell you the truth it's one of the things that made America acceptable to me. How can I explain? It's the way you may love a troublesome child only when he is asleep." Laughing, he pointed at my father's portrait. "This fellow, on the other hand, didn't care for the game. I tried so many times to convert him but he remained as stubborn as a mullah."

At that moment, Omid arrived with a lanky, long-haired teenager in a Frank Zappa T-shirt who seemed a stranger to this crowd. With his hands stuffed in his pockets and his refusal to smile, the boy's face nevertheless contained a trace of my brother's gentleness.

"My son, Arash," Omid said.

I shook the boy's hand. "*Hot Rats* is still one of the best albums of all time," I said.

He gave me a blank look.

"Don't get ahead of yourself," Omid said to me. "Kids nowadays wear the T-shirts of the old bands but no one actually listens to the music."

"There was a time when Zappa was more than a logo," I said. "Have a listen," I told the kid. "It'll be worth your while."

He nodded and looked down at the paisley motif on the carpet under his sneakered foot.

"Is your speech ready?" Omid said.

"It was, until I got here. Now I'm rewriting it in my head. Yours?"

"I was never a performer," he said. "I'm dreading this."

Someone began tinkering on the piano, Mozart's *"Eine kleine Nachtmusik—a little night music."* When he finished a few guests lightly applauded. "Can anyone really play?" a woman in a tobacco-brown dress called out.

"Hamid can play," my mother said. "He played like an angel when he was a child, but God only knows what happened since."

Conversations dissolved into whispers; everyone knew my story, or at least their own version of it. I had been laid bare as the son with the malignant past. I looked to my brother for guidance but found none; his face—part pity, part indignation—had nothing left to offer.

"Well? Will you play something for us?" my mother continued. "In memory of your father, whom you loved so much."

I had anticipated my mother's bitterness, but had not expected it to be so public. I kept my composure as best I could and sat down at the piano, resting my fingers on the cold and unyielding keys. Through the throat-clearing in the room I sensed the guests preparing themselves to witness a man's familial bankruptcy with both dread and glee. I shut my eyes, and what came to me was a piece I had played one winter morning when my father, just returned from Uncle Majid's funeral, had sat on the sofa and said to me, "Play something to get me through this black day."

I had been sitting at the piano, practicing as I was expected to do for hours every weekend. From the kitchen came the scent of butter and eggs and chives; it was almost lunchtime and I was hungry. Not knowing what my father was asking of me, I turned the pages of my exercise book, given to me by Mme Petrossian—the Armenian lady who had fled Ottoman Anatolia and who offered me lessons every Wednesday afternoon—and stopped at *Moonlight* Sonata. I played the first movement, which I had only recently learned and which made me think of the crippled cat I had loved and lost the night I had slept under the apricot tree with my uncle. My father sat with eyes closed and though I made many mistakes, he listened until the end. "Hamid," he said. "It's a terrible thing, losing a brother."

Now, sweating under my new suit, I glanced at Omid, then at my mother. I pressed one key, then another, and another, until both hands were obeying my memory of the notes and I fell into the adagio of the sonata, the melody hushed and full of things unsaid. I was overtaken by memories of bygone summers, of our old house in Tehran, of the cool scent of wet earth after a morning rain and of the lacecap hydrangeas, of my father and my mother and Omid. I thought, too, of Noushin—of how I had once loved her—and of Golnaz, my absent daughter. I did not play for myself or for them or even for grief at things lost, but for the disappointment that united us, for the constellation of our heartbreak, for the betrayal, the love, the destruction.

When I was done I heard my mother crying in the kitchen and another voice, a woman's, offering words that failed to console. Omid, lost in thought, stared at a cigarette burn on the carpet. I looked up, not at the room but out the window—at the city beyond. Twilight separated the horizon now like the bones of a catfish. My mother emerged from the kitchen, and directed the guests to the dining room. "Everyone must be hungry," she said. People stretched limbs and resumed talking, released at last from the talons of grief.

Ali Rahimi excused himself. He couldn't stay for dinner, he said. "The children . . ." he added, pointing at the girls. "It's a school night." My mother, who had reclaimed her good cheer, intervened. "Nonsense," she said. "You must eat something." But he was already putting on his jacket and his wife was tightening the laces of the girls' suede Adidas.

"Let the man go," Omid said. "He must have a good reason to go home."

Ali thanked my mother, mumbled some condolences, and left.

TRAYS OF RICE AND STEW arrived from the kitchen, followed by pitchers of *doogh*—which the younger guests didn't recognize. "It's a yogurt drink with mint," my mother explained, and everyone, in deference to the deceased, forwent gluten sensitivities and lactose intolerances and agreed to eat and drink with abandon. I sat at the table next to Omid, who remained silent.

"You played beautifully," Doctor Albert said.

"Maybe he is still an angel," an old woman said in a bitter, cutting voice. I recognized her downturned mouth and realized it was Azar, Uncle Majid's wife. She wore a homemade peach macramé cardigan and was holding her fork with a tissue. She was, apparently, still a germophobe.

"What a table you've laid out, madame," said a blue-eyed old man. "Your husband would have been happy."

"Thank you, Jacques," said my mother. "Please eat well to make me happy also."

Jacques—the Frenchman I had nicknamed M. Hulot—was one of my father's researchers from his encyclopedia days. How they were all resurfacing from his past.

"I was surprised when I heard you had chosen cremation," Jacques said, in the matter-of-fact style of a Frenchman. "That's uncommon, no?"

Utensils clinked in the room's silence. "It's what he wanted," my mother said.

"Better than ending up in one of those sad graves along the Long Island Expressway," Doctor Albert said.

"The ultimate cemetery is the Cimitero Monumentale di Milano," Azar said. "The most magnificent mausoleums you'll ever see. All of Milan's important families are buried there. What luck," she said, sighing, "to find yourself there at the end."

"Surely they can make room for you, Azar-*khanoum*," another woman said. "With your talent you should have long graced the runways of Milan." She was also wearing a macramé cardigan, only in pearl white. I noticed that several of the octogenarian women had on versions of this dreadful sweater, and I understood that Azar must have sprouted some kind of homespun fashion business in her old age.

"But nothing beats the Okunoin Cemetery in Mount Koya, Japan," a youngish man said. "I was there last year for our company's merger and a Japanese colleague took me there for a visit. Imagine, ten thousand lanterns illuminating the mausoleum of Kobo Daishi, the founder of Shingon Buddhism. Truly breathtaking."

"How lucky," Azar said. "You were in Japan?"

"Yes," the man said. "And actually all over East and South Asia. China, Thailand, Cambodia, Indonesia . . ."

"If you ask me, the most beautiful cemetery is Père Lachaise in Paris," my mother said. "Think of it, Balzac and Oscar Wilde debating the human condition while Piaf croons 'Je ne regrette rien' in the background. And nearby there is Proust."

My mother, I was quite certain, had not read a word of Balzac, Wilde, or Proust. When I was a child she read only the newspaper and the occasional magazine, and I doubted that this habit had been reversed once she had arrived in America. To be sure, her guests were no better informed than she was, and so everyone nodded in agreement that a place holding the bones of so many luminaries must indeed be a fine destination.

"I think Hedayat is there, too," said Doctor Albert.

Several people confirmed this, referring to the grave of Sadegh Hedayat, the modernist writer whose work no one read or understood. Still, everyone, even expats, had heard of *Boof-e-koour*—*The Blind Owl*, the writer's best-known and least comprehensible book, and most knew that the author had gassed himself in his rented Parisian apartment in 1951. These two factoids were sufficient to give any dinner party an air of intellectual gravitas, and this one was no exception.

"When were you in Paris?" Jacques asked my mother.

"We were there the first time with the boys," my mother said, gesturing at us—the boys—men in our fifties silent at the dinner table, still hoping our mother would speak well of us to others. "I think it was 1972. From there we went to Rome, then Venice, then Vienna, and finally Munich. It would have been a fabulous summer, were it not for Hamid's outbursts."

That summer had nearly killed me. My father, from the beginning, declared that on this trip he was going to be a free agent because he planned to spend half a day in front of each Titian and Caravaggio, and he didn't believe any of us would have the stamina to accompany him. So we were stuck with my mother. In France we hopped from one château to another, from one Louis to another, royal antechamber to piss-chamber. Rome became a race to see the highest number of artworks possible, and by the end of the week I had visions of the Madonna and Child, in streaks of gold and lapis lazuli, every time I shut my eyes. Venice was a tiresome serenade of gondoliers who convinced my mother that life in Italy consisted of handsome men in striped shirts singing *O sole mio* to swooning ladies, and Vienna and Munich, those Teutonic lands of self-flagellating ostriches, were a sad parade of Baroque palaces and indigestible servings of blood sausage and memorials.

"Hamid is awfully quiet," Azar said with a catty smile.

"Tell us, Hamid," said the dentist. "Which is your favorite cemetery?"

I looked up from my plate and saw all faces—some reproachful, others embarrassed—turned in my direction. Clearing my throat I said, "The most incredible gravesite, in my opinion, is that of the old prime minister Mossadegh. His tomb is at his old residence, where for many years he had lived under house arrest."

No one replied. I knew that they did not wish to engage me in a political discussion. I was yellowcake at their dinner table.

"I visited his house last year," I continued. "It's in Ahmadabad, not far from Karaj. A quiet place, unmarked and barely visited. Everything is as he left it, even his old pistachio-colored car, still parked in the garage. The land around the house has grown wild, and on the morning I visited, crows were cawing and a wet wind was blowing. Inside the living room, at the center, sits the coffin, like a coffee table. It's covered with a dark cloth and a vase full of roses, candles, and the like. All around there are framed black-and-white photographs of the man, and as I stood there, so close to his bones, I thought it was the most mysterious thing, not only where one ends up but *how* one ends up. So much depends on the story," I continued nervously. "And who gets to tell it. When he died many newspapers said his death had gone unnoticed. They said that as his ambulance brought his body from the hospital to his home for the burial, everyone was busy shopping in the bazaar as though it were a day like any other. What they failed to mention was that the Shah had forbidden his family to put a death notice in the papers."

"But he has since gotten his due, wouldn't you agree?" Jacques said.

"Nowadays," I said, "he is both a legend, and forgotten. Historians hail him, but ask anyone in Tehran to tell you where his house is and they will look at you as though you had asked for directions to Middle Earth. We are obsessed with him and we also want to forget him. I think that like most humans he was magnificent as an idea but he failed as a man. And so we love him, but we are also bitter, like the progeny of a noble patriarch who was, in the end, unable to protect his disloyal family."

"Enough, Hamid," said my mother. "No one wants to hear about your visit to Mossadegh's house. Or your theories either. Next thing I know you are going to convict those of us who moved to America of being retroactively guilty of the coup."

A few guests chuckled.

"I convict you of no such thing," I said. "In fact, what people rarely mention is that the Americans and the British weren't the only ones at fault. We, the nation, also failed the old man. So many were complicit with the Shah and his backers . . . So many, including the clerics."

"The clerics?" the businessman said. "But haven't they always been against the monarchy?"

"Like everyone else," I said, "the clerics, throughout history, have switched sides back and forth as it suited them. In that instance a monarch was better than a so-called Communist."

"All this shape-shifting is too confusing," my mother said. "Who can keep up?"

"What everyone knows," I carried on, staring now into my mother's bloodshot eyes, "is that America was the ring leader of that coup. And you must have made your peace with it, since you carry an American passport."

"This country took us in," she said.

"Yes, it took you in. But it's also part of the reason you had to leave yours in the first place. It's like the cigarette corporation that sells you the cigarette first, then the nicotine patch."

"You are one to teach history lessons," my mother said under her breath.

"Why did you invite me here tonight?" I said.

She gave no answer.

"You invited me," I said, "because I am an extra in your farce, just as I had been when I was a boy. Without me your stage is incomplete. And yet you never could stand me, because I was unable to behave as you wished me to. I don't blame you for resenting me. The truth is I have embarrassed you time and time again. Mother," I added, "you and I are fire and water. We cancel each other out."

"I invited you," said my mother, "because you are my son."

We were trapped in an ache from which there could be no exit. Omid looked pale and impassive, just as he had on his last night in Tehran, nearly four decades earlier, when he had stood in our bedroom and conducted a triage of his belongings, condensing his life into one suitcase.

"I was asked to make a speech tonight in memory of my father,"

I said. "And I had prepared just such a speech, about fathers and sons, disappointment and love, absences and reunions. It was, I think, a beautiful speech, and it may have momentarily offered us all a feeling of warmth, maybe even harmony. But I will give no such speech. Instead I will tell you something . . ."

My mother swirled her drink, the ice clinking against the glass. "Good," she said. "I'm glad you won't give a speech. You've already talked too much and no one wants to hear any more from you."

I took a breath and considered leaving. My face felt hot; my eyes, too, were cinders. A cold sweat was breaking on my forehead. I reached into my pocket for a tissue, but instead grabbed the tin candy box, which felt soothing and cool against my clammy palm. "As I was saying," I continued as I settled back into my chair, "instead of the prepared speech I will tell you something that I have never before revealed to anyone, except to my wife, who no longer speaks to me. It's about a crime, not in the legal sense, but in the human sense. Perhaps then, the right word for it is sin. Only one other man knows of this misdeed, and that's the man who carried it out on my behalf. Mother, I was the one who orchestrated the seizure of *bābā*'s encyclopedia papers, the wiping out of his life's work. I asked a fellow revolutionary to do it."

My mother's face drained of all its color. Leaden half-moons cradled her eyes.

"I know you wish me to leave now but are too stunned to say so." I folded my napkin and got up. "Goodbye," I said. "I am sorry, for us both."

No one moved as I made my way across the living room and out the door. In the hallway, as I waited for the elevator, I heard chairs stirring and voices murmuring; it felt like the aftermath of a robbery. Someone double-bolted the door from inside. I thought of lingering to eavesdrop but didn't. What difference did it make, what they said about me, when everything had already been said, so long ago?

I stood still, my reflection in the stainless-steel elevator doors distorted and alien, like a face gleaned in the lid of a pan. The doors opened at last and I pressed the lobby button. When I turned, I saw Omid standing before me. Looking at his face, his long lashes and the skin under his jaw only beginning to slack, I was filled with an aching love for this brother I had failed.

"All this time . . . It was you? *You* destroyed *bābā*'s life-work?" His voice trembled as he spoke and the veins on his temples bulged alarmingly. "Why did you make this confession?" he continued as the doors shut and the elevator cables inched downward.

"I thought it was time for you and Mother to know."

"Why now?"

"I don't want to live a lie anymore."

"That's what you tell yourself," he said. "But Hamid, everything you do, everything you have ever done, has been for your own benefit, and your own benefit alone." Shutting his eyes, he added, "How many people you have destroyed . . ."

As he spoke something ruptured in my ear and a ringing sound echoed in my head. "Omid," I said, "I never killed."

"There are many ways to annihilate a life," he said.

The ringing intensified, buzzing in my head. "I committed my share of misdeeds," I said. "But there are things you don't know. About *bābā*."

"What things? How dare you vilify the man any more than you already have?"

"This is the truth, Omid. I learned it from Yasser the day

before the Black Friday demonstrations. *Bābā* was arrested after the Mossadegh coup, and under pressure he ratted on many, including his best friend Houshang, the artist. Later, when he worked for the Ministry of Culture, he threatened on multiple occasions to have Houshang arrested. Omid, I've seen the letters. They carry his signature . . ."

The elevator opened and I stepped into the marbled lobby. For some time Omid stood quiet, but as the doors began to shut he held them open and said, "Why don't you focus on your own actions? What you did tonight was the culmination of a project you began decades ago. Tonight, on your father's memorial, you laid the final brick in your life's masterwork, which has been the destruction of your family. Well done, brother. Your magnum opus is complete."

PART
—◆—
TWO

31

WE WERE GOING back empty-handed. The past disowned, the future rebuffed. And Reza Abbasi's sixteenth-century drawing of the pilgrim still captive in a warehouse in Queens.

From the plane's oval window I watched New York dissolving. Steel, glass, velocity. I imagined the millions pushing against one another, and my brother among them. I thought again of his kitchenette and his dead dog and his lemon tree. And his final words to me. Throughout my life I had been called so many things—glass boy, fighting cock, revolutionary, Captain Prick, prosecutor's shadow, Minister's vizier, woeful destroyer. I was, in fact, all of these.

The mood on the plane back to Tehran was manic. Food was circulated and teacups refilled. Lurid jokes were exchanged as in a boys' locker room and spitballs were tossed across the cabin. The Minister, drafting a letter, ignored the chaos.

"They're all so pleased to be released from the diplomatic drudgery and to be going home," I said. "Look at them. You'd think it was the eve of Eid."

"When we land they'll be reminded that Eid has to be validated by the Ayatollah," said the Minister.

It's true that the end of Ramadan wasn't certified by a calendar, but by experts sent by the Ayatollah throughout the country to witness the new moon's crescent, marking the start of the lunar month. "Yes," I said, "the Ayatollah supervises even the moon."

As I spoke I noticed a security agent in a corner of the plane eyeing me. He was from the old guard; I recognized the type as a reformed junkie spots his own kind.

In every revolution the old guard, once feared, becomes over time as anodyne as an uncapped bottle of acetone. Remembering the hotel concierge's cuff links, I wondered how Mao, for instance, ended up on cuff links, wallets, and teacups designed by the chic fashion houses of Shanghai. One way to lighten the world's mistrust of our country, I thought, might be to emblazon a neon-tinted image of the Ayatollah on a pair of cuff links or on a stylish gym bag. That would surely rid the man's image of the dread it inspired. For who, after all, would be scared of a Warhol-style mullah?

LIKE CHILDREN COLLAPSING after a sugar rush, the men suddenly fell into silence and the engine's drone filled the cabin.

There was a time, decades before, when a flight held the excitement of elsewhere. Now, no matter the direction, it was only a reminder of nowhere. My father's ashes, heavy in my breast pocket, made me think of the coffee dregs stuck to the bottom of my overturned fortune cup when I was a boy. "A stain at the bottom means sorrow in the heart," my fortune-telling mother would say every time she read my cup.

I shut my eyes and saw Noushin and Golnaz in court before a judge with their catalog of grievances.

My last memory of my wife was of the lilacs I found crushed on the sidewalk on the day she left. A quarter of an hour after she was gone, when I began sensing the funereal stillness of the house, I rushed downstairs, and seeing the flattened petals on the pavement—Golnaz had tucked a few stems from our garden in her mother's purse that morning—I ran down several streets to the deserted bus stop, calling out her name in the noontime hush of a city sitting down to lunch. I stood for some time on the street corner, foolish and lost. An old man asked me if I was all right and for some inexplicable reason I said, "My father used to call me a fighting cock." The man's milky eyes were unhurried. "What they call you is of no importance," he said. "What matters is who you are." He walked on, his body a museum of bone and loneliness.

Well, who was I? I was the one who had designed Noushin's departure from the get-go, carving an exit for her—slowly, imperceptibly, chiseling centimeters off the cement of our togetherness with chronic bouts of absence. The first time I abandoned her she was four months pregnant with Golnaz. My vanishing was neither premeditated nor impromptu, say, in the style of an Updikean antihero stepping out for a pack of cigarettes and never returning. It was somewhere in between. By this I mean that it was an act I could have foretold, though no exact timing was ever assigned.

The night in question was not unlike any other. Insomnia—mine, which always triggered hers. Between us the whistle of the teakettle on the stove, the sweet smell of boiling milk, our nightly ritual of appeasement and pacification. The reading of poetry out loud, which we did together during these bouts of sleeplessness, taking turns, each mothering the other until one would fall back asleep and the other would follow.

I was lying groggy on the sofa, my head on her bare lap, feeling the bulge of the baby against my forehead. Noushin repositioned herself, moving her stomach away to make more room for me, as though apologetic, somehow, for the child growing inside her. She read a Shamlou poem to me, and as I sensed my eyes shutting to the sound of her voice, I woke up in a panic, breathless, and feeling myself penned in by the walls of our apartment, I put on some clothes and headed out. "Where are you going?" she said. "I need air," I said. She asked if she should come with me and I said no, there was no need, I would be back in a few minutes. "Just need some air," I said again, and she nodded, understanding no doubt that air was akin to a void and could include neither her, nor the baby.

Even as I ignited the engine on my motorcycle—a secondhand Yamaha I had bought when my old Harley finally collapsed—and rode in the blackness of that November night, I believed I would be back before long, as I had promised. But as I rode on, past the construction cranes on Arjantin Square and the unlit shops of Valiasr Street, I merged onto Hakim Expressway, and sensing my own momentum with my unhelmeted head I pressed the gas, going faster and farther, mosquitoes colliding with my bare forehead, the city limits vanishing behind me. In Karaj, at dawn, I stopped at Emamzadeh Taher cemetery, where Shamlou had been buried a few months earlier. Flashing my Swiss Army light on the graves, I found my way to his, and I watched the day breaking, despite everything.

I rode north through lonely villages, reveling in the smell of cow manure and earth, and parked my motorcycle on a side road, taking a piss in an open field and relishing the landscape, free of humans and their burdens.

By the time I arrived at the seaside the sun was high in the damp northern sky, the air full of saltwater and fish, seaweed and grief. I stopped at a teahouse for breakfast, and as food and drink warmed my stomach I considered again what I had done. I may have been heartless, but no one, I convinced myself, could accuse me of being thoughtless. I was three months into my fortieth year. On my birthday, as Noushin and I had walked home from dinner, the news of her pregnancy still convulsing in the stifling August night between us, I had looked for the first time into my future. Finding only the black shadow of a wasted man, I had understood that the kindest act I was capable of was to fabricate for Noushin and the baby an escape route from me.

I rode along the coast as far as Bandar Anzali, which happened to be H.'s hometown. The Caspian seaport, free of holiday-makers, stood sober and dignified. Teahouses were shuttered and summer villas locked for the season. By the misty lagoon, where fishing boats were unloading the morning's haul, a boy's kite fluttered low in the sky like a woman's headscarf. I thought of H. and the fake story I had shown him about the fire in Anzali. I thought of his face. Always his face, his stabbing eyes and his impish goatee.

Behind the clouds the sun was still making its midmorning ascent. Eleven in the morning—this was the hour when Noushin would normally call me from the gallery. Had she gone to work that morning? Did she tell anyone that I had disappeared? I thought of Akbari, and his intolerance for disappearances orchestrated by anyone but himself.

My absence from my shoddy life made me feel like a child peering at the plastic replica of his own city through a snow globe discovered in some dusty souvenir shop. At the harbor, the whitewashed nineteenth-century clock tower—once a lighthouse—stood tall and solitary. I took long sips from my bottle, followed by deep breaths afterward. Seagulls descended along the seashore, indifferent to me and free of judgment. How long had I looked for a place far away, one like this with a lighthouse that was once a beacon for seafarers in the blackness of a Caspian night? Standing at the foot of the edifice I asked it for direction with the goodwill of a novice pilgrim at prayer, but all I got was a silent announcement of the hour—twelve minutes past noon. The day had already half vanished.

At a pay phone I called Noushin. "It's me," I said stupidly when she picked up.

"Oh, you're alive," she said, her voice breaking.

"I hate to disappoint," I said.

"I'm in no mood for jokes," she said. "I thought you were dead, with that junk motorcycle of yours." She blew her nose. "Where are you?"

"I am in the most tranquil place on earth," I said between sips. "Before me are a sea, a lagoon, fishermen, a clock tower, and the mist of an autumn day."

"Stop that fake poetic nonsense," she said. "You rode all the way to Anzali?"

"Noushin," I said. "You and the baby will be better off without me."

She was quiet for some time. In the background I could hear *khanoum* Modaress, the gallery owner with an assortment of Hermès scarves, bossing around some underling.

"We will be better off without you?" she said. "You should have thought of that before you slept with me and certainly before you married me."

"This baby wasn't in the plans," I said.

"Accidents happen," she said. "I believe you had something to do with it."

"I need air," I said. "I need to be away from all that city soot and corruption."

"So what are you going to do? Rent a cabin and live by the sea? Become a fisherman?" She laughed mirthlessly.

"Why not?" I said.

"Hamid," she said. "You say you want to get away from the soot and corruption. But these have nothing to do with the city."

"What, then?" I said.

"The soot is from the life you've lived," she said.

"The life I've lived suited you just fine until now," I said. "Who's been supporting you while you work part-time for next to nothing in that stupid gallery, and who's been funding you while you go out and pursue your grand photography projects? The source never bothered you before, *khanoumeh* Taheri, so why the sudden crisis of conscience?" Never before had I called her by her maiden name.

"I never liked the life you chose," she said.

"I don't give a damn that you didn't like it," I said, with such abandon that the seagull feasting on a breadcrumb near me leapt away. "The point is you never objected."

"I objected many times, and you know it. And each time you told me you're doing it because you're influencing things from inside. Hamid, it's enough. Get out of there and let's start over, with the baby." She paused for a minute. "I love you," she said.

"Noushin, I'm sorry," I said, and hung up without saying goodbye, knowing well that once the ashes of our conversation had scattered, my longing for her would return. Why was it that I could only love her in absence?

MY DISAPPEARANCE PROMPTED rumors that I had become unhinged. I, too, wondered if I was losing my mind. Akbari inquired if he should pay me a visit. "I just need time to clear my head," I said. But I was not sure what that meant or how one goes about accomplishing such a task.

I rented a studio overlooking the port, listening to foghorns and fishing boats drawing near and sleeping long hours on the flat mattress of an old wooden bed that creaked every time I turned this way or that. The apartment was scarcely furnished: a kitchenette with a working gas stove; a sink; a fridge; a square table with a naked lightbulb above it; two snuff-colored chairs, vestiges of the 1970s—that decisive decade of my youth—and an ottoman with stains that I preferred not to think about. A gray mouse occasionally appeared from behind the stove; in time, I looked forward to his visits.

Each day I sat at the kitchen table for hours with a glass of tea, under the glare of the lone bulb, contemplating my present through the progression of my history. If I examined my life through the prism of a dossier—as I had grown accustomed to examining all lives—then I could have said that mine, the entire arc of it, had been a misprint. I, Hamid Mozaffarian, promising art student, deemed by professors as "clever"—son of Sadegh Mozaffarian, founder of the Art Encyclopedia, and Monir Farahani, so-called offspring of Qajar kings—had ended up, somehow, as an interrogator, the arbiter of others' guilt and innocence, greasing the pulleys of Akbari's apparatus of law and order. But when I contemplated myself as a man and not a dossier, then the incongruousness of my present no longer perplexed me: my life, as so many before mine, was but a series of wrong turns.

I wondered what I would have become had I resumed my studies at the university. For the first time I questioned the prophecy Akbari had given me decades earlier, that on the day I betrayed my father, I had embarked on a one-way road. Had there truly been no going back? It was now too late for such ruminations. I was a veteran of the penal system, and far too old to return to university. In any case, Akbari, who could not abide the escape of one of his protégés, would retaliate for my desertion by charging me with the death, all those years ago, of the judge. Our legal system knew nothing of statutes of limitation. We were in servitude to a divine order, where sins have no expiration dates.

All of this I wrote off as life's regrets.

What I could not write off was the reality of my forthcoming child. The perpetuation of myself in the form of a baby nearly drove me to madness. That this decision was not in my own hands but in those of another human being, a woman who claimed to love me, added to my torment. I considered writing a letter to my father. Maybe, I thought, in going back I could go forward. I wanted not only to confess but also to explain. But after the salutations, what would my first sentence be? The first sentence sets the intent, everyone knows that. Apology or indignation? Acknowledgment or expiation? What does a man who isn't there say to a man who vanished?

On a walk by the lagoon early one morning I remembered

swimming in the Caspian with my father, who once reached out to me in the water, his colossal fingers encircling my wrist. I let him maneuver me back to the beach, back to my mother, who lay on a towel in her yellow swimsuit, her skin devouring the sun. "You are quite a sorry sight, Monir," my father said. "You look like a burned chicken." My mother looked up, squinting, and shut her eyes again, resuming her interrupted bliss. But interruptions can't be erased. Soon her eyes opened and she got up. "I'm going for a walk," she said without waiting for a response. I looked at my mother's disappearing body as she headed for the water, then at my father's hand, feeling myself alternating between the two, and as I got up to run after my mother I heard my father say, "Sit with me, Hamid. For once, just sit with me." We sat together wrapped in our towels, listening to the conversations of others.

"How old are you?" my father said.

I thought it possible that he truly didn't know. "Turning nine in August," I said. I reached for my glass marble, the one with the snow owl, tucked in my mother's beach bag.

"I'd like you to tell me a story," said my father.

"What kind of story?" I said.

"Any story," he said. "Something interesting."

My mind was a blank as I felt my wet swimsuit cling to my skin. "I don't know any . . ."

"Come on," he said. "You never speak, unless poked. You live in your own absentminded head. Make yourself known, my son! Or at the very least, heard."

"A real story?" I said. "Or a made-up tale?"

"It doesn't matter," he said with a loud sigh. "Whatever you prefer."

I plundered my mind for a story, anything to save me from this tribunal I had been summoned to, with no warning. But it was as though someone had pillaged what little might have existed inside my head. I found nothing there, and nothing is what I offered my father.

A vendor approached with cones of ice cream.

"No, thank you," my father said to him. "There is no pleasure eating an ice cream alone." The man looked at me with pity in his eyes, and walked away.

SO MY FATHER WAS A COLD MAN, and perhaps something worse, if one were to take into account his betrayal of his friend H. But wasn't I, in comparison, hoarfrost? If cruelty had a hierarchy, I had outperformed my father fiftyfold. A billion cold fathers must have walked this earth; few produced sons such as I. Of course, blame at the father's feet was the psychologist's justification, while absolution of the father was the geneticist's vocation. Where then, was the truth?

AFTER THE FIRST MONTH, the mouse, finding me an agreeable roommate, never left. He slept in a crevice under the stove and came out when he was hungry or bored. Often I left him crumbs of bread and cheese, and I watched him as he gnawed a sliver of food, content. On a few occasions I woke up in the morning to find him sleeping on my mattress, his tiny body curled under the arch of my foot. That he neither knew nor cared about my past comforted me. I thought it absurd that I had formed a friendship with a mouse. But this, too, is what a man is made of.

WHEN I RETURNED to Tehran I was four weeks away from becoming a father. For Noushin's sake—and the baby's—I should have kept my distance. After all, if I had gotten nothing else from my seclusion in Anzali, I had gotten this much: I understood the mayhem I was capable of. But I was not willful enough to stay away. Instead I made a vow—even briefly believing it— that I would become, as they say, a better man.

Noushin, naturally, didn't let me back into the apartment. I rented a run-down room downtown, offering her the illusion of choice, but I persisted with my quest to regain entry into my former life with the same stubbornness that months earlier had propelled my absence. I showed up nightly with tins of caviar I had brought back from Anzali, along with sweets and massage oils and the best wine I could manage. I cooked dinner for her, rubbed her swollen feet, rested my lawless head on the baby's heartbeat. And I sang to them both, usually one of my old Dariush tunes, which I used to sing when Noushin and I were courting: *Kouho mizāram roo dousham / rakhte har jango mipousham / mowjo az daryā migiram / shireyeh sango midousham / ageh cheshmāt began āreh, hich kodoum kari nadāreh . . . I will put the mountain on my shoulder / wear any war uniform / take the wave from the sea / milk the sap of a stone / If your eyes say yes, none of these will be difficult . . .*

SLOWLY SHE RELENTED, and by the time she was giving birth, on a rainy night in April, I was fretting and pacing in the fluorescent-lit hallway of the hospital like any husband who has been there all along.

When I saw the baby, twelve hours later, it was spring in the hospital room. Lilacs by Noushin's bed. White curtains fluttering by a sunlit window. And the baby, a red poppy, in her bassinet. But the first thing I felt for the child was not love but pity; I was the seedbed of her existence, the hollow ground from which her life would have to germinate.

32

FOR THE FIRST TWO YEARS OF HER LIFE I was attached to the baby with a terrifying ferocity. Often, when holding her head, I would touch the fontanelle and think how easy it would be to break her. At such times I would place her back in her crib, admonishing myself for harboring such thoughts. Noushin interpreted my interactions with the baby as lack of devotion.

Still, for those two years we spent in the three-room apartment we shared on Arjantin Square, we cooked and ate, slept and laughed. The pop songs rotating in our CD player made us believe in the possibility of belonging, to each other and to the idea of our family. With hand puppets that I constructed with foam and Ping-Pong balls and bird feathers—a bespectacled cat, a bearded dog, a long-lashed canary, and a classic Pahlevan Kachal, the bald-headed hero of the puppetry of yore—I performed for them nightly, dressing up the figurines as mullahs, fighters, professors, and princesses, and making up stories of love, loss, valor, and honor that would have pleased my father that day on the beach. In this makeshift world love didn't always survive but loss always had meaning, and valor sometimes faltered but honor, above all, prevailed.

As I watched the laughing faces of my wife and daughter during those nights I marveled at my own capacity for transient love, and I wondered how long this love could be sustained. To keep our story going I created ever more complicated adventures for our puppets, so much so that they began overtaking our lives: Noushin and I talked in their voices and accents even when communicating with each other during the day, and the baby, just beginning to speak, was learning to imitate them all. What harm was there in living life as a play? None, I convinced myself, but another voice—the sober one excluded from the game— never tired of reminding me that all plays must come to an end.

33

THE PUPPETRY ENDED, as most things, with a confession. Up at dawn as usual, hours before work and world, I sat in bed, tilting my limbs toward gravity, one foot to the floor, then the other. A body trapped in its own trance. I watched Noushin, asleep after another night spent soothing the child. Our child, sleepless, like us.

ON THE STREET, at that hour, company could be found in strays—dogs and men. On a sycamore tree by the newspaper kiosk I noticed an engraved heart, lovers' initials locked inside.

No doubt the heart would soon vanish along with the tree, cut down to make room for another government building.

At sunrise kiosk shutters were unrolled and vans unloaded newspapers, thousands of words adding up to naught. People trickled out of homes, sleepwalking toward their daily newspapers. I did the same, then walked to a nearby café, just opened for the day.

Along with reports of a workers' strike in Abadan and Ahvaz, and of hundreds arrested in Khorasan for partaking in "corruption networks," I read this headline:

CLERIC CALLS FOR ARRESTING DOG OWNERS

Hojatoleslam Hasani, a Friday prayer leader in Orumieh,
has denounced the *moral depravity* of dog ownership
and called upon the judiciary to arrest all dogs and their
owners, saying, "I demand the judiciary arrest all dogs
with long, medium, or short legs together with their
long-legged owners, otherwise I will arrest them myself."
In June, the police banned the sale of dogs and stipulated
penalties for dog walking in public, which has become
fashionable in some neighborhoods, in North Tehran
especially . . .

Were we living inside a prank? Some dreamed-up cartoon strip with no end?

ACROSS THE STREET Noushin was heading to the grocery store with the pram. I almost hid behind the curtain, but it was too late; she had seen me and was walking toward the café.

She sat across from me, struggling to fit the pram in the tight space between tables. "You left so early," she said. "God forbid you should help me with the baby. Did you forget I had a photo shoot this morning? I had to cancel it and reschedule."

"What photo shoot?"

"For the series I've been working on, about how all the old houses of Tehran are being destroyed to make room for high-rises. This morning I had arranged to photograph the house of Anis al-Dowleh, the favorite wife of Naser al-Din Shah. It's that building on Mowlavi Street that's now the headquarters of the butchers' union. I told you about it already."

"I'm sorry, I forgot. I have a lot on my mind."

"Hamid, you need to help me out," she said. "I don't know how long . . ."

The waiter interrupted her. She ordered tea and looked out the window.

"What don't you know?" I asked.

"I don't know how long I can carry on, like this."

I watched her, the lavaliere kissing the crater of her throat—an Italian cameo that she never removed, not even when we made love. It was a memento from her father, who had abandoned her and her mother in the winter of 1984, when Noushin was twelve. She had told me about the necklace one night early on in our relationship. Her father, she said, had offered it to her before he left the country for what he claimed would be a one-month business trip but what would turn out to be for good. He had picked her up from school on a Thursday, and they had driven to the video store to select a movie for the weekend, as they often did. They settled on *Being There*, with Peter Sellers as Chance the gardener, with the raunchy scenes naturally censored out. On the way home he had bought her ice cream, and in the car he had presented the cameo necklace—a portrait of a woman carved into a sardonyx shell. That evening they had watched the movie with her mother, and had laughed together at Chance's unlikely rise from gardener to Washington insider. The next morning, before dawn, her father was gone.

The tea arrived and she stirred it absentmindedly as she looked out the window, at a woman shouting at a motorcyclist who had nearly run her over. "I don't know how long I can carry on," she said again, this time mostly to herself.

"Noushin," I said. "Please don't complicate my life. You know what I have to contend with in that hellhole every day."

"Ever since we met you've been telling me that you are there because you are 'undermining the system from inside.' I think I let myself believe you, because of our own first encounter. After all, you let me go so easily, and all my friends, too. But you can't possibly be releasing everyone. So what do you do with the ones you keep? . . . Hamid, how do you live with yourself? Please quit. Get a decent job."

"This isn't a sports game," I said. "I can't switch sides, just like that."

The baby's squeals and her plastic giraffe banging against my chair earned us the peeved gazes of others. I picked her up and sat her on my lap, and this, the illusion of being safe, was enough to calm her.

That's when I told Noushin everything. My betrayal of my father—the germinal act of my downfall. The judge, the bubblegum soapsuds, Akbari's threats to arrest me for the judge's death each time I spoke of quitting. And H. His face, always that diabolical face.

Beads of sweat formed on her neck as I spoke; in a different time and place, I would have kissed them. When I was done she looked at the baby, now asleep, then stared at me, as if for the first time. I don't think she had ever allowed herself to imagine to what lengths I had gone, in that dark room where she, too, had once sat, and in which our romance had perversely been born.

"The answer to your question," I said, "is that I don't live with myself, not really. But I have a question for you, too: how have *you* lived with me, all this time?"

She looked around the café and didn't speak. After a while she said, "Being in the presence of violence that chooses not to harm you is its own kind of drug. Getting up each morning with the knowledge that you've been spared can fill you with a kind of elation. In this type of existence, each outlived moment is accompanied by the thrill of averted annihilation. It's a bizarre way of being, a teetering between the desire to be harmed and the desire to be spared."

"But why are you teetering between these two desires?" I asked.

"I don't know," she said. "For the same reason you are, I suppose? Each morning when you show up in that hellhole, as you call it, you, too, are in the presence of violence that has chosen not to annihilate you, but could."

I reached for her hand across the table and squeezed it, and we held on to each other, as two porcupines hugging.

Sunken in revelation as in quicksand, she let go of my hand and sat back, the sun in her face, tapping her teaspoon on the wooden table. The sound dissolved in the din of the café, where the day was now unfolding, as any other.

34

M Y BREAK WITH AKBARI occurred over a dead goldfish. It was Nowruz 2009—the vernal equinox, another new year. My daughter, just a month shy of nine years, had for some time been downhearted, so much so that the school principal had asked to see us before the holiday. "The girl is withdrawn and solitary," she said, stiff as a starched laboratory coat, tortoiseshell glasses at the edge of her nose—the kind of woman for whom the memory of good sex was as dusty as the underside of Margaret Thatcher's bedframe. "Golnaz no longer interacts with her friends and her grades are suffering. Maybe life at home is difficult?" I thought it a clever trap to have said, "Life at home is difficult," and not "*her* life at home is difficult," an invitation to us to expose the jagged intimacies of our family.

Noushin sat brooding in her chair, staring down at the linoleum tiles; I knew she was on the verge of confessing to a decade of acrimony. Leaning forward to preempt my wife's eruptions, I said, "It's possible that I haven't been as present at home as I should have been. Because of work, you see? Nothing that should concern you in the least, I assure you, *khanoum*."

The principal seemed to recoil at the mention of my occupation; she was well aware of my involvement with the Ministry of Intelligence. "I understand," she said. "I have no doubt that Golnaz is in a loving home, and that this is just a phase." Closing the child's dossier and forcing a smile, she continued, "Well, *eideh shomā mobārak*, happy new year to you."

OUTSIDE, in the cool sunlight of a March afternoon, a burst blood vessel swam in Noushin's right eye. She brought a ridged fingernail to her mouth and chewed on it, pacifying herself. Somewhere, I imagined, far beyond where we stood, orange blossoms bloomed and rosewater was distilled from newborn petals. And we, what had we to show for this new season?

I held her hand and she held mine as we always had, and we walked together down the narrow street, where a group of bicyclists, surely younger than we, sped past us, propelled by their still immaculate belief in their own possibility.

"I'll get a goldfish for Golnaz this Nowruz," I said. "Each year she asks for one and we never get it."

"You know how I feel about that," she said. "After every new year people dump their goldfish in the rivers and thousands end up dying. It's a cruel tradition."

"So we won't dump it," I said. "I'm sure Golnaz would love to keep it."

"Do as you like," she said. "At least you're finally interested in the child."

Across the street a vendor stood behind his cart of fire-roasted beets, filling the afternoon with sweet steam. "Do you want a beet?" I asked her.

"A beet?" she asked incredulously as she picked up her pace.

"Noushin," I said. "I'm sorry for my ways."

We walked home, the spring in our nostrils indifferent to our diminishing options.

GOLNAZ NAMED THE GOLDFISH Bolour and in the two weeks leading up to the new year she was less solitary, cheerful even. She placed the fish in a glass bowl that she decorated with gravel of different colors, and she talked to it and fed it and sang to it when she thought no one was looking. I found it mysterious that a creature so tiny and delicate could ignite in a child such joy, but remembering the three-legged cat in our garden I understood that the fish was lovable because it was blameless. Encouraged by her good humor—however short-lived—I decided to celebrate the new year properly, with all the heraldry the occasion required—the apple, the green grass, the vinegar, the *samanoo*, the *senjed*, the coins, the garlic, the mirror.

Noushin was not around much that week; her first photography book, whose publication had been delayed for four years, was at last scheduled to be released later that month, but was at the last minute again preempted by the Ministry of Culture and Islamic Guidance, which deemed several images—her self-portraits—"questionable" and "subject to further examination."

The problem was the lavaliere that appeared around her neck in every photograph. For one thing, the officials objected, the woman carved into the cameo had a seductive gaze, not to mention that sweetheart neckline of her dress, which suggested cleavage. Furthermore, the cameo's repetition in so many photographs was in itself suspicious. Was it supposed to symbolize something? Noushin insisted there was nothing subversive about the object's repetition—in her father's absence the necklace had simply become an extension of herself, like a phantom limb. The officials, not renowned for sentimentality, remained unmoved and suggested that she Photoshop the necklace out of the images. This was not possible, she countered, since the Ministry had previously approved the photographs and one thousand copies of the book were already printed. "Well, *khanoum*," one of the officials said, "the previous administration left us in 2005. It's now four years later and it's about time you bid farewell to our predecessors' lax ways. *They* may have approved, but *we* disapprove—it's as simple as that. However, bear in mind that when all options have failed, there is always the magic marker. You could, very easily, just black out your neck."

Undeterred, she returned daily to the Ministry, where she submitted herself to an interview that concluded vaguely and offered nothing but a postponement of a definitive verdict regarding the acceptability of the book. It was—she said one night between sips of the borage infusion that she drank for her frayed nerves—like being stopped at a border, neither apprehended nor admitted.

It was up to me, then, to create for Golnaz a new year's celebration that would not interrupt the calm she had found in her cohabitation with the fish. I spent two days shopping and chopping, cooking and cleaning, and that afternoon, when Golnaz arrived home from school, I felt no shame greeting her, as I usually did. I had placed the goldfish in the center of the table, next to the mirror, which shimmered in the spring sunlight, and it was this reflection of the red fish and the harmony around it that brightened my daughter's face as she entered the room.

I DIDN'T NOTICE when Akbari came in; in the daytime we left the front door unlocked. Golnaz was in the living room playing Pokémon and I was finishing up the cooking in the kitchen. From the open windows came the sound of a ball bouncing against a wall and the laughter of children freed from the confines of school. As I stood by the simmering pots contemplating my strange and accidental happiness, I heard a man's voice resonating in the living room. I ran out and was startled to find Akbari in his newsboy cap, arms crossed against his chest, cheering on as Golnaz stabbed the keys on her pocket Nintendo.

"To what do I owe this honor?" I said.

"Where are your manners?" he said. "You don't wish me a happy new year?"

"Yes, *eideh shomā mobārak*. Well?"

"Have you made up your mind about my offer?"

The day before he had informed me that he would be moving to Mashhad to help run one of the country's biggest charitable foundations, with stakes in scores of businesses. He had offered me a position at the helm of one of these, a fruit canning factory. "Hamid," he had said, grabbing a handful of *noghl*—sugar-coated almonds—from a bowl on his desk and pouring them into his mouth, "if you accept, you could become a rich man faster than I can swallow these almonds." The almonds were from his son's wedding a week earlier, an event that I could not attend because of a sudden and embarrassing pain in my scrotum.

The money I could gain by accepting his offer was naturally a lure. Charitable foundations had become the economy's chieftains. Having been, for centuries, beneficiaries of gifts and donations—known as *waqfs*—they had further expanded their assets after the revolution through the confiscation of factories and land whose owners had fled, disappeared, or been imprisoned. With their vast holdings they collected rent from hotels, shops, and farms, and through their construction division they built everything from airports and bridges, to roads and industrial water pipes. Many of the bosses were clerics with deep ties to Sepah Pasdaran—the Revolutionary Guard—though at times these very bosses also competed with Sepah. The entire affair was a labyrinth no one fully grasped, and I imagined that being involved with one of these foundations would be like running Disneyland, where everything a visitor saw, touched, ate, heard, or even smelled was owned or operated by Mickey Mouse.

When Akbari proposed the job, I did—at least initially—imagine myself in a vintage Porsche Carrera, pressing the gas pedal with the tip of a Ferragamo boot, driving with my family by the Mediterranean Sea on a road overlooking the Cap Canaille—Noushin's dream destination. But as I stood before him with my testicles on fire, I was reminded of the reality of my life and the lassitude of my middle-aged bones. There was, too, the old dogged question I could never be rid of, *How far are you willing to stray?* "I'll think about the offer," I had said.

His appearance on the new year was his way of demonstrating his displeasure at my hesitation. He turned now to Golnaz, who was still slumped in the corner of the sofa, her fingers banging on the Nintendo keys even more fiercely than before. "What do you think?" he said to her. "How would you like to live in a big house in Mashhad?" She ignored him and kept on playing. But when he added, with that loud, commanding voice that was so familiar to me, "Listen when someone is talking to you!" she dropped the game and looked up, her brown eyes wide and repentant.

Seeing the two of them face-to-face agitated me; I sensed the dual sides of my life catastrophically colliding. The pain, which had dulled since morning, shot once more into my scrotum.

"I'm not going to Mashhad," I said.

He raised a bushy eyebrow. "Maybe you don't realize that I am granting you a great honor," he said.

"I didn't become a revolutionary all those decades ago to end up canning peaches in some factory in Mashhad," I said.

"The factory is part of something far bigger, and more powerful," he said. "You know that very well."

"Maybe I don't want to be part of something big and powerful anymore," I said. I looked at Golnaz, and at our new year's spread, interrupted.

"What's the matter with you?" he said. "Have you had those balls checked yet?"

The previous evening, as we were both heading home, I had stupidly told him of my pain, forgetting that one must never share intimacies with a man like Akbari. A memory now came to me: a breathless moth in an airtight jar on my bedside table. I, a boy of eleven, sleepless in bed, watching its struggle with a flashlight, listening to its muffled wings through the glass.

"My balls are fine," I said. "I am just tired."

"We spent decades sowing seeds," he said. "Don't give up before the harvest, you fool. This is our reward." He gripped my forearm and leaned toward me. "Besides," he continued, "we've become brothers, you and I. We've been in this together, at every step, haven't we?"

This last invocation sickened me most perhaps because it was the truest. Yes, we had been in *this* together. For how could I deny that though my fascination with Akbari had over the years transformed into revulsion, there remained something of the original pull, a certain attraction to his lawlessness and cruelty? That his vulgarity, which so contrasted with my own polished and privileged upbringing, freed me from myself, and erased my ineffectual boyhood . . . That in his presence I became blind to suffering and could do with impunity what I dared not do when alone . . . That even as I learned to defy him by releasing increasing numbers of detainees, I remained, in the end, forever in his debt, for he was the one who had taught me how to play God . . . The idea that a goldfish and a new year's meal could turn me into a different man now seemed laughable; how could the life I had traced on this earth be so easily undone?

"Let us be," I said to Akbari. The shooting pain was now radiating into my gut and I collapsed on the sofa, next to Golnaz, who was holding on to a throw pillow with a torn seam. "Please," I said. "Let us be."

"From the day I met you," he said, "I knew you would falter. There was a piece missing in you, an essential piece. I tried, all these years, to fill you out, make you more substantial. But you are a hollow man, and a waste of my time."

"Get out of my house," I said. "You are nothing more than a provincial mercenary, and no matter how many ladders you climb, you will remain the lizard that you always were."

For some time he stood, staring me down with black eyes as he had done, decades earlier, with my father. Then he leaned over the coffee table, reached into the fishbowl with his liver-spotted hand, and pulled out the goldfish, which writhed in his tightening grip. Golnaz watched him, voiceless, and by the time she buried her face in the sofa armrest, the goldfish lay dead on the coffee table, and Akbari was gone.

35

LATE IN THAT SUMMER OF 2009, Noushin left me for the first time. It was the summer of mass demonstrations against a rigged reelection, the summer of bloodshed and batons. Each night she would congregate at Tehran University or Azadi Square with her friends, among them an artist she seemed enamored with, a fellow named Bahman, one of the originators of public art in Tehran in the 1990s. He had staged throughout his career bold exhibits on roadsides, in the backs of trucks, and inside abandoned warehouses designated for demolition. His most popular feat was a reproduction in a condemned warehouse of his childhood home: linoleum-floored kitchen, blue gingham vinyl tablecloth, tarnished samovar, white lace curtains—the surfaces that furnished a man's memory. Thousands came to see the exhibit before a demolition truck arrived one morning at dawn as scheduled, knocking down the decrepit building and with it Bahman's replica of his past. Interviewers asked him why he had selected a site doomed for extinction and he had said, "Without the extinction the artwork would have been nothing more than a banal exercise in nostalgia."

The night Noushin met him at some art reception, a few weeks after the goldfish incident, she tucked Golnaz in bed with a song—I think it was something by Shajarian—and an origami she had made with newspaper; I remember the word *compensation* imprinted on the bird's wing. Afterward, she began spending time with him, meeting for coffee and going to museums, encounters that I initially encouraged because they took the onus off me, but whose frequency was beginning to vex me.

During those summer riots their mobile phone exchanges multiplied; a nation's collective discontent, they seemed to believe, somehow sanctioned their private transgressions. Though I was pleased with the demonstrations—for I, too, wanted to be rid of the incompetent president—I was also in my legal right to have my wife arrested for partaking in them. Naturally, she was aware of this, and it was with defiance that she put on her green headband each evening and sent breathless texts to her lover to arrange the night's rendezvous, right under my nose. Often I wondered if she was protesting the government, or her life with me. To spare us both the embarrassment of our marital collapse, I watched her in silence and chose to say nothing.

Akbari, meanwhile, was as contented as a man who stumbles onto an unannounced banquet. In his final hour, just as he was preparing for his grand move to Mashhad, scores of demonstrators were put before him, awaiting his investigation. He postponed his departure. *The nation needs me*, he said.

On the morning of July 22, when the alarm clock rang, I opened my eyes to an empty bed. It was five o'clock and Noushin had not come home. I lay in bed, feeling under my calves the mattress's tired ribs. The familiar pain, which had diminished since the new year and for which I had yet to seek medical care, was suddenly back in force, a jackhammer in my scrotum.

She appeared in the doorway after dawn, a tear in her sleeve, a bruise on her right cheek. When she opened her mouth to speak I saw that she had a chipped tooth. "They got Bahman," she said. She walked to the bed and sat on the edge, smelling of caked blood and gasoline. "Hamid," she continued. "Will you help him?"

"There are people above me," I said.

"I know you can get him off if you want to," she said.

I cupped her bruised cheek in my palm. "Why would I want to?" I said.

She pushed away my hand. "It was never like that," she said.

"You think I'm an ass? All this time, right under my nose."

"This isn't about me, *it's about a man's life*."

"There are thousands more, like him," I said. "Why should I save this one?"

Looking down at the floor she said, "Because I love this one."

I STARED AT THE CEILING as she got up and packed a bag, opening drawers and armoires, removing from our shared space foundations for a life apart—clothes, underwear, hairbrush, face creams, books.

"Where are you going?" I said.

"To my mother's. I'll take Golnaz with me."

"How long are you going for?"

"I don't know," she said. "I need time to think."

"Think about what?"

"Just think," she said.

"You pick up and leave, just like that?"

"*You*, of all people ask me this?" she said. "How many times did you pack a bag?"

"So this is retribution?"

"Oh, Hamid," she sighed. "Not everyone thinks like you."

I STAYED IN BED as she went to Golnaz's room and listened to their muted voices—Noushin explaining, Golnaz protesting, the sound of drawers opening and shutting, bags being zipped— echoes of another absence being born.

She ran a bath, as she did every morning. The sound of water filling the tub made me believe that this was a day like any other. She wouldn't leave me, I reassured myself, not for long, in any case. Let her have her little adventure. God knows I had had my own over the years. Sooner or later she would tire of it and come home.

I made myself get out of bed and stumbled to the bathroom, steamy from her bath, and I watched her naked body as she lay in the water, her eyes shut. Bruises marked her rib cage and forearm. I wondered who had dealt these blows and whether it was someone I knew. Something propelled me to shave, an act that I knew would cause a small uproar: a government man walking around with the face of a Gillette salesman. At the sink I reached for my razor, but no matter how many times I wiped the mirror, the steam rose again, erasing my face. I could have opened the door but the last thing I wanted was to ruin Noushin's bath.

I shaved without a reflection, finally, tracing the blade along my chin from memory. Naturally I missed a few spots and cut myself more than once. When I was done I stood over the toilet, and as urine burned its way along my penis and dribbled into the bowl, I saw drops of blood accompanying it. The terror of demise liberated me from my reality.

ON MY DESK, that morning, his dossier was among the dozens stacked, waiting for my attention. I read through it—he was born in Shiraz, had received his art degree at Tehran University and his masters in London. Divorced, no children. His public art projects had been written about internationally, deemed by the foreign press as "groundbreaking," and "conflating the private space with the public realm in a highly dichotomous society." This man had not only stolen my wife, he had also stolen the life I had meant to live. I called him in.

"State your name," I said.

"Bahman Borumand," he said. He had the calm, obstinate face of a man with a grievance; I had once carried the same face.

"You have been charged with vandalism, acting against national security, and disturbing public order. What do you say in response?"

"I am innocent," he said.

"*Aghaye* Borumand," I said, "do you know a woman named Noushin Mozaffarian?"

"No."

"Don't try to protect her. By lying you exacerbate the situation. So I ask you again. Do you know Noushin, who works at Anahita Gallery?"

"I don't."

"Tell me the truth, you fool. Because I already know the

answer. It's right here in your dossier. If you deny it you'll make things worse for both of you."

"I know a Noushin who works at Anahita Gallery," he said, hesitating. "But her surname isn't Mozaffarian."

"Taheri, then?"

His earlier defiance gave way to alarm in the manner of a lover. "Is she all right?" he said. I could barely hear him.

With my chin burning from the razor cuts, I was sure I looked ridiculous—a man who can't even shave properly. "She is fine," I said. "Don't worry about her. She was taking a bath when I last saw her."

"You are familiar with Noushin?" he said.

"That's one way of putting it," I said, shutting the dossier. "She is my wife."

He swallowed so hard that his Adam's apple bobbed along his throat like a sinusoid.

"You still claim you are innocent?"

"What is this interrogation about, exactly?" he said.

I sat back in my chair and watched him. He was tapping a foot on the floor, his ears sticking out like a fly's antennae. Poor stupid man. If I hadn't felt that finishing him off would be akin to doing away with myself, I would have sent him to Akbari at once.

"Get out of here," I said.

He must have thought I was bluffing because he didn't move.

"Didn't you hear me? You're free. Go, and quietly."

He got up. "Thank you . . ." he started.

"Don't thank me," I said. "Just get the hell out of here."

AT MY DESK for the rest of that morning I did nothing but read a growing pile of dossiers. Around noon I got on my bike for air and tea. I rode up to the local café, where people had already be-gun streaming in for lunch, mostly the regulars from the prison and some new faces—no doubt families of the detainees. Akbari was there, on the terrace, biting into a sandwich. By the time I had started a U-turn he had already seen me. He made a strange gesture—part military salute, part requisition—and called out my name. "Have a bite," he said. "I want to talk to you."

I parked my bike and walked to his table. It was a faultless summer afternoon, the mountain air crisp.

"Sit down."

I did as he asked.

"May I order you some food?"

"I have no appetite. I just came out for air."

"What's with the close shave?" he said. "Your face looks like a baby's ass."

"It was time for a change," I said.

"Making progress with the dossiers?" he said as he chewed the last bite of his tongue sandwich.

"Coming along," I said.

"Rumor has it that you're stalling," he continued, slurping his Zamzam cola with a straw.

"That's why it's called a rumor," I said.

"Hamid," he said. "I'm watching."

"Watch all you like," I said. "There is nothing to see."

"But you are wrong: there is always something to see," he said.

I RODE NORTH ALONG THE RIVER, soothed by the sound of the stream. I thought of Bahman Borumand, roaming free, no doubt at that very moment exchanging sweet words with my wife. I thought of their reunion, later, and of their tender embraces. But instead of jealousy I felt only exhaustion, the weariness of a man trapped in the wrong life.

I rode some ten kilometers north to another teahouse, and as I settled on a carpeted banquette in the silence of plane trees, the pain resurfaced, knifing me now in the left flank. I cursed myself for my terror of doctors. Nauseated, I doubled over and vomited my breakfast, which I had eaten alone that morning at the dining room table as Noushin and Golnaz paraded before me, back and forth, gathering their belongings—one last pair of shoes, one more doll, and the identical turquoise necklaces I had bought them both one summer from Neyshabur, on my way to Mashhad with Akbari. The image that replayed before me now was of the two of them standing before me with their suitcases, looking like matryoshka dolls, indistinguishable in every way except in size.

The waiter offered me a kitchen towel to wipe my mouth. "Forgive me," I said. "I think I must be very ill."

"STONE," SAID THE DOCTOR, to my relief. "Kidney stone. Go home and wait until you pass it." He handed me painkillers and recommended I drink fluids. "But only water and infusions," he said. "Leave the other stuff for a better hour."

I returned to the empty house and spent the rest of the day in bed sipping Noushin's borage tea while the city convulsed around me. I remembered my father's gallstones, his "knife attacks," as he used to call them. We, Mozaffarian men, were skilled at one thing: making stones.

I stayed home that evening and didn't turn on the lights at sundown. Lying in the clotting darkness I pinched my own skin, remembering my youthful body from my revolutionary days. I missed my old self as one may miss a dead friend.

Before dawn it came—the stone—crushed gravel streaming into the toilet along with my urine and blood. Returning to bed and lying on Noushin's empty side, I allowed myself an hour of sleep then woke up, relieved but agitated, to scour the house like an ambush predator. I am not sure what I was looking for—perhaps after so many years employed by the Ministry of Information, snooping had simply become a way of being. I found nothing remarkable—crayons, notebooks, poorly folded clothes, half-filled handbags carrying the remnants of a forgotten day: dry-cleaning receipts, crumpled tissues, tampons, lip gloss, hair bands. But in Noushin's closet, next to her row of boots that stood guard like an army, I saw stacked crates of photographs, among them a box bearing my name and below it, in quotes, "The Interrogator." Inside were photographs of me, in black-and-white, chronicling my transformation from baffled revolutionary to aging captive of a life gone wrong.

I laid out the photographs on the floor in chronological order. The first, which Noushin had taken when she had been arrested, on that summer night a decade earlier, stunned me. Though I had seen it countless times before, I now noticed a pleading in the eyes, the kind you see in nineteenth-century photographs of people in ill-fitting suits staring helplessly at the camera. Engorged veins along my temples and the sides of my neck threatened to erupt at any moment.

The photographs that followed, twenty-seven in total, portrayed me in various positions of struggle. In one, taken in our living room, I was standing by the console, my arms crossed, wearing the tan python camo military jacket I had purchased from a Chinese website, looking down at Akbari—he was at least a head shorter than I—and nodding to him in absentminded deference. In another, dated February 2009—just a few weeks before the goldfish episode—I was holding my daughter's hand outside the prison gate, a yellow grocery bag filled with dossiers hanging from my arm. In this photograph I was looking to the side, and Golnaz, in her school uniform, was looking up at me.

I lay down on the floor, on top of the photographs, my body still convulsing from the passed stone. I shut my eyes, and the world became distilled to sound: the neighbor's hammer pinning a nail into the wall; the gurgle of the toilet tank replenishing itself; a leak in the faucet; the hum of car engines on the street below; glasses jingling in the kitchen cabinet next to the refrigerator. And, suddenly, this: my father's voice as he called out my name from the departure gate at the airport, *Hamid! Hamid!*

36

AFTER THE PASSING OF THE STONE and a week of indolence, I submitted my resignation, aware that Akbari could checkmate me at any moment, as he had threatened for decades, with the judge's death.

For a month I browsed the classifieds, each listing offering me alternate versions of myself—car mechanic, accountant, schoolteacher, magazine illustrator. Corpse washer, even. This last one seemed the most just for a man with my corpus of wrongdoing. In the end, having settled on becoming a gardener, I enrolled in an evening horticulture class that began in the fall and allowed me to immerse myself, on Mondays and Wednesdays, in fantasies of a life preoccupied with plants and bulbs. My classmates—housewives, amateur ecologists, and a few earnest young men eager to learn a craft—quickly bonded with one another but seemed unsure of what to make of me. Their wariness only grew when the teacher asked us to introduce ourselves and I said, "Hamid Mozaffarian, hoping to find a way."

In class, as the students discussed cycles of renewal and death, I would doodle in my notebook as I used to in school. Often, unexpected memories would grip me—the chipped snow owl encased in my vanished marble, for example, or the star jasmine vine that Uncle Majid planted one spring for my father's birthday along the south wall of our house. I remembered how the following winter, when all else was dead or dormant, the jasmines turned red.

FOR THE DURATION of that fall and early winter, I was a bona fide gardener. In the backyard of our apartment complex I planted perennials reputed to survive in confined spaces—little lantern columbines, two-tone lavender with silver foliage, and in the sunniest section, where Golnaz used to host tea parties for her dolls, a row of paper-white narcissus flowers. For some time I debated including tulips, those ubiquitous symbols of martyrdom whose image marked our murals, our stamps, even our flag. After digging the soil with the garden fork one afternoon I held the tulip bulb in my hand, remembering that this crescent-shaped flower had once been more than a symbol: it was simply a flower—Uncle Majid's favorite. I added a bed of red and yellow tulips, ten in total.

I didn't read newspapers, and turned on the radio only for the music programs. My bank account was depleting, especially as

Noushin had withdrawn a large portion of the funds. Thoughts of livelihood were expelled from my life along with the noise of the world. So when the phone rang one December morning and I heard Akbari's scratchy voice on the other end of the receiver, I held my breath, aware that reality had finally caught up with me.

"Dead," he said.

I had not spoken to another human being since the fall, except for the occasional exchanges with my classmates and the shop girl who advised me on bulbs and soil. "Who's dead?"

"You haven't heard?" he said. "The Cat! They've turned his funeral in Qom into a mass protest, but it will blow over soon. Son of a dog has been pestering us for twenty years. Well, no more *gorbeh nareh*. The Cat has finally exhausted his lives."

Images of that sticky summer afternoon looped in my mind. Flies around the fruit bowl. The blowfly inspecting flesh. And the Cat appealing to us to spare the prisoners' lives.

"But that's not why I called," he continued. "I wanted to tell you that I'm sorry things got so bitter between us. What are you doing with yourself? You disappeared again."

"I've been here," I said. "Gardening and studying horticulture."

He laughed. "At least come up with a lie that suits you."

"I've never been more truthful," I said.

"Are you well?"

"Well enough."

"Happy?"

"Enough," I said.

"Holding up financially?"

As was his habit, he had cracked the eggshell of my reserve. "I'm broke," I said.

"I'll bring you some cash."

"What is it you want?" I said. "A man like you doesn't just bring cash."

He paused. "Friendship means nothing to you," he said.

"Friendship?"

"You jackass. Thirty years, we've known each other."

"I'm sorry," I said.

"I will be over soon."

So it had always been with Akbari: I surrendered to him every time.

I made myself a cup of coffee and went down to the backyard, where I sat on a lawn chair, next to the narcissi. I spotted a milky white lizard—Akbari's namesake—climbing along the brick wall in the winter sun. I watched its spasmodic movements as it reached the top and returned to the ground, avoiding the glass shards left behind by the building's residents who, lured by the promise of the flowering backyard, had been congregating there nightly with food and drink. They came even though they knew that no flower would blossom until spring.

Akbari arrived with aviator sunglasses and an orange down jacket; he looked as though he were headed for a ski trip in Dizin. He pulled an empty chair next to me, sat down, and handed me a heavy envelope.

"Who knew you were also a gardener," he said. "But is it imaginary? Where are your flowers?"

"I've been planting bulbs," I said. "They'll bloom in the spring, assuming I've done everything right." As I spoke I felt ashamed of this time lapse between the planting and the promised bloom, a period of absence that could only be negated by hope.

He watched me like a parent indulging a child's preoccupation with a new toy.

"Thanks for the loan," I said. "I'll reimburse you."

"Never mind," he said. "I won't need the money once I get to Mashhad."

"And when would that be?"

"When this business with the demonstrations is finished. Today it flared up again, on account of the Cat's funeral. But it won't last. These things have a way of running their course."

Removing his glasses, he leaned back in his chair and shut his eyes against the sunlight. He had the rosy cheeks of a man who sleeps soundly through the night.

"You'd never believe what I found today," he said. "I was cleaning an old drawer in my office and there, crumpled in the back, was a piece of paper I had picked up from your console the day I came for your father's papers. On it was the General's phone number. It brought back some old memories!"

"What general?"

"The landlord at your family's house. The air force man, the guy with the polo shirts who liked horseback riding and Italian crime novels."

"My God, the General . . . But I thought he escaped. Anyway, that phone number was useless . . ."

"The number was useless, but it was written on the back of a receipt from a telephone store. We decided to check it out and see where it would lead. And that's where we found him! He was hiding in the shop basement crouched in a corner, surrounded by hundreds of receivers and wires. He looked like something out of a cartoon." Akbari chuckled and tapped his knee. "When we ambushed him I said, 'Expecting a call, General?' He didn't appreciate the joke."

"Well, it isn't funny."

"Idiot," he said, crushing a few shards of glass under his boot.

"If it weren't for me you would have ended up like him. The prosecutor was on your tail back then, because of your doodles all over town. I was the one who sang your praises and kept him from arresting you."

"I know. But why did you do that?"

"For one thing, I admired what you did to your father. Not many men would have had the guts. But there was more."

"More?"

"You were a prize catch. That a man of your background should serve in our ranks somehow satisfied me. Being among us went against every grain in your body, and yet I could tell that a part of you enjoyed it. What greater suffering is there, tell me, than a clash between a man's façade and his interior? I dangled the judge's death over your head all those years so you wouldn't quit."

"So you enjoyed seeing me suffer?"

"I never thought of it like that," he said. "But yes, we all did."

"Who's *we*?"

"All of us—the whole gang. Those of us who lived our entire lives in the backwaters that you only visited for a month or two on that storied Che Guevara motorcycle of yours. 'Here comes *aghaye philosophe*, with his French books and his *Star Trek* stories!' we would say when we saw you. You believed yourself superior to us, and we knew it. You were like a great salamander in a field of lizards, similar in appearance but in truth of a different species."

"Why tell me all this?" I said.

"Why not? You've defected. And besides, maybe I like you a little bit."

I thought of my daughter's mournful face as she watched her goldfish wiggling wildly in Akbari's fat hand. "What a vocation you've made," I said, "of the pain of others."

"You're no holy person either," he said.

A neighbor from the second floor—a recent divorcee who I knew had been taking maximum advantage of her new status as a single woman—arrived in the garden with a book. But seeing Akbari, whose prosecutorial face everyone recognized from the newspapers, she turned back around and disappeared into the building.

"It's a fine feeling," Akbari said with a coy smile, "to be feared."

"Do you ever have misgivings?" I asked him.

"Misgivings? About what?"

"Everything," I said. "For example, not heeding the Cat, on that summer afternoon."

"Let it go already," he said. "Why lose sleep over the death of people whose organization was repeatedly bombing us?"

"The organization, yes. It would bomb us to this day if it could. But those who were killed that summer weren't the actual bombers; they had been in prison for a long time and had no hand in the plot."

"That's a technicality," he said. "They belonged to an organization that did have a hand in it, don't you see? Maybe that's where you and I have differed, all along. You believe that each man is responsible for his own actions and nothing more; I believe that a man doesn't exist in a vacuum, that his affiliations either condemn or exonerate him."

I thought of Khavaran, that cemetery of unmarked mass graves where the bodies had been dumped, afterward. It had once been a cemetery for religious minorities, but after that summer it became something else. I had never had the courage to visit, and in any case, what was there to see? People said it looked nothing like a cemetery, that there were no tombstones, no signs, no markers, that it was a wasteland, nothing but clods of soil clumsily turned over. They called it *la'natabad*—the place of the damned.

"But what about all the others who were detained?" I said. "Many of them had no affiliations whatsoever."

"Every person has some kind of affiliation," he said, "whether or not he carries a card. Whoever was arrested was detained for a good reason."

"You know that's bullshit," I said.

"All this tree-hugging is turning you into a sentimentalist," Akbari said. "It doesn't suit you." He slapped my cheek. "Get it together, Hamid. You're better than this."

"What's wrong with this?"

He got up and straightened his puffer, which was a size too large. "What are you going to live on, your flowers?"

"There is no shame in that," I said. "My uncle . . ."

"Listen, Hamid. Some people create and others destroy," he said. "That's the way of the universe. With all your so-called erudition, you haven't understood this yet? You and I are among the destroyers. Stop trying to negate it, you'll only make yourself more miserable." He put on his shades. "So long, brother," he said.

37

As I RODE THE MOTORCYCLE words looped in my mind. *Noushin, I've been making changes. I've quit the job. I'm taking horticulture classes. Don't laugh, but I am becoming a gardener. Please give me another chance.*

The sun was blinding, and as usual I'd forgotten my sunglasses. I struggled to keep my eyes open but in the harsh light tears started falling.

"You . . ." was all she could bring herself to say when she opened the door. She was in a bathrobe, her hair wrapped in a towel. "You're so thin . . ." she added.

"I'm sorry to show up unexpectedly," I said. "Can I come in?"

She sighed but stepped aside.

The first thing I noticed when I entered was Golnaz's purple barrette on the coffee table. And a doll on the floor.

"She's at school," Noushin said. "And my mother is out for groceries."

She sat on the sofa facing me, crossed her legs, then leaned back. "Well?" she said.

As I tried to retrieve my prepared speech I couldn't help staring at her bare legs. How many times had I kissed those kneecaps, which now seemed unknown to me, as though they belonged to a woman I had just met? I diverted my eyes and tried to concentrate. *I've been making some changes*, I rehearsed in my head, as I had done the night before in bed and that morning in the shower. But somehow the rest of the words had deserted me.

"Do you want tea?" she said. "Or lunch, maybe?"

I had no intention to linger; her mother was bound to return at any moment. "I've been making some changes," I said.

"Oh?" she said, standing up.

My faintheartedness disturbed me; for decades, my entire adult life, I had been the one before whom people scrambled to remember prepared speeches. What was happening to me? I cleared my throat. "I'm asking you to come back," I said.

She tightened the bathrobe sash around her waist.

I told her of my foray into horticulture and the garden I had planted in the backyard, and of how the neighbors were assembling there nightly. Naturally I didn't say how, late into the night, people sometimes got rowdy or melancholic or belligerent, how their voices traveled up to my bedroom, aggravating my sleeplessness. To inject reality into my creation would be to strip it of its wonder.

"So you've become Chance the gardener," she said, laughing.

"I suppose so," I said. "But in reverse! I've gone from government insider to gardener."

As we laughed together I sensed the distance between us beginning to fill. But soon she added, "You sound like a deposed dictator promising reforms. It's too late, Hamid."

"It can't be too late," I said. "Are you still in love with that artist friend of yours?"

"That's over," she said.

"Then why haven't you come home?"

"I didn't leave you to be with Bahman," she said. "I was with him just so I *could* leave you."

"You succeeded. Now come back."

"We'll see," she said as she ushered me out, as cagey as the clerks she contended with at the Ministry of Culture and Islamic Guidance.

THAT AFTERNOON I RODE to the cemetery to visit Uncle Majid's grave, something I hadn't done in years. In the decades since his death the cemetery had filled up nearly to capacity, causing administrators to stretch its boundaries and offer multi-tiered plots. I avoided the crammed martyrs' section, dedicated to those fallen in war and combat, and with the help of my mobile phone and the cemetery's Bluetooth system, I was able to locate my uncle's grave.

I tiptoed through the maze of tombstones. A dry winter wind shook the branches of the pine trees, carrying with it a faint smell of tar. Several funerals were taking place at the same time and I avoided these as discreetly as I could. I walked on until I found Uncle Majid's grave, visible through dust and a pile of rotting leaves. I dispersed the leaves, wiped the grave with my winter scarf, and sat on the ground next to my uncle's grave, knowing that it was empty but for the scattered bones of a foot. I was sorry for the way he died, and the way he lived. I was sorry for his loneliness.

From a parked car outside the cemetery walls came the sound of a lone setār, the wistful notes of the stringed instrument puncturing my heart with a cleft of light; it was, I thought, a recording of Ostad Ahmad Ebadi, among my father's favorites. I looked at the two empty plots next to my uncle's, purchased decades earlier by my father for himself and my mother. For the first time since their departure I remembered my parents not as my adversaries, but as human beings with whom I had, once upon a time, shared a home.

38

W E FOUND A WAY BACK TO EACH OTHER, Noushin and
I. Or so it seemed during the first months after she returned. In the carapace of the apartment, we held on all winter,
suppressing vicissitudes with sleeping pills and poetry. Modest
gardening commissions came from acquaintances, and as the
first breezes of March thawed the earth, I believed that I was, at
last, finding my way out of my past.

Frequently newspapers featured articles about Akbari's work
at the foundation in Mashhad—a new hospital, a refurbished
school, more housing for the poor. What no one wrote about
were the accompanying photographs and the gradual shifting of

his appearance—manicured nails, tasseled suede loafers, Rolex watch. Next to him in these images stood the foundation's custodian, a cleric whose religious credentials were as mutable as Akbari's veneer: though for years he had claimed on his website to be an ayatollah, he had downgraded himself to hojatoleslam after the press had begun poking at his seminary records and his mysteriously absent theological theses.

I remembered a trip to Mashhad with Akbari some four years earlier. We had gone to visit his youngest brother, Mohsen—the last of ten children—enrolled at the famed seminary the Mashhad *hawza*. Akbari claimed to barely know his brother; the boy, he said, was still in diapers by the time he had left home at twenty. But he remained fond of Mohsen, because he found him unblemished and earnest, and therefore, he added—amusing.

We met Mohsen at a restaurant near the Imam Reza shrine, drowned by the sound of cranes and drilling at a construction site nearby. Throughout the meal Akbari, who had had a few months of seminary training after the revolution, teased his brother, whom he called the Theologian, on his research for a senior cleric who was writing a book on gender justice in religious law. "All teachings," Mohsen said defensively, "have as many interpretations as there are interpreters. You could have a patriarchal interpretation, a humanist one, a feminist one . . ." Akbari pinched Mohsen's cheek as he used to do with me. "Feminist interpretation?" he said, laughing.

Afterward we attended nocturnal prayers at the shrine, where we sat on red carpets in the majestic courtyard under a cool October moon, surrounded by thousands of pilgrims, the lights of the blue dome and the minarets glinting in the night sky. When the prayers concluded around two in the morning, scores of volunteers emerged with their brooms, sweeping in tandem like

Viennese waltzers. I shut my eyes, remembering that Attar himself had walked these very courtyards in the twelfth century, and sensing Akbari's body next to me—the pungent scent of his Davidoff cologne mixed with his sweaty socks, I felt a strange sadness over the cohabitation, in a single city, of so much beauty and so much deceit.

Now, settled in my refurbished life as gardener and family man, I encountered Akbari's photographs in the newspapers with the equanimity of a retired hunting dog.

"A GALLERY IN NEW YORK has offered me a show," Noushin said one morning in June as we sat at the breakfast table, between us bread and jam.

"All of a sudden?" I said.

"No . . . I've been talking to them for some time." She crushed a lavender flower in her hand and brought her palm to her nose.

Dread had already flared up inside me. I sensed her announcement as a harbinger of doom.

"You don't seem pleased," she said.

"I am," I said. "Congratulations." The sound of my knife scraping butter on bread slowed down time.

"There is one thing," she said, twirling her teaspoon now. "They want my Interrogator Series."

"Your *Interrogator Series*? You mean the photographs of me?"

"Yes, those," she said.

I had read somewhere that during the reign of Henry the Eighth the punishment for a toilet cleaner who had dumped filth on the street was to stand knee-deep in one of his own buckets of shit, wearing a headdress declaring his crime. Noushin's announcement struck me as similar—a postmodern pillorying.

"You can't," I said. "Give them something else. You have so many other series. The one of the Tehran metro, for example. The one about street art, or the one about the destruction of old houses and the rise of skyscrapers."

"I've proposed all of them. The Interrogator is what they want."

"Of course it is."

"I knew you would react like this," she said. "But why do you care? It's in New York City, the other side of the earth. And the gallery is obscure. How many people do you think will see it?"

"If you make someone stand naked in a public square, it doesn't matter if one person sees him or one thousand. It doesn't even matter if no one comes. It's the act itself that counts."

"I'm sorry," she said. "But I must do this. It could be my big break."

"I won't allow it," I said.

"You won't *allow* it? They are *my* photographs."

"They are *my* photographs!" I said.

"You are mistaken," she said. "They are photographs *of* you. But they are my creation and they belong to me."

She left the table, dumping the lavender in her teacup.

IN A CAFÉ that afternoon I sat with a newspaper I didn't read. Around me swirled gossip, soccer scores, politics, philosophy, the folding and unfolding of love affairs. Before me was a glass of freshly brewed tea with a mint leaf inside, reminding me once more of H. *You may try to put me out of sight, but you will see me every time you bring a glass of tea to your mouth, because I will be right there, sitting across from you, a face you will be unable to get rid of. For the rest of your days,* aghaye *Mozaffarian, you will be having a discourse with me.*

Now, twenty-seven years later, my reply to H. formed itself in my mind: *You could say that we are like the Greek symbolon, a single coin broken in half—a witness to an exchange.*

39

H OW EASILY THEY FIT INTO MY BACKPACK, her prints
and the electronic drive! An incorrigible Luddite, Noushin
had, over the years, delegated to me the task of backing up
her work. That night, as she slept, her mobile phone lighting
up with texts from Bahman Borumand—the bastard I should
not have saved—I slipped out of the house with the backpack,
and rode to my old office, where a shredder sat, ready for its
one task.

Though my pass had long expired, the guards recognized me
and let me through. The old grooves turned in the keyhole of my
office door, and I was back, the desk nearly as I had left it; with

the exception of seven model airplanes, all replicas of the Mirage F-1. My replacement was clearly war-obsessed.

I sat in my old *Star Trek* chair. Here I was again, Capitān Kir. I unzipped the bag and pulled out the hard drive, crushing it with a rolling pin I had brought for the occasion. Then I slipped the print photographs into the shredder's mouth, one by one, and I watched, with relief and fear, as slivers of my black-and-white self rained down in the bin.

The next morning, Noushin left me. This time for good.

PART

———◆———

THREE

40

"*AGHAYE* MOZAFFARIAN, you, of all people?" the interrogator said.

The window blinds of his office, drawn all the way, blocked out the afternoon sun. I recognized his face but couldn't immediately place him. Soon it came to me. I used to see him jogging in Park-e Mellat on the weekends, back when I would take my daughter there to see the first tulips. He had renounced his Caesar haircut in favor of a classic taper.

"Let's begin with your biography," he said as he extended pen and paper. "You're familiar with the routine."

"You already know me," I said, jetlagged from the long flight from New York.

"We know you in a different capacity," he said. "In this capacity we are strangers."

"That's absurd," I said. "I am the same man."

The mint candy box sat between us. On the lid was a picture of a bow-tied penguin in a clean, white, minty world. Only then did I realize how stupid the box was.

"Don't make this difficult," he said. "You have pen and paper. I'll leave you to it."

I sat before the empty page, pen in hand. I wrote down my name, my address, the schools I had attended, my work history, my position at the Ministry, and the reason for my trip to New York. I didn't mention Noushin and Golnaz—my interrogator already knew I had a family. I didn't include the names of friends either; I had so few left. When I was done, I sat waiting, tapping the pen on the desk. The senselessness of my life echoed in the room, and I wondered how long my interrogator would leave me there; among the most basic tactics, I knew, was keeping the detainee in a chronic state of uncertainty.

He returned some thirty minutes later with a glass of water, which he placed before me. I thanked him and took a sip—it was tepid and tasted of leeched plastic.

He scanned my so-called biography then looked up. "How did you, of all people, stray in this way?"

"I am as fallible as any man," I said.

"You have to do better than that."

"How shall I explain?" I said. "My story must be put into context."

"Just give me the story, plain and simple," he said. "I have no patience for context. The security man reported that for the duration of the flight you fidgeted with your pocket, which, it turns out, contained this." He pointed at the candy box. "Contraband?"

"Mints," I said, attempting humor.

"Suffering from a dry mouth?"

"Let it go, *sarkār.*"

He opened the box, stared at it perplexed, and as he dipped his index finger in the ash and brought it up to his mouth, I almost let him. *Let one man poison the other,* I thought for a moment before I held back his hand. "For the love of God," I said, "don't taste it!"

"Contraband?" he said again.

"Yes, contraband," I said. "But not the kind you think."

"Well?"

"It's my father," I told him.

He stared at the bits of bone mixed with ash glinting under the yellow glare of the table lamp. "Your father? . . ."

"He wanted to be buried here," I said. "I am merely a son honoring his father's final wish. And it's only a small portion of him."

"Where is the rest?"

"The rest is exiled, in America," I said.

HE LEFT ME ALONE again to seek further guidance—the matter was beyond his jurisdiction. I sat once more, taking inventory of the items on his desk. I was not sure what I hoped to find—a child's photograph, a handwritten letter—but there was no such object. Other than a glass of tea gone cold, the only item on the desk was a mechanical clock.

The room was hot. Night fell as I waited, and my travel clothes, already wrinkled and sweaty, now clung to my skin. A moth fluttered by the lamp, restless. It made a hissing sound each time it got too close to the bulb. I shut my eyes but sleep would not come. Which was just as well. For some time Golnaz had been appearing in my dreams as a baby, night after night. In one dream, I forgot her in the luggage compartment of a train, in another I dropped her in a soapy bathtub and watched helplessly as she was sucked into the drain along with the dirty water.

Outside the interrogation room, dim voices approached and disappeared. No one came. I got up, feverish, and paced, circling around myself like the mosquitoes I used to trap in glass jars when I was a boy.

Around midnight the interrogator finally returned with a piece of paper. "I spoke with Hojatoleslam Karimi," he said, and read the note: "*Breaking a dead man's bone is like breaking it when he is alive. Cremation is a great sin.*"

"A sin isn't necessarily a crime," I said. "What does the law have to say about it?"

"Don't play the fool," he said. "As you know, there are two sets of laws. You can argue all that with the judge."

"May I keep the box in the meantime?" I said.

"Keep it," he said. "But if you scatter even a particle of that dust, things will end badly for you. We've weighed it, down to the last speck."

ESCORTED THROUGH CORRIDORS more familiar to me than the lines etched into my palm, I was shoved into a cell, and put in solitary.

How many men had I sent to this room? How many had spent their final night on this very mattress? My own father, I nearly sent. When I shut my eyes, a memory came, of me and my father playing backgammon under the apricot tree in the garden. It was the summer after the revolution, the summer of idleness and waiting, the summer that would end in betrayal and exile. With his friends and associates dead or gone and his encyclopedia sitting untouched in his study—papers in a state of chaos he no longer knew how to contain—he seemed to have lost something essential, that martial confidence with which he had made sense of himself. He sat silent for hours, moonstone *tasbih* in hand, prayer beads bouncing in a loop, playing backgammon when I invited him to play. He neither lectured nor listened to the discourses of others. On a few occasions he said, "God knows what became of H. . . ." I wondered if his betrayal of his old friend and the convictions of his youth were tormenting him, and I interpreted his private torment as a communal victory, for the revolution and for myself.

BUT VICTORY IS as saccharine and short-lived as a stick of chewing gum. Once you grasped the workings of the new regime, you understood, as so many had before you, that to survive was to comply. What no one warned you was that while you were busy surviving, you were witnessing the exquisite power of your own indignation blazing through your fellow men. You asked yourself, *Is this destruction truly my doing?* When you saw that it was, you dropped your head in disgrace, but you also congratulated yourself, for having become the demiurge you always believed yourself to be. You had grown, at last, into your own mythology.

41

SOMEONE IN A NEARBY CELL cleared his throat every few minutes. The mattress gave off a dank, putrid smell, of sweat and sorrow, dread and grief. That mine should be added to it seemed like poetic justice, a Dantean *contrapasso*. But I was not afraid, not in the classical sense. My fate within these walls did not preoccupy me; I had lived enough, and outlived even more.

What I did fear was a voice that began corroding the inside of my brain—my daughter's voice. Three years had gone by since she had left, but the night of her departure haunted me like one of those dreams in which you show up, late, at your own funeral.

How can I explain? To explain would in itself be an act of indecency. I will, therefore, only recount.

A WINTER NIGHT, unremarkable at first. Dinner preparations, the evening news, the rattling of windows against the February wind. Despite this normality, which veered, almost, toward dullness, I felt a foreboding I could not name. As Golnaz and I sat through dinner and ate our *fesenjoon*, and even later, as we watched television for the latest soccer scores, I knew something was not right. She carried her phone nervously, stroking it and glancing at it when she thought I wasn't looking. "What's going on, Golnaz?" I finally said. She blushed, as she used to when she was a child, that good-natured girl who would follow me around the house with a straw in her mouth to inhale my cigarette smoke, and would accompany me every morning to the bakery for our daily *sangak* bread. "What? Nothing," she said. "Give me that phone," I said.

She looked at me the way those star-crossed men had back in the old days. Terror. Sorrow. A supplication for mercy. Those looks made me feel like God, *astaghforallah*—may God forgive me.

"Give me that phone," I said again as I walked over to her. She was slumped in the love seat in her jeans and frayed Coldplay T-shirt, the scalloped lace rim of her pink bra peeking from her low-cut neckline. Underneath her thick black hair—disheveled as usual—was a face that frightened me with its nascent female beauty. "Leave it, *bābā*," she said, clutching her phone. "Please."

It was that "please" that nearly did me in, the sweet invocation, so helpless and almost heartbreaking. But I was a veteran, by that point, a succession of pleases dotting my past like medals. I confiscated her phone the way I would wrestle an object from an opponent's grip.

The phone was locked. "Your password," I commanded against her stunned silence. She refused to comply. This, too, I was used to. And this much I had learned: most people comply, in the end. I only hoped to God she would make it easy.

If I had to name one memory from the moment my hand gripped her upper arm to the moment she revealed the password some ten minutes later, it would be the delicacy of her bones. Having rarely touched her since she was a child—except for occasional kisses on her forehead—I had forgotten that she had been, and still was, small-boned, almost elfin. This realization did not stop me from lifting her and laying her, facedown, on the sofa, pressing her body into the pillow, allowing her to come up for air every minute or so only to reconsider her refusal. In those final moments before she surrendered, as I held her down and watched her back heaving like her goldfish of yore, I began crying for the first time in decades but still could not let go. I remembered how I used to be afraid of embracing her when she was a baby, how I had known, even then, that I would one day break her.

FOR SOME TIME afterward she remained curled up on the sofa, taking deep breaths and mumbling to herself. Lacking the courage to face her, I went to bed, tears running from my eyes. Had I nearly suffocated my own daughter? And for what? Text exchanges with some boy, an adolescent crush gone sour. What else had I expected to find? As I lay in the dark, I heard her bedroom door creak open, and the sound of her catlike footsteps scurrying across the living room and out the door. I let my daughter slip out of my life, just like that.

42

F ROM THE HALLWAY came the familiar voice of the warden distributing breakfast. That he should find me in this cell, waiting for his offering, embarrassed me. To preserve dignity I decided to refuse food; sustenance and sleep were necessities I had been known to do without, far longer than most. The footsteps approached and the rattling of metal echoed louder.

When the door was opened, I was surprised to see the Minister. "I talked them into letting you go," he said.

"Just like that?" I said.

"You know this place much better than I do," he said. "Anything is possible here, isn't it?"

"And my father's ashes?"

"You can take them with you, but don't speak of it to anyone."

"How can I thank you?" I said.

"Don't," he said. "But listen, Hamid, you can't return to the Ministry."

"I understand," I said. "In any case, I think I am done."

We hugged as the old friends we should have been, and the scent of his aftershave filled my nostrils. I wished him well for the rest of his term. "Do you think things will turn out all right, in the end?" I asked, and he said, "I think not, as the world is inclining toward darkness." I put on my shoes, straightened myself up as best I could; if I hurried, I could still make it to the divorce hearing. "So why bother?" I said. "I mean all this effort, the diplomacy, the meetings with this or that official. For what, really?" The Minister stood for some time, his eyes examining the scribbling on the walls—fragments of prisoners' writings which must have added up to some kind of narrative. "What else can we do," he finally said, "but try to act, if only for the historical record?"

NOUSHIN LOOKED WELL. Her skin had a youthful glow and her black eyes were clear and luminous. Being away from me had done her much good.

"*Haj-agha*," she said to the judge. "This is my fourth attempt to get a divorce from this man. It's enough."

"Why do you seek a divorce?" said the judge.

She sighed. "I've already explained so many times. I seek a divorce because he has devastation implanted in him, and he makes it impossible for anyone to love him. *Haj-agha*, this man is radioactive."

"What have you to say?" the judge asked me.

Words had abandoned me.

"My daughter is waiting in the corridor," Noushin continued. "If he denies his brutality once again, I ask that she be allowed to come in and testify. *Haj-agha*, he is a selfish creature, an evil character, he . . ."

"*Khanoum*," the judge said. "This man is a respected official in the Ministry of Foreign Affairs. Please watch your tongue." He turned to me once more. "What have you to say for yourself?" he asked again.

"As of this morning I am no longer with the Ministry," I said.

"Very well," said the judge. "But that isn't our concern at the moment. Please respond to the lady's characterization of you."

The lady's *characterization*. How could I argue with it? Clutching the tin box in my pocket I thought again of my daughter, and the idea of facing her here, in this courtroom, hearing her account of that accursed night, was more than even I could bear. "Yes, *Haj-agha*," I said. "Everything the lady says is true."

The judge waited, as though offering me a chance to reconsider. "You seem unwell," he finally said. "Perhaps you wish to reconvene?"

Noushin knew better than to contest verbally. She crossed and recrossed her legs, unable to find for herself a calming position. She was wearing marine-striped espadrilles. I remembered her fondness for marine stripes, emblems of the Mediterranean summer vacations that she believed we would one day take together. For so long she had wanted picnics at the beach with white sundresses and wicker hampers, but the reality was always the same—sweat, city soot, wrinkled headscarves, clammy thighs, disappointment, the countdown back to the fall, to another winter, cold and dreary, when she would start again to dream of the summer, believing somehow that this one would be different, that this one, against all odds, would be dipped in the perfect shade of Mediterranean blue.

"No need to reconvene, *Haj-agha*," I said. "As I mentioned, everything the lady says is true."

Noushin looked at the judge, her face flushed and confused. She brought a cupped hand to her mouth and held it there.

"Fine," the judge said. "Then the rest is merely paperwork."

GOLNAZ WAS IN the corridor on a bench. No longer the elfin girl, she was seventeen years old, and she looked it. When she saw me her face changed, from defiance to alarm and back to defiance again. She looked away from me.

It occurred to me that never before had she seen me with a shaved head, and this must have further stunned her—this appearance of a tall bald-headed man, who was once known to her as her father. I walked toward her, my heartbeat heavy and irregular. "Golnaz," I said as I stood over the bench. "I'm sorry."

She didn't speak. Her hands were interlocked on her knees as though in prayer; her fingernails were painted hibiscus. Up close, she resembled her mother as I first knew her, and this was a strange thing, to be so confronted with the physicality of a past that was no more.

Noushin came out of the restroom and caught up with us. She was peaceful, like someone who has been offered shelter after years of wandering the earth. "I suppose this is it," she said.

"Yes," I said.

"Goodbye," she said softly. I remembered how once, when she was pregnant with Golnaz and we both lay sleepless in bed, I had turned to her and said, "So much sorrow . . ." She stared at me, her eyes full of a love I was incapable of reciprocating. "You mean so much sorrow in this world?" she said. "No," I said. "I mean in this bed."

I held her hand now for a fleeting moment, and she let me. "Goodbye," I said.

43

IT WOULD BE TEMPTING, even for me, to interpret the absence of enmity during my final interaction with my wife and daughter as an indication of redemption for my character. After all, as the reformed sinner Saint Augustine, author of *The Confessions*—the first confessional book and as such the original autobiography—long ago contended, in order to write about the form of your life, you must first die, albeit symbolically. Only when born again through a process of conversion, argued the Doctor of Grace, are you able to make sense of your own story.

Centuries later the Florentine Dante Alighieri reincarnated the autobiography with a twist: instead of a conversion there would be a divine encounter, carrying the narrator from Inferno to Purgatory to Paradise, a full circle that would begin in ignorance and end in knowledge. The point is that in the autobiography there is a time-honored tradition of redemption and repentance, which is a concept dear to all: *towbeh* for Muslims, *teshuvah* for Jews, *penance* for Christians—who doesn't appreciate a good metamorphosis story, a passage from wickedness to virtue? Even the contemporary secular tale, say, of the disillusioned drunk or the wayward hustler, hasn't escaped this familiar trajectory, of darkness to light, anguish to liberation.

But I, Hamid Mozaffarian, despite my fondness for redemptive tales, had no such conversion. For those who live their lives through narratives of improvement, this may be a disappointment, perhaps even a betrayal. Still, I am not entirely arc-less. If what prompted the change in my behavior fell short of repentance, it was nonetheless a final acknowledgment of who I was, and a longing to shelter others from what I was capable of. My improvement, if you can call it that, lay not in an actual betterment of my character, but in the absolute acceptance of what the world had made of me, and of what I had made of it.

BUT AS I MENTIONED, the temptation for hopeful interpretation is a powerful elixir, and my daughter was among those who initially succumbed to it. One week after our encounter in the courthouse she sent me a letter, handwritten in a careful script.

Bābā,
For the first fourteen years of my life, I tiptoed past you. I skulked in the darkness of your sleepless nights, the infinite depths of your whiskey, the silence of your

taciturn past. I was a makeshift child, in exile long even before my birth. When I left, on that cold morning in February, in a stranger's unheated taxi, the road signs dim in the fog, I knew that from that moment on all signs would direct me away from home, from you.

Seeing you at the courthouse the other day unleashed something in me.

I don't know where we can go from here, or if.

But I would like to find out. In two weeks I will be performing in a play at a small underground theater. (It seems I have a knack for acting.) I am inviting you to come. Details will follow.

Golnaz

44

INVITING ME TO AN "underground theater" was, I understood, my daughter's reaction to my metamorphosis: *underground* meant illegal, and as such was not approved by the censors at the Ministry of Culture and Islamic Guidance. Was she daring me?

We gathered in an old bathhouse turned playhouse—two dozen spectators crammed along the brick corridors. Noushin, too, was there. She nodded at me coolly; this was no reconciliation. I sat in a corner, removed from the others, most of whom were university students.

The play, titled "Six Ministers in Search of a Government,"

recounted the story of six actors who survive the crash of a Tupolev Tu-154 aircraft carrying the entire troupe of a theater ensemble. The five men and one woman—my daughter—who had been on their way to a festival to perform their roles as six ministers in a cabinet, now find themselves in a strange land, where the population lives harmoniously and where a rotating panel of advisers administers the affairs of the state. The actors introduce themselves: the Minister of Happiness, the Minister of Loneliness, the Minister of Morality, the Minister of Privacy, the Minister of Authenticity, and the Minister of Fury, this last one played by Golnaz. They explain that as they have no identity other than their assigned ministerial roles, they must, in order to live, find a government to serve in. The attendants of the unnamed state reluctantly agree to let them form a cabinet and to dispense nonbinding recommendations. Over time, as the ministers' counsel seeps into the citizens' lives, the ad hoc cabinet begins to contradict the laws of the state, until no one—the six ministers included—knows whom to believe.

I watched my daughter—the Minister of Fury—managing rage onstage by offering the people farcical concessions—permission to laugh before sunrise, permission to sing in the shower, permission to pick one's nose between the hours of nine in the evening and midnight. Her face was red from all the collective fury she could not contain, the smudged eyeliner on her lower lids leaving the appearance of faint bruises below her eyes, making her look sleepless or injured. As I watched her, an image of her as a baby in her bassinet appeared before me. Spring. Lilacs. White curtains quivering in the hospital room. It occurred to me that I would miss her more than anyone after I was dead, but soon I grasped the absurdity of this thought. Despite all my years on this earth, I was not cured of my solipsism.

AFTERWARD, AS HER FRIENDS surrounded her, praising her performance, I stood aside, waiting. She glanced at me from time to time, her eyes black and full of anger, but something else, too—a longing. She reminded me of myself at the Campbell's soup party, all those decades ago, when I had lashed out at my father and Yasser about the government's corruption.

Noushin whispered something in Golnaz's ear and walked out. Was I to stand there all evening, waiting for my daughter to make time for me? I waved at her from a distance and headed toward the exit.

Footsteps followed me. I turned around.

"You aren't going to talk to me?" she said.

"You seem very busy," I said.

"Busy?" she said. "I was just chatting with friends. What did you think of the play?"

"It was a fine Pirandellian attempt."

"That's all you have to say about it?"

"What else would you have me say? You've been giving me black looks all evening. Or just ignoring me."

"What did you expect? A red carpet?"

"Look, Golnaz," I said. "I am no fool. I know what you're doing."

"What am I doing?"

"You are full of rage, and you need me to witness it. I lived a version of this with my own father."

It was there, in an unlit corner of the theater, that my daughter fell to her knees, her voice breaking under the ochre brick vaults of the old bathhouse. Curled up on the tile floor, her silent, convulsing body became smaller, shrinking into itself. I stood for some time, unsure of what to do, watching her and surveying the exit. But something—maybe my father's ashes, which I had been carrying wherever I went, or just exhaustion, an inability to keep on running—made me kneel beside her. I held her and brought her head to my chest, a forgotten gesture. I remembered how once, after her mother was gone, as she had sat at the kitchen table crafting a paper menagerie for her art class, she had intentionally pricked her forearm with the scissors and watched with fascination as blood surfaced from her skin. As I confiscated the scissors and yelled at her never to do that again, she—transfixed by the immediacy of her own mortality—smiled with something close to delight.

I held on to her now, more so for myself than for her. She smelled, as she had when she was a child, of powder and honey, vanilla and salt. She would not let go.

45

TEN—THAT'S THE NUMBER OF TIMES I saw Golnaz after our encounter in the old bathhouse. We had tea twice, took walks in Laleh Park four times, met for dinner three times, rode once on my motorbike to Tajrish, where we ate steamed beets and chargrilled corn. On our final encounter we browsed a bookshop (she bought a translation of Cormac McCarthy's *Blood Meridian* and I bought nothing), then devised our way out of a makeshift quarantine with three other players at the Tehran Escape Room near Mostafa Khomeini Street, formerly known as Cyrus Street. I had assumed, given the nature of the game, that I would be the one to excel at it, but it was she who ended up unraveling most of the clues and deciphering the codes for our escape. "Never assume," she advised our team, "that a watch is a watch or a pen a pen. In this universe nothing is what it seems."

Our meetings were at first cordial affairs, nearly balletic in their decorum and restraint, but on the afternoon we rode to Tajrish she began to disclose more of herself, her circumspection giving way to undeserved trust. This pattern was not unfamiliar to me: I had long discovered that those who had lived their lives with caution often became reckless during interrogation. To protect her I tried, on multiple occasions, to steer her back to herself, to shelter her from forsaking words that she could not retrieve once spoken. But she viewed any such attempt on my part as a negation of who she was, which she equated to another form of assault.

For some time after leaving home, she said, she became obsessed with the Rubik's Cube she had found in the drawer of our living room console and taken with her to her mother's. "That cube," I said, "helped me pass many hours at the job . . . back in the old days, you understand, when every now and again we would have downtime . . ."

We had left the bazaar and were walking toward the square, the snowcapped Alborz Mountains visible in the distance. "I understand," she said. "Did you ever solve it?" I remembered how, whenever I could not bring myself to read one more dossier or walk into one more interrogation room, I would pull out the cube and rotate the columns, the endless combinations driving me into a trance that contained neither man nor file, only colored blocks, spinning, spinning, spinning. "I solved it just once," I said. "In those days the advertisement claimed there were three billion configurations and only one solution. But it turns out there are multiple solutions . . . And you? Did you solve it?" She laughed. "Once I had solved it I could not unsolve it," she said. "Which frustrated me. Because I wanted to go back to a state of not knowing, when anything was still possible."

It was on the afternoon when we went to the bookshop and later to the Escape Room that we had our most intimate, and, as it turned out—final—conversation. "I took something else from your desk drawer the night I left," she said as we walked along the edges of the old Oudlajan neighborhood. "Your notebook of drawings from high school. You had a character named Everyman Jamshid that was on nearly every page. He made me laugh—there was something so pensive yet sweet and earnest about him, with his sideburns and upturned collar and cigarette. And there were so many other drawings besides: caricatures of army generals as pigs, and garish kings trapped on Ferris wheels. And one that I liked in particular: a dandy riding a donkey, wearing house slippers with the image of Cyrus the Great woven into them. I could not believe that you were the creator of these images, that a man such as you had once upon a time been capable of humor." She placed her hand on my arm—it was the first time, since "the incident" as she called it, that she had initiated any physical contact between us. "Did you miss the notebook?" she said.

"No," I said. "I didn't even notice it was gone."

She was silent for some time. "That's what's absent nowadays," she said. "Humor, and lightness."

"How do you retrieve humor, and lightness?" I said.

"I think," she said, "that they only come once you have traveled a sufficient distance from your own grief."

"How far is sufficient?" I said.

"Farther than you'll ever travel again," she said.

"Do you remember the puppet shows I used to perform for

you and your mother?" I asked. "Maybe you were too young, and have no recollection."

"I have vague memories," she said. "Flashes of the puppets and their squeaky voices and all of us laughing. But maybe this isn't my own memory, but an echo of Mom's recollections, because she never tires of speaking about that period, of the nightly plays and the familial laughter. 'Back then,' she always says, as though to appease herself for her lost years, 'we were truly happy.' But maybe she is right, maybe we were truly happy. Maybe that was the last time you allowed lightness to live through you. I wonder if it can happen like this, that grace can just take leave of a person one afternoon . . ."

I said nothing. Her indictment of me was brutal yet just.

"I did find the puppets," she continued, "in that same drawer from which I took the Rubik's Cube and the notebook. There was a bald one with a T-shirt that read *Pahlevan Kachal* . . ."

"Oh yes," I said. "He was my favorite—the protagonist of most of the plays. The bald hero who saved the day. It's too bad you don't remember."

"Well, here you are, so many years later," she said. "You've turned into Pahlevan Kachal, except you didn't manage to save the day, did you?"

"Golnaz," I said. "Do you think you will ever forgive me?"

"Forgiveness isn't the point," she said. "The best I can do is try to understand. But I am not sure I am able to."

Night was falling. A clean, black winter sky masked the day's pollution. "When I was young," I said, "after my family left, I slept on the roof whenever I could. The stars in their multitude comforted me when I felt very alone. I believed that we were all connected, somehow, in our separateness."

"The problem with your generation," she said, "is that it suffered too much and inflicted too much suffering. There isn't any way for us to undo that history. We are all trapped inside it."

I COULD NOT HAVE KNOWN, as we said goodbye by the metro station, that this would be the last time I would see her. In fact, we had made plans to meet the following Thursday for a movie. But as she descended the stairs and disappeared underground— she was on her way to meet friends for dinner—I was besieged by a restlessness I hadn't felt since our reconciliation had begun.

46

WHEN I GOT HOME a rotten taste swam on my tongue, vanishing after a glass of water but soon resurfacing from deep within my throat. I grabbed some cheese and a loaf of bread and sat at the kitchen table by the open window. I ate voraciously, satisfying a cavernous hunger. The night whirled around me. I had pain all over, pain I could not explain, in my back, along my calves, in my bones, even in my groin. Heartache swells in the body, like lost time. Someone in the apartment upstairs was again rearranging furniture. The ceiling rumbled with the vibration of tables and chairs being dragged back and forth.

Before me I saw H., his keen eyes, his goatee, and his grit.

Of the countless men and women who had over the years sat before me, his was the last human face I remembered. Those who followed had transformed, over time, into a faceless composite, reduced to nothing but colors and forms. If H. had lived in me as a painting by Goya, the others added up to a Rothko, as a mirror held up to my very marrow.

I knew what I had to do. I knew it because I had used up all other possibilities. It was time for the past—that black decade that began after our revolution and culminated in the summer of 1988—to infiltrate the future. In the console drawer, where I had kept the Rubik's Cube and the old notebook and the puppets, was the recording of the Cat admonishing us. I was going to release the tape, even though I was well aware that the release would make no imprint, as those involved, chief among them Akbari, would deny the past with a shrug, as they had all along. And the population, riveted for a day or two, would soon let the matter slip back into the blackout from which it emerged. You could not call it oblivion, because in order to forget one first has to remember. And we, inheritors of an unclaimed past, could not be faulted for misremembering when denial was our primary language.

But what of Golnaz? No doubt after hearing the recording she would refuse to speak to me. She had already overstretched her heart; to stretch it any further would cause a rupture. Yet it was my last conversation with her that had triggered in me a desire to release the tape, to act, in the words of the Minister, *if for nothing else than the historical record.*

I had the recording converted to an electronic file the next day. Later, at my computer, as I reviewed the e-mail I had prepared for a dozen newspaper editors—reading and rereading it, the audio file attached as an ampersand—I felt incapable of pressing Send. Was my impulse to act for the sake of archival testimony worth the loss of my relationship with my daughter? But if, as she had concluded, the suffering that my generation had borne and inflicted could not be undone, then should we not, at the very least, offer our progeny this smallest of courtesies: the truth? What else was left for me, other than bearing witness?

THE TAPE'S RELEASE, as I had predicted, caused a minor uproar, followed by uniform disavowal. No crime could stick, because the fortress had been built in Teflon. On the third day after the news broke, I received a letter from Akbari:

> As I said long ago, from the moment I met you, I knew
> you would falter. Well, you've done it at last. This time
> for real. *Mobārak*—congratulations!
>
> Instinct dictated that I retaliate against you. But
> I reconsidered, not for charity (as you well know),
> but because your grand attempt at righteousness is
> inconsequential, not only here, but everywhere. This, my
> brother, is the reason: the world—that very world that
> for decades condemned us for our actions and denials—is
> now outranking us in both cruelty and duplicity. Look
> around you. From the Americas to the Caucasus, the
> world is draped in malice. Massacres, migrations, the
> exodus of people and their dignity—no one gives a damn!
> And in a great sea of darkness, what chance is there for
> the little goldfish that wanted to prove the possibility for
> justice?
>
> If I were a man prone to sentimentality, I would have
> harbored resentment over your betrayal of our friendship.

But sentimentality is not my trade. And if anyone is at fault, perhaps it is I, as you showed me your true colors early on. Didn't our friendship, after all, begin with betrayal on the day you invited me to liquidate your father's encyclopedia?

To end with one of your own favorite expressions: *bāz gardad be asleh khod har cheez*—everything goes back to its origin.

Mostafa Akbari

47

I WOKE UP TO AN ORDINARY DAY. Kettle whistling, milk boiling. To say that what I had done offered me quietude would be a falsehood. But I did sense a correction in the alignment of my compass, and this felt like a compensation, however small. The recording was already fading into entropy. No matter. I had acted, for once, in deference to the future.

I stood before the sink, reached for the razor for the daily grooming ritual. But something propelled me to rummage through the bathroom vanity to find the shaving brush my parents had offered me on my eighteenth birthday, the last birthday we would be together. Declaring a truce for one night, we had

had dinner at Café Naderi, then, at Omid's request, had driven in my mother's Fiat to Karaj for ice cream. My mother had sung in the car, an old Delkash tune, and my father had joined her with his untrained voice. The August night was heavy with their honeyed duet, the rosewater-saffron ice cream, and the scent of embarkations and farewells. We were, all of us, at our kindest, not wishing to undo the goodness that had so suddenly been born among us, a goodness that, like a queen of the night flower, would die by daybreak.

I removed the brush from its dusty packaging and held it under the faucet, warm water softening the bristles. I lathered it and brought it to my chin, the white badger hair against my skin a reminder of indulgences of times past. How different my life had turned out from the one my parents had wished for me at eighteen, the life of a man who would greet each day with a German-made black silvertip shaving brush, a man like my father.

The question of the ashes, I had yet to resolve. Now that I had them, I didn't want to let them go. But I had promised my mother and Omid that I would scatter them. Where? The Caspian Sea? This struck me as hackneyed. The grounds of our old house would have been seemly, were it not for the fact that after I moved out the property was confiscated by a charitable foundation and was offered to a Basiji militiaman, whom I knew too well. What of the empty grave next to Uncle Majid's, which my father had purchased for himself long ago? This last option seemed the most apt, but to bestow to the earth a handful of his ash in place of his body seemed wrong even to me.

MY PHONE BEEPED from the kitchen. I rinsed my face—I had cut my chin as usual—and hurried to it. I hadn't heard from

Golnaz since the tape's release and had a premonition that the text was hers. It was. This is what she wrote in an attached letter:

I've come to the conclusion that I can't understand.
On one of our walks you said, "The revolution was the expression of an impulse to create something new, not just a duplicate of Plato's Republic, or the Magna Carta, or the French Revolution, or whatever else existed before. The revolution was a gesture toward self-realization, a manifestation of a people's desire to honor itself." This, I accept. But how does one account for what happened after?

Leave us now. We, your inheritors, don't want to hear about your old revolution anymore. We want good friends, devoted lovers, nights of music, days of discourse and ideas. It's life we want, and love . . . I'm sorry, bābā, for us both. Take care of yourself.

48

ON THE IDLING TRAIN TO TABRIZ a vendor walked in with a tray of sweets. I bought a walnut *koloucheh*, placed it on top of my cup of tea. Steam slowly softened the dough, and I took a bite. Butter, walnut, sugar, cardamom. A memory of my father's writings being spirited away in the garbage bags circled my mind like a noose.

As the train pulled out of the station, a young man, breathless, walked into my compartment and placed his suitcase overhead. "I almost didn't make it," he said in a thick Azeri Turkish accent as he sat across from me. "My family would have been disappointed if I were to miss the celebrations."

"Celebrations?" I said.

"Tomorrow is the winter solstice, *shabeh yaldā*," he said. "Did you forget?"

I wanted to ask about his family but I was tired. The air was heavy with the smell of frying meat that wafted in through the half-open window. Somewhere on the platform, children were arguing.

IT HAD BEEN three months since I had put the ashes in my pocket. I had been to parks, the old bowling alley, the kiosk where my father bought his morning newspaper, and our family apartment, where I saw the current occupants, the Basiji with his wife and three children, the youngest still a baby, setting off together on some weekend excursion. I didn't understand how a few grams of ash in a pocket could offer a man such condolence. But for the first time in decades, I felt accompanied, and safe.

I was headed to Tabriz because I wanted to see the Aladaglar Mountains, the presumed site of Uncle Majid's demise, in the company of my father. When we reached Qazvin I walked to the dining car, propelled not by hunger but jitters. On the way I passed the diminutive tea vendor tucked into a compartment the size of a janitor's closet. A tarnished samovar behind him, he was surrounded by tea, sugar cubes, and extra pillows and blankets. The old man appeared to have shrunk to accommodate the size of his room. I said hello as I passed, but he looked at me perplexed, his capacity for speech reduced to the necessities of a tea transaction.

In the dining car I shared a table with a mullah in a *qabā* eating chocolate pudding and playing a game on his smartphone, his fingers pounding the keypad. Every now and again he would say, "Damn, I died again . . ." Then he'd look up, take a breath, have a spoonful or two of pudding, and launch another game with redoubled resolve. I ordered a pomegranate soup, which arrived fast. It was the color of rotten cherries.

I looked out the window, at the docile cows, the pickle-green pastures of late fall, the sandstone houses, and the snowcapped mountain ranges of Qazvin becoming visible. My familiar aversion toward myself was matched at that moment only by my scorn for the world's indifference to my actions. I pulled out the tin box and placed it on the table; the cleric was too engrossed in his game to notice.

Sadegh Mozaffarian—for this was my father's name—the man I had failed to know. Son of Ahmad Mozaffarian, shift supervisor at the oil refinery in Abadan and census taker in Tehran, and of Nasrin Mozaffarian. I saw him as a newborn, his ill-timed arrival landing him in a raft teetering in contested waters, neither here nor there. And as a boy, running barefoot along the palm trees of the Karun, his birth certificate the only testament to his legitimacy as citizen and persona grata. Or later, as a young man in Tehran, wearing his first pinstriped suit and Oxford shoes, studying Caravaggio and Delacroix while listening to a recording of a lute, his favored musical instrument throughout his life. And later still, now husband and father, drinking Cointreau at some ministerial dinner, his monogrammed cigarette lighter kindling his Dunhills as he bequeathed to his fellow diners one of his famed monologues on the amaranthine history of art.

Here he is in Isfahan, where we traveled with Uncle Majid in my eighth year, at Ali Qapu, the portal to Safavid palaces. As we walk through the seventeenth-century edifice, where Shah Abbas received guests and dignitaries, my father falls into one of his homilies. Shah Abbas, he tells us when we reach the sixth floor, known as the Music Hall, that mightiest of the Safavid kings, in the process of uniting the country—politically, socially, economically, and religiously—also urged the artists of his day to create a uniform style, reflected in everything, from the tiles and murals that graced his palaces, to mosques and shrines and public squares, to carpets and textiles and book arts. As my father speaks, his voice amplified by the circular niches of the room, a crowd swells around us, tourists and locals passing through, all enthralled by the speech of the professor contextualizing for them a fragmented patrimony they are expected to make sense of. The more the crowd surges the more thespian my father becomes, and as he discourses on the expanded scale of ornamental motifs, say, the split-leaf palmette arabesque on the dome of the mosque of Sheikh Lotfollah, he seems to me clownish, a parody of himself. The apogee of his speech is the homage to Reza Abbasi, whose frescoes of rose-lipped, almond-eyed youths in rich textiles encircle us. These portraits, my father clarifies, were painted before the artist broke free of the court and evolved his own style, his subjects no longer the idealized youths of Safavid splendor but the everyman he encountered in the town square—the scribe, the horse groom, the pilgrim. The form of the paintings, my father continues, reflected the content, and vice versa. But by this point his audience is dwindling, and attention has shifted from art history to lunch. And we, captive family of the orator, hungry and silenced, linger with him in the deserted music room.

So the Safavids had created a narrative of themselves, and their art was designed to express this chimera. That is, after all, what humans have done since the beginning of known time, offering meaning to their existence where no meaning exists.

Every dynasty, religion, government, tribe, generation, and family compiles a story of itself. Some succeed in fooling themselves and others about the authenticity of their tale, others falter. What I failed to see as I stood trapped in the Music Hall of Ali Qapu was that my father, too, as all men, had all along been constructing a chronicle of himself. He did this through the compilation of his encyclopedia, legitimizing his origins by turning himself into the lexicographer of our national heritage. Would he have succeeded, had I not ransacked his mythmaking? I, his son, who had undone him in a single act of biblioclasm, had not foreseen that annihilating his narrative would annihilate a part of my own.

BACK IN THE overheated train compartment my young roommate had already fallen asleep, beads of sweat on his brow. I draped my coat over the heater and opened the window, but its levers were loose and it kept closing. "It's so hot I could cook an egg on my bald head," I said to the old tea vendor as he made another round through the train. "Wait until we get to Zanjan," he said. "Your bald head will be as stiff as a popsicle."

In the heat, I, too, fell asleep and dreamed that I was young again. I was checking into a run-down hotel with H., somewhere by a sea, maybe it was Anzali. The clerk gave us two keys, but once upstairs we saw that the rooms assigned to us did not exist. We walked along the dark corridors, a lightbulb flickering on and off. H. put down his suitcase, and as he sat in the musty hallway he said, "Hamid, I'm very tired." I said, "I know," and sat down next to him. I held his hand, which was burning. *I am holding H.'s hand*, I thought in the dream. *So he isn't dead, after all, he is alive, he is here.* Then he dissolved and I screamed, the way one screams in a dream, like a choking animal. When I opened my eyes the old tea vendor was holding a glass of water out to me.

As predicted, an icy wind swept through the compartment once we reached Zanjan. The train began its ascent, and the window banged open and shut, open and shut, heat and cold alternating, making us shiver. Suddenly, there it was, the tip of the rainbow mountain, which in my mind belonged to Uncle Majid. A "giant birthday cake," as he had once called it. *Look, bābā*, I whispered to the tin box, *we are here, together again with Majid*. I shut my eyes and saw my father place a Märklin passenger car on a rail, oblivious of me, as was his way. But I didn't mind his indifference, as I once had. I enjoyed watching him, and this, the knowledge that I could go on watching him for the rest of my days, consoled me. Remembering the seventeenth-century picture book my father had once offered me, I whispered the lines I had long ago memorized, *The Memory, under the hinder part of the head, layeth up every thing and fetcheth them out: it loseth some, and this is forgetfulness.*

At the Tabriz train station I said goodbye to my young companion, who had slept the entire trip, then bought a return ticket back on the night train. It was dawn in Tehran when I arrived, yet people were already shopping for the evening's festivities. I found my motorcycle where I had parked it near the bazaar, and rode northward, craving air. But in the miasma of rush-hour traffic the day grew thick around me, turning each breath into something I had to think about. Bikes, mine included, snaked through cars with little regard for traffic lights. Pedestrians cursed at vehicles and at one another.

Uptown the air was cleaner, carrying within it a scent of oblivion. After breakfast I browsed the chic shops, postponing as long as I could the hour of my return to my ghostly home.

In one shop I found flour sacks fashioned into designer pillows. "The rustic look," the saleswoman said. In another shop, Swiss-themed, I considered dozens of watches but bought none. I did buy a cuckoo clock, maybe in memory of my mother and the Swiss boarding school of her romanticized girlhood, her edelweiss days at the Collège Beau Soleil in Villars-sur-Ollon, amid thermal baths and chalets overlooking Mont Blanc, just a short drive—as she liked to tell us—from the lakeside towns of Montreux, Vevey, and yes, Evian.

In one more café, instead of ordering the tea I had intended to drink, I asked for hot chocolate, the drink of my boyhood. Three women on the far edges of youth, smooth ponytails visible through sheer headscarves, sat at the café's opposite end. With their bracelets jingling like wind chimes, they left lip-glossed stains on the rims of teacups that would soon be washed and refilled and offered to those who would come later in the day, and later still—a succession of washed-out kisses that would never meet.

BY THE TIME I left the café daylight was already dulling. A woman asked me for the time. "Almost five o'clock," I said. She thanked me and walked away, but turned back. "Would you like to come with me?" she said. "An ensemble of young musicians is giving a concert in Parvaz Park for the winter solstice." I thanked her and told her I could not attend, though by refusing the invitation I felt I was rejecting life. A grimace must have reflected my ambivalence. "Don't worry," she said, laughing. "It isn't so serious, I assure you!"

As she walked away I surprised myself by calling after her. "I changed my mind," I said. "I'll join you." We headed together to the park. She was fortyish, pretty. Angelic dimples and whimsical gray eyes. "Is that a bird in your bag?" she said. "A cuckoo clock," I said. "How quaint," she said. "You must be a romantic." We entered the park in the half-light of dusk. "It's possible that I once was," I said.

The concert was under way when we arrived. An ensemble of five musicians with santoor, setar, kamancheh, ney, and daf. As I sat listening, music carrying me back to my own beginning, I felt myself a misplaced man. Were I, for instance, some forgotten hat, left behind in a train compartment, or a glove, dropped from a pocket of an unsuspecting traveler, I would no better understand my location in the world. But no matter. I was still here, after everything. I thought of that winter solstice of decades past, when I had sat for the last time with Minoo in the mirror shop.

A boy walked among the listeners, offering rosebud garlands for sale. I bought two, one for the woman and one for my daughter, though I knew that I would not be seeing Golnaz again. I placed one over the woman's neck. She smiled, pleased with her decoration, then took the other garland from my hand and slipped it over my head.

"When I was a child in Khorramshahr during the war," she said, "my parents and I would huddle next to the record player during the blackouts. Music would drown out the air raids. I don't know why this memory came to me now."

I gently kissed her forehead. "Everything will be all right," I said, for lack of anything better.

The setar player was now riffing solo. The sound of his pear-shaped instrument vibrated in the winter night, convincing me, as nothing else had managed to do, to let my father go. I turned to my companion. "Excuse me," I said. "But I must take care of something."

She nodded and gave me a sweet dimpled smile. In a different time I would have tried to woo her. But I was too bone-weary for that.

I walked to the edge of the park. Below me, the outstretched city, lights flickering in the night. I remembered the city of sand Omid and I had once built on the beach in Babolsar, *the dwellings, the date grove, the clay pit, and even the temple of Ishtar.* I took out the tin box and opened it. My father's ashes, like a flock of snowbirds, flew into the winter branches of a sycamore tree. Under my tired breath I said, *Then I wept for seven days for the lost past with Enkidu, and for my future death surely so soon to come.*

I RODE HOME, the rose garland around my neck shedding petals along the way. In the kitchen, as I poured myself a drink, my phone rang. It was Omid.

"There was an article in the paper this morning," he said. "About that tape you released."

I didn't reply.

"You did the right thing," he said.

"One right in a landslide of wrongs," I said.

"*Bābā* would have been pleased," he said.

"By the way," I said. "Where did you scatter his ashes?"

"I couldn't think of a place in America that had any particular meaning for him. In the end I poured them in one of the giant planters in the lobby of the Metropolitan Museum."

"Well done, brother! I also released the ashes tonight. In a park overlooking the city."

"I think he would have liked that."

"There was a concert for *shabeh yaldā*. An ensemble of young musicians."

"It's all theirs now," Omid said.

"What about us?" I said.

"We are a skipped generation."

Yes, we were a skipped generation, a hiccup in history. I held the phone and let myself feel our age—my brother's and my own—not only in years, but in our increasing irrelevance.

"Omid," I said. "Do you celebrate *shabeh yaldā* over there?"

"We don't," he said. "Here the winter solstice means organ recitals in grand cathedrals. Usually Bach."

"What time is it there?"

"It's almost three in the afternoon."

"Isn't it strange," I said, "that our solstice is almost over and yours is just beginning?"

"Are you high?" he said, laughing. "You sound like a teenager on weed."

AT THE KITCHEN TABLE, drink in hand, I stared for some time at the mint candy box. I pictured my father as a suited figurine inside a Märklin dining car, riding from a planter in the Metropolitan Museum to a sycamore tree in Tehran, and back again—in a timeless loop. When I noticed the cuckoo bird sticking out of my bag, I pulled out the clock, hung it on a bare nail on the wall, wound the chains, and watched the yellow pendulum sway back and forth. Leaning toward the table, I laid my head on my forearms and fell asleep. The red bird bounced out of its cage and called out the time at the top of every hour. I let it. I longed for daylight.

ACKNOWLEDGMENTS

I would like to thank Ileene Smith, whose intelligence, insight, and dedication made our work together feel like a true collaboration; I feel so fortunate to have had the experience. I am also indebted to Jonathan Galassi and Mitzi Angel for their vote of confidence, and to everyone at FSG for continued support and enthusiasm. And my deep thanks to David McCormick, steadfast agent and friend, who has stuck by me through good times and bad.

Over the years I have been sustained by the generosity of many organizations, including the Whiting Foundation, PEN America, the Jewish Book Council, the Sami Rohr Jewish Literary Institute, the Sirenland Fellowship, the Santa Maddalena

Foundation, and the Corporation of Yaddo, which has on multiple occasions offered me not only the luxury of uninterrupted time but also a bridge to beautiful, lasting friendships.

A big thanks to the Encyclopædia Iranica—an unparalleled resource on Iranian history and culture—made possible by Professor Ehsan Yarshater and his team of scholars. I am also indebted to Salvatore Quasimodo for his poem "Man of My Time" (*Uomo del mio tempo*), from which the title of this novel is derived, and to Ardeshir Mohassess, whose wry and satirical illustrations offered me inspiration as I wrote; having one of these illustrations on the cover of this book is a dream I dared not think possible.

To my dear friend Giorgio van Straten—thank you for your unconditional affection and for standing by me no matter what, especially when it counted most. And to my longtime friends Joy Jacobson (who read multiple drafts of this novel and offered insights every step of the way) and Sophie Arnold—I am grateful, and I cherish our long hours of quiet conversation. I also thank Gary Lippman for his thoughtfulness and boundless generosity, and Lucy Rosenthal for more than two decades of support and friendship.

Finally, to Salar: thank you for reconnecting me to the pulse of Tehran—a city that continues to live and breathe in my heart—and for so much more. I'm grateful to Nina, Tanya, Prudy, Marc, and Carol for their enduring kindness, and to Stephanie, Andrew, Maya, Ellie, Leah, and Simon for making me turn to the future despite my propensity to dig the past. To Ymelda I remain indebted for her big heart and humanity. And above all, to my dear siblings—Joseph, Alfred, and Orly—I thank you for showing me, again and again, that home transcends geography. I am also forever grateful to my mother, Farah, for her tenderness, grace, and strength, and to my father, Simon, who, while no longer here, continues to walk with me.